QUEEN AMONG *the* DEAD

QUEEN AMONG the DEAD

LESLEY LIVINGSTON

zando
YOUNG
readers

NEW YORK

zando young readers

The characters and events in this book are fictitious. Any similarity to real persons, living or dead, is coincidental and not intended by the author.

Copyright © 2023 by Lesley Livingston

Zando
zandoprojects.com

First Edition: January 2023

Text design by Pauline Neuwirth, Neuwirth & Associates
Cover design by Evan Gaffney
Cover illustration by Tal Goretsky

The publisher does not have control over and is not responsible for author or other third-party websites (or their content).

LCCN: 2022939791

ISBN 978-1-63893-018-1
eISBN 978-1-63893-019-8

10 9 8 7 6 5 4 3 2 1

Manufactured in the United States of America

For my mother,
Margo Elizabeth Rose Livingston

THE FOLK OF EIRE

FIR BOLG – *the Folk of the Land*
  Inhabitants since before the first days of the coming of the
  Tuatha Dé to Eire.

FIR DOMNANN – *the Folk of the Sea*
  A splinter tribe of raiders descended from Fir Bolg driven
  across the Eirish Sea in the first days.

FOMORI – *a near-mythical race of shapeshifters*
  Defeated and driven from Eire by the Scathach Queen in the
  first days of the coming of the Tuatha Dé to Eire.

FAOLADH – *a sisterhood of elite Fomori warriors*
  Their powerful shapeshifting abilities, the *riastrad*, were taken
  from them after their defeat by the Scathach Queen in the
  first days, at the battle of An Bhearú.

FÉ FÍADA – *Mist Lords of the Fomori*
  Fomori royalty, driven to extinction by the Scathach Queen
  in the first days.

TUATHA DÉ – *the Tribe of Gods, descendants of the Scathach Queen and her folk*
    Ruled by the Dagda, the "Good God," a leader chosen by the Lia Fail, the so-called Stone of Destiny.

HORSE LORDS – *descendants of the Scathach Queen's Scythian cavalry*
    Lords of the Golden Vale in the south, keepers of the Dagda's herds.

I

"NEVE ANANN ERIU . . ."

The Dagda's voice rolled like low thunder through the great stone gathering hall of his palace. The sound swept over Neve and she winced. Ruad Rofhessa, Dagda of the Tuatha Dé, only ever used his youngest daughter's full name when he was furious with her. Although such occasions weren't exactly uncommon.

"Give Lorcan back his tooth."

Neve lifted her chin and gazed up at her father on his granite throne, flanked by a pair of tall, bronze *carnyx*, the wolf-headed war horns blown in times of strife to call the *tuaths*—tribes—to the field of battle. There was mud on Neve's tunic and blood on her knuckles, but at least her cheeks were dry. The boy standing beside her had tear tracks staining his. And a blossoming purple bruise on his jaw.

The Dagda leaned forward, one massive hand clenched on the war club that was the emblem of his kingship, stained dark with ancient blood. "I thought we'd been over this."

1

Neve opened her mouth to defend herself, but the Dagda heaved a sigh and waved her silent, slouching back in his throne as if he simply couldn't summon the energy to sustain his anger. As if his mind was already turning to other matters. As if he was already somewhere else . . .

"There is to be *no* fighting, Neve," he said.

"I wasn't fighting. I was defending the honor of the Dagda's mighty throne."

"I have warriors and priests to perform that duty." Ruad Rofhessa looked down at his daughter where she stood before the great hearth, a defiant gleam in her dark golden eyes. "You've seen ten whole circles of the seasons come and go. Next Samhain it will be eleven. You are almost a young woman now, Neve, and I expect you to start acting like the daughter of the Dagda and not like some brawling Faoladh she-devil."

Neve bit her lip to keep from grinning at the comparison. The Faoladh were legendary women warriors devoted to the fearsome goddess Macha the Warbringer, and in ancient times they had been revered—and feared—throughout all of Eire for the mystical battle madness that was said to magically transform them into raging beasts.

"I'm sorry, Father," Neve said, dipping her head in an effort to look sincere. "Lorcan, I'm sorry I knocked you down."

"Twice," Lorcan said.

"*Three* times," she muttered under her breath. Then she lifted her head and smiled her best, most brilliant smile at him, extending a hand to clasp.

Lorcan warily reached out and the two gripped each other's wrists. With that, Neve spun on the heel of her beaded sandal.

"Neve."

She stopped midstep and turned back around. "Yes, Father?"

"Give Lorcan back his tooth."

"What tooth?" she asked innocently.

"*Neve . . .*"

"All right."

Lorcan held out his hand and she reluctantly dropped the bloody molar into his palm. Neve grinned.

"He told me it was loose yesterday. I was only helping." She shrugged, her grin turning just a bit predatory.

The boy's face flushed a deep shade of red as Neve spun back toward the massive gilded oak doors. This time no one stopped her from leaving. She headed to the wing of the palace where she shared a many-roomed apartment with her older sister, the crown princess Úna.

The sky overhead was an ominous shade of violet, the threatening promise of an approaching thunderstorm. The corridors were deserted by the time Neve shouldered open the carved ash-wood doors to her quarters.

"Where is your sandal? And why are you such a mess?" Úna's perfectly shaped brows knit together beneath her silver circlet. "What happened?"

"I lost my sandal when I threw it at Lorcan's head," Neve told her. "I'm a mess because fighting is messy business. And I was fighting because the gods demanded it."

"Did they?"

Neve nodded and stripped off her one remaining leather sandal and her torn and dirt-stained tunic. "We were playing 'invasion' and stupid Lorcan told me I couldn't win the battle because

I was a girl and girls can't fight," she explained as she stalked toward an alabaster washbasin. "I proved him wrong and now he is my sworn enemy. I wanted to offer his tooth to Khenti-Amentiu the wolf god of the Tuatha Dé in tribute because I am his favorite. But Father made me give it back . . ." Neve frowned, realizing her father had seemed more preoccupied than usual. "He's going away again, isn't he?" she asked Úna as she scrubbed Lorcan's blood from her fingers and the courtyard dirt from her face.

"Not far." Úna smiled at her gently. "And not for long. He's going to the Great Barrow."

"Pff. I don't like that stupid pile of rocks." Neve shrugged into a linen shift and combed her fingers through her damp hair. "I don't like that architect. And every time Father comes back from there, I don't like *him*."

"Neve." Úna sat up straight on the couch and her expression became serious. Her glance darted around the room, empty save for the two of them. Not even Úna's bondswoman, Emer, was around to hear, but she lowered her voice anyway. "Listen to me and listen well. You cannot say things like that. Not ever. Not even to me. Gofannon isn't just an architect. He's a Druid and a *very* powerful man. There are things you don't understand yet."

Úna sighed and reached for a blue glass goblet full of mead set on a low table. Although just three years older than Neve, the Dagda's firstborn already seemed as if she'd passed well beyond girlhood into womanhood. She took a delicate sip.

"Politics is one of those things," she continued. "Power is another. Here in the halls of Temair, the two are inseparable, and one day your life may depend on how well you are able to navigate those twin rivers."

Neve bit her tongue. She knew there was truth in what her sister said. The Druids were neither of the Fir Bolg peasant tribes nor from Neve's own people, the Tuatha Dé, who ruled over them. But the Druids held sway over both, because the order of wandering priests had in recent years begun hoarding the ancient magic of the land. Magic that her father—at Gofannon's urging—had decreed forbidden to any but the Order, and the decree was enforced harshly, even violently at times. Especially among the Fir Bolg, where even the smallest of magics made a harsh life just a bit more bearable.

Before Neve was even born, Gofannon came to court to become the Dagda's chief architect and monument builder. As the story went, he'd once been a high Druid from the land of the Cymru, just across the Eirish Sea. Neve had heard whispers of deeds that had led to his banishment from that land, but she didn't know whether to believe them or not. All she knew was that even in her father's Great Hall with a fire blazing in the hearth, the presence of the tall man with the red beard and the piercing blue eyes cast a tomb-like chill she could feel in her bones.

Still. Neve wasn't *afraid* of him. Not really . . .

"Come on, my little wolf cub." Úna rose and held out a hand to her sister. "Time for sleep. There's a thunderstorm brewing on the horizon and I should think that after the day you've had, you'd need a bit of rest."

"It's still light out," Neve muttered, then brightened. "When you're Dagda, we can stay up all night. We'll watch the moon sail across the sky until morning."

Úna tilted her head and regarded her sister. "I can't be the Dagda, Neve," she said. "And neither can you. You know that."

5

"You take the western half and I'll take the eastern," Neve continued, ignoring Úna. "Or the other way around. I don't mind. I'll command the *óglach* and protect us from invasions of hordes of beastly Fomori." She propped herself up on her elbow and grinned at her sister. "The Horse Lords will breed magic horses for us swifter than the winds—just like in the old stories—and we'll race our chariots from one shore to the other. It'll be glorious."

Úna rolled her eyes. "The Fomori were driven from the land by our ancestors," she said. "If they ever truly did exist. They're just a story now, told to frighten little children. And the Dagda's horses are already the swiftest in the land. Without any magic at all."

"You're starting to sound like that horrid old Gofan—" Neve's mouth snapped shut at the stern look Úna gave her. "Never mind . . ."

"Go to *sleep*, Neve." Úna padded over to her own couch. "Then you can dream all you want about donning armor and driving dreadful beast people all the way back across the water."

That was a dream Neve would welcome, she thought as she flopped on her side. But Neve was flush with her resounding victory over Lorcan and sleep eluded her like a wily fox.

"*Girls can't fight*," he'd taunted her. She'd shown him. The most famous fighters in all the old stories were girls. Warriors like the Scathach Queen herself. And her greatest adversaries, the Faoladh, a secret sisterhood of Fomori warriors, the last of their kind, who long ago wielded their shape-shifting powers on the field of battle to devastating effect.

Outside the wind began to moan and the sound of it made her restless. She climbed silently out of bed. Carrying a pair of plain sandals, she slipped out, padding silently through the winding breezeways to a disused stable yard overgrown with ivy. A forgotten place and Neve's secret refuge within the palace walls.

Lorcan was standing just inside the gate as if he'd been expecting her.

"You were going to keep my tooth," he snapped, round face flushed.

Neve snorted at his attempt to look menacing.

"What if I *died*? What if the Druids'd had to stick me in a barrow without it? What if they'd buried me without all my parts?"

"Then I suppose your soul-wraith would have wandered the afterlife looking as ridiculous as you do now," she said.

"At least I'm not so ugly that my own mother tried to drown me!" Lorcan spat.

Neve felt the blood drain from her cheeks and she rocked back a step.

"You take that back, Lorcan," she gasped. "Take it back! Or I'll—"

"You'll *what*?" The boy's face was blotched crimson. "Look at you! No wonder the queen left Temair in shame. She wanted to give the mighty Dagda a son. You'll never be a warrior. It's hard to believe you're even Tuatha Dé!"

Neve felt as though she'd been punched in the stomach. And this time, she couldn't make herself punch back. She spun on her heels and pelted across the deserted yard toward the gate leading to the royal stables, Lorcan's mockery ringing in her ears. Neve grabbed the halter of her favorite mare and threw a leg over the pony's bare back, setting her heels to its flanks and urging it to run, out into the wide fields beyond the walls of Temair.

The storm was nearly upon them before Neve had even reached the farthest edge of the necropolis to the north. Barrow graves rose up like blisters from the green land all around her, lifeless and foreboding. Grass and dirt, driven by the wind, clung to the tear tracks on Neve's cheeks as the last dim light of the sun faded and the shadowed hills turned the color of old, dark blood. She cast a blurred glance skyward at the dark clouds filled with the bull-headed sky god Taranis's wrath. Storms like this could sometimes last for hours or even days, and if she was caught outside in it, the hailstones could flay the skin from her bones.

She didn't care.

It isn't true! Lorcan's a liar . . .

Neve knew the story like she knew her own name. The bards sang of it! On the night of her birth, a *ban sidhe* demon had crept over the palace walls and spirited her away, hurling her out into the dark waters of An Bhóinn, where she would have drowned, were it not for the divine will of the gods. Of course she'd heard snatches of hideous court gossip. The whispers that it was Queen Anann herself who'd thrown her child into the river. But no one had ever dared utter those filthy lies in Neve's presence.

Neve buried her tear-streaked face in her pony's shaggy mane as it ran.

A monster tried to kill me that night. Not my mother . . .

"No!" The pony, already skittish with the storm, reared to a stop in the lee of a barrow and tossed its head, snorting and stamping. Neve slid from its back, sobbing, and fell to her knees. "It wasn't her! It was a ban sidhe . . ."

The tears spilling down her cheeks splashed the front of her tunic and vanished into the earth. The sound of her weeping echoed off stones and turf. Neve should have known better than to weep on Dead Ground. Known better than to utter those words, like a summoning.

She fell silent as the storm winds shrieked and the long grasses in front of her began to spin, funneling up from the ground, coalescing into the grotesque, ghoulish shape of a ban sidhe demon. Its eyes burned with pale green fire and its gaping mouth was a cavernous maw, hungry to devour her soul.

"*Neeeve Anaaannn Eriiuuu . . .*"

Neve screamed and clapped her hands over her ears as the wraith's voice tore at her mind like teeth and claws, ravaging the sound of her name. The sky turned black as pitch. She would die there, she knew, alone among the dead, and no one would ever know what happened to her.

As fate would have it, she wasn't alone.

The barrow grounds hadn't seen another living soul that day, except for one.

At thirteen years old, Ronan was still lean and wiry enough to be able to cut away a square of turf, shift a stone or two, and navigate the passageways of most of the tombs without leaving behind obvious signs of desecration.

This evening, the boy's leather satchel bulged with a cache of stone fragments carved with spells and prayers that he'd liberated from the tomb of the recently interred chief óglach—leader of the Dagda's own personal guard. The boy felt no twinge of remorse o r the pillaging. The man was dead—and, by all accounts, had been of an odious disposition—so what need had he of incantations? At least, that's what the lad told himself.

The óglach's tomb had been rich and stoutly constructed, the stones cunningly laid, and it had taken some doing to get in and out again, even for a practiced tomb robber. Now, with a storm coming on fast over the hills, Ronan decided against a trek back to Blackwater Town, where he shared a hut with a handful of river rats and outcasts. Instead, he stashed his pickaxe and spoils in a half-finished cairn he found, then curled up, sheltered by stone and earth, to wait out the deluge.

As the sun sank below the horizon and the winds began to howl, he heard a noise.

A thin, high shriek that raised his hackles.

Ronan poked his head out of the depression where he hid and, shielding his eyes from the biting gale, peered into the purple-tinged gloom. About thirty paces off to his left, there was a small shape cowering before a whirlwind rising up from the ground.

A wash of poison-green light spilled out over the barrows, and a terrifying wail erupted. The boy saw the hunched shape throw an arm up in defense and realized it was a young girl crouching in front of what looked like . . . a ban sidhe demon.

Ronan swore under his breath.

One scrawny urchin missing from the muddy streets of Blackwater wasn't his problem. *But a ban sidhe on the loose with a taste for fresh blood is*, he thought. *Or, at least, it will be if I don't do something.*

He'd never actually seen a real demon before, but—having studied under the harsh tutelage of the Druid priests since he could barely walk—he knew the wraith would feed on any living thing it came into contact with and, unchecked, grow stronger and more deadly. Just like the thunderstorm bearing down on the valley. Eventually, the Druids would have to be called upon to banish the ban sidhe back to its forsaken realm.

And, in the meantime, that would cut into *his* profits. Maybe even his life expectancy . . .

The girl screamed again. Ronan raked his fingers through his dark hair in frustration, then dropped back down into the dugout. He reached for his satchel and rifled through his bounty of sharp-edged stone strips, careful not to nick his fingertips. Spilling even a drop of blood into that bag full of magic would have been . . . unwise.

As he'd pilfered spells from the óglach's barrow earlier that evening, he'd noticed that one of them had borne the mark of a *fuath*—a particularly nasty kind of water demon whose name literally meant "hate"—which, under normal circumstances, was *not* something to be trifled with. And even if the boy were reckless enough to want to trifle, the barrows were too far from any water source normally required for a successful conjuring. But circumstances that night were hardly normal.

As Ronan held the spell stone up in front of his face, and the girl screamed again, the skies opened up and the fury of the thunderstorm poured down upon them both.

Plenty enough water.

Now, all he needed was the hate.

Ronan peered at the slashes and knots chiseled on the stone and hissed through his teeth to think that some "mourner" had placed such a vile spell stone in someone's grave. Designed not to soothe or protect, but to torment the soul of the barrow's inhabitant. It would fetch him a good price if he sold it in the dark market of Blackwater Town—

Focus! Time enough to think about profit later. *If* he managed to survive.

"Good thing I'm a quick study," he muttered, scanning the lines of symbols. The incantation was crafted with a complexity beyond what the boy had learned from the Druid priests. "I hope . . ."

Lightning lashed the underbellies of the thunderheads as Ronan heaved himself up out of the trench and ran, throwing himself in front of the girl right as the ban sidhe demon lunged for her.

The demon's taloned hand scraped Ronan's shoulder, sending agony rippling down his arm. The girl shouted a startled warning, and the sound was enough to distract the monster for an instant—barely—but a string of word shapes plucked from the carvings on the spell stone was already forming on the boy's tongue and in his mind.

"Fuath!" he cried, his voice cracking. "Hear my summons, Hated and Hating!"

Above Ronan's head, the torrential rain twisted into tortured skeins, winding and weaving into a monstrous shape—half horse, half serpent, all malevolence—a feral creature of darkness and evil. Rage given form and purpose. A shriek split the air as Ronan's conjuring became reality, and the fuath's head canted on its sinewy neck, fixing a baleful glare on the boy. Ronan knew in that moment he was meddling with forces beyond what even a skilled Druid should. He wasn't even quite sure how he'd managed it. But he had, and he only had a moment to act.

He swallowed the tight knot of fear in his throat. *Now, to set the fuath upon the ban sidhe like a hungry beast on a baited trap,* he thought. With any luck at all, the two demons would duel to their mutual destruction.

"Obey my command!" he shouted. "Release your fury on one deserving of it!"

Ronan swept his arm in the direction of the ban sidhe as it loomed over the girl. The fuath shrieked again and charged. The ban sidhe's head whipped around, green-fire eyes peeled wide, howling as the ghostly serpent-horse bore down on it. Flickering veins of indigo darklight raced across the fuath's sickly pale, scaley hide, crackling in its mane and tail as it pawed at the air and reared back to strike at the ban sidhe.

In that moment, the boy ran for the girl and grabbed her by the wrist, yanking her out of the way of the two spectral combatants. They ran, stumbling, across the grass, slamming into a moss-robed stone. The boy threw his arm up to shield them from both storm and spells and, in the gloom, he saw the girl's face—a handsbreadth from his—and was caught, suddenly. Snared like a rabbit in the circles of her dark golden eyes.

She stared back at him as large glistening tears spilled down her cheeks. Without thinking, Ronan reached up and caught them on the pads of his thumbs.

"Stop that!" he said. "Do you want to summon another one?"

Then he squeezed his fists shut around his thumbs. He stared in wonder as her tears sizzled and vanished, sending tiny flares of indigo light sparking between his fingers. In that very same moment, the ban sidhe shrieked and exploded into nothingness and a sudden void of silence.

The girl's mouth fell open, and Ronan blinked in astonishment at the demon's sudden demise. His masters had always told him that strong human emotions—manifested in blood or tears or even, sometimes, sweat—were keys to unlocking powerful enchantments. At least they were safe now. From the ban sidhe, at least . . .

The fuath was another matter. Ronan tensed as he felt the flickering threads of the enchantment that held the demon bound—just barely—to his will begin to fray. The bonds were snapping, one by one, and in another moment, the boy's own conjuring would turn and devour them both.

"Run!" Ronan scrambled back as the serpent-horse struck at him. Missed shattering his skull by a hairsbreadth. Reared back to strike again—

And then, suddenly, the *girl* was there.

With a shout, she brought down Ronan's pickaxe with all her strength onto the serpent-horse's head. The boy watched, frozen, as the sharp iron spike pierced between the thing's eyes, stabbing down through the roof of its gaping mouth.

The fuath shrieked and writhed . . .

And shattered into sparkling dust blown away by a gust of wind.

Ronan collapsed onto his knees. The thunderstorm quieted down all around them as if it, too, had been fueled by some kind of demon energy now banished. Ronan offered up a brief heartfelt prayer to whatever god watched over blacksmiths. Iron was not only an exceptionally rare commodity but also one of the *only* material elements that could disrupt a magical conjuring. That morning, Ronan had, on impulse, stolen the pickaxe—a fine tool, clearly intended for a rich patron—from a blacksmith's hut on his way to the necropolis. He offered up a second prayer to the protector of thieves.

"How . . . ," he panted, "how did you know that iron would disrupt the fuath spell?"

The girl shook her head, equally winded. "I didn't," she said. "I just thought I'd try hitting it with something sharp."

The two of them looked at each other and burst into laughter.

"What's your name?" he asked when their laughter subsided.

When the girl hesitated, he held out his hand.

"I'm Ronan," he said. "Apprentice Druid priest. One day I'll practice real magic in the stone temples and oak groves, and I'm going to have to remember that fuath spell. It's a good one."

"You'll have to get it right if you want to serve the gods," she answered, but not in a dismissive way. Just sort of matter-of-factly, as if she believed that one day he actually might. "I'm Neve," she said, reaching for his wrist. "And if you ever tell anyone *ever* that I was crying, I'll summon another demon and command it to drag you down into the darkness and fires of Teg Duinn."

He stared at her and she turned away.

"Now where's my pony gone?" She put her fingers to her lips to whistle. There was an answering neigh from behind the near barrow, and she started in that direction.

As he watched her go, Ronan felt a sharp sting pulsing on his palm and glanced down to see a thin line of crimson welling up. A few paces away, he found the fuath spell stone lying in the grass where he'd dropped it. His heart stopped cold when he realized that the shard bore a bright trickle of blood along its jagged edge.

Ronan held it up in front of his face, not daring to move or speak or even *think* until the rain had washed the stone clean.

When he looked around, Ronan realized he stood all alone in the darkness and the dying storm. No girl, no demons.

It would be many years before he would see either girl or demon again. And when he did, Ronan would come to realize that once he'd managed to conjure one, the other would soon follow.

II

Seven Years Later

*T*HE THIEF SMILED disarmingly. "Forgive me, but . . . have we met?"

Neve's gaze flicked from the young man's face, framed by wavy black hair tied back in a tail, down to the laces of his worn sandals. He was half a head taller than she was and wore only a tunic and simple woolen kilt with a travel bag slung across his chest. There was nothing in particular that would mark him as different from any other peasant. Still, she knew he was a thief—not because of how he was dressed, but because she had just watched him expertly cut a coin purse from another man's belt while the man haggled over a bolt of brightly checkered cloth at a market stall.

She tilted her head as she regarded him. "I can't imagine under what circumstance I would have ever come into contact with the likes of you, thief."

"I'm a thief?" he asked. "You're the one holding the knife and demanding money."

"Is stealing from a thief really stealing?" Neve grinned and tightened her grip on the blade that she held against the thief's throat. "Now hand over your coins."

The long walk to the bustling marketplace of the town of Blackwater had made Neve thirsty for a tall mug of cool mead but she didn't have any money. Why should she? She was a princess. She had no need of coins. Unless, of course, she'd sneaked out of her father's palace without permission that morning . . . which was why she'd followed the thief and his purse of ill-gotten coins and cornered him in this alley.

Neve slid the blade right up under the point of his jaw, where she could see his pulse beating rapidly and looked him directly in the face.

"Wait!" he gasped. "We *have* met—I remember now. I remember your eyes. It was years ago and there was a storm rising. You were little and scrawny and your name was, uh . . . Neve!"

"I'm not—"

"You *are*," he interrupted her, something Neve wasn't used to. "You were. I'd spent that day, uh, selling prayers for the dead at the necropolis. You were crying and there was a—"

The knife bit into his throat. Enough to draw blood and a hiss of pain from between his teeth.

"I don't cry."

"*That's* what you said that night." The thief swallowed, the muscles of his throat moving against the edge of the blade. "You see? I *do* know you, Neve—"

"*Princess* Neve."

He blinked, his jaw drifting open. "Prin . . . cess . . ."

"Everyone knows me." She grinned coldly at him. "I'm the daughter of the Dagda. Beloved of the Wolf. She for whom the sun sets and the moon rises—"

"You told me you'd kill me if I ever told anyone!" he interrupted her again. "About you weeping. And I didn't." The thief shook his head, as much as the blade at his throat would let him. "I mean, it wouldn't have mattered if I *had*, because I didn't know who you were then. You neglected to mention the princess part." He glanced down at her knife and then back up to her face. "Princess Neve. I kept your secret. Surely that counts for something, right?"

Neve looked at him more closely. His eyes were a stormy shade of dark gray—flecked with silver like the blade of her fine iron dagger—and his face . . . his face had lost the childish softness of that night. He'd been young then, too, and she *had* cried in front of him, she remembered.

". . . Ronan . . ."

Behind the shock of black hair that fell in front of his face, Ronan's gray eyes went wide with surprise. "You do remember," he said. He smiled, but Neve could discern a hint of wariness in the expression. "That's flattering."

"It was a rather memorable occasion," she said. "*You* just happened to be there."

"To save your life. You're welcome."

Neve suppressed a shiver as a long-submerged fragment of that night drifted to the surface of her memory—of the ban sidhe, the pale-green fire in its empty eye sockets and the ghostly hands reaching for her.

She lowered her knife, spun the blade in her hand, and sheathed it at her belt.

"You were lucky," she said. "You lost control of your fuath spell and that thing almost killed us both. Are you a full-fledged Druid priest now? I would have thought you'd be a bit better dressed. And less inclined to thievery."

"I left the Order." Ronan shrugged.

"They kicked you out."

"And *then* I left."

"What was your crime?"

"Curiosity. A restless spirit. Somehow, I get the feeling that's something you can understand, Princess Neve." He regarded her frankly. "Huh. I would have thought *you'd* be a bit better dressed. And less inclined to thievery."

"I was thirsty," she said with a shrug. "And I can't just walk into any *bruidean* and demand beer without coin, so . . ."

Ronan held up a hand. "Say no more." He drew the pilfered money purse from the pouch at his belt and hefted it. "Come. I know a quiet place. I'll buy you a drink. I'm sure the Dagda's daughter has a fascinating story or two to tell, and my ears are as thirsty as your tongue."

Of course, it was against Neve's better judgement to go with him. But her entire venture into Blackwater Town had already set that boat adrift. It was near impossible for her to resist the place, so different from the confines of the palace. So *alive*. She found the plain speech and easy laughter of the Fir Bolg villagers much more invigorating than the mannered, measured ways of the Tuatha Dé. Temair was like a vase of carefully cultivated blooms set down in a meadow full of wildflowers. The chaos of the latter spoke to Neve's restless spirit, regardless of the possibility of weeds or thorns, so the prospect of a drink with a thief was hardly going to send her running home.

Neve twitched the edge of her long shawl back up over her head and gestured for Ronan to lead the way.

<hr />

As THEY WALKED through the narrow winding streets, Ronan stole another glance at the girl at his side, his chest tightening. He remembered how Neve had disappeared that stormy night, vanished back into the mists almost as if she'd been a wraith herself. Now here she was again. After Ronan had spent the last seven years searching the face of every dark-haired girl in Blackwater and beyond for a flash of those golden eyes. Promising himself that one day he *would* find the girl from the barrow grounds—and make her pay for what had happened to him.

Ronan's fingers curled into a fist around the thin ridge of an old scar on his palm. To be fair, after so long, he'd never really expected to find Neve again. And he certainly wouldn't have expected her to be the Dagda's daughter. And not the good one, either. But here she was, walking beside him. At his invitation.

Mórr's blessed light! What do you think you're doing? Ronan asked himself as he led the princess through the twisting alleys and laneways of Blackwater. *This girl was trouble back when you didn't even know who she was. Now?*

Now, she was the kind of trouble that—good daughter or no—would mean his summary execution if any of Ruad Rofhessa's wretched óglach were to catch him in her company. And thanks to the decrees of his Druid adviser Gofannon—

who, if gossip was to be believed, was acting more like a king than the Dagda himself—Blackwater was riddled with óglach, searching out illicit magic practitioners and spell scavengers. One of the reasons Ronan rarely, if ever, turned to dealing these days. He'd lost one too many friends to the jaws of a harrow hound. Coin purses were boring bounty, but safe. At least, on *most* days, he thought, putting a hand to his neck where Neve's blade had nicked him.

They approached the curtained doorway of a thoroughly disreputable drinking establishment, the only bruidean in town that Ronan hadn't been thrown out of recently. Neve had drawn her shawl up over her head and wrapped it over the lower half of her face so that only her eyes were visible, that fearless golden gaze that had haunted his dreams for years—and occasionally his nightmares. She walked with her head held high, chin tilted upward, with an unconscious arrogance befitting the daughter of the Dagda.

"Does your father know you're here in Bla—"

"No."

"Oh." He pushed aside the curtain, holding it for her to pass through before him.

"*No one* knows. My father would flay the commander of his óglach alive if he knew. And I like the commander of the óglach, so I'm careful." She paused before stepping inside. "I know I said everyone knows me, but they only *know* me when I'm dressed in gold and jewels and traveling in a gilded chariot with a fawning retinue. Even in Temair, no one ever looks me in the face. No one except you."

"I didn't mean—"

"No." She shook her head. "It's actually a nice change. I'm sick of talking to the tops of people's heads."

"Then I promise to keep your secret—again. And keep my bowing and scraping to a minimum."

"See that you do. Now. I'm not getting any less thirsty standing here." She ducked through the doorway, heading for a table tucked away in a corner.

They sat down and Ronan signaled the *bruigu* for a round of beer. There was a moment of silence that stretched out between them as he cast about for something—anything—to say. Something that wouldn't make him sound like one of those poor haunted souls that wandered down by the docks. The ones said to have been touched too hard by the magic of the land and lost their wits to it.

Ronan prided himself on having kept his wits even if he hadn't been *touched* so much as *pummeled* by magic. A thing only he—and the girl sitting across from him—knew. He felt a surge of long-buried emotion rise up and threaten to swamp his studied indifference. The scar on his palm pulsed, a memory of the fuath spell.

"Tell me something . . . ," he said, an edge to his voice that, even to his own ears, bordered on insult. "You are called Beloved of the Wolf—among, uh, other things—but I've never really understood what that means. It's hard to think of those beasts as particularly affectionate."

"You're wrong," Neve said curtly. "They're fiercely protective. Very gentle with their offspring. In fact, both mothers and fathers carry their young in their mouths."

Ronan shrugged, struggling with the sudden rawness he felt inside. "I suppose that's gentle," he said, reaching for the mugs on the tray carried over by the bruigu and placing one in front of Neve. "If you aren't overly clumsy."

Neve regarded him coolly for a moment, as if trying to decide whether he mocked her in earnest, then reached for her drink.

"The night I was born," she said, after a long pull on her beer that drained a good third of the mug, "I was stolen from my cradle and flung into the waters of An Bhóinn. The wailing of the royal women shook the walls, they say. But the next morning, a fisherman came across a great black wolf sleeping on the riverbank, a tiny human baby asleep in the cradle of its forepaws."

"You."

She nodded. "Me."

He cocked his head and peered at her through narrowed eyes. "And that *really* happened."

She cocked her head in the other direction and raised an eyebrow. "You would question the story of my divine birth?"

"Well, no . . ."

"The fisherman was terrified, of course." Neve shrugged. "But he knew he had to act or face the wrath of the gods. So he paddled his skiff as close to the beast as he dared and plucked me from the wolf's embrace. The wolf opened its eyes and snarled and he almost dropped me. But then the great beast stood and padded back into the forest. Almost as if the wolf had just been waiting there for someone to come fetch me."

"And who was it that stole you from the palace in the first place?"

Shadows flitted behind Neve's eyes, and for a moment Ronan thought she wasn't going to answer him. But then she took another sip of beer and lifted her chin.

"A ban sidhe demon," she said finally.

"You do seem to attract those, I've noticed."

Neve rolled her eyes. "Clearly there were those among the gods who were jealous of my beauty," she explained patiently. "And so they sent the demon to drown me."

Ronan didn't ask *whose* gods, exactly, she meant. That in it-self was a contentious topic of conversation in Eire, a land that had long since been conquered by Neve's ancestors—the Tuatha Dé had brought their own strange, outlandish deities with them from across the seas to a land already rife with so-called gods. Gods of war and water, wolves and wildflowers, day, night, light, dark . . . anything and everything that man could claim held a little bit of power he could pray to borrow. Most of those old gods of Eire had faded into the mists and mountains, leaving only their names behind. Ronan, for his part, didn't believe that they'd ever existed at all. He didn't believe in gods.

"It was obviously Khenti-Amentiu who saved me," Neve con-tinued. "For he is wise and a lover of beauty."

"Khenti . . ."

"Amentiu." She looked at him like he was soft in his brain. "The wolf-headed god of the dead? The wanderer of the sands? He who guided my ancestress, the Scathach Queen, to lead the Tuatha Dé from their far-off desert home into the West, to this rich green land in the first days—"

"I don't know," Ronan interrupted before Neve began to fully wax into strident poetical rote like a Druid master. "How jealous could these other gods have been? Your gods all have the heads of beasts and you were only a day old. Probably still red and wrinkly and—"

"*Don't* make me summon the óglach, thief."

"Right." He took a sip of his beer. The thick brown stuff was cool and sweet and refreshing. It almost made it possible for him—*almost*—to forget that he was sitting, matching wits with the girl who'd torn a hole in the darkness one night long ago and

25

let a fuath demon seep under his skin. "I'm sure you were quite striking. And the fisherman? What happened to him?"

"My father rewarded him with a good stout roundhouse with stone walls and a thatched roof in Baile Sláine." She shrugged. "He lives there now and wants for nothing."

"Have you ever spoken with him?"

"Why would I grant an audience with a fisherman?"

"The same reason you'd take refreshment with a thief, I suppose," Ronan said. "We both saved your life and—" A heavy hand fell on his shoulder in that moment. Ronan heard the rasp of a drawn sword.

Neve's eyes went wide as she glanced up from her drink. "Perhaps it's time I returned the favor . . ."

She shot to her feet, flipping over the trestle table as she did so. Mugs and crockery flew, shattering against the walls and floor and spilling beer and oysters everywhere. Neve put her head down and charged straight at the shocked óglach with his horned bronze helmet and breastplate, shouldering him into a rack of clay jars that collapsed on him in a clattering heap.

"Run, fool!" Neve shouted as she pelted for the low door of the bruidean.

For the first frantic moments as they raced through the alleys and laneways between market stalls, Neve thought *she* was the one the óglach had been searching for. She'd recognized the face beneath the brim of the bronze helmet as belonging to Fintan, the chief commander of the Dagda's guard. She'd been swiftly disabused of that notion, though, once she'd heard the bellowing howls of hounds on the hunt.

Not just any hounds—harrow hounds.

The spell-harrows of Temair, at a glance, resembled ordinary wolfhounds—huge, shaggy beasts with great long legs and angular heads—except for their heavy silver collars. And—when they were under the influence of their cursefire—their crimson eyes.

Neve felt the small hairs on the back of her neck rise at the sound of their eerie, spectral howls. The harrows were monstrous conjurings, magically bred by the Druids to sniff out and hunt down the illicit magic users and spell traders outlawed by the Dagda. Once the hounds had run their prey to ground . . . Well. Neve had been on a stag hunt once when she was a child, with her father and his *ordinary* wolfhounds, and had seen firsthand what their jaws and claws were capable of. She shuddered to think of the same situation when the quarry was a man. And the hound, a monster.

But that was somehow the exact circumstance she presently found herself in. And it was all the thief's fault. As she dragged Ronan into the shadowed archway of a weathered storehouse, she briefly contemplated leaving him to his fate.

But then she remembered that, once, the circumstances had been reversed.

And Ronan had *not* left her to her fate.

"Damn all," she muttered, heaving the rust-hinged door closed behind them.

She sprinted across the rotting wood floor toward the dock that sagged perilously over a reed-choked stretch of the Blackwater. As she glanced out over the dark surface of the river, Neve shuddered. There was a reason it didn't have a true name, like An Bhóinn. Blackwater, it was said, had grown so full of monsters, the gods had abandoned it, taking its name with them.

When Neve was younger, magical things—creatures of both darkness and light—could be found roaming almost everywhere in Eire, if only you looked hard enough to find them. Now, only a few scattered places were still like that—mostly groves and hollows and caves—places one treaded lightly through, if at all. It was as if, because the Druids had outlawed mortal magic, the wild magic of the land had grown scarce and sullen without it. Wary of human interaction. Dangerous . . .

Out in the middle of the sluggish current, Neve saw an oily, iridescent flicker of movement twisting beneath the surface. She retreated a step back into the dingy little hovel, but there was no other way out except the front door, which wasn't an option. If Fintan caught her, her father would lock her away for the rest of her life. There had to be some way for them to escape . . .

The barks and belling of the hounds grew nearer. Ronan came up beside her, and she rounded on him. Neve's chest was heaving with exertion and her face felt hot from their mad dash, but the thief wasn't even slightly winded.

"Are you all right?" he asked. "Are you angry or just out of breath?"

She hauled off and punched Ronan's shoulder. Hard.

"Angry." Ronan nodded to himself, wincing. "You're definitely angry."

"You told me you left the Druid order!" Neve snarled.

"They kicked *me* out, remember?" he snapped.

Neve felt a cold finger brush her spine. "You don't just steal coins, do you? That night among the barrows. You were tomb robbing. You were *twelve* and a tomb robber."

"I was *thirteen* and I was alive," Ronan shot back. "Something I wouldn't have been otherwise. Some of us haven't grown up with your advantages in life, Princess. And if you want the honest truth, I sold my last incantation at the beginning of the summer. I'm fresh out. This land is *starved* for magic lately, Princess, in case you haven't noticed. Thanks to your da and his decree. Even I can't beg or borrow—or even *steal* it—on my life."

She didn't believe that. Why else would the harrows be on the hunt for a common thief? You couldn't swing a turnip in Blackwater without hitting three. So this thief wasn't just a thief. He was a liar, too. He carried magic. She knew it. She could almost feel it coming off of him, pulsing like the heat from a firebrand . . .

The baying of the harrow hounds grew closer, more frenzied, cracking the fragile bubble of silence around them.

"Tell me the truth!" Neve whispered frantically. "You've got a spell with you now, don't you? Is it that fuath you conjured all those years ago?"

"It's not—"

"Get rid of it!" Neve snapped. "Throw it into the river or—"

"I can't."

"Yes, you can!" She grabbed the satchel that he wore slung across his torso. "Steal another one. Another day. It's not worth your life—or mine!"

She turned the bag upside down, but the only things that fell out were a half-eaten leek and a tiny wooden carving. There were no chiseled stone shards. No scrolls or woven incantations.

Neve held up the crude little carving that resembled a fox or a dog, or maybe a wolf, if you squinted at it just right. "Is *this* it?" she asked, looking for the symbols that would have spelled out an incantation.

"No!" Ronan snatched it back and shoved it into his satchel. "Of course not."

"Then *what?*" The baying of the hounds was getting louder. Closer . . .

Ronan thrust his hand up in front of her face, palm toward her, long fingers splayed wide. "*This* is."

"Blessed Light!" Neve gasped and rocked back a step. "What—"

There were marks—lines and patterns—writhing like eels just beneath the surface of his skin, blue-black and glowing faintly with a shimmering, darkling light. The markings slithered in slow-crawling lines of twisting sigils—like living versions of the woad tattoos the Tuatha Dé marked their skin with—spiraling out from a thin, faded scar at the center of Ronan's palm, moving toward the tips of his fingers, winding down the inside of his wrist . . .

Neve had never seen anything like it.

She held her breath and stepped toward him, slowly, tentatively, reaching out to touch his palm. Wordlessly, she traced the glowing lines with her fingertip down the soft underside of his wrist, over the place where his pulse beat.

Ronan swallowed thickly against the sensation and closed his eyes. "Stop," he whispered hoarsely.

When he opened his eyes again, Neve still stood, staring up at him.

"Tickles," he said, pulling his hand back, wrapping the sigils in a clenched fist.

Suddenly, there was a thunderous hammering on the door of the storehouse. The harrow hounds barked and snarled, claws shredding the wood. Neve spun around in a panic, grappling for the knife at her belt—as if she might actually use it to cut the hand from his wrist and fling it away—but Ronan lunged for her before she could draw the blade and wrapped his arms around her. Tightly.

It was, Neve thought fleetingly, a death sentence for him to manhandle the daughter of the Dagda in such fashion. But, then again, since he'd more likely than not be dead anyway in the next few moments, he didn't really seem to care.

Neve could feel the warmth of Ronan's skin radiating through his tunic. Knew that he could probably feel the wild beating of her heart against his chest. She glanced down to see the writhing sigils on his wrist suddenly glow brighter . . . and then burn dark, flowing together and rippling outward across his skin like spilled ink, flowing up the arm he had wrapped around her. A rising mist seeped in from the river, creeping across the warped wooden floor planks.

Without warning, Ronan leaped, launching them both off the edge of the sagging river dock. Neve uttered a tiny scream as they arced through the air and broke the surface of the water with no more splash than a leaping salmon, before swiftly sinking into the cool dark depths of the Blackwater.

In that same moment, the óglach and their harrow hounds burst through the door to find nothing but sunlight and dust motes dancing in the shadow-striped air.

III

*T*HE CURRENT WRAPPED around the princess and the thief, dragging them downstream toward where the Blackwater emptied into An Bhóinn. Neve struggled to peer through the tangles of weeds and her own dark hair—and instantly wished she'd kept her eyes shut tight. Not far behind them, following in their wake, she could make out monstrous shapes, dark and glimmering and cloaked in swirling clouds of silt, writhing up from the river bottom. She caught gleaming eyes and gaping mouths flashing rows of serrated teeth.

Water-wights . . .

Neve knew instantly what they were even though she'd only ever heard stories—of water-wights and forest-wights and barrow-wights—tales told to frighten children away from dangerous places. She'd fought countless imaginary monsters like that when she was a girl—pretending Lorcan and some of the other sons of chieftains were strange, sharp-toothed terrors and chasing them around the courtyards of Temair with sticks.

But at the all-too-real sight of the otherworldly nightmares, Neve felt a surge of panic and struggled to break free of Ronan's hold. She dug her nails into his forearm and kicked, but his grip was unrelenting, stronger than it should have been. Something reached out and grabbed her foot and she screamed—a muted burst of silver bubbles in the green gloom. Even though he couldn't possibly have heard her, Ronan spun around in the water and released his grip, flinging her downstream as he fought the current to position himself between her and their pursuers.

As she was swept away from him, Neve saw Ronan lift a fist and punch at the darkness. A booming echo swept over her and she lost sight of him.

Neve thrashed in the water—trying to reach him, to help—but she was too far away, and her desperation for air too great. She kicked, thrusting upward with her arms and legs, until she was gulping mouthfuls of air. She spun around, treading water and calling frantically for her thief. For a long moment, there was nothing. Stillness.

And then, twenty or more full lengths of a man upstream from her, the surface of the river churned like a boiling cauldron over a roaring fire. The water foamed white, peaked with waves from thrashing bodies, and she saw Ronan's dark hair whip up in an arc as his head broke the surface.

"Go!" he shouted when he saw her. "Swim, damn you!"

Then he disappeared again beneath the water. Neve angled for the nearest bank, swimming for all she was worth, but the river had other ideas. The current caught her up in its teeth once more and carried her to its confluence with An Bhóinn, where it spat her out into clearer, calmer waters. The oily, clammy-cold feeling of the Blackwater sloughed away and Neve stretched out her arms, treading the waves at the mouth of the tributary, anxiously waiting for Ronan to reappear.

But it wasn't Ronan she saw first. Another dark plume of hair whipped through the air, but this head was long and angular with wide, dark, upswept eyes and shimmering silvery skin. Long, muscular arms stroked through the water and legs fishtailed with a splash as the water-wight submerged again. It shot like an arrow toward Neve, shedding dark streamers like spilled ink in its wake as it entered the purer flow of An Bhóinn—as if the creature was made of shadows, melting in sunlight. Fading, but not fast enough.

Neve thrashed through the shallows toward the bend of the southern shore, feet sinking in the soft riverbed as she scrambled for the weedy bank. She felt talons graze her calf and she mule-kicked backward, landing a glancing blow, but she was still too far from solid ground.

She would be dragged under. Devoured . . .

A vicious snarl shredded the air. For a terrified instant, Neve thought the spell-harrows had tracked them down. But it wasn't a hound that had found her. A massive black wolf the size of one of her chariot ponies exploded out from the bushes of the riverbank and, with another snarl, leaped over Neve's head into the river.

Neve scrambled out of the way as the creature landed with a tremendous splash, jaws snapping as it fended off the water-wight. As they fought, she couldn't tell where one creature ended and the other began as the caldera of river water thrown up in the struggle cloaked them in green and white foam, but the frightful contest was over in a matter of moments. The sheeting water fell back into the river, ripples dissipating, as Neve clung to the riverbank, staring at the wolf that stood flank-deep in the water, mouth open and pink tongue lolling out as it panted with exertion.

The wight was gone.

When the wolf swung its huge head around to look at her, its eyes shone yellow-gold in the late afternoon sun and Neve held her breath.

"Khenti-Amentiu?" she whispered, not daring to believe. "Are you—"

The creature huffed and shook itself, thick fur sending water droplets flying, and then it loped past her, leaping gracefully up the bank, where it shook itself dry again. At the sound of splashing behind her, Neve half turned to see Ronan staggering waist deep through the river toward shore, water streaming from his chest and arms, his satchel somehow still slung across his torso, over the shreds of what was left of the tunic clinging to his lean-muscled body. He shook the hair back from his face and froze abruptly.

The wolf locked eyes with him and its lips curled back from long white teeth, quivering as it snarled, a low rumbling growl building in the creature's chest. Neve could feel the echoing vibrations deep inside her own ribcage.

She heard Ronan suck in a breath. "Neve . . ."

"It's all right." She put up a hand, gesturing for him to stay where he was. "I'm all right . . ."

Neve could see the fur on the wolf's neck rising as its head lowered and ears flattened back against its skull. Tail twitching, it looked as though it was about to leap back into the river. The water-wight might have survived the encounter, Neve thought—she couldn't be certain one way or the other—but it was doubtful Ronan would.

"Ronan's . . . a friend," Neve said in a low voice. "My friend."

The wolf's eyes shifted to Neve's face and Neve swore if the creature could have spoken in that moment, it would have asked, "*Are you sure of that?*"

Neve swallowed her own flutter of uncertainty and nodded slowly, keeping her eyes locked on those of the wolf. All around her it seemed as if the world grew quiet and held its breath. The breeze off the river died and the birdsong in the trees fell silent. Even the river seemed to mute the murmur of its music. Without looking at him, she knew that Ronan had gone stone-still in the water. The wolf's nostrils flared as if trying to scent danger. The growl rumbled louder in its chest . . . and then subsided.

The wolf looked out at Ronan and opened its mouth in a wide yawn that served to emphasize the sharpness and strength of teeth and jaws. Then it uttered a low howl that sounded distinctly like a warning and turned to vanish into the trees. The tension flowed from Neve's limbs and left her wobbly with relief.

"It's all right," Neve called out to Ronan. "We're safe now. Khenti-Amentiu—"

"It was no wolf god that saved us," Ronan snapped. "It was luck. Luck and a plain old wolf defending its territory. The hills around Blackwater are littered with their dens. We're just fortunate that beast decided it wasn't hungry enough to feast on a pair of soggy humans."

Neve ignored him, her eyes fixed on the place where the wolf had disappeared beneath the trees. She could hardly expect a Fir Bolg peasant to understand a visitation from the divine. She barely understood it herself. After a long moment had passed and the wolf didn't reappear, she glanced over her shoulder and saw that Ronan was still out in the middle of the stream.

"It's gone," she said, waving him toward shore.

"I know . . ." He stayed where he was, unmoving.

"What is it? Are you hurt?" She started to wade back into the river. "Do you need help?"

"No!"

"Ronan—"

"My kilt." He let out an exasperated sigh.

"What about it?"

"I've lost my kilt. And my belt. With my money." He sank farther down, until he was chest deep in the water. "And my dagger. And here I thought this day was going so well. Of course, that was before *you* turned up."

The otherworldliness of the encounter vanished like mist on a breeze and Neve burst out laughing. The more dour Ronan's expression, the harder she laughed, until she was gasping for breath and her sides hurt.

"I'm glad I'm able to entertain you, Princess. I really am." Ronan glared at her. "But, under the circumstances, I'm feeling a bit vulnerable this close to the Blackwater, so perhaps you could, uh . . . help. Somehow . . ."

Neve fought back her laughter as she glanced around for a nice big lily pad or the like with which to preserve Ronan's modesty. She spotted a length of sodden cloth twisting in an eddy at the water's edge—the wayward kilt—and ran, splashing through the shallows, to retrieve it. Still giggling, she hooked the thing with a fallen branch and waded back, holding it out to Ronan, who snatched it from twiggy fingers.

"I can't do anything about the money," Neve said, directing her gaze skyward while he salvaged what was left of his dignity. "But you can have my belt and dagger."

"No. Thank you. I don't need any more of your help," he muttered.

"Take it." She waded toward him, unfastening her belt with the sheathed dagger hanging from it. "It's an old hand-me-down anyway. I can always get another, but it's hard to cut a purse without a blade."

Ronan stood and reluctantly reached out to take the belt and blade. Suddenly realizing his tunic had been reduced to rags, he stripped it off and threw it into the middle of the river with disgust. As he slung her leather belt around his waist and adjusted the hang of the dagger on his hip, Neve couldn't help but notice that, for all his shirt had been torn to shreds, there wasn't a scratch on Ronan's torso . . .

"What?"

Her attention snapped back up to his face at the question. "Hm?"

"You were staring. Is there a leech on me?"

"Oh. Oh! No . . ." She turned away, realizing that she had indeed been staring. "I just . . . I should go. Someone might start looking for me."

That was unlikely, she knew. Still, she didn't want to push her luck.

Neve was fairly certain Fintan hadn't had the chance to recognize her, because the óglach commander never would have dared to set cursefired harrow hounds on the daughter of the Dagda—even the wayward one. But she feared she'd been a fool to tell the thief her real name. What if she couldn't trust him? What if he turned loose-lipped over drink, or with friends? A single breath of gossip, she knew, could grow wide wings, and her father had threatened on more than one occasion to lock her up in the women's wing of the palace if she didn't start behaving like a good little second-born princess—which meant biddable, demure, marriageable, destined to be shipped off one day to seal an alliance with some petty Cymric warlord or other.

Either fate would be infinitely worse than a whole sea full of water-wights, as far as she was concerned. The boredom alone would kill her in a handful of days. Today . . . had not been boring. She didn't know exactly what it had been.

"Well, then." Ronan nodded. "Princess. I'd say we should do this again sometime, but I really don't think we should. And as long as we keep each other's secrets, let's hope we never have to."

As he turned away, Neve felt a brief, startling sensation—as if a thread stretched tight between them had suddenly snapped—leaving her stung, unbalanced. She hesitated as Ronan settled himself on the bank and pushed his hair from his face, squeezing the water out so it ran in rivulets down his back. The places on his arm and hand where the glimmering lines had appeared beneath his skin were normal now. Unmarked. Unscathed . . .

Druid tricks, she thought, frowning.

That's all it had been.

She glanced back to the riverbank, a sliver of doubt now lodging in her mind about the wolf. Had that been an illusion, too? For all she knew, Ronan had simply been trying to lull her into his confidence once he'd figured out who she was, maybe capture her and hold her for ransom, but the spell-harrows had sniffed out his cheap conjuration and spoiled the attempt, and now he'd soured on the idea. Deemed her more trouble than she was worth . . .

Neve knew that her imagination was running wild. Ronan was a thief, yes. But a harmless one. *Nothing* else. One that was now pointedly ignoring her.

She shrugged and—wishing she hadn't been quite so hasty with her generosity in handing over her belt—gathered the hem of her tunic up with one hand and clambered awkwardly up the bank. She stood there for a moment more, wanting to say . . . something. Thank him, maybe, for saving her life again. Except that was ridiculous. Neve was a princess and *she'd* just saved *his* life, too. So, really, they were even. Again. And maybe he was right. Maybe the scales between them, such as they were, had finally balanced after almost seven years. Perhaps they should just count themselves fortunate if they managed to never darken each other's pathways again.

"So be it," Neve whispered.

She turned her back on Ronan, too, then, even as she felt an unaccustomed sting of regret and pushed her way through the scrub growth in the place the wolf had disappeared. Her sandals squished as she walked and her damp breeches chafed uncomfortably, but soon enough Neve was able to pick up a game path threading through the woods that led, eventually, back home to the palace.

IV

I N NEED OF a crossing?"

Ronan's head snapped up at the sound of a voice calling out to him from the middle of the river. He turned to see a little wooden fishing skiff with painted bright-yellow eyes on the bow bobbing on the surface of the lapping waves. Its lone occupant peered at him from beneath the wide brim of a woven wicker hat.

"Sorry?" Ronan asked, wondering how long the man had been there, floating on the river. And how much he'd seen . . .

"To the other side."

"Other side of . . ."

"Back to Blackwater Town, if that's where you're going. I can see you've already tried swimming." The man grinned and his face folded into weatherworn creases. "Looks like it worked out a bit better for you'n most folk. By which I mean, you're still in one whole piece. This close to the Blackwater, that's a rare thing. You find your way into the water 'round here, you don't usually find your way back out again."

41

Frowning, Ronan looked back at the murky river mouth.

"Ride's free," the old man continued, "if you work the oars. You've strong wrists from the look of you."

Ronan glanced down, relieved to see that the spell marks had fully faded from beneath his skin. The feeling of them was gone too, even though he could still feel the tingling heat of Neve's fingertips where she'd traced the lines . . . He glanced back over his shoulder, half hoping—and half dreading—that he'd see the princess standing there still. After so many years of looking to find her again, had he really just let her walk away?

No, a voice in his head answered. *You* pushed *her away. For good or ill.*

The boat drew closer and Ronan rose to his feet, wading carefully out into the shallows to climb aboard. He took up the oars and pushed off, guiding the little craft back into deeper water.

"Heard the óglach dogs earlier," the old man said. "That you they were hunting?"

Ronan kept his gaze fixed over his shoulder, in the direction he was rowing. "Why would you think that?" he asked.

"Well, like I said"—the old man chuckled—"only thing that goes into the river that comes back out again still breathing is something the river respects. Or recognizes as one of its own, at least."

Ronan's head snapped around. What was *that* supposed to mean?

But the fisherman wasn't looking at him. He was staring over the side of the boat, at the water that reflected his wrinkled visage back up to him. "Did you know that the Blackwater used to have a name?" he said. "A proper one, I mean. In the days before the Tuatha Dé came to the shores of this fair isle."

Ronan shook his head and turned back to his rowing. "What was it called?"

"I don't know. No one does. It's a lost thing." Again the chuckle. "Lot of lost things, these days. Like poor lost lads on lonely riverbanks."

The water turned dark and soupy beneath the bow of the skiff and they entered the Blackwater tributary. Ronan decided to shift the topic away from himself. "Do *you* have a name?"

A pause. "Call me Swift."

"Is that your name?"

"As good enough as." Swift shrugged. "Swift of Baile Sláine, if you need specifics. Fisherman, healer and dealer in fortunes, yours to command. River used to run clear as a maiden's tears, too. Now it's as full of darkness as Donn the death god's charnel house. Good fish, though. Brown trout. Tasty. That's if you can catch 'em before the wee beasties do."

The old man spat over the side of the skiff. Where the gob of spittle punched into the murky water, it began to foam and bubble. He picked up a short, stout club from the bottom of the little boat and smacked the surface a few times, barking a string of cheerful obscenities.

"We have an understanding," Swift explained. "I don't get out of the boat, and they don't eat me."

"That's not really . . ." The water abruptly stopped churning and Ronan shrugged. "I mean, fair enough. Seems to have worked out for you so far."

"So far. How's your bargain working out for you?"

Ronan blinked at him. "I don't know what you mean."

"I think you do." Swift tilted his hat up and peered at Ronan, as if he was trying to see clearly something in Ronan's face that he'd only half glimpsed. "Who's your mother, boy?"

"Dead and buried," Ronan said, his voice flat and cold.

"Didn't ask *where*." The fisherman snorted. "Asked *who*. Never mind. Your da?"

The current began nudging them back downstream again, but Ronan's hands went still, clenched tight on the oars. He felt the blood rushing in his ears as a wave of memory rose up from somewhere deep inside of him.

"I don't have one."

"Ah." Swift's eyes narrowed at Ronan. "Orphan then. Raised by the Druids, maybe?" It wasn't a great leap in reasoning to think so. A fair few orphans his age—left in the wake of a wave of particularly devastating coastal village raids—had been taken in by the Order as babies, to apprentice or serve.

"For a while." Ronan shrugged, taking up the oars again. The sooner he could reach the docks and leave the old man to his boat, the better. "Until I didn't need them anymore."

"Kicked you out, did they?"

Ronan grunted in annoyance. "Why does everyone think that?"

Swift grinned. "What did you do?"

"I wanted to learn things." Ronan heaved a frustrated sigh, remembering the soul-deep longing that had kept him in the Order far longer than it should have. "Magic. *Real* magic. Not just Fir Bolg peasant spells and cattle curses. The Druids wouldn't teach—"

"Bah." Swift slapped a gnarled hand on the boat bench, his mouth twisting in disgust. "Druids. Frauds and swindlers, more like. Think they're all so clever . . . You don't learn magic so much as find it, boy." He waved at the trees and hills and river. "Or it finds *you*. This land is a land made of magic—wild magic, the kind you don't need spells and tokens for—and it is the birthplace of gods and monsters. Before the Tuatha Dé, before even the Fir Bolg settled here—"

"I don't believe in gods," Ronan snapped. "Ours or theirs."

"Ah." The fisherman nodded. "How then of monsters? D'you believe in those?"

Monsters? Yes. Ronan believed in those. The Dagda and his Tuatha Dé were as monstrous as they came, as far as he was concerned. But he also knew that wasn't what the old man was referring to. Swift was talking about the Fomori.

That, at least, the Druids had taught him. He'd learned that when the Tuatha Dé first came to the land of Eire, it was rife with the wild dangerous magic Swift spoke of, bound by darkling mist and shadows and overrun by the Fomori, a race of shapeshifters. Back then, Eire was only inhabited by a few scattered tribes—collectively called the Fir Bolg—who lived in both reverence and fear of the Fomori.

The Tuatha Dé had made an end of that. On the point of many swords. They'd been led in those long-ago days not by a Dagda—a "good god," as it were—but by a mad and mighty queen. Her folk had called her the Scathach, because she rode a horse and drove a chariot like one of her Scythian Horse Lords. The Fir Bolg peasants called her Scota and spat on the ground. Her real name was Neith, and in the years since she'd led her invasion force to those shores, the Tuatha Dé had transformed the land. Built a civilization of enlightenment, raised palaces and reaped plentiful harvests from fields that had never before been sown. But they'd had to conquer first, and that meant the death or banishment of every last one of the Fomori—along with those of the Fir Bolg who refused to bend beneath the Tuatha Dé yoke. The specter of those first bloody years had haunted the kingdom of Eire ever since.

That part of history Ronan hadn't had to learn from the Druids. He'd learned it when he was only a few days old. From marauders who called themselves the Fir Domnann—a splinter tribe, descendants of Fir Bolg who'd been driven to flee across the narrow Eirish Sea, and who had been trying to cross back over to reclaim Eire ever since. Instead of calling themselves Fir Bolg—folk of the land—they called themselves Fir Domnann—folk of the sea—to show their disdain for their fellows who'd stayed in Eire and made the best of it. To the Fir Domnann raiders, any Fir Bolg in Eire who managed to live peacefully under the yoke of the hated Tuatha Dé deserved to burn.

They had turned Ronan's tiny village into a pile of smoldering ash.

And the Dagda and his war chiefs had let them torch too many settlements before finally rousing themselves out of their gorgeous palaces to fight back. Seething with the dull familiar ache of his life-long hatred, Ronan wondered if the Tuatha Dé would ever be called on to pay the full price for their ancient transgressions. Only a day earlier, he would have cheered such a thing on.

Now? *Now* . . . he had other concerns. Complications.

One complication, really.

He closed his eyes for a moment and pictured Neve's face. Pictured the way her eyes—those remarkable golden eyes—had glittered with defiance in the moment before she'd leaped to her feet and shoved the óglach out of the way. So that *he* could escape. Almost as if she cared about what happened to him.

And *that* wasn't something Ronan was accustomed to.

Especially not from someone like Neve. *Princess* Neve.

"Well, believe in monsters or no," Swift's voice jolted Ronan back to the present, "it's shallow enough here that the beasts won't drag you out and drown you. Probably . . ."

The bottom of the little skiff scraped on stone as Ronan pulled up the oars and threw a leg over the side. He could see threads of smoke just over the treetops from cooking fires spiraling up into the dusky air. Blackwater was just a short stroll away.

"As for gods, lad?" Swift called out, pushing the skiff back out into deeper water. "You don't have to believe in them. But you might, at least, pay them a little mind once you find that *they* believe in *you*."

—————

"MACHA'S GENTLE MERCIES. You look like proper hell."

Ronan had finally made his way back to the cramped little roundhouse at the very edge of town, where he shared a dirt-floor room with an apprentice blacksmith named Cavall. As he'd shouldered past the flap of ragged leather curtaining their doorway, a *zang-zang* sound reached his ears. Cavall—who was also Ronan's occasional comrade-in-theft—was perched on a low stool near a glowing brazier with a whetstone and a blade. Unless he was asleep or eating, Cavall was almost always sharpening something.

"Been adventuring, then?" he asked, pausing to take in Ronan's appearance.

"You've a keen eye, Cavall."

Cavall snorted. "Better ha' been worth it. You're supposed to be saving up your strength for the Samhain revels tonight."

Ronan cast a wan eyeroll at his friend as he crossed the room and dug around in the little wooden trunk for his second-best—now first-best and only—tunic.

"Cavall, my lad"—Ronan shrugged the shirt on over his head and re-fastened Neve's leather belt around his waist—"you have *no* idea."

"Well, unless I'm mistaken, you've no purse to show for it." Cavall waved a hand at the place on Ronan's hip where a fat bag of coin had rested for a brief glorious moment that afternoon.

"That I haven't." Ronan sighed. "Lost it in the Blackwater, if you can believe that."

Cavall chuckled. "Thieving filthy town."

"Filthier river."

"You lost it *in* the river?" Cavall shook his head. "You mean *on*. Or, perhaps, beside."

"Definitely in."

"And you're not dead! We'll celebrate your miraculous survival at tonight's festival!"

"About that—"

"You're *not* missing it." Cavall shoved the blade he'd been working on into a heavy leather rucksack.

Ronan eyed the leather pack. "How much is Cliona offering this time?"

Cavall flashed a grin. "More than usual. Enough to keep us in mead for a month. And maybe even a bit of nice meat. Good thing my bastard master is drunk more than half the time and sleeping or puking the rest, else he might have noticed I've been skimming off his wares."

He hefted the straps of the sack over his shoulders. The contents made a clanking, discordant music, appropriate to the occasion. The Festival of Samhain also marked the anniversary of the Faoladh's historic defeat in the war against the Tuatha Dé. At the Battle of An Bhearú, when the river had run crimson for three days.

Ronan could tell the tale by heart. The Scathach, in her victory, had been so impressed by the fierceness of that one small band of female warriors, she'd granted them the kind of mercy she denied all the others. Which was to say, she let them live, in exchange for their absolute sworn fealty. Not just to her, but to the Lia Fail—the Stone of Destiny—itself. The most sacred, most mysterious and powerful treasure the Tuatha Dé possessed, the Stone was the chooser of kings. So what the Scathach, in truth, demanded was loyal servitude to whichever ruler the Lia Fail chose, down through all eternity.

The Faoladh swore their oath. She accepted. And then the Scathach, using the power of that sworn blood oath, had her court sorcerer—a Scythian possessed of great and terrible magic—cast an enchantment that stripped the Faoladh of their *riastrad*, the shape-shifting battle-madness magic they commanded. And so the Faoladh—and their descendants—remained, bound by eternal servitude to the throne of Temair. Compelled to defend their conquerors to the death should they ever be needed.

Of course, they never had been, because the Fomori had never returned.

Yes, Ronan could tell the tale by heart. Every Fir Bolg could.

Cavall shrugged. "Where's the harm in keeping the fires of an old legend or two stoked? Give the rabble something to look forward to. Me? I look forward to getting paid." Cavall hefted a pair of earthen jugs from an alcove and handed them over to Ronan, then fished out two more to carry himself. "You can earn your cut with an entertaining telling of your day's adventurous deeds while we walk."

"You won't believe any of it."

"I don't have to. I just have to get in a good laugh or two. Come on." He paused as he noticed his friend's new finery. "Nice belt."

"Aye. Fit for a princess."

Cavall raised an eyebrow at Ronan. Then his gaze narrowed and he whistled low as he set the mead jugs down and plucked Neve's dagger from the sheath at Ronan's belt. He ran a practiced thumb along the edge, inspecting the polished ebony hilt wrapped in fine silver wire, and the pommel—also silver—carved to look like a flower, petals fanning outward, with a small blue jewel at the center. But it was the blade itself that captivated the apprentice smith. Finest iron, dark gray with a silvery sheen that flowed in a pattern like waves along its surface. Even Ronan could tell the thing had been crafted by a master weapons maker.

Cavall held out the dagger, one blunt finger tapping the blade just below the hilt, where the iron bore a mark that looked like the head of a wolf, with a long, tapered snout and high, pointed ears.

"Like I said"—Ronan took back the blade and returned it to its sheath—"you won't believe any of it."

"Add it to the tale." Cavall headed to the door and pushed aside the curtain. "Let's go."

V

"I DON'T FARM AND I don't pray," Ronan grumbled as he and Cavall made their way along a little-used path heading away from town into the forest, "so I don't really see the point in these harvest rituals . . ."

Cavall laughed. "Don't be so prickly," he said. "Where there's a ritual, there's food. And drink. And girls." He fell silent for a moment, and then added, "And salvagers . . ."

Ronan stopped abruptly on the path. Cavall winced at his reaction.

"Now, come on—"

"*No.*" Ronan glared at him. "No salvagers. I told you. I'm out of that trade. There were *harrow hounds* in Blackwater today, Cavall."

"So I heard."

The way the apprentice smith looked at him, Ronan wondered for a fleeting instant if Cavall knew *he'd* been the ones they'd been hunting. Him and the princess. Cavall had seen the dagger blade marked with the wolf head. He was smart enough to figure out something strange had happened to Ronan that day. And he was clever enough to try to use it to get Ronan to throw his lot in with the salvagers.

"Just talk to them, that's all I'm saying. The salvagers have coin—who knows where from, I don't ask—and they have conviction." He put a hand on Ronan's shoulder. "You're a minor legend to these folk. The rogue Druid's apprentice! What's wrong with giving them a little bit of hope even if you can't ferret out any *actual* magic? You know enough tricks—I've seen you do it before. Why let all that Druid lore that's stuffed up in your head go to waste? You don't owe the Tuatha Dé anything."

Ronan glanced down at the old pale scar on his palm and felt the stirrings of the magic that lay sleeping beneath his skin. Cavall may have seen him cast a few small—*so* small—magics. Barely more than herb and stone spells. Mostly because Ronan had spent most of his young life trying very hard not to attract the sort of attention he'd garnered that day.

He shook his head and let the matter drop as they entered a clearing. A few handfuls of folks from both the town and nearby farming hamlets had set up trestle tables, lit fires, and hung sheaves of grain and autumn boughs between the trees.

"Cavall!" They both turned to see a young woman striding toward them, arms stretched wide in greeting. "Ronan! A blessed harvest to you both. What a day!"

"Can't argue there." Ronan shook his head, grinning at the sight of Cliona, leaves in her hair, mud on her boots, fresh from the forest like some kind of fierce woodland spirit. Her eyes sparkled and her cheeks were flushed as if she'd sprinted to get there.

"We just had the most excellent Samhain hunt . . ." She wrapped Cavall in a heartily bone-crushing embrace until he uttered a creaky whimper of surrender and then let him go with a shove. "The stag was glorious! What a chase he gave us!" she continued, turning her attention to Ronan.

"Uh!" He ducked the embrace. "I'm fragile, Cliona. You know that."

"Ha! Sleek as a weasel you are, but hardly delicate. You'll survive us all somehow, I dare say."

"I am good at escaping traps. Were I your stag, you never would have caught me."

Cliona shot him a sharp glance at what, he realized belatedly, was very nearly an unspoken dare. Ronan breathed a little easier when Cliona laughed, slapped him on the back, and reached past him for a large, heavy jug of beer. Cliona swung the jug up on her hip as if it weighed no more than a basket of carded wool, and walked back toward the bonfire. The dwindling daylight tinted Cliona's hair—a pale, silvery-blond mane bound up in winding plaits—a rose-gold shade, and cast shadows that emphasized the long, strong muscles beneath her fitted leather tunic and leggings.

It wasn't everyone who could get away with joking about Faoladh rituals in her presence. But Ronan had known Cliona for years—ever since he'd left the Druid order—and he was well aware she took her sacred duty as leader of the Faoladh, and her dedication in particular to the warrior goddess Macha, very seriously.

The truth was, Ronan thought, if he didn't like Cliona as much as he did, he'd be outright terrified of her. Her and her band of feral sisters. He'd learned most of what he knew about their sisterhood from his time in the Order. In fact, the Faoladh were—indirectly—the very reason Ronan was no longer *in* the Order. As an apprentice, he'd stumbled over a reference to them in one of the forbidden histories stored in the Druid archives he'd been wont to peruse in secret. The stories of the ancient sect of shape-changing women warriors had intrigued young Ronan enough that he'd relaxed his vigilance on one of his late-night forays into the locked cell full of scrolls and tablets. His Druid master, Eolas, had caught him and banished him from the Order.

Just as well, he thought, not willing to admit the sting of his banishment was still sharp, after all those years. But then he cast a glance in the direction of the ragged revelers—about a dozen men and women—that he'd pegged as Cavall's salvagers. They huddled together beneath an ancient oak, all mutterings and furtive glances. *Who needs Druid spells when you've got* those *hardy souls keeping magic alive in the land?*

"Salvagers" were, in essence, the remnants of the spell dealers that had scattered after the óglach had found and raided Blackwater's dark market, back when they'd first started to crack down on the use of magic. A shady, loosely allied band of Fir Bolg folk, the salvagers were intent on gathering and hoarding any bits of stray magic they could find, by any means necessary. They'd tried—with varying degrees of success over the years—to recruit Ronan, with his particular skills and knowledge, to their cause. A few years back he'd disavowed them when they started to become more erratic and dangerous—taking the kinds of chances that prompted brutal reprisals by the óglach and their spell-harrows. Ronan used to know a handful of salvagers by name. These few strays he didn't know at all.

Among the lot of them, Ronan thought, *they look as though they could barely farm a turnip, let alone coax magic from springs and groves.*

"That's Nym. And Gwylon." Cavall came up beside him and nodded his chin first to a slim, sandy-haired man with eyes that looked everywhere all at once; then to an older, broad-chested man with an open, guileless grin and a baldric sheathed with half a dozen bronze-bladed throwing knives. "They're the ones I've talked to. Seem normal enough—relatively speaking."

Ronan grunted in reply.

"The twitchy one over there," Cavall continued, "is Sparrow. Dunno the names of the others."

Ronan glanced at the girl with the delicate, pointed features and wide dark eyes perched—very like her namesake—on a tree stump, the toes of her boots curled around a sawed-off branch. With his Druid training, Ronan could tell in an instant that she had old blood. Traces of Fomori somewhere in her lineage. Not enough to give her any actual Fomori magic. Just enough to make her yearn for it. He had no doubt that, somewhere in her family history, there'd been a shapeshifting ancestor who hadn't just *resembled* a bird. He felt a welling of pity for Sparrow. He'd known others like her over the years who would have killed for the power to fully manifest what their blood whispered to them they *might* have been . . .

Sparrow tilted her head and glared at him. "What are you lookin' at?" she called in a high, harsh voice.

He didn't answer, just went to pour himself a libation.

Hopeless, Ronan thought. Did they actually think they could prevail over the Dagda and the Tuatha Dé? Somehow wrest back control of Eire's fading magic and usher in a return to an idyllic age? The salvagers were fools. Just as deluded, in their own way, as the Faoladh. Only the Faoladh, for their part, were blameless, doomed to spend their lives mourning a magical gift that would remain forever trapped in their blood, waiting for a call from the Dagda that would never come—

"We're going to war with the Tuatha Dé."

Ronan was startled out of his reverie. "You're what?" he asked, looking down to see Sparrow standing before him, fists on her hips.

"Cavall said you can get us more magic," she said.

Well, that was the thing, really, Ronan thought. It wasn't as if magic had just up and vanished from the land. More like, the ability to *access* it had. Wild magic still roamed the forests, swam in the rivers—he'd recent firsthand experience with that—and lurked in mountain caves and sea coves. But it took spells and skills to harness it, and the Druids had hoarded the spells and set harrow hounds on those with the skills to craft them. Ronan had noticed that the less magic was called upon, the scarcer it seemed to be, even in its wild guise. One day soon there would be none among the Fir Bolg with the ability to carve a stone or stick or weave words on a cloth that would call the magic into use. It was as if the magic was a well to dip into . . . only the Druids had stolen all the ladles for their own use. Whatever *that* might be, Ronan thought darkly.

With a start, he realized Sparrow was still talking to him. "We're salvaging it—"

"Yes, I know. Hence why you call yourself 'salvagers.'"

"We're saving it up for *battle*," she said. "We're going to burn Temair to the ground. Release all the stolen magic. Cavall said you could find us more spells. Good ones—"

"Cavall has obviously been drinking. Heavily." Ronan glowered over at where Cavall was just that moment unstoppering a jug of mead, and then back down at the strange girl. She looked as though she might bite him. "And maybe you have, too. You don't go to war with the Tuatha Dé."

"Really?" Sparrow nodded back in Cavall's direction. "Looks like *they* might . . ."

A handful of Faoladh stood in a loose circle around the smith as he shrugged the rucksack off his shoulders and hefted it up onto a trestle table. Cliona reached inside and drew out a pair of long daggers with elegant, leaf-shaped blades.

Ronan sighed. "When *they* go to war, they'll be *with* the Tuatha Dé, as is their calling. And that, alone, should be enough to make you and your friends rethink your grand plans."

"We'll see about that," Sparrow said, arms crossed over her thin chest, defiance pulsing in her big, bird-black eyes.

"All twelve of you? Well. Good luck, then." He shook his head and left Sparrow to join his less mad friends. *Slightly* less mad . . .

"That's quite a cache," he remarked, peering over Cavall's shoulder as he unrolled leather wrap after leather wrap, each containing an assortment of bronze-bladed weaponry, expertly crafted. "Don't tell me *this* is the Samhain the Dagda has finally called you to his service, Cliona."

"If he did, we wouldn't need *these*," she said flatly. "On that day, the riastrad returns to the Faoladh. And on that day, we won't need weapons any longer. We will *be* weapons. Until such time, it is our duty to stay alive."

"And that's what you need all these blades for? Basic survival?"

Cliona's voice lowered to barely above a whisper. "Aevinn has had glimpses." Then she went back to examining Cavall's wares by the light of the roaring fire.

"Glimpses . . . ?" Ronan waited. Then gave in. "Of what?" he asked.

Aevinn walked up to them. "Of water, fire . . . blood."

He exchanged a glance with Cavall, who barely suppressed a smirk. Aevinn was the Faoladh's seeress, a diviner who claimed to receive visions from their goddess. Ronan and Cavall humored her more often than not, but even Cliona usually barely indulged her.

"Water, fire, blood," Cavall said. "Bit general, that, don't you think—"

"*Darkness*," Aevinn added emphatically. And then her gaze turned inward, focusing on something only she could see. "A dark power rising, making its way toward Teg Duinn. A wolf on a wide green hill howling at a blood red moon . . ."

That sent a shiver down Ronan's spine in spite of himself.

Teg Duinn—the mythical House of Darkness—was another thing he'd read about in the forbidden Druid archives: the Fir Bolg name for a legendary portal, foretold by oracles and augers, that would, in the last days of Eire, yawn wide and devour all those who lived, dragging them down into the Otherworld. Apparently.

As for the wolf in Aevinn's fevered dreaming, well, Ronan figured he'd had a close enough brush with wolves already that day.

"I won't leave this life without a fight," Cliona said as she picked up a sword and a dagger, spinning each in her hands before stepping back and slashing the blades through the air.

"Stories," Ronan muttered. Cautionary tales to frighten children. Reasons to keep the Faoladh busy. To give them purpose. But tonight, he reminded himself, was no time to argue. It was Samhain. A celebration. There was mead enough and no need to beg.

Ronan fetched himself a cup and drank it down. He closed his eyes as the liquid seared a sweet trail down his throat into his belly, and he grinned at the tingle in his fingertips that had nothing to do with marks beneath his skin. Unbidden, the image of Neve's face, a warmth in her golden eyes to rival the mead's fire, came to his mind. His breath caught in his throat.

But when he opened his eyes again, it was Cliona's face that was a handsbreadth from his, and the bright spark in her blue eyes was like the glint of a blade's edge.

"Fighting can wait till the morrow," she said. "Tonight is a night for a different kind of dancing." Cliona tilted her head toward the bonfire, a challenge in her gaze. Ronan snorted and—after a moment's hesitation—grabbed her hand. Together, they ran toward the roaring fire, leaped high over the flames, and landed, tumbling across the ground, on the other side.

Laughing wildly, Cliona slapped at the smoldering edge of Ronan's tunic, then at her pale hair wreathed in smoke and embers. Others followed and soon the whole of the gathering was leaping and dancing and singing as they piled the firewood higher so the flames could push back the coming night.

It was Samhain. The turning of the year.

On that night, light and darkness balanced on the edge of a blade.

Ronan wondered on which side his own fate might fall.

VI

NEVE APPROACHED THE palace warily. The gate she had used for her escape from Temair earlier that morning stood ajar. She was certain she'd shut it behind her and was also certain she was the only one who even remembered that there was a gate there at all. The stone wall and small arched portal were so overgrown with ivy that it was near invisible. Rather like some of the other portals scattered about Eire, Neve had always imagined. The magical ones that led to the Otherworld, to the realms of the long-forgotten gods. Doorways hidden in plain sight . . .

The entire palace compound of Temair had been originally built with magic—and not just to raise the walls and halls. Small spells had been woven into the delicate stone carvings and intricately painted murals to keep the lamps lit and the rooms fresh and fragrant, the gardens lush and fruitful year-round. But those days were gone. Now the palace required pitch torches and servants to keep the rooms lit and livable. The painted murals had started to flake away in places, and the hangings had grown faded and frayed at the edges. One day, it would all crumble to nothing, Neve feared, leaving no trace of its elegant grandeur behind.

Still, Neve liked to imagine some stray leftover enchantment had kept her secret escape hidden from the other palace dwellers. As she eased the wooden gate open farther, just enough to pass through, Neve felt the small hairs on the back of her neck lift. Inside the stable yard, she tilted her face to the breeze and sniffed at the air. No smoke. No smells. No cooking . . .

And that wasn't right.

It was close enough to evening meal time that there should have been a multitude of aromas drifting through the palace courtyards as roasting spits were turned and cauldrons of soup and stews set to swing over fires. Also, Temair—even in this overgrown, forgotten hollow curve of it—was never this silent. All she heard in that moment was a lonely crow call.

And then a voice: "It will be moonrise soon enough. I'd hurry if I were you."

Without her dagger at her hip, Neve had her fist cocked and ready to strike almost before she realized it.

"I'm sorry, Princess, I didn't mean to startle you." The owner of the voice stepped out from behind the spreading branches of a yew tree and Neve exhaled in relief.

"It's just *you*," she said, annoyed, lowering her arm.

Sakir, the only son of Farsa, the Dagda's Horse Lord and stable master, was a descendant of the Scythian warriors who had accompanied the Scathach Queen to Eire and been granted dominion over the Golden Vale—a wide, sweeping valley in the south to breed and raise war horses for the Tuatha Dé—far enough away from Temair to be its own little kingdom. Neve and Úna had made the journey once with their father when Neve was about five years old. Ruad Rofhessa had lifted Neve up onto the back of a sweet little mare to trot in circles swinging a wooden toy sword, and the Fir Bolg freedmen had called her "Little Scota."

In recent years, Farsa had brought his son from the Vale to live with him in Temair. Sakir had been assigned as Neve's tutor in all things horse-related. Which Neve had loosely interpreted as including learning to fight from both horseback and the deck of a bucking chariot. Sakir was only a few years older than Neve, but he was a gifted charioteer and skilled warrior and, when she'd demanded lessons, he'd taught her archery and how to wield a sword herself. Reluctantly, at first. The women of Temair weren't tutored in the arts of warcraft—indeed, it was an unspoken rule that those skills were essentially forbidden them—and Sakir had been surprised when she'd taken to her lessons with both enthusiasm and aptitude. So much so that he'd even recently begun to show her how to use a *sagaris*—the slender, two-headed Scythian war axe Sakir had been named for.

"What do you mean, 'hurry'?" she asked, pretending he hadn't just caught her sneaking back into the palace. She glanced around the deserted courtyard and her mind doubled back on what Sakir had said about the moon rising.

"Oh no," she murmured, sprinting over to the outbuilding where the Dagda's chariots were stored. She could see, even from a distance, that it was empty. "No, no, *no*."

"The king is on his way to Brú na Bóinne," Sakir called after her. "Along with your sister and the whole of the Tuatha Dé,

Princess. Lords, ladies, bondsfolk, the whole court. They've all gone for the—"

"The Stone Singing. Of course—damn! It completely slipped my mind!" Neve whirled in a circle, panic climbing up from her belly into her throat. "He'll *kill* me . . ."

"Not if you get there before the ritual begins," Sakir said. "I have your own chariot ready and waiting." He paused and his hazel eyes flicked over her, head to toe. Neve was still damp from her plunge into the Blackwater, her clothes streaked with mud and algae. "You should, perhaps . . . change first."

"Stay here!" Neve snapped, and dashed off toward her palace quarters.

Neve ran past the kennels and saw that the harrow hounds had all been penned in for the night, each stall locked up tight with an iron bar inscribed with a silver sigil to keep them under control.

Samhain was one of those times when—from sundown to sunrise the next morning—the walls between the mortal and Otherworldly realms grew thin in places and stray magic roamed free. The dogs would be restless until the dawn broke, but harmless in their pens. One howled mournfully as Neve sprinted past, sending a shiver up her spine. She glanced at the sky, as if the moon had already risen, but she knew Sakir was right.

There's still time . . .

She burst through the doors into her quarters to see that her good heavy gown with the patterned hem and sleeves had been laid out on her couch, beside the green and purple checked cloak for special occasions. Úna must have been hoping she'd make it back to the palace in time, Neve thought as she stripped out of her stained, dripping tunic and breeches.

There was no one to help Neve dress. Because of the ritual—and the fact that, this time, it coincided with Samhain, the Fir Bolg festival of the turning year—Úna's bondswoman, Emer, would have been permitted to leave the palace and celebrate with her own folk. Neve made do as best she could, tying the laces loosely before wriggling into her gown, jamming her feet into a pair of soft doe-skin boots, and slinging on a few bangles and a jeweled torc to make it seem as if she'd made an effort.

She flung her cloak on over her shoulders and fumbled with the garnet-studded silver cloak pin as she pelted back to the stables. Sakir was waiting for her, perched on the deck of the sleek wicker racing chariot Úna had gifted Neve on her fifteenth birthday. As she ran across the stable yard, he stood and took up the reins.

"Go!" she urged, slapping him on his shoulder as she jumped up behind him.

He snapped the reins smartly and the ponies broke into a trot, pulling the swift, light chariot along the palace avenues and out the main gateway. The palace watch—the only other living souls left in Temair—let them pass with disapproving glares and then shut the bronze-bound heavy oak gates behind them. Once outside the walls, Neve kept her eyes fixed on Sakir's shoulder, ignoring glimpses of shadowy shapes and gleaming eyes beneath the trees, as he urged the ponies to a full gallop. They headed north and east, toward the place where the An Bhóinn curved like a cupped hand around the sprawling burial ground for generations of Tuatha Dé.

In spite of Neve's urge to roam far beyond the walls of Temair, it was a place she avoided most of the time. Except for when she couldn't. Which was every full moon for the last three years, when the Dagda would drag the whole of his court out in a procession to Brú na Bóinne so they could witness the raising of the next in a series of standing stones. Massive, rough-hewn slabs of stone quarried from sacred sites scattered throughout the realm and transported to the floodplain, the stones—thirty-six of them—would ultimately form a ring of silent sentinels encircling Ruad Rofhessa's massive mortuary temple.

A temple that was finally nearing completion after ten long years.

A temple, some whispered, that wasn't really a temple at all.

The air was warm and silky on Neve's face, ruffling her hair as the chariot raced across the downs. "Did my father see you when he left?" Neve asked Sakir as they approached the carved stone bridge that forded An Bhóinn. She almost had to shout in his ear so he could hear over the rushing wind of their passage.

"No, Princess," Sakir answered over his shoulder. "I kept out of sight with the cart and your ponies and waited for you in the old paddock beside your secret gate."

"Why?" she asked, not understanding. "Why would you do that?" Never mind the fact that he was clearly familiar with her habit of sneaking out of the palace.

He hesitated before answering, shortening up the reins as the wide, winding avenue leading to their destination came into view.

"Because I saw you leave Temair this morning," Sakir said. "And when you didn't return in due time, I thought it might be prudent to provide you with, uh . . ."

"An excuse?"

"An explanation." He shrugged. "This way you can tell your father you were practicing your horsemanship in the far fields under my tutelage, and I failed to return you to the palace in time."

"No," Neve said. "Absolutely not. My father will have you flogged with your own horse whip if he thinks this is your fault."

"Then I have nothing to fear, Princess." He grinned wryly at her. "You know I don't use a whip on my horses."

The Dagda had never intended for his youngest daughter's equestrian lessons to turn martial. As far as he or anyone else at court knew, Sakir might as well have been her nursemaid, Neve often thought, bristling at the indignity. For his part, the young Scythian horseman somehow managed to remain both deferential and aloof in his role. Neve had never actually seen him lose his temper or show anything approaching fear—not even when faced with the task of taming an unbroken stallion.

As they slowed to a stop, Neve's billowing cloak settled back down around her shoulders. Although earlier in the day it had been almost stifling with the humidity, the air had grown precipitously cooler. Now a damp chill breeze whorled toward them from the direction of the barrow downs, where an ambient glow from fire pits and torchlight burnished the lowering sky. A ground mist was rising and Neve suppressed a shiver. Sakir wore no cloak—he rarely did—but she noticed even the sun-bleached hairs on his arms standing up against his summer-tanned skin. She put a hand on his shoulder.

"Stay here. I'll walk the rest of the way."

"Princess—"

"That wasn't a request, Sakir."

With a warning glance, Neve stepped down from the chariot and, drawing the hood of her cloak up over her head, walked swiftly—and, she hoped, discreetly—toward the hundreds of Tuatha Dé gathered in the clearing before the Dagda's great monument, Brú na Bóinne.

The sun was almost gone behind the far green hills and the sky in the west was a riot of crimson and amethyst clouds trailing like war banners across the skies. In the eastern gloaming, bright-white pinpricks of stars began to wink in the sky. The shadows of the gathered crowd, grown long upon the ground, began to merge into a deeper darkness. Like a wraith herself, Neve slipped past the ring of torches that circled the assembled folk of Temair and, weaving through ranks of bejeweled and perfumed bodies, managed to find Úna. She stood and slipped into place beside her just as the Druids began their chant.

"Where in the great wide world have you been?" Úna whispered out of the side of her mouth. Without looking away from the ritual, she reached up and tugged down the hood of Neve's cloak. Everyone except the Druids in their cowled robes was bare-headed in reverence to the Dagda's monumental achievement.

The drone of the Druid chants hummed like drowsy bees in Neve's ears. She put a hand up to smooth her wind-twisted hair.

"I . . . the far fields," she whispered back. "Practicing with my chariot. I lost track of time . . ."

"The far fields." Úna pulled a long strand of limp green river weed out of Neve's tresses. "Mm-hm."

"Did he notice?"

Úna shook her head in disbelief. "He's *furious*, Neve." Of course Ruad Rofhessa had noticed his youngest daughter's absence. This time, and how many others before?

Neve swallowed thickly. "Oh."

Damn you, thief, she cursed silently. It was *his* fault she'd arrived late.

She stood there, fingers knotting anxiously behind her back, as the chanting of the Druids swelled and the folk of Temair raised their voices in soaring harmonies. A faintly luminous mist piled up in drifts all around them—as it did every time—and the singing of the stone into its sentinel place commenced. The singing was the only thing Neve could stomach about the ritual. The songs of the Tuatha Dé were glorious, as intricate and complex and intertwining as the tattoos they worked into their skin, and she felt the tightness in her chest loosen—just a little—as she lent her own voice to the melody. To the invitation of the mystery within the music.

The temple itself, however, was an *un*inviting mystery to Neve.

Its secrets—unlike most of the secrets Neve encountered—held no allure for her whatsoever. In fact, Brú na Bóinne stirred a kind of uneasy revulsion in her each time she had to participate in the ritual, watching a new sentinel stone be sung into place.

The ceremony was supposed to evoke a sense of the mystical. But even though the Dagda's Druids were the only ones for whom magic hadn't been outlawed, they seemed disinclined to waste their efforts on actually making giant rocks fly. Gofannon and his priests relied, instead, on a clever system of ropes and sloping sand hills and wooden posts that made it seem, in the shadowy twilight, *almost* as if the stone was floating, drifting upright to a standing position before sliding down gracefully into the hole dug to receive it.

The Singing of the Stones.

Neve knew, of course—as they all did—that it wasn't *really* magic that moved the giant sentinels. But the effect still managed to send a shiver down her spine.

The latest stone to be sung into place was positioned near the front of the temple where the single entrance stood—a gaping black maw—in the middle of the curved white stone wall that comprised the structure's edifice. The monument rose up out of the floodplain like a low, lone, perfectly circular hill. The shallow dome of its roof was covered with lush green turf and encircled with kerbstones, each one longer than a man is tall, laid end to end and carved with intricate spirals and knotwork designs. Then the whole of the structure was encircled by the outer ring of standing stones, placed at intervals, like guardians. At least, it would be. The one the Tuatha Dé sang to standing that evening was the second-to-last stone.

Once the circle was complete, there would be a final dedication ceremony, performed at Midwinter, at sunrise after the longest night of the year, and then Brú na Bóinne would be finished. And the Dagda's legacy would be . . . what? Neve didn't really know, exactly. She didn't know why, but the prospect of that circle finally closing filled her with a kind of vague, unnamed dread.

But more likely, the mound of stones would sit there, curled like a sleeping dragon in the wide green valley, for all time. Then, maybe her father would finally come back to himself and become just Ruad Rofhessa once more. A father and a king. Not a monument builder.

At last, the stone tipped forward as the song swelled and slid down into the deep hole dug in the earth. The mist rolled away as the stone settled with a thunderous boom that echoed across the plain and Neve flinched, feeling the thrum in the very marrow of her bones. For a moment, she thought she saw something. Something she'd never seen before at a Singing. As the mist faded, she glimpsed a faint indigo light emanating from the surface of the stones. Like a flicker of lightning flashing—and then . . .

Nothing. Stillness.

Neve glanced sideways at her father where he stood in the midst of all his chieftains. His expression was feverishly intense but the strong angles of his profile made it seem as if he, too, were carved out of rock. The gold on his brow and at his throat shone, garnets and amethyst sparking like embers in the torchlight, and his eyes were fixed, unblinking, on the yawning temple maw.

Neve had a sense the Dagda could see things in that darkness no one else could. Or maybe only *one* other member of that gathering could see those things, too . . .

She looked past her father at the architect responsible for designing and building the Dagda's temple, from every stone stacked and laid to every pattern carved, line and curve. Gofannon. His gaze was equally fixed on the same darkness as the king's. And his expression was one that Neve could only describe as . . . *hunger*.

She shuddered and looked away from him.

In truth, she never found it easy to look at the man, even though there was nothing discomfiting about his appearance. Rather the opposite. He was handsome, with mild blue eyes and a thick copper mane swept back off a high forehead, falling in braids woven together and fastened with gold rings. Around his neck, he wore a silver torc, fashioned like a serpent, with moon-white pearls for eyes. He was well-mannered and fiercely intelligent, a gifted Druid.

He's more than a common Druid. He's a sorcerer.

That was the whispered rumor, at least. That he controlled magic beyond what a normal human—with runes and rites and lore—could. Or should. A sorcerer, Neve had heard, held power even over life and death. Úna scoffed whenever Neve brought it up, though, saying that Gofannon's power was political in nature and *that* was more than enough. Bru na Bóinne was his idea. Such was his sway over the Dagda.

As the song of the Tuatha Dé died away on the evening breeze, the lightless maw of the barrow seemed as if it opened wide in a toothless howl. Neve felt as if it would swallow her whole and she would tumble down its gullet into endless darkness.

With a great effort, she tore her gaze away and squeezed her eyes shut.

She opened them again when she heard Úna's sharp intake of breath.

The Dagda was striding toward them, stalking through pools of light and shadow cast by the fire pits, the ever-present war club in his hand swinging like the tail of an angry cat. Neve wished she had something to grip, too—her sword or sagaris or bow—something that would make her feel less like a defenseless child. Even the dagger she'd given Ronan would have helped.

She took a step back and stumbled against Úna, who put her hands on Neve's shoulders to steady her. Together they stood as their father glared down at them, his broad chest expanding and contracting like a bellows. The tuath marks tattooed on his cheeks, above his dark, braided beard, appeared almost black against his ruddy complexion and made him look even more fearsome.

"Neve—"

"*Lovely* singing tonight, Princess."

Startled, Neve turned to see Gofannon standing beside her, seemingly oblivious that he had just dared to interrupt the Dagda on the cusp of a tirade. While Ruad Rofhessa was rendered momentarily speechless, Gofannon reached out to take Neve's hand. The pearl eyes of the snake torc coiled around his neck seemed to wink at her in the torchlight.

"Simply lovely. Your voice is a gift to this glorious endeavor," he continued smoothly. He bowed his head at Úna. "Both of you, of course, my lady."

Úna returned the bow with a graceful nod. "Thank you, Gofannon," she said. "You're very kind."

"Not at all." His gaze lingered on Úna for a moment, then shifted back to Neve. "You are both blessed by the gods. But I must commend you, Lady Neve—I could hear *your* voice rising above the crowd. I could sense the magic in it." He turned his attention to the Dagda. "I feel, my lord, that perhaps we should dedicate the stone we raised this night to your youngest daughter."

Neve watched, astonished, as her father's mighty ire boiled away like steam, leaving an empty cauldron behind. He muttered something that sounded like "Perhaps . . ."

"Perhaps in the shape of one of your tuath marks, lady?" Gofannon continued blithely, as if Ruad Rofhessa had enthusiastically agreed.

Neve's throat went dry. "I . . ."

"You *have* received at least one mark at your age, haven't you?"

"I . . . no. Not yet." Neve stammered. "I—"

"Oh," Gofannon said, a faint frown crossing his brow. "I see . . ."

To commemorate their triumph in conquering the Fomori, the Scathach had ordained that the Tuatha Dé would mark their bodies with the sigils they'd found carved on stones throughout their new land, forbidding the use of those same marks to the Fir Bolg. The thought had always made Neve uneasy, like theft—not of riches or cattle—but of something more important than that.

"It's far past time you did," her father said, looking for all the world as if he might drag her off that very moment to have the needle pressed into her flesh.

"No matter, my king." Gofannon smiled benignly at Neve. "I will dream a symbol for her myself and have it carved into the stone we raised this night. Maybe it will inspire the princess to take her first mark."

"I'm sure it will," the Dagda said pointedly to Neve.

A cold, oily shiver ran down Neve's spine. As grateful as she was for the distraction, why did it feel like the sorcerer was trying to subtly lay some kind of claim to her?

Stop it, she admonished herself silently. He was simply trying to deflect her father's anger so that the king wouldn't mar the ritual and lose face in front of the whole court of Temair. Gofannon was a master of that kind of politic persuasion. Neve had seen him quench fires between certain tuath chieftains without their even realizing it. Seen him kindle blazes between others the same way. And Brú na Bóinne was his glory.

"And then," Gofannon went on, "when the final stone is sung into place, I move we dedicate it to our next queen. To you, Lady Úna." He took up Úna's hand and, as her wide sleeve fell back from her delicate wrist, he smiled. "I myself shall carve a mark on the stone for her," he said. "One that echoes her great beauty. One like *this* . . ."

He pressed his finger against the spiraling design on Úna's forearm, the first tuath mark her sister had ever received. Neve remembered the day that Úna had ridden off to the blind tattooist's cave early one morning not long after her eleventh birthday, so that he could dream her mark for her: a concentric spiral, simple at a glance, but to Neve it always looked as though there was some kind of goddess or spirit at the center of the symbol, projecting power . . . or constrained by it. She couldn't tell.

For a moment, Neve's thoughts returned—as they seemed to keep doing—to the thief Ronan, and to the strange, darkling marks she'd seen moving *beneath* his skin.

As lords and ladies began to drift past, Gofannon let go of Úna's wrist and stepped back with a bow before taking his leave. The court was heading back to the palace now that the ritual was done. Neve gazed around and was struck by the ethereal sight of the richly dressed lords and ladies, attendants bearing torchlight, bathed in moon and star gleam, weaving silently through the waving grass and night-blooming flowers back toward the river crossing. They looked almost godlike. As if the veil between Eire and the Otherworld had parted and the denizens of the spirit realms wandered free.

When the final stone is sung into place . . .

"You will both attend me in the Great Hall when you arrive back at Temair." Her father's voice broke her reverie. "The *moment* you arrive. Do I make myself clear?"

Úna took her younger sister firmly by the hand and said, "Clear as spring water, Father," before leading her away.

The Dagda called to his chiefs and his charioteer and led the procession back home, his green cloak billowing behind him. Neve glanced back over her shoulder. The pale stones of the barrow seemed almost to glow in the darkness.

Why did it feel, Neve wondered, that with each stone guardian raised at Brú na Bóinne . . . with each step closer to the completion of the temple . . . a noose was tightening? Stone circles were supposed to keep the things within them safe. But they were also supposed to keep the things within them contained.

Which purpose did this one serve, she wondered?

VII

WHAT *EXACTLY* DID Sparrow mean by 'going to war with the Tuatha Dé'?" Ronan raised an eyebrow at Cavall as the two of them rested against an ancient oak at the edge of the clearing with their mugs. After his third or fourth leap over the fires, Ronan had begun to feel a bit like a haunch of roasted boar in need of a good basting. Cool beer had seemed a reasonable remedy. "She can't be entirely serious. Can she?"

Cavall shrugged in that way he had when discussing matters more weighty than whatever blade he was currently forging. "Hear them tell it," he said, "the scavengers aren't just hunting and gathering for themselves anymore. And they're trading in more than just healing spells and petty hexes."

That confirmed what Sparrow had told Ronan. Up to a point. "*Who* are they gathering for?" he pressed.

Cavall hesitated. Then he said with a sigh, "Fir Domnann. Apparently."

"Death and Darkness, Cavall!" Ronan swore, feeling a rush of heat to his head. The mere mention of the splinter tribe made Ronan's blood boil. "Those bastards burned my village to the ground when I was a babe. How are they any better than the Tuatha Dé? How could *they*"—he flung out an arm in the direction of the salvagers—"have honestly expected me to go along with their idiotic scheme? I'll not be a part of it."

"That's what I told them, once I knew." Cavall held up his hands. "They still thought it was worth a try convincing you."

"You tell them there's nothing to convince me of," Ronan said through clenched teeth. "I'm done with magic and I want nothing to do with their little wars. War and the Tuatha Dé don't end well for—"

Cavall hissed and jerked his head in the direction of something over Ronan's shoulder. When Ronan saw Cliona striding toward them across the glade, he muscled his expression into a casual smile.

"You boys fighting?" she asked.

Ronan snorted. "I'm a lamb, Cliona. Remember?"

"One day, lambkin, I'll see you bare your predator's teeth, I think." She smiled, but her blue eyes stared into his as she murmured, "We all will . . ."

Ronan didn't know what she meant by that, but it sent a ghost-breath shiver across his skin. Cavall made a show of pretending to hear his name called and excused himself from the conversation— almost running to get away—as the air between Faoladh and thief crackled with unseen sparks. A moment later, Cliona blinked and those sparks flew up and away into the night.

"Come on then, tender morsel." She bared her teeth in a grin and grabbed Ronan by the wrist. "I find myself in need of some excitement."

She stepped sideways—and Ronan ducked hastily—to avoid a pair of her sisters swinging wildly at each other with flaming torches, cheered on by the crowd, in a ritual representation of the Battle of An Bhearú that had devolved into a rollicking brawl. Ronan couldn't fathom what other kind of excitement Cliona craved that night as she dragged him away from the festivities, toward a pony cart standing off at a distance beneath the trees.

"You've been to one Samhain revel, you've been to them all," she said. With a glance at the revelers, she hopped up and took up the reins. "We'll bring it back before they need it again," she said when he hesitated. "Come *on.*"

As she urged the ponies into a trot, following the curve of the river north and east, Ronan sat back and soaked in the lush, twilight-rich scenery rolling past. In those liminal moments between light and darkness, Eire was heartbreaking in its beauty. Folded hills and meadows saturated with deep purples and rich, crimson-tinged shadows, languid beneath a luminous sky.

The sounds of festivities quickly faded behind them to be replaced with a deep silence broken only by the mournful calls of late geese flying home and the clatter of the cart wheels on the track as they headed . . . somewhere. Flickering, wispy sprites danced in the gloaming shadows beneath the trees, shy and curious. Like he'd told Cavall earlier, Ronan didn't really have much use for harvest rituals, and he was curious what Cliona had in mind. After a short while, she pulled the cart to a stop in a thick copse of hazel trees.

"This way," she said as she reached into the cart bed for a dark woolen cloak. She shrugged it on and, drawing it close over her leathers, silently beckoned Ronan to follow her as she wove through the trees toward distant flickerings of torchlight.

On the plain of An Bhóinn.

At the edge of a crowd gathered before the Dagda's great mortuary barrow.

Ronan's heart crawled up toward his throat.

The sight and sound of Druids chanting filled Ronan with a surge of conflicting emotions. Even as he'd disavowed magic to Cavall earlier, Ronan had felt the lie. Just like he felt the darklight sigils writhing unseen beneath his skin. The place where Neve had laid a fingertip against his wrist still burned like a guttering torch. All of it enough to get him torn to pieces by harrow hounds. So it was probably fortunate that the only person who knew his secret for absolute certain was the one person Ronan was unlikely to get within slingshot range of ever again.

"Ah, gods . . . ," he muttered. "I should have known I'd never be *that* lucky."

It was the tilt of her head that first caught his attention as he and Cliona slipped through the edges of the crowd for a better view of the ritual. But even if he'd been blindfolded, Ronan would have known she was there. Almost close enough to reach out and touch. Standing beside her coolly elegant sister, Neve was mussed and hectic—hair tangled around her face, her cloak and gown hanging askew—and still somehow wildly beautiful. The sight of her almost made Ronan grin, recalling their mad adventures of the afternoon, and that night so long ago . . .

But then he remembered he'd decided not to ever think of her again.

So don't.

She shook back her hair from her face and the last lingering twilight seemed to caress her cheeks and the long lines of her neck . . .

Fool.

Ronan wrenched his attention back to where the robed and hooded Druids ranged around the entrance to the Great Barrow, chanting verses that rolled with familiar cadences. He could feel the power, sense it in the rising pale-blue fog that swept toward the gathered crowd of glittering Tuatha Dé nobles. When they all began to sing, a chill ran up his spine and made his scalp prickle.

There was magic there. Real magic. A *lot* of it.

But Ronan was confused. He could see the huge, carved stone was cradled by a series of ropes and scaffolding . . . all of which did nothing. The ropes weren't taut in the way they would be if they had, indeed, been lifting up the great stone, and the scaffolding and support structures looked impressive but, in reality, were just for show. Something which, Ronan noted, the obscuring mist conveniently disguised.

No. It really was the singing that moved the stones. The actual *singing*.

Ronan shut his eyes tight for a moment and listened in the way he'd learned to when he'd been in the Order. A way of listening that went beyond just sounds heard with the ears, to meaning—and magic—heard with the mind and heart . . . One voice in particular rang out in the gathering darkness, accompanied by an answering echo, like the distant cry of a lone wolf. The sound of it cut through Ronan's mind, and he could feel the cursed magic in his own blood stirring in answer.

His eyes flew open as he sought out Neve's face again in the crowd. Her eyes were closed, her face tilted upward. And the breath that escaped her lips in song, misty with the chill in the air, shone with a subtle luminescence.

Magic . . .

He could see scattered glimmer-wisps of enchantment rising with the voices of others gathered there, too, all of them much fainter than Neve's. Ronan's head swam with confusion. Why would the Druid Order arrange the *trappings* of a ritual in order to disguise the *actual power* of the ritual, allowing the participants to wink and nod to each other about how it was their "singing" that raised the stones?

Ronan glanced over at Cliona and saw that her eyes were narrowed, her nostrils quivering, as if her Faoladh senses caught the scent of magic, pungent in the air. "They want them to believe it's just fakery," she whispered. "But it's *real . . .*"

Ronan felt himself tense. "Cliona. Why did we come here?"

"I wanted to see for myself what Aevinn dreams about," she said. "I wanted to see Teg Duinn."

"And you think *that's* it?" Ronan nodded at the grassy dome of the Dagda's monument. "The—what was it, now—the 'wide green hill' from her visions? Eire is rife with wide green hills, in case you hadn't noticed."

"Something is coming, lambkin," she said, her eyes fixed on Brú na Bóinne. "Look. Closely. What do your Druid eyes see?"

Ronan stifled an impatient sigh, but he focused his attention on the barrow in the way the Druids had taught him.

And felt a chill race across his skin.

"The sigils on the kerbstones." He nodded at the monument. "It looks like every spell the damned Druids have ever confiscated has been carved into the patterns of those stones. Broken down into the elements of pure distilled magic."

The barrow was a giant's cauldron, filled to the brim with simmering power.

"We knew the Druids were hoarding magic. Now we know where. But why?" Ronan whispered. "And why all the misdirection?"

"Maybe they don't want anyone to know just how much *actual* power they're gathering and pouring into this temple," Cliona whispered back. "If the Tuatha Dé ever realize this isn't just something built to assuage their Dagda's vanity, they might begin to wonder why they aren't quite living like the gods they once believed themselves to be. They might start to wonder, too, where all the magic has disappeared to. And why. This way, they don't question until it's too late."

Right. Create a distraction with one hand, cut a purse with the other . . .

That much Ronan understood.

"Too late for what?"

"The wolf to find the wide green hill," she murmured, "and howl at a blood red moon . . . Teg Duinn."

"But why—"

The song swelled as the sentinel stone tipped forward and settled into the pit with an echoing boom. Silence descended. The spell was broken. The Tuatha Dé stirred and shook themselves as if from a dreaming sleep.

"Well. Now we know one thing at least," Cliona said.

"What's that?" Ronan asked.

"Who throws the better party." She punched his shoulder and grinned. "Come on. I've seen enough for now. Let's get back before Cavall drains all the beer jugs dry."

The eerie solemnity of what they'd just witnessed, the puzzling strangeness of it, vanished as she turned on her heel and started back in the direction of the pony cart. When Ronan hesitated to follow, Cliona arched a pale eyebrow at him.

"Go ahead and I'll meet you back there." He pulled her close and whispered in her ear, "There's got to be a rich purse or two in this lordly crowd worth cutting."

"Don't get caught in any traps you can't wriggle out of, my thief," she said. "Remember, I've put bets on you outliving us all."

"And I'd hate to disappoint you, love," he said with a wink.

The troop of glittering nobles bunched up near the narrowing of the path leading to the river crossing and, beneath his cloak, Ronan slid his newly acquired knife from its sheath. A few "careless" bumps in the crowd, a purse here, a bit of loose finery there, and Ronan could recoup his day's losses in only a few moments. All without going anywhere near the head of the procession and the royal entourage who led the way.

A cloak brooch and two full coin purses had already found their way into the inside pocket of Ronan's cloak when he spied a particularly rich, jeweled silver cuff circling a lady's wrist peeking out beneath the hem of a wide sleeve. Weaving his way through the crowd, Ronan sidled up to the cloaked woman and reached with light, nimble fingers for his prize. But when his fingertips brushed against her skin, Ronan felt as though he'd been struck by lightning and his hand closed convulsively around hers.

His target gasped in surprise and spun around and—of course, Ronan cursed silently—it was Neve, her hood falling back to reveal her face. Sparks of bright gold flared in her eyes as she realized who it was that had dared lay a hand on the Dagda's daughter.

"Teeth and talons!" she hissed. "What are you *doing* here?"

Before he could answer—in truth, he really had no *earthly* idea what he was doing in that moment, or why he hadn't just left with Cliona in the first place—Ronan glanced down at where he held Neve's slender fingers. He sucked in a sharp breath and Neve followed his gaze. The palm of her hand shone faintly with a pale, golden glow in lines that seemed to form a pattern. The markings disappeared before he could fully tell what it was.

Ronan snatched his hand back like she'd suddenly turned to molten metal. He could feel the old scar on his own palm suddenly pulsing with darkling fire. He clenched his fingers into a tight fist, as if to keep that light from leaking out.

"What am I doing here?" he whispered in a dry rasp. "What are *you* doing here?" He glanced toward the head of the entourage, where he could see the Dagda in his chariot. "You're supposed to be up there. With your people."

Neve's golden eyes were wide, staring down at the swiftly fading marks on her palm. "What did you *do* to me?"

Ronan peered at her hand. What *had* he done? He hadn't done anything. Had he? All he knew was the mark was already vanishing and he had no raging desire for Neve to raise a ruckus. "Uh. That? Just a trick. A bit of Samhain fun . . ."

Neve thrust her hand deep inside her other sleeve. "I understand. You have a persistent death wish. That's the only thing that could possibly explain this behavior. My father's óglach couldn't catch you today, so you thought you'd make it easy and just hand yourself over to him directly. Shall I whistle his chariot ponies over?"

In truth, that made about as much sense as anything. How else was Ronan supposed to explain it to Neve? Especially after what he'd said to her on the riverbank? And what he'd said *had* been true. Attending the Tuatha Dé ritual hadn't even been his idea. He was starting to think that it hadn't been Cliona's idea, either. Not entirely. No. Something else was at work in Ronan's destiny that Samhain Eve. Something that seemed determined to keep throwing him into the path of the daughter of the Dagda. But for what reason, Ronan couldn't even begin to fathom.

When he didn't respond, Neve snorted with derision. "You're damned lucky the harrow hounds are kenneled back at Temair this night, thief."

"Why is that?" he asked. "I mean—why aren't they here?"

"Because they are not needed at Brú na Bóinne. This is a protected place."

"Is *that* what you think?" Ronan pressed. "Truly? Or is it because there is so much magic here in this place—on *this* night—that it might ignite a cursefire blaze in them so strong they would burn to ash?"

Neve looked at him like he'd lost his mind.

"You mean *that*?" She threw a hand back toward Brú na Bóinne. "I can see now why they chased you out of the Druid order if that's what you think—"

"Stop." He resisted the urge to lay hands on her again. Barely. "You're not that blind or that stupid, Neve." He winced. "Uh. Princess Neve. You can't be. Yes, the ropes, the scaffolding, all designed to make it look like an illusion. But *you* felt it. I know you did. The real magic."

Neve's eyes flicked down to Ronan's clenched fist, where he could still feel the sting of his curse. For a moment, her haughty demeanor wavered and slipped, and the girl from the bruidean who'd saved him from the óglach looked at him again through the windows of Neve's golden eyes.

"Yours is the only *real* magic I've seen in years," she whispered.

His fingers unclenched and he lifted his hand. Her hand raised to meet it, fingertips poised to touch. Ronan waited, breathless, to see if the glimmering mark would flare again on her palm . . . But

Neve pulled away from him as if from a burning torch, dropping her arm.

"What do you want of me, Ronan?" she asked.

The question caught him off guard. What *did* he want? "I don't know," he said.

Her eyes closed and she huffed a sharp sigh.

"I *don't*." The frustration he felt at his own inability to explain boiled over. "All I know is something's happening. Something in this realm has . . . *shifted*. I can feel it, Neve."

Neve stepped back. "I don't know what you mean."

"You do, too. I know you do. There is danger waiting—"

"Enough." It was too late. The royal mask slipped back into place. "The only danger waiting for *me* is back at the palace. Thanks, in large part, to *you*."

"Me? Wha—"

"And the longer I stand here talking to you, the deeper the peril."

Before he could think of what to say to that, Neve whirled around and sprinted off to catch up with the royal entourage, leaving Ronan with a hollow feeling in the pit of his stomach.

What had Neve been doing, lagging so far back in the crowd? And why had Ronan reached for *her* of all people? Coincidence was something he'd never believed in, but, even if he had, this was all too much for just one day. What was it the old man had said about the gods?

"You don't have to believe in them. But you might, at least, pay them a little mind once you find that they believe in you."

VIII

NEVE CAUGHT UP with Úna before her sister had the chance to become even angrier, and the Dagda's two daughters rode back to Temair together in Neve's chariot. Sakir did a remarkable job, Neve thought, of making himself virtually invisible as he drove, calling only to the horses in a quiet voice, and that as little as possible.

Úna didn't say much either on the ride home, and Neve silently cursed the wretched Fir Bolg thief. She hated disappointing her sister—especially when it wasn't her fault—but it wasn't as though she could explain herself. Not this time.

"I *said* I was sorry," Neve muttered as the torch-lit palace appeared, rising over the treetops.

"No, you didn't." Úna sighed, a weary sound. "And I know you aren't."

"Úna—"

"I don't think you should be, if you want the truth," her sister cut her short. "I *don't* think Father's right, or reasonable in this matter. But Ruad Rofhessa is not just our father, he's the bloody *king*! Death and Darkness, Neve—you can't keep defying him like this!"

Neve blinked at her sister in astonishment. She'd never heard her speak like that—on the very edge of cursing like a Fir Bolg fishwife. Úna was grace and good manners in every situation and always, always the one to make peace. But her reaction told Neve something—that she wasn't the only one who would suffer under their father's wrath. And Neve would rather cut off her own hand than cause her sister hurt.

"I *am* sorry," she said again. And this time she meant it.

Úna's expression softened, and, after a moment, she kissed Neve's forehead. "I am, too, little cub. Maybe . . . just stay silent and let me handle Father, all right?"

"That," Sakir said dryly as they drove through the gates of the palace, "is an excellent plan."

But once they found themselves standing in front of the Dagda in the Great Hall, there wasn't much chance for either of them to speak. They'd entered the vaulting, cavernous chamber to find him alone, sitting on his great chair, hunched over his knees with a large mug of mead clutched tight in his fist.

"I don't know what you were thinking, Neve," he said by way of greeting. "I never do. It's like your mother left a cursed piece of her soul behind in you when she went away. Just to torment me. You're exactly like her."

"I'm sorry, Father." Neve avoided her father's angry stare, fixing her eyes firmly on a hacked and split battle shield hanging from the carved wooden post at the center of the hall—a trophy of war, taken from the dead hands of a legendary Fir Domnann warrior named Sengann, vanquished in battle by Ruad Rofhessa himself before Neve was even born.

"Determined to embarrass me in front of the whole of my court," her father railed. "I will not stand for it."

"I said I was—"

"You are Tuatha Dé!" he roared.

Neve ground her teeth together and kept her mouth shut. She'd never seen her father like that. As if the heat of his fury was something that came from outside himself.

"What in this great green world compels you to go tearing around the countryside like some wildling thing?" He thrust himself up out of his chair and off the dais, stalking back and forth in front of his daughters. "Like some kind of animal, without any regard for your dignity—let alone mine—like one of *them*—"

"*Them?*" At the derision in her father's voice, suddenly all Neve's promises to behave flew out of her head like so many sparrows from a broken bird cage. She thought of Ronan. A thief, yes—an infuriating one—but *not* an animal. Belonging to folk who'd been made lesser by the way her own folk treated them. Neve felt a prickling rush of shame for the way she'd reacted that afternoon and it stoked a fire in her, fed by her father's contempt. "You mean those filthy Fir Bolg?" she said. "The folk of this land that our people *conquered*? The ones you rule over as king?"

Úna grabbed for her. "Neve—"

"*No*, Úna." Neve wrenched her sleeve from her sister's grip. "Say what you like about me, Father. But a king—a Dagda—

rules over his people equally, peasant and princess alike, or he is a tyrant."

"Don't push me, Neve!" her father thundered, towering over his daughters. "You think you know what it is to rule? You know nothing of kingship. You think I haven't noticed, but I've seen you racing your chariot and swinging your axe around like some kind of hero from a bard's tale. You want to be like the Scathach? Is *that* what you want? You want to crack the Lia Fail to dust with your reckless will? I have spent the last ten years of my life raising a legacy out of the flesh and bones of this very land in order to keep it safe from the darkness that threatens to devour us."

Neve stared at her father wide-eyed. What on earth did the Lia Fail have to do with her—or the Scathach, for that matter? What darkness? What was he talking about? Her father spoke as if there were hordes of invaders beaching ships, hammering at the very gates of Temair, instead of a few scattered disorganized raids quickly suppressed by the óglach. He spoke as if the gates of the Otherworld were on the cusp of yawning wide to spew forth horrors.

By her side, she could sense that Úna was just as confused as she was.

"Do you think the gods sent me this monumental task to taunt me?" Ruad Rofhessa continued, his gaze roving above her head, almost as if he wasn't even talking to her in that moment. "To mock the greatness of the Tuatha Dé? We are the kings of this land and we will rule eternal. I will see to it. I *will* keep all our people—*all* the people of this green isle—safe." He stopped and spun back around. "You, Neve Anann Eriu, will *not* be a stone in that road. I have been warned and now so have you."

Warned? Neve wondered, stunned. *By who? Why?*

"Father . . . please." Úna moved toward him, her voice low and soothing. "Calm yourself—"

"And *you.*" The Dagda rounded on his elder daughter, one blunt finger pointing at her face. "Don't think I don't see your mother in you, too, my gentle girl. Gentle as a hunting cat, you are. Don't think I don't know the schemes behind that demure smile."

The Dagda threw back his head, pouring what seemed like half a cauldronful of mead down his throat.

"I know what to do with *you,*" he said, wiping his mouth with the back of one hand and fixing Úna with a pointed glare. "You, my child, will marry."

Úna made a choking sound. "What—"

"Now. A husband. As soon as it can be arranged. It's time the throne of Temair had a proper heir. A prince to sit on the throne after me . . ."

Úna's hands clenched once, and then she swallowed hard and lifted her chin. "You are my father and my king," she said, her voice quiet and clear. "You are the Dagda of the Tuatha Dé. I will, of course, do as you say."

Neve started to sputter in outrage, but Úna gripped her arm. Painfully.

"Only *I* will be the one to choose my husband."

Neve bit down on her lip to keep silent. Úna had told her that she would handle their father and suddenly Neve believed her wholeheartedly. The Dagda regarded his eldest daughter warily, like a hunted beast sensing a hidden snare.

"Not you," Úna continued. "Not the Druids, nor your chieftains, nor advisers. I alone will decide who will share my bed and board and, on the far-off day when the gods call on you to cross the Great Dark River and take your place at their side in the Otherworld, who will sit on the throne of Temair."

"You—"

"*I* will decide," she said again, cutting Ruad Rofhessa's protest short. "And if you don't agree, then you can send me to live locked behind the women's walls with Neve, marry a worthy suitor yourself to be your prince-consort, and the gods give you good luck birthing a babe to be your heir. You'll leave a legacy to an empty line."

And that, Neve understood, was that.

Ruad Rofhessa understood it, too. He had experience with Tuatha Dé women.

"Failing that," Úna continued, "I suppose you could always beseech our mother to return to court . . ."

The Dagda actually blanched a bit at the suggestion. But then an eerie calm seemed to settle upon him like a cloak. He gazed at his eldest with an expression that was indecipherable. Neve tried to find respect there, but all she managed to glean was a calculated understanding of his options—which Úna had just laid out to him quite clearly.

"So be it," he said, and took a rather more measured sip of his mead.

Úna tilted her head in a gesture of acceptance of the agreement. She reached for Neve's hand to lead her away before he changed his mind.

"Choose wisely, daughter," Ruad Rofhessa said. He shot Neve a flat, gray glare over the rim of his mug. "I don't think any one of us here would want the responsibility for the Tuatha Dé's blessed continuance to fall on your sister's shoulders, now, would we?"

That last barb delivered with the precision of one of his óglach archers, the Dagda turned and stalked out of the room by way of the door behind the throne that led to his private dwelling. Neve swallowed the hurt that swelled in her chest. Theirs had never been an effusively affectionate relationship, to be sure, but Ruad Rofhessa hadn't ever looked at her like she was an actual *adversary*. Something to be fought. Or feared . . .

No, she thought. *That's ridiculous. The Dagda fears nothing. Certainly not me . . .*

"He's gone mad," she said as she and Úna made their way through the silent corridors of the palace back to their rooms.

"He hasn't," Úna said, but her brows knit in a deep frown. "He's just . . . not thinking clearly. Perhaps the stress of building Brú na Bóinne . . ."

"More madness! Some of the common folk are calling it Teg Duinn, you know, claiming it leads to the Otherworld," Neve said. "*They* say it's cursed." That was the way of most things in Eire: one thing to the Tuatha Dé meant something else entirely to the Fir Bolg.

Úna lifted an eyebrow but didn't bother to ask how Neve knew what the common folk said. "It's a covenant between the Dagda and the gods. An offering to beseech their benevolence and help keep all of Eire safe. That's all."

That sounds like Gofannon talking, Neve thought.

"What do we need safekeeping from?" she asked.

Úna stopped and turned a smile on Neve that was supposed to be reassuring. It was anything but. Neve was well aware that if anyone understood the actual state of the kingdom—and whether or not it was in any peril—it was Úna. Over the course of the past year, while their father had become occupied to the exclusion of all other matters with his monument, the tuaths had quietly begun to turn more and more to Úna for tacit leadership. It seemed to Neve her sister had taken advantage of that role, carefully gathering threads from the corners of the kingdom to weave a tapestry that would afford her influence, no matter who wound up sitting on the Dagda's throne beside her. There were, Neve realized, more ways to rule than vanquishing enemies with club or sword.

"What have you heard?" Neve asked. "Tell me. I'm not a child."

The smile faded. "Rumors. That's all." Úna rubbed a hand over her forehead as if she could erase the furrows. "Whispers of more raids to come. Bigger ones. Sightings that could mean ships massing off the north coast, between Eire and Alba . . . *maybe*. Then again, it may be nothing."

"The Fomori are returning," Neve murmured.

"Oh, Neve, no . . ." Úna shook her head. "Listen to me. You're *not* a child and the Fomori are a story for children. These are just raiders—like that wicked old brute Sengann's raiders, the Fir Domnann—remember them? And they can be defeated just the same. No need for magic. Just plain old swords and spears."

For once, Úna didn't sound so very certain.

"Is Father readying the chieftains?" Neve asked. "Will he sound the carnyx and call up the warriors of the other tuaths to prepare for battle?"

Úna hesitated. "No, that's just it. He's not doing anything except . . ."

"Except building his damned temple to himself."

They reached the entrance to their sprawling apartments, where an óglach stood guard about thirty paces down the corridor, trying to look inconspicuous in spite of the massive gray-furred hound that stood leashed at his side. Ruad Rofhessa was clearly serious about making sure his daughters didn't test his patience any further that night. The doors to their private rooms swung inward and Úna's handmaiden, Emer, appeared before them, a heap of ruined garments—the clothes Neve had hastily discarded on the floor—piled over one arm.

"Oh!" Emer exclaimed, startled. Then her dark-eyed gaze narrowed at the óglach in the hall. "Away, beast!" she snapped, flapping a hand at him like a fierce, tiny bird defending its nest from a hovering hawk. "Go harass some other poor soul, and take that bloody great magic-eating abomination with you." The guard glowered at her and a low rumble sounded in the hound's chest, but Emer was undaunted. "*Off*, I said!"

The óglach retreated around the corner of the hallway as Emer ushered her royal charges into their apartments and slammed the heavy oak door shut behind them with a snort of disdain. The Fir Bolg bondswoman was near in age to Úna but sometimes treated the princess—both princesses—as if she were their nursemaid. To say she took her serving duties seriously was a vast understatement. And Neve knew well Emer's thoughts on the subject of the óglach and their hounds.

Her mother had been a skilled Fir Bolg healer in Baile Sláine—one who hadn't been above calling up a little small magic here and there to help her ease aches and ills—until the Dagda's spell-catchers decided that her "small" magics had grown too great. She'd left the village in the dead of night, just steps ahead of the harrow hounds that had come howling to the door of her hut—who found nothing but an infant girl, left wide-eyed and barefoot, clutching a little straw doll. They'd brought the abandoned child back to Temair and she'd been put to work in the gardens, where the flowers and herbs had thrived under her touch. When Úna had chosen her as a handmaiden, Emer had thrown herself diligently into the role.

Still muttering crossly, Emer set about helping her mistress divest herself of her ritual finery as Úna held out her arms, clearly lost in thought. Neve, suddenly exhausted, kicked off her boots. Bare feet chilled on cold stone, she drifted out onto the terrace of their private walled garden and sank down to sit at the tiled edge of the little pool, staring at her own pale reflection in the dark water as the moon sailed on overhead and the stars pulsed with light. In the distance, she could hear the night watch call to each other, and a hunting owl glided overhead on silent wings.

In the fields and in the forests, scattered throughout the kingdom, folk came together around bonfires to celebrate Samhain that night, but Neve was trapped inside Temair, with no hope of escape. She held her hand out over the water, half hoping—half dreading—she would see the strange glimmering light reflected there, but her palm remained unmarked. Neve wondered what Ronan was doing in that same moment. Wondered if he'd gone back to his own ritual gathering after intruding upon hers.

He's probably laughing with his friends at the strange ways of the Tuatha Dé right now, she thought. *Drinking beer, and holding the hand of some Blackwater girl with long hair and loose skirts that don't tangle round her legs when she wants to run and jump and . . .* Neve heaved a thick sigh. She wondered if she'd ever even see Ronan again. She felt a strange hollowness in her chest when she realized how unlikely that was.

The air had grown cold enough that Neve could see her breath, and she drifted back inside to find Úna was almost ready for sleep.

Neve watched for a moment as Emer combed out her sister's long hair, wondering how Úna could seem so composed after what had just happened.

"Who do you think you might choose?" Neve asked, tugging at the uneven lacing on her own gown. "For a husband, I mean?"

The carved bone comb in Emer's hand paused for a startled instant before continuing its strokes through Úna's thick shining tresses.

"I don't have to think," Úna said. "I've already made my choice."

"I really have to start paying more attention," Neve said dryly, certain her sister was joking. "Well, are you going to tell me or not?"

"I've chosen Lorcan," Úna said, wincing as Emer worried the comb through a snarl.

"Lorcan?" Neve snorted. "Very funny." She rolled her eyes toward the murals on the chamber ceiling. "All right, I deserve your anger, I know. It's my fault Father is making you marry, but I'll help make it right, Úna, I swear. Never mind that hedgepig Lorcan. I'll help you find someone worthy of your—"

"Neve!" Úna turned and snatched the comb from Emer's hand, slamming it down on the little table as she rounded on her sister, eyes blazing. "Would you for once in your life shut your mouth and listen!"

Neve's jaw dropped open but no sound came out. Thankfully.

"I *love* Lorcan," Úna said quietly.

Neve swallowed her astonishment before she responded. Carefully. "Lorcan," she said. "The son of Father's First Spear chief, Lorcan . . ."

Úna's gaze was withering. "You haven't even bothered to notice a single thing about him since you were children and he made an easy target for your sorely misplaced anger," she said. "*He's* grown up, Neve."

"I—"

"I know that's hard for you to grasp because *you* seem so very unwilling to undertake that same task," Úna cut her short. "But he's grown. He's tall and strong and a warrior. He's thoughtful. He talks to me and he *listens* to me and I love him."

"I meant no insult," Neve said stiffly.

"Of course you did." Úna sighed and her shoulders dropped as the anger lifted from her as swiftly as it had descended. She picked her comb back up and handed it to Emer again, waving a hand for her to continue. Neve had quite forgotten she was there. Like all good servants, Neve supposed, Emer had that uncanny knack of blending into the shadows when the need arose. "You always do. It's the first place you always go, little cub. A cave of sharp teeth, full of sharper words and a razor tongue. It's where you're most at home."

"It's not my fault *you* scooped up all the manners the gods allotted to us before I was even born," Neve muttered.

Emer had to stifle a grin at that and even Úna laughed, if a bit wearily.

"Mother always thought I was *too* mild," she said. "In you, though, I think Anann saw herself. Even when you were just a tiny baby. Rebellious, restless. A clenched fist and a kicking foot. A king in the body of a queen, just like her."

Úna stood and plucked up a throw, draping it around Neve's shoulders, and led her over to one of the sleeping couches. The sisters sat side by side on the couch as Emer flitted about the room, dousing torches and banking the coals in the braziers so they would stay warm throughout the night without burning out.

"Why did she leave?" Neve asked. "Mother. Was it because of me?"

"Oh, cub." Úna wrapped an arm around her sister. "Why would you think that? No. She left because she left. One day you might find her and ask her. But—and you must remember this no matter what the Dagda or the chieftains or any other *man* of the tribe says—Anann had every right to do what she did. No matter the why of it. And the only reason the Tuatha Dé have any kind of realm at *all* to be the lords of is because of a beautiful and powerful queen."

"The Scathach."

Úna nodded her chin against the top of Neve's head. "The Scathach."

Neve knew the story of their ancestress almost as well as she knew her own. She was her namesake, after all. *My mother must have had delusions of grandeur when she dreamed my name*, Neve thought bitterly.

The grandeur of a queen who long ago reigned over the White-Walled City of Ankh-Tawy in a far-off desert land known as Kemet. She was renowned for her warlike tendencies and her unsurpassed skill with horse and chariot, taught by her consort, a Scythian prince known as Elchmar the Horse Lord.

In the flickering torchlight, Neve gazed up at the fading murals painted high up on the walls and ceiling of their chambers. Chambers that used to belong to the war-hungry Scathach herself, shown riding a silver stallion at the head of a procession of ethereal beings in flowing robes and armor. She wore a long black and gold cloak with the hood pulled up to hide her countenance. Neve had always wondered what her face looked like. Whether she was beautiful, or simply irresistible. Powerful.

In the old tales, she had been still a princess around Neve's age when her brother, the god-king of Kemet, was murdered by his rivals. Her grief nearly drove her mad and carved a darkness upon her heart. She swore revenge and dedicated her soul to Khenti-Amentiu, the wolf-headed God of the Dead, and promised him blood in exchange for vengeance. Then she commanded Elchmar's brother—a man so dangerously clever they called him a sorcerer—to design a lavish underground banquet hall beside the sacred river of Hapi, and invited her brother's conspirators to a feast, where she sealed them inside and opened a portal that diverted the river waters into the hall, drowning her enemies.

Neve shivered at the thought and couldn't help remembering the feeling of almost drowning earlier that day in the Blackwater, wrapped in the arms of a presumptuous thief.

That act had made the princess a queen, but her own people rose up against her in fear and horror. So she fled Kemet, along with her Horse Lord and his brother the sorcerer, and those of the royal court and their warriors who remained loyal. They sailed into the west, almost to the edge of the world, with horses and chariots and all the riches they could carry in an armada of one hundred ships. They brought with them powerful relics, chief among them an obelisk known as the Lia Fail, the Stone of Destiny, carved with symbols of power, gilded with precious electrum that glowed white-gold under the sun and moon.

And when, finally, the Scathach and her followers reached the shores of Eire, they called themselves the Tuatha Dé. The Tribe of Gods. They set about conquering the inhabitants of the lush, mystical green island at the end of the known world, driving the monstrous Fomori shapeshifters into the sea.

But the Scathach's lust for rule went too far. She sought to increase her power with dark magic stolen from the Beyond Realms. She cut off Elchmar's hand and declared him no longer fit to reign at her side, and proclaimed that the Lia Fail had told her that she should rule supreme over all the folk of Eire. She shed the title of the Scathach and chose, instead, the title of "the Dagda"—"the Good God"—in part because she wanted her rule to transcend her womanhood. Her humanity, even.

But the Scathach was anything but good. Soon, even her loyal Scythians turned against her. Elchmar's brother used his sorcery to restore his brother's hand, fashioning one of living silver. Together, they turned the power of the Lia Fail against her and used it to banish her from Eire—from the mortal realm itself. Elchmar was proclaimed Dagda instead and decreed that no woman should ever hold power over the tribe again.

"They still need to marry us to claim the throne, but our womanly souls are too prone to corruption to ever sit upon the throne ourselves," Neve said dryly. "That's what the Scathach's tale tells us, isn't it?"

"A tale told by *men*, little cub," Úna said. "The magic and the mystery, that's all nonsense. The heart of the tale is a woman. A woman who loved and grieved and wanted—*and took for herself*—what men have always taken for granted. Power." A smile tugged at the corners of her lips. "And don't forget the end of the story. Even though he became Dagda, Elchmar was overcome with the anguish of what he'd done, and the magic that had restored him physically eventually unraveled his mind. He wandered into the wilderness and disappeared forever, diminished and dishonored."

"At least Father isn't *that* far gone," Neve snorted. "Yet."

Úna laughed. "I suppose I should thank you for making him so angry," she said. "I don't think he would have agreed to my choice any other way."

I wouldn't blame him, Neve thought, although she wisely held her tongue.

"Now?" Úna continued. "I'll be queen on *my* terms. I'll rule the way I want . . ."

Úna's gaze turned inward, her smile fading to something else. Something that, on someone else, might have looked almost predatory. "*Gentle as a hunting cat, you are,*" Ruad Rofhessa had said. And in the flickering light, Neve saw—for the first time—what her mother might have seen: her father looking out from her sister's eyes.

"What happened to the Lia Fail?" Neve asked.

"Hm?" Úna's mind snapped back from whatever unseen path it wandered.

"The Stone of Destiny. What became of it?"

"Oh . . . I don't know." Úna shrugged. "It used to stand in the circle court outside the Great Hall. I remember—at least, I think I remember—seeing it when I was very small. The sunlight looked like fire reflecting off its surface."

"I wonder where it is now," Neve murmured.

"Who knows?" Úna lay down on her own sleeping couch, dark hair fanning out on the pillow. "It's probably in a storeroom somewhere in a forgotten corner of the palace." She yawned and turned on her side, her voice muffled. "No one at court really believes the stories about that silly stone . . ."

She was snoring softly in a moment and Emer pulled the bed-clothes up over her, flitting above Úna like a phantom in the flickering glow of the brazier.

Neve wasn't so sure about *no one* believing in the power of the Stone of Destiny. She had clearly heard their father when he'd said: "*You want to be like the Scathach? Is that what you want? You want to crack the Lia Fail to dust with your reckless will?*"

She pictured Ruad Rofhessa's face as he'd said those words. And she realized she'd been right. Her father—the mighty Dagda—had been afraid. And, as impossible as it was to fully wrap her mind around it, Neve knew what he was afraid of. It wasn't the stone, or the old dead queen. It wasn't even Úna, with her carefully guarded, soft-spoken aspirations. It was *her*.

Neve Anann Eriu. Beloved of the Wolf.

She for whom the sun set and the moon rose.

And she was glad of it.

IX

ONCE ÚNA'S WEDDING announcement rang out, the ladies of Temair mobilized with the kind of speed and ferocity that the warriors of Temair could scarcely marvel at. Neve observed the joyous whirlwind from a safe distance, convinced that the decrees against Tuatha Dé women ruling and riding into battle were exceedingly wrong-headed. They would have brought the whole of the world to heel in a moon and a day.

But even with the palace humming like a happy, busy beehive, Neve somehow felt more alone than ever. It seemed she wasn't the only one. On a morning when the sun burned sullen and orange through the autumn fog, Neve rose and dressed to walk the gardens as she'd done every day since the Dagda had threatened dire consequences should she leave the palace grounds again without his permission. She paced restlessly along the pathways between the many palace courtyards, her heavy cloak sweeping the frost-crisped stalks of the flowers that rustled at her passage like whispered secrets.

But on that day, over the crunch of her boots on fallen leaves, Neve heard the sound of muffled weeping. Even strained with sorrow and at a distance, she recognized Emer's voice. Neve followed the sound, turning onto a path that was barely discernible, overgrown with moss and creeping thyme. She followed it to a small, circular enclosure—a private little walled garden off what had once been her mother's apartments.

Neve faintly remembered playing there when she was very small. For years her father had threatened to raze it to the ground to build something more sensible there—like a chicken coop or a midden pit, he would sneer—but he never had. The heart that Anann had so deeply bruised with her departure had never *quite* allowed it. What it *had* allowed was for the place to fade from memory. Like Queen Anann herself.

Neve walked toward the apple tree standing in the middle of the neglected enclosure. Its trunk was shedding bark, the branches withered and black, brittle as old grief. Blighted. The tree would not survive the winter.

And Emer, kneeling at its roots, was clearly heartbroken because of it.

Neve went and silently knelt beside Emer as her narrow shoulders shook. Neve wanted to comfort her but she didn't quite know what to say. *It's just a tree, Emer,* she could have said. But it clearly wasn't. It had been something special to a Fir Bolg peasant girl.

The tree had been one Emer had grown from a sapling, planted when she was barely more than a twig herself, new to court and all alone. Under the care of her nurturing hands, the tree had flourished, grown, and produced sweet golden apples. In the spring, the perfume of its blossoms and the humming of lazy bees in its branches had filled the little courtyard, now silent except for Emer's sadness.

Neve reached out to the poor tree and, as she laid her hand on its weathered trunk, she felt a strange, shimmering sensation fluttering along the surface of her palm. In the same place Ronan had touched her the night of the Stone Singing, she could feel that very same fire. With a shock, Neve knew with a certainty that, if she turned over her hand, she would see a mark, glowing pale and golden, beneath her skin. She snatched her hand back into her sleeve before Emer noticed.

Neve's heart was pounding in her ears. There was wild magic pulsing beneath the withered tree bark. Faint, fading, barely there . . . But Neve had felt it. She was no Druid; she shouldn't have been able to *feel* magic. But she had. And she'd be in deep trouble if anyone found out she could. Ruad Rofhessa would probably feed her to the harrow hounds. Gleefully.

Stop it. You're imagining things.

"Lady?" Emer sniffed, turning her head to look at Neve, her expression quizzical.

"I'm just so sorry, Emer. For the tree."

"It's just a tree, lady," Emer said, wiping her eyes with the corner of her shawl. "The Tuatha Dé can always get their apples, no matter the death of one small tree."

"My mother didn't think that way."

"Your mother was a good woman. Wise." She picked up a handful of earth and let it sift through her fingers. "She shouldn't have left us."

No, Neve thought. *She shouldn't have left any of us . . .*

Emer brushed the rest of the dirt from her hands and stood. "The queen-to-be has told me I'll be staying on as your hand-maiden, lady," she said.

"What? Why?" Neve clambered to her feet, her skirts catching around her knees.

Emer put out a hand to steady her. "As queen, she'll have ample bondswomen to look after her," she explained.

Neve had always thought her sister looked on Emer as friend first and servant second. Now to hand her off like an outgrown gown . . . She wondered how Emer felt about that.

"Is there anything you'll be needing in the next while, lady?" she asked. "I'll be gone from court for a day or two. There are merchants in Baile Sláine I need to see. I want to make something special for the queen-to-be's wedding."

Neve told her no, she'd be fine, and watched as Emer hurried away, shawl flapping behind her like wings. When Neve reached out a tentative hand to the tree again, laying her palm flat against the trunk, she felt nothing at all. As if the faint, flickering magic had been drained utterly.

Or there never was any magic there at all, she chided herself. *Fool.*

She turned over her hand to see her palm was pale and smooth, crisscrossed with only the lines that had always been there. Unmarked by a secret sigil. Magic, it seemed, was a fickle thing.

A nonsense thing, Úna would have told her.

A *dangerous* thing. Neve thrust her hands back into her sleeves and headed toward her chambers, giving the harrow hound kennels a wide berth, just in case. She passed Emer, perched on the back of a merchant wagon heading through the main courtyard, as she went. Even the palace bondswomen had more freedom to travel beyond the palace walls than she did, Neve thought bitterly. But then she felt the shadow of a smile tug at her mouth.

Well, why not? Neve thought. *Someone ought to have it, if not me.*

She decided that on the eve of Úna's wedding, instead of accepting Emer's service, she would give the Fir Bolg maid her freedom. Her *real* freedom. Something Úna—who stood on the cusp of ruling as Dagda in everything but name—hadn't even granted her.

The thought filled Neve with a sense of righteous purpose. And then another thought—a wilder, wayward thought—occurred to her. So long as she was thinking of making amends on behalf of her fellow Tuatha Dé, why should she stop at Emer? What of the other Fir Bolg? A strange, dangerous notion, to be sure, and one that would send her father into a paroxysm of wrath should he find out. Maybe even draw her sister's ire down upon her.

But something was stirring in Neve's soul.

Neve thought of Ronan, probably the only soul in Eire who could help her understand what was happening to her. And who would likely never speak to her again. Unless she could somehow make him understand, after everything she'd already said, that she wasn't his enemy.

Unless she brought him a peace offering to prove it.

Neve changed direction and made her way to the Great Hall of Temair. The chamber was empty—of course it was; the Dagda and his chief advisers were all at the Great Barrow—but Neve still felt as if she wasn't quite alone. She glanced around before dragging a carved bench over to the pillar where the battered shield of Sengann the Raider hung.

What better peace offering than a war trophy? And if the shield itself didn't speak to his Fir Bolg heart, she thought, perhaps the shield's gold- and amethyst-studded embellishments might speak to his thief's purse.

Emer had only been three or four years old when the óglach had brought her to court. Neve had been too young at the time to remember much about those days, other than that she wasn't allowed to go outside the walls of Temair then, either. Because of the Fir Domnann raiding parties that had roamed the country-side at the time, burning villages and wreaking havoc, season after season. That is, until the warriors of the Tuatha Dé finally met them in pitched battle and the Dagda himself fought and killed their leader, Sengann. Neve had been proud of her father for killing the Fir Domnann invader.

It wasn't until years later that she learned from Emer that the Fir Domnann had once been part of the peaceful Fir Bolg tribes. Caught up in the Scathach's war of conquest, some of the Fir Bolg had chosen to fight alongside the fearsome Fomori. Some fled across the Eirish Sea to Cymru, and the rest had been left with no choice but to accept the Tuatha Dé as their new rulers. What Sengann had done, generations later, had been to gather a band of exiles in Cymru and attempt to retake their ancestral home. But without the terrible, shapeshifting magic of the Fomori, the Fir Domnann were powerless to do much more than burn a few coastal villages. And they'd suffered mightily in retribution at the Dagda's hands.

Learning *that* had made Neve less proud of the Dagda. And of the Tuatha Dé.

She stood in the middle of the hall staring up at the shield, just like she had when she was little. Its design was still visible beneath an ancient crust of blood and battlefield muck, a triple spiral famously inscribed there in defiance of the Tuatha Dé decree that only *they* could bear those marks.

Neve reached up and tugged the relic from the nail that held it. For a long moment, she held the thing up in front of her, equally mesmerized by the painted spirals and blood stains. Sengann had once stalked across the green fields of Eire with that shield, like her father had with his war club, Neve thought. Furious and full of life. Had he really deserved such an ending? For leading his folk to reclaim their land?

Yes. Because he lost.

Neve froze and looked around the hall. But the whisper had only been in her mind. She gave her head a shake and hurried from the chamber, hiding the broken shield beneath the heavy folds of her cloak. To reach her secret gate, she had to risk skirting around the back of the royal kennels on the south side of the palace compound. Behind the stout fences hung with silver charms, the spell-harrows lay in the shade, long pink tongues lolling out of their toothy muzzles. When they weren't actively on the hunt for illicit magic, the hounds resembled nothing so much as great silly dogs. But the moment they sensed anything more powerful than a meadow sprite in a mushroom ring, their big black eyes burned red and they transformed into something monstrous.

"Lady Neve?"

She nearly jumped out of her skin. "Fintan!" she exclaimed, shifting so the shield beneath her cloak was on the opposite side from where he stood. "You startled me."

The óglach chief dipped his head, his weathered face bending into an apologetic smile. "Very sorry, lady. Didn't look to find anyone out here by the kennels. Most folk avoid the beasts."

Thorn, Fintan's lead dog, roused herself and loped over, pushing her head between the fence rails. Neve froze as Thorn sniffed at her hand, nostrils flaring. She pushed her big black nose into Neve's palm—where the glimmering mark had so recently flared—and whined, a mournful sound. Sweat broke out on the back on Neve's neck. And then . . . nothing. The dog's eyes stayed dark as deep mountain pools as she lay down and flopped over onto her side on a bare patch of dirt.

"Sorry to disappoint," Neve murmured, her mouth gone dust dry.

Fintan cocked his head at her. "Lady?"

"Oh. Uh, I . . . ," she stammered, "I just meant . . . the dogs must get bored. Now that there hardly seem to be any spells left in the land to hunt. Don't they? Don't *you*?"

Fintan chuckled. "That's the way it's *supposed* to be, lady," he said.

"But the óglach are hunters. Warriors . . ."

"Aye," Fintan agreed. He nodded at the dogs. "And before *they* were harrow hounds, they were just hounds. Some days, I swear, I wish they still were. The cursefire is hard on 'em. But magic—even spells that *seem* harmless—can be frightful dangerous, lady. I've lost hounds on the hunt before. And that's never an easy thing."

Thorn stood and shook herself, then loped over to a trough that had originally been meant for horses. She was more than tall enough to lap at the water, drinking noisily and sending a shower of droplets flying.

"The hounds are fine so long as they're watered and fed," Fintan continued. "And so are we, lady. The gods willing, I'll die of boredom before I die of battle . . ."

I won't, Neve thought. *I know it. I can almost smell the blood of a battlefield the way a hound scents quarry. It's near. And getting nearer . . .*

"Lady?"

Neve looked up with a start, having forgotten him—and herself—for a moment. Fintan had raised a hand and looked as though he would lay it on her shoulder, before dropping it back down to rest on his sword hilt.

"Is there anything you need, lady?" he asked quietly. "Anything I can help you with?" The way he asked made it seem as if he sensed she was troubled.

For a brief, mad moment, Neve teetered on the verge of telling him exactly how troubled she was—*Remember that day in Blackwater, Fintan? In the bruidean, and then down by the docks? When the quarry you were hunting was me?*—but thought better of it. Fintan was, for good or ill, the man responsible for eradicating the magic of the realm. The very thing she suspected was at the root of her troubles.

No. There was only one person Neve trusted with her troubles. And she didn't actually trust *him* at all.

X

The clearing at the center of the Blackwater market rang with shouts and the clash of blades. The cold, crisp air held a tang of wood smoke and roasting fowl, with just a faint hint of fresh blood—Ronan's blood.

Shirtless, weaponless, clad only in his kilt and laced boots, with a pair of leather bracers protecting his forearms and nothing else, the thief had already taken a dozen shallow cuts to his upper arms and torso from his adversary's sword.

He glimpsed a flurry of wagers changing hands from the corner of his eye, but his attention was focused on the woman half crouched before him, wielding the very sharp, expertly crafted bronze short sword.

"Hold, Grian!" Ronan whispered frantically, gasping for breath.

"The only thing I'll hold is you," the redhead snarled back, "squirming on the point of my blade, wee bunny . . ."

Then she swung her blade at his head. Again. Grian was a stickler for realism.

Never mind the fact that their contest of Hare and Hunter—an autumnal market ritual that was more entertainment than anything—was just meant to be a distraction while Cavall and a few of his friends, including one or two Faoladh, lightened the pockets and purses of the gathered crowd.

"Mórr's blessed eyes!" Ronan cursed and dove forward, rolling across the scrubby grass as the rope snare looped around his ankle tightened painfully. "Why do *I* always have to be the Hare?"

There was a burst of laughter from the watchers at the edge of the clearing.

"Three silver pieces on the Hare," a female voice called out from the crowd.

Ronan paused, momentarily distracted. An unusually high wager in Blackwater—enough to draw even Grian's attention for an instant. And in that instant, Ronan swung himself up into a crouch, dropped his head, and charged past her guard, catching her square in the ribcage with his right shoulder. The breath left Grian's lungs with a *woof,* and she crumpled backward, hitting the ground hard. In a flash, Ronan looped the snare rope around her throat and bounced back up, kicking out with his snared foot to tighten the line like a noose and stepping on it with his other foot to keep it taut.

The laughter turned to shouts of outrage as Grian writhed on the ground, her face mottling crimson with anger, and Ronan threw his arms in the air in a triumphant gesture. The Hare was supposed to lose, if only to propitiate the gods for an easy winter. But, inasmuch as Ronan didn't believe in gods . . .

"These dark days'll be hungry ones this year, I fear." The Hare grinned down at the Hunter, triumphant. "With only turnips for the stew pot and no meat!"

Then someone tackled him from behind.

Ronan found himself facedown in a drift of fallen leaves, the point of a dagger pressing not so gently into the soft hollow at the base of his skull.

"You forget," Cliona growled in his ear, "we Faoladh hunt in packs . . ."

They'd performed this dance a dozen times. And yet. He went very still, waiting to see if this would be the time Cliona took the ritual one step further and spilled his blood onto the thirsty ground. She grabbed him by the arm and flipped him over onto his back, still straddling his bare chest, then placed the knife at his jugular.

Her eyes glinted, and then she spun the blade in her hand and sheathed it at her belt. She stood and held out her other hand to help him to his feet.

The crowd grumbled, and there were scattered exclamations from those with lightened fortunes, but nothing that sparked into anger. It was Blackwater. What was stolen from you today you'd just steal back on the morrow. In a matter of moments, the market was back to normal, buying and selling and bartering and stealing.

"You're getting better at avoiding the pot, Hare," Cliona said.

Ronan rolled the shoulder she'd nearly dislocated. "Sorry to leave you hungry, love."

He reached past her to retrieve the dagger he'd placed on a bench before his contest with Grian—hares weren't exactly armed, after all—and cut through the rope that looped around his ankle.

"I didn't give you that blade so you could leave it behind in a fight, you know . . ."

Damn. The three-silver-piece wager. It *had* been her voice. He'd known it.

Ronan turned slowly and let out a long sigh when his gaze met hers, golden and gleaming, staring out at him from the depths of a hood that cast a deep shadow over her lovely face. The princess had a large carrying bag slung over one shoulder and was dressed in fitted leather leggings and a tunic. Ronan dipped his head in a mockery of a courtly bow and tugged at the laces of one of his wrist bracers, ignoring how her gaze drifted over his bare chest.

"Princess," he said in a voice low enough that Cliona, still standing nearby, wouldn't hear. "I see you managed to avoid all that courtly peril looming over our last encounter."

"If that's what you see, then you're as unobservant as you are irritating," she snapped. "I've had nothing but disasters for days because of you. My *sister* is to be *married.*"

He arched an eyebrow at her. "And?"

"I don't expect you to understand," Neve said sharply. "But you do understand *this*, don't you?" She thrust her palm up between them, almost brushing his nose.

Ronan took a long look at her hand, and then reached up to move it aside so he could look into her eyes. "If you're going to slap my face," he said, "you'll have to work on your aim, Princess."

"What?" She glanced at her palm and then back at him, teeth clenching in frustration. "No. It's not there now. But it *was*. Again. The mark on my skin. How do I get rid of it?"

"I don't know what you're talking about," he said flatly and glanced over his shoulder. Her voice was rising in volume—enough to attract attention. "We Fir Bolg aren't allowed to mark *our* skin. But if your hands are dirty, Princess, try a good scrubbing back at the palace. We've no fancy baths here in Blackwater."

She ignored his sarcasm, hitching the leather bag she carried higher on her shoulder and standing her ground. "You did this—*you* have to help me!" There was a note of almost pleading in her voice. "My chamber garden is close enough to the harrow kennels that I can hear them howl when it's time to be fed. I'd rather not be their next meal."

She actually meant it, Ronan realized. She was as close to being frightened as he'd ever seen her. "Neve—"

"Who's your little friend, Hare?" Cliona asked, walking toward them. "She owes me three pieces of silver." She was flanked by a loose assortment of her Faoladh sisters, most of them with mugs from the beer seller's stall, bought with stolen coin. In the light of day, they looked less like legendary warriors and more like a pack of stray hungry dogs—untamed and shabby, wary but dangerous if provoked.

Provocation being a particular skill of Neve's.

"That was dishonorable of you," she said, swinging around to face Cliona, her tone so casually haughty that Ronan nearly laughed out loud. "Attacking him from behind like that. And he was unarmed."

Her rebuke actually pulled the Faoladh leader up short. Cliona stared at Neve, bemused—the ill-tempered cur, its nose bloodied by the swipe of a kitten's paw—but her indulgence was short-lived. Before Ronan could step between them, Cliona had drawn a knife and slashed it across Neve's body—only to find her blade hooked and twisted out of her grip by the long-handled axe that had suddenly appeared in Neve's fist.

"Death and Darkness, Cliona—no!" Ronan lunged for the Faoladh leader. "Leave this! *Leave* it. You don't want this fight—"

"*I* do!" Grian said as she shouldered both of them aside and tackled Neve to the ground. Neve slammed hard into the dirt, her eyes widening with fury as her axe flew from her hand.

Ronan very much doubted Neve had ever been in a fight—much less a grappling brawl—in the whole of her princess life, and he feared Grian would pummel her to paste. Neve proved him wrong in less time than it took him to form the thought, wriggling out from under her assailant like a river eel and leaping to her feet to deliver a swift, sharp kick to Grian's ribs. Grian responded by taking her out at the knees and the two of them crashed to the ground, a dust cloud rising as they rolled and rained vicious blows on each other.

Neve scrambled to her knees and delivered a wild swing that connected with Grian's jaw. Grian's head snapped back, a thread of bright blood arcing through the air from her split lip.

Then her eyes went black.

Even without her riastrad, a bloodied Grian was a dangerous Grian. And a dead daughter of the Dagda—even *that* one—would just give the Tuatha Dé an excuse to raze Blackwater to the ground. Ronan whispered frantically to Cliona and then lunged between the two combatants, arms thrust out to hold them both at bay.

"That's enough!" Ronan snapped at Neve over his shoulder.

Cliona wrapped an arm around Grian's chest and murmured in her ear.

Ronan saw Grian's jaw clench and her fists tighten in spite of what Cliona was whispering. Her bloodied lip lifted in a snarl.

"Do not forget yourself." Cliona's voice was a low guttural warning. "We are no common brawlers. We are the Dagda's wolves. That is our only true fight."

"Aye." Grian spat crimson on the ground and backed off at last. "Whether we wish it or no."

Neve went very still. "Wait. You're what?" Her glance swept Cliona and her sisters. "*You* . . . are Faoladh?"

Grian wiped the back of her bloodied hand across her mouth. "That's what they tell us."

Cliona's mouth twitched in a sardonic smile. "At the Dagda's eternal command," she said, spreading her hands out and inclining her head in an almost-bow.

"Then you eternally serve no one," Neve said. "The Dagda will never call upon you."

"There are Dagdas and there are Dagdas, young cub," Aevinn said, stepping up beside Cliona, her voice like a whetstone dragged over a blade's edge. "Ruad Rofhessa may not ever call upon us, that much is true. And yet we *will* serve the Chosen of the Lia Fail again. One day—in this life, with this generation—or the next."

Neve looked from one Faoladh to the other. "You seem awfully certain of that."

"I am Aevinn, seeress of the Faoladh."

"What do you see?"

"War approaching. Darkness descending. Challenges a Dagda must rise to . . ."

"Rag-end raiding parties setting fire to fishing skiffs hardly constitute the makings of a war," Neve said, but it didn't really sound as if she believed it. More like she was repeating something she'd heard time and again by rote. "And Midwinter means darkness always." She took a step toward Cliona. "You are pledged in service to the throne of the Tuatha Dé in times of strife with the Fomori. The Fomori are dead and done. That should render your oath moot, I should think." She turned and walked over to where her axe lay on the ground, alongside the bulky leather satchel she'd dropped in the fight. "You would do yourselves all a favor to forget it. Live your lives."

"This is our life," Cliona said flatly. "When the Dagda of Eire comes to find us, the Sisters of the Wolf will be ready."

She turned on her heel and, plucking a mug from the nearest Faoladh, tossed back her head and drained it dry. Neve watched the band of warrior sisters follow Ciona, and as they disappeared beneath the trees at the edge of town, Ronan thought he saw a surge of longing sweep across Neve's face. She glanced down at the blood on her knuckles.

"I didn't know you could do that," Ronan said.

"What?" Neve wiped the blood off with the hem of her cloak. "Defend myself?"

"Fight."

"I can fight just fine," she snapped. "Just ask my sister's betrothed and maybe he'll show you the tooth I knocked out of his head when we were children."

"What are you doing here?" Ronan asked, pushing the hair back from her brow to examine a bruise beginning to blossom on her forehead. "Other than starting brawls with my friends? Didn't your last foray into Blackwater impart anything meaningful about maybe staying away from this place?"

She batted away his hand. "That's rich wisdom coming from you, when *you* appeared at Brú na Bóinne—after telling me we should stay away from each other."

Ronan pinched the bridge of his nose. "That wasn't my idea," he said. "And yes. You're right. We should." He put his hands up in a gesture of surrender and backed away. "Why don't I start this time? Goodbye again, Princess Neve—"

"Wait!" There was an edge of panic to her voice. "Stop. I demand it."

"You demand it."

"I . . . request it."

"A request from Tuatha Dé royalty of a Fir Bolg peasant is a demand and you know it." He could feel his jaw clenching, even though he knew he was being hard on Neve. She hadn't personally subjugated his folk. And she would never get the opportunity to, especially now that Úna was to be married. But she was Tuatha Dé.

"Please," she said. "There is a reason I came here. A real reason. I need you to help me understand this." She thrust her hand out toward him again.

Ronan leaned forward to peer at it.

This still proved to be nothing. Ronan raised an eyebrow at her.

Neve uttered a guttural sound of pure frustration and, before Ronan realized what she was doing, she slapped her palm flat against his sweat-slick chest, just above his heart. Ronan hissed in pain as a sudden, searing heat bloomed beneath Neve's hand.

Neve pulled her hand away with a gasp and they both stared down to see lines of shimmering golden light appear on her palm—as if the creases had split open. The gleaming lines snaked out and joined together to form a faint, gleaming sigil, three pointed, the points shaped like flames, maybe, or something else—Ronan couldn't quite make out the image before it all blurred together, pooling like liquid fire in the cup of her hand.

Ronan slammed his hand down over hers, extinguishing the fire with a flash of his own indigo-hued darklight. He clasped her hand tightly until the sensation of icy heat faded. He could feel Neve's pulse pounding and her golden eyes held a tangled mess of fear and excitement when she gazed up at him.

And sparks of what he could only identify as pure, wild magic.

"Never!" Ronan spat through clenched teeth. "*Never* do that again. Do you understand me?"

He glanced around to see the salvagers Nym and Gwylon in the distance, haggling with a fish seller. He half expected to see Sparrow with them—she usually was—but it was just those two and Ronan was glad of it. Sparrow seemed to be the one among the salvagers who could sniff out magic at work no matter how small or hidden. Neve's little display had been neither.

"Is this what *yours* feel like?" she whispered. "The fire—"

"No, this has nothing to do with me," he said. "I can't help you. We are *not* the same."

Her gaze pierced him. "If you were as bad a thief as you are a liar," Neve said, "you'd have starved long ago."

Ronan closed his eyes and took a breath to try to calm himself. "Neve . . . let it alone."

"I can't. I *could* have, if not for you. This is not something I have ever known before, but now . . . it's like the ban sidhe demon from that night so long ago has been sleeping under my skin all this time. And it only woke up because *you* woke it up again that day in Blackwater."

Her words cut through him to the marrow. Because that was the way he'd felt since the very *first* night he'd met her. Saved her. Tapped into something far more dangerous and powerful than either of them could conceive of because of her . . . As if they had both been cursed that night. And now their curses called out, each to each.

"You need to forget about this," Ronan said. "Forget how it feels. Forget how it makes *you* feel." It was like Ronan was counseling himself. And not just about *that*. About her. He hoped she hadn't heard that in his voice. "Forget all of it, Neve."

Her golden eyes shone too brightly. "I just thought . . ." She blinked rapidly and looked away, her hand clenched into a fist between them. "I just thought it might be a good idea to find someone who could make it make sense. It's my misfortune yours was the only name that came to mind."

"And so you thought you'd just wave *that* around in a crowded marketplace in broad daylight." Ronan wondered if not having to live by your wits meant not ever bothering to use them. "Just like you thought goading a Faoladh into a fight was a good idea—"

"The vaunted Faoladh." Neve scoffed. "It seems my father was right about them after all. They are useless."

"Not useless," Ronan snapped, suddenly angry at her arrogance. At the fact that she just thought everything could be fixed with a snap of her princess fingers. "They're purposeless. And nobler still than others I can think of. *They* accept their fate with as much grace and dignity as they are allowed." The tone of his voice held a rebuke. And a challenge. The fate of Cliona and her mad band of she-wolves was one of the very rare things in his life that Ronan actually gave a damn about. "Imagine if it was you."

"I don't have to imagine," she said quietly. "I'm the second daughter of the Dagda. The one he wishes a ban sidhe would rid him of again—only with more success this time. I am the very embodiment of a purposeless soul."

Ronan groaned inwardly, having clearly managed to hurt one of the only *other* things he might actually give a damn about.

"I can fight, too," she said. "And I'm good. But I'm not allowed—will *never* be allowed—Fomori or no. I could be a king, but I'm a woman. I could be a queen, but I have a sister. I can conjure a flame in the palm of my hand, but no one will tell me how. Or why. Eire is my home and my heart, but I don't belong in Temair, which is the only place I'm allowed to be. Until the day when my father will no doubt find me a fine, doddering old lord from a kingdom on the other side of the Eirish Sea to seal an alliance whenever he deems it useful. So I suppose I have that to look forward to . . ."

"Neve—"

"Here." She slipped the strap of the leather sack off her shoulder and tossed it to him. "I had meant to deliver this as a peace offering between us, Fir Bolg. It belongs with you." She nodded her chin at the market folk. "With them."

Ronan reached inside the bag and pulled out a warrior's shield, the wood hacked and split, the painted design faded and filthy. And unmistakable. He recognized the triple spiral immediately. Any Fir Bolg would. He turned his gaze back to Neve, his feelings for her swinging back toward blunt, baleful anger.

He shoved the relic back into the bag.

"Don't you even want to know—"

"What this is?" He dropped the satchel at her feet with a dull thud. "This is the battle shield of Sengann, the Fir Domnann warlord."

Neve frowned, unbalanced by his reaction. "It's been hanging—"

"He burned my village and murdered my family when I was just a babe."

"I . . ." The color drained from Neve's face. "I didn't know. I thought—"

"You should go."

Neve slumped and without another word, turned and walked away from him. He watched her go. Saw how the folk of Blackwater watched her pass with furtive glances, knowing instinctively she was not one of them, but sensing perhaps that she wasn't entirely Tuatha Dé, either. Not in the same way that the other lords and ladies of Temair were. A terrible sense of foreboding clutched at Ronan's heart.

He was right. Had been right all along. The two of them would never truly be able to understand each other. Or each other's worlds. They both carried hidden fire, but they were not the same. Unleashed, Ronan's would be snuffed out by harrow hounds.

Neve's, he feared, might just burn until the whole realm was on fire.

XI

*T*UATHA DÉ MEANT "tribe of gods." Neve was beloved of a god, daughter of the "Good God" . . . Wouldn't that mean she was a goddess? Even a little bit?

"No?" she asked her hand. Her normal, not-fiery hand.

After her last disastrous foray into Blackwater, it had occurred to Neve that maybe Ronan had actually, inadvertently, taught her something about how to ignite the glimmering mark: anger. Only that couldn't be it. Not entirely. Not when she'd been angry at just about everyone at court since her unjust confinement. If that *was* it, she might have already set Ruad Rofhessa ablaze with a glance. Still, it made her anxious to find herself in any kind of crowd.

But that wasn't something she could avoid on that particular morning, when the equivalent of a war council of chieftains had convened in the women's wing of the palace, and Neve's presence there was *non*negotiable. Úna's robes were nearly finished after

weeks of intricate labor by a legion of supremely skilled artisans. The final fitting—and Úna's last day as an unmarried maiden— was to be an occasion of great celebration among the court ladies.

The wedding dress looked like something a goddess would wear.

Layers of pale-blue linen, so finely spun they were almost translucent, floated over top of beaten-gold tissue that sparkled like rain at sunrise. The sleeves, loose and flowing, were fashioned so that when Úna lifted her arms, the gesture would reveal her other tuath marks. On the day of the actual ceremony, those tattoos would be highlighted with fresh bright-blue woad and gold dust. The whole gown was covered in a delicate web of glittering beads, green and blue and amber glass, that shimmered as she walked, like some kind of magical creature caught in an enchanted net.

"At least there's *one* goddess in the family," Neve muttered wryly, running her thumb over her palm. She stood watching from the edges of the gathering, absently swirling a goblet of spiced cider as Úna turned circles on the tiny dais so the women crouched at her feet could finish the hem. The fitting took place in a wide room filled with couches, doors open to a small orchard filled with sunlight and bright laughter.

"That must be what the Fé Fíada looked like when they used to walk the green hills of this blessed isle," sighed a silver-haired matron from the kitchens named Glynnis, gazing at Úna. Her face was seamed with age, but her eyes were still bright, and her strong hands carried a tray laden with piles of delicate cakes.

"Don't be a silly fool, Glynn," Emer snorted, carrying a tray of her own. "There was nothing delicate about *them*."

"What are Fé Fíada?" Neve asked.

"*Were.* They were shapeshifters," Glynnis whispered, as if the very word was forbidden. "All Fomori were, to some measure. Only these ones were dreadful powerful."

That piqued Neve's interest. "Like the Faoladh," she said.

"No, not like those brawling brutes." The old matron's nose wrinkled. "The Fé Fíada had mastery over the very *elements*, look you, without even need of spell nor speech. They were like"—she paused, searching for the right description—"Fomori royalty, if you can imagine."

"Aye," Emer said. "And a sight to see, sure. But they were ne' butterfly-winged and barefoot prancing over the meadows. More like, the beauty of a thunderstorm, or a waterfall from a high cliff." She nodded in the direction of Úna's sparkling gown. "Fierce, not fancy."

"You're just sour because yon dress was stitched without a whisper of magic," Glynnis said and rolled her eyes. "Just pure human mastery."

Emer cast a sharp glance at her. "And why do you think I'd be sour over that?"

Glynnis fell silent and Neve was reminded that Emer's healer mother had augmented the mastery she'd had over her own craft with—if the óglach were to be believed—more than just a whisper of magic. The two women moved off to deliver the cakes, and the court ladies fell upon Úna like a swooping murmuration of starlings.

She will make a formidable ruler, Neve thought as she watched Úna effortlessly navigate the subtle, sometimes treacherous seas of unspoken rivalries and shifting loyalties among the court ladies better than the most politically astute chieftain wrangling warring freedmen to his cause. *A Dagda in all but name . . .*

"Lorcan doesn't know what he's getting himself into," she murmured to herself.

Neve had seen him early that morning, looking harried and half asleep, buckling on a sword belt as he hurried through the main courtyard to lead a band of óglach out on patrol. There had, Neve thought, been a lot of óglach patrols in recent days, mostly in response to rumors of more coastal raids. A lost shipment of wine meant for the wedding feast had prompted an outcry in the kitchens, but Neve had overheard Farsa telling Sakir that same ship had been carrying a load of Cymric ore bound for Temair's weapons makers. And so Lorcan rode out with his warriors, even though he was getting married on the morrow.

"Don't look so grim. You'll be prince-consort soon enough," Neve had mockingly consoled him. "And then you can laze about all you want while *your* First Spear leads patrols."

He'd cocked his head at her, a bemused expression on his sleep-creased face. "I'll still go," he said. "Even if I become king."

"Why?" Neve asked, in spite of her promises to Úna to at least try and be friendly to her former adversary. She'd never quite forgiven Lorcan for what he'd said to her when they were children. Stubborn and petty, maybe, to hold a grudge for something Lorcan probably didn't even remember saying, and yet . . .

"Because Eire comes first" was his answer. "Before anything or anyone."

Neve rolled her eyes. "My sister will be so pleased to hear that."

Lorcan snorted, then vaulted onto his mount's back. "Your *sister* was the one who said it to *me*."

He signaled to his patrol to move out and Neve watched them go, harrow hounds loping along beside the men and horses.

Now, stuck in a corner of Úna's dressing chamber, hemmed in by battalions of bright dresses, Neve wished she had begged Lorcan to take her along on his patrol. She excused herself and fled, just as another round of trays loaded with nectar and sweet-cakes appeared.

"I was wondering how long you'd last," Sakir said by way of greeting as she nearly lunged through the garden gate, pulling it closed behind her with a bang. "I'm impressed. I thought you would have bolted like a wild colt long ago."

Neve grinned as Sakir held out a small round shield and a pair of sagaris to her. He had already strapped his own shield to his left forearm, and his long chestnut hair was tied back from his face with a leather thong. Neve hefted the sagaris with a satisfied sigh. An entire morning spent in the women's wing, holding her tongue, had Neve dying to bury her axe blade in the nearest available target.

Sakir led the way to the small stable yard, where, for once, Neve's secret gate stayed solidly shut, hidden behind overgrown ivy. Neve shrugged out of her skirts—she'd worn a pair of fitted suede leggings beneath, just in case—and she and Sakir ran through a series of drills, first with sword, then sagaris, then sagaris and shield. They fought until her arms felt jellied.

When he finally called a halt, Neve collapsed on a bench, eyes closed, gulping for air. The sweat ran down her face and when she felt the chill nudge of a clay water flask against her shoulder, she reached for it without opening her eyes, pouring the cool, sweet water down her throat. When she opened her eyes, it wasn't Sakir who sat on the bench beside her, smiling.

It was Gofannon.

Sakir must have taken the weapons into the barn to clean them, and Neve felt, for a moment, like a vole alone in a meadow spotted by a fox. She nodded politely at her father's high Druid and forced a tight smile. "Thank you. For the water."

Gofannon sighed at her reaction, his blue gaze shadowed with an earnest concern. "You're most welcome," he said. And then after a moment, added, "I would wish for us to be friends, Lady Neve."

"What makes you think we aren't?" Neve asked, trying to smile like Úna.

He didn't answer her question. Not exactly. "I know it must be difficult," he said instead. "Your father spends so much of his time and attention on the Great Barrow. I feel responsible for having diverted his energies away from you and your sister these past years. But you must believe me, lady, it *is* for the greater good. For the glory of the Tuatha Dé and the safety and security of all of Eire."

"So I've been told," Neve said. "Since the day the first stone was laid."

She tucked her hand beneath her. She had no idea if a Druid like Gofannon could sense the glimmering mark, invisible beneath her skin, but the sooner she could get away from him the better.

"Do you believe?"

"What I believe," she said, echoing what Lorcan had said to her earlier that day, "is that Eire comes first. Before anything or anyone."

Gofannon nodded. "You are wise for one so young," he said. "As is your sister. I think it gives Ruad Rofhessa great peace in his mind to know that his daughter has stepped into her divine role toward the continuance of the Tuatha Dé."

"Yes, he's a bit less grumpy these days, I've noticed," Neve said dryly.

To her great surprise, Gofannon laughed heartily at her observation. It was a nice laugh, pleasant sounding.

"And you're right, of course," she continued. "Úna will make an excellent queen."

"I wasn't speaking of Úna," Gofannon said.

Neve stared at him, not understanding.

He nodded in the direction of the barn, where Sakir was cleaning their weapons. "The sagaris suits you, lady. The Druids often say that the soul of a weapon finds the hand for whom it was wrought. Yours is a powerful yet elegant instrument."

"It certainly weighs less than my father's war club."

"Do you know it has its origins as the traditional weapon of a god?"

"Does it?" Neve glanced again at the barn, wishing desperately for Sakir.

"There is a place—an island kingdom, far away in the east, in the middle of a bright-blue sea—where the double axe is a powerful symbol. It belongs to a god who is half man, half beast. The folk of the island call it—the axe—a *labrys*," Gofannon continued. "And the symbol, carved into stone, marked the passage to the home of the god. The labyrinth."

Talk of symbols made her hand knot into a fist at her side. She took a deep breath to calm her rabbiting pulse. Gofannon had given no indication he'd sensed anything strange about her. It would be foolish to give him a reason to. "And what is the . . . labyrinth?" she asked politely. "A palace?"

Gofannon's gaze drifted up over the stable yard walls. "It's more a fortress. Or even a prison, some might say. It was a place of judgement, built of many halls," he said, winding his hand through the space between them as if conjuring an image of a labyrinth from thin air. "Many corridors. Winding around and twisting in on themselves. A Spiral Path, only made of stone, underground. Easy to get lost in. Hard to find your way. But once discovered, the path leads to . . ." He paused, blinking as if waking himself from a dream or vision. "Well. No one knows, really. The legends say no one has ever returned once they've entered. Not even heroes."

The way the sunlight angled into the stable yard in that moment carved deep shadows and sharp planes on Gofannon's face, making him seem far older.

"Is that where you come from, Gofannon?" she asked. "This island?"

"No, Princess." He smiled, his mild blue gaze the exact shade of the late-autumn sky. The scales of the serpent torc he wore around his neck shimmered, its pearl eyes glimmering as he took a breath. "But I traveled much and far over this great wide world before I came into the service of the Dagda."

"Sounds more exciting than boring old Temair," Neve said.

"Dear lady." He frowned at her in gentle admonishment. "The kingdom of Eire is a place of plenty and great beauty. And power. Why else do you think your ancestress led her ships to the shores of this island?"

"Because if they'd sailed any farther," Sakir said, walking up—finally—to stand before Neve, "they'd have sailed into an endless sea. And the Scathach knew well enough that horses run better than they swim. Not that this island is much drier . . ."

Neve laughed with nervous relief. "He doesn't like rain."

"Not me, my bones." Sakir shrugged.

"They say the bones of a Scythian are hollow so that his horse can outrun the wind, unburdened by his rider's weight," Gofannon said.

"Here, the wind whistles through my bones like the breath of a drunkard playing on a flute," Sakir countered. "Heavy and wet."

Gofannon grinned in amusement, but his eyes seemed to focus on some distant vista as he said, "Spoken like a true Son of Elchmar."

"What, Master Gofannon, do you know of my tribe?" Sakir asked. "If you don't mind my asking. I am simply curious. There are only a handful of us in Temair, the rest in the south lands with the herds. I've never seen you break bread with my father in his house . . ."

"As I told the princess, I have traveled." Gofannon put his fists on his knees and pushed himself to standing. "I had the privilege of caravanning across Scythian lands when I was a boy. But you are right. It was presumptuous of me to say such a thing, Prince. I meant no offense."

"Nor I. And I am no prince here. Only a charioteer." Sakir spread his hands in a humble gesture that somehow only served to emphasize his proud bearing.

Gofannon flashed him a cool, courtly smile and turned back to Neve. "Your father has summoned me to attend him at Brú na Bóinne, lady. With your leave."

As the Druid architect strode away, Neve felt the tension flow like water from her limbs. "Come," she said to Sakir. "Fetch my bow. I need to shoot at something."

But Sakir was still staring off in the direction Gofannon had gone. "He's lying."

"You don't think he's traveled with Scythians?"

"No, Princess." He shook his head. "I think he *is* Scythian."

"What makes you think that?"

"He knows our sayings. His eyes always search for the horizon. And he walks like he wishes he were riding," Sakir said. "But he is not from the Golden Vale, or I would have known him there."

"He was not born in Eire. He said so."

"Which makes me curious." Sakir shrugged. "And him . . . dangerous."

"Why dangerous?"

"Because Scythians are dangerous," he said, and headed back toward the stables.

They passed the harrow kennels on the way. They were empty— the óglach and their hounds, Sakir told her, having been called away to Blackwater on the rumor of some magical transgression or other. Neve thought of Emer's mother and wondered if the hounds' quarry was a village healer, like she had been. As much as she got on with Fintan, Neve didn't agree with him. Enchanting bees to make more potent honey mead surely wasn't the same as blighting the cattle herd of a rival chieftain for spite or conjuring a fuath demon. And yet . . .

At the stables, Sakir hitched up his own chariot that day, because the last time they'd taken hers, Neve had shattered a wheel spoke driving recklessly over rocky terrain. The stable wheelwrights had yet to repair it because they'd been busy with the increased activity of the óglach in recent days. Sakir drove toward the starting point of the lane he'd set up in the south meadow with targets placed intermittently for Neve to shoot. She arranged her quiver and checked the tension of her bowstring, settled herself into a wide, braced stance on the deck of the chariot.

And then the ground began to shake.

The air trembled with a muted thunder, and Neve saw a cloud of dust rising from the direction of the main gates of Temair. The small contingent of Scythian cavalry the Dagda kept stationed at Temair—mostly for ceremonial occasions—was riding out, horses and chariots both, moving fast.

And they were heading in the direction of Brú na Bóinne.

As they thundered past, Neve saw Lorcan at their head, riding on the same horse he'd taken that morning. The animal was lathered and steaming—Lorcan'd clearly ridden hard back to Temair to gather warriors, not stopping to change mounts before leading them back out. Sakir watched them go, a cold fire burning in his hazel eyes. Neve could tell just by looking at him that the young Horse Lord wanted—more than anything—to ride out with the warband.

"Let's follow them!" Neve urged.

Almost more than anything. "Absolutely *not*."

"But—"

Sakir rounded on her, the cold fire suddenly blazing hot. "*That* is not a scouting party or a patrol, Princess," he snapped. "Those are Scythians and that is a *warband*. There must have been another raid. Maybe even a Fir Domnann attack, judging from the haste of those chariots. And there is nothing you can possibly say that will convince me to drive you anywhere near that."

Neve fell silent and heard a dry chuckle, and a voice, rustling like fallen leaves, in her mind.

You would let this Scythian stable boy keep you from the fray? Perhaps the sorcerer was wrong about you. Your weapon has not found its hand.

"You once told me the women of Scythia fight alongside their men," Neve said. "There was pride in your voice when you said it."

"Neve—"

"I only want to watch, Sakir. From a distance. I want to see a real battle with my own eyes."

She held his gaze as if daring him to look away from her in that moment.

Finally, with a muttered curse, Sakir reached for his bronze helmet, hanging from its hook on the chariot rail. "From a *distance*," he said, and tugged it down over Neve's dark hair.

"What will you wear?" she asked, tying the lacings under her chin. The helmet would keep her protected—and disguised—but it would leave him vulnerable.

"If we get close enough to the fight that I need a helmet," Sakir said, "I'll ask some raider to hit me over the head with a sword and make an end of it, nice and quick. Because if either of our fathers finds out about this, they'll just kill me anyway. And it *won't* be nice and quick. Hang on."

He slapped the reins and they thundered off in the wake of the warband.

The attack was happening between the banks of An Bhóinn and Brú na Bóinne, near a cluster of barrow hills to the east of the Dagda's monument. The attackers were only thirty, maybe forty in number. Not a large party by any means, but until Lorcan and the Horse Lords had arrived, they'd been fighting only a handful of

Tuatha Dé lords—the Dagda's usual retinue when he left court—and a scattering of stone carvers and white-robed Druids. Sakir drove the chariot up onto a low ridge so they could look down on the field, close enough to see, far enough to stay safe.

"Fir Domnann," Sakir confirmed.

Neve peered over his shoulder and saw that he was right. Most of the raiders had bare torsos and limbs painted with bright-green swirling designs of spirals and knots and braided lines. The Fir Bolg of Eire might have been forbidden to mark their bodies in such a fashion, but the long-exiled Fir Domnann did so with bold defiance. Neve felt a stirring of pity for them. Like she had for Sengann. Eire had been their home.

And the Dagda would show them not a shred of mercy.

Neve had seen her father hunt. She had seen him compete in the summer games against champions from the other tuaths, wrestling and shooting his bow and racing his scythe-wheeled chariot as if demon-driven, and because of that, she had thought she knew just how fierce a warrior he would prove on the battlefield. But all that was pale shadows and puppetry compared to what she witnessed on the plain of An Bhóinn.

Ruad Rofhessa was not just fierce—he was ruthless.

From the raised hillock where Sakir had pulled the horses to a stop, she could see the small band of Tuatha Dé warriors fighting in ranks, maneuvering seamlessly between shield wall formations and attacking wedges of spear- and swordsmen, while the newly arrived Scythian chariots harried the flanks of the attacking raiders.

But not the Dagda. The king of Temair followed no such rules of engagement. Instead, he harangued his charioteer to plunge directly into the heart of the fray as he swung his mighty war club and howled at the top of his lungs.

He was, Neve thought, a fuath demon made flesh.

Hated and Hating . . .

Ruad flung himself from the deck of his scythe-wheeled chariot into a clot of invaders only to climb back aboard moments later when they all lay strewn on the ground at his feet. There was blood in his hair and matted in his beard. Neve shuddered to think that, once interred in his Great Barrow, it would be *his* spirit that would be the one that would protect the land forever.

Unless he died before Brú na Bóinne was completed.

Which was clearly what the Fir Domnann intended.

A chill of something close to premonition came over her, and Neve had a sudden, horrid feeling she knew *how* they meant to accomplish that. But before she could say anything to Sakir, a horse suddenly careened across the field, just below them, and Neve saw a painted, howling Fir Domnann warrior had leaped onto its back, clutching at the rider, who hung on desperately, fist knotted in his mount's mane. It was Lorcan, his shoulder bloodied from what looked like a spear wound. Another moment and the raider would have him on the ground and dead.

Neve didn't think. Didn't hesitate.

She drew an arrow from her quiver, nocked and sighted and loosed, the way Sakir had taught her. She missed her mark—hitting the raider in the thigh, rather than through his heart—but it was enough to make him lose his grip, and he fell, screaming and flailing. Lorcan's head whipped around to see who it was that had saved him, but Neve was hidden by her helmet, and Sakir gave the ponies their head to get Neve farther away from the fray.

But as Lorcan's attacker fell beneath the hooves of his horse, something caught Neve's eye. The painted marking on the Fir Domnann's skin flared with a faint, flickering glow. Only for a moment, but that glow had been answered by a corresponding flash that Neve caught out of the corner of her eye. It had come from the hill of Dubhadh—an ancient barrow to the east of Brú na Bóinne. She slapped Sakir on the shoulder and pointed.

He saw it too. She knew because she heard him swear.

Thin wisps of mist snaked down the sides of Dubhadh, slithering through the long grass toward the ranks of the invaders. The Fir Domnann raiders stood frozen as the marks on their bodies began, ever so faintly, to glow . . . and then their battle cries turned to bone-chilling, otherworldly shrieks and howls. Neve watched in horror as they surged toward the Tuatha Dé, seemingly consumed with unnatural battle fury. Lorcan and the Dagda and the warband would be cut down and there was nothing she, with a handful of arrows, could do about it. She felt her heart thud painfully in her chest. She'd wanted to see a battle. She was about to witness a massacre.

And then Neve saw something else.

Ronan of Blackwater.

Darting from the cover of the trees and climbing up the far side of Dubhadh.

XII

RONAN HAD WOKEN up that morning with a feeling like he'd quaffed far too much mead with Cavall the night before. Which would have been entirely unremarkable, except for the fact that Cavall had been nowhere to be found after the sun had gone down, and Ronan had retired early to his pallet without having had so much as a single measure of mild brown beer.

Even still, he'd spent the morning feeling as if something in Blackwater was . . . *off*. In places, here and there, it felt like walking into a gathering storm—close and humid—even though the day was cold and biting dry. Other places, it felt as if his skin was pulled too tight over his flesh. Still others made him feel like he was being watched . . . He wasn't. He had a thief's surety of that. But when he spotted the óglach and their infernal hounds on the prowl, it was clear to Ronan that they were certainly looking for someone. Or some*thing*.

For that reason, Ronan spent a few hours dodging in and out of his usual haunts, checking for stirrings of the darkling marks under his skin that would tell him he was in trouble and listening to the dogs in the distance, who, it seemed, were growing increasingly frustrated on the hunt. Not once had he heard their customary bone-chilling howl, but they were also clearly catching scents—and then losing them just as fast. His own particular magic remained, thankfully—especially after his last little run-in with Neve—dormant. It was almost, Ronan mused, as if someone was playing a prank on the óglach. But to what end?

He only eventually figured it out because of his Druid training, some portion of which had been in augury. When the óglach turned up one dusty alley, Ronan turned down another and found himself by the river. The day around him fell still. Silent. And there he saw, standing beneath the oak trees on the opposite bank, a black-furred, golden-eyed wolf with a sparrow held lifeless between its jaws. The wolf stared at him, and he felt as though a cloud passed over the sun, although the sky was clear.

He closed his eyes, and the meaning of the portent was startlingly apparent.

"*Damn* . . . ," Ronan whispered as the wolf loped away, disappearing into the shadows with its catch. "Damn them all . . ."

He ran, filled with the dread certainty of why the óglach's hounds were so very preoccupied that day chasing wild phantom geese all over Blackwater. When he got to the docks, Ronan was less than surprised to see a fishing skiff with bright, painted yellow eyes on the bow.

"Where have those salvaging idiots gone?" he called out to the old fisherman at the tiller.

Swift grimly nodded his wicker hat in the direction of An Bhóinn.

"Oh *no* . . ." A wave of sick apprehension flooded over Ronan.

"I can get you there," Swift said, his mouth set in a hard line. "But you'd best hurry. There's not much time."

Madness, but Ronan didn't have much choice, other than going back home and pretending none of this was his business. *And then you can live with the knowledge that you let her die . . .*

Swearing through his teeth, Ronan cast off the line, shoved the skiff out into the murky shallows of the Blackwater, and climbed aboard, taking up the oars. He realized he hadn't needed the old man to tell him where Sparrow and the rest of the salvagers had gone. He'd already known.

A wolf on a wide green hill . . .

A dark power rising, making its way toward Teg Duinn.

The only thing was . . . he didn't know which side that dark power was on.

From the river, they could hear the fighting as the watercourse curved to the south, around the plain where the Great Barrow rose up from the green land. Through the winter-barren branches of the trees, they could see where the fighting was thickest, and Ronan rowed past it, farther downstream to the east so that he could double back. He had a strong suspicion he knew where Sparrow and her mad folk would have set themselves up. A place already steeped in dormant power with a clear view of the field.

He should have believed her, Ronan thought as he steered the boat into the shallows, hidden by a screen of brush, and slipped over the side to wade ashore. Sparrow had told him the salvagers planned to join with a band of Fir Domnann raiders and offer them the magic they had gleaned so they could war with the Tuatha Dé. He should have taken her seriously, instead of laughing at her when she'd asked for his help. Magic or no, Sparrow and her salvagers would soon be destroyed by the Dagda's forces, along with the rest of the raiders.

The last thing Ronan wanted was Sparrow's blood on his hands. The image of the wolf with the sparrow in its jaws flashed in his mind. There was no way Neve would be allowed to fight in this battle, he thought. She'd told him as much the last time he'd seen her. But he also knew—without a shred of doubt—that she was *there*. Somewhere. And he'd be damned if he'd see blood on *her* hands either.

So Ronan's aim was simple: find Sparrow. Or, failing that, find Neve.

But either way, cheat death out of at least one soul that day.

Pry the bird out of the wolf's jaws.

He broke into a run, and then a climb, as he reached the place where the salvagers had positioned themselves, on top of the hill of Dubhadh to the east of Brú na Bóinne. The highest of an overgrown clump of barrow graves, their occupants long forgotten, with a clear view of the battle raging on the floodplain. He could see them huddled up there. Could almost smell the acrid tang of the ragged bundle of small magics they'd gathered—made even smaller by all the phantom spells they would have had to leave lying around Blackwater as distractions, just to keep the óglach otherwise engaged that afternoon.

Clever, Ronan begrudgingly admitted. Yet still so very stupid.

Because their plans hadn't taken into consideration the chaotic nature of the power they drew upon. As Ronan had always known, chaos attracted more chaos. He reached the summit of the barrow, where the salvagers huddled, casting their curse and sending it forth, too engaged to notice his arrival. And the most chaotic thing he knew was racing toward them in that very moment, feet braced wide on the deck of a bucking chariot.

Ronan glanced down and saw a lone chariot driving along a low ridge at the perimeter of the skirmish, separate from the rest of the Dagda's warband. Even from that distance, he could tell. The charioteer was bareheaded, and the helmeted archer standing behind him, wearing an axe and carrying a bow, could be no other than Neve. Ronan could sense her presence like a blazing torch in his mind. The sounds of battle below faded into nothingness as he saw her yew bow swing up into position, aimed at the summit of Dubhadh, the curve of the bow bending like a reed in the wind, the string pulled taut . . .

The arrow glinted in the sun like fire . . .

. . . and then it *was* fire.

Bursting into pale golden flame, trailing crimson smoke, the slender missile arced through the air toward the cloaked figure on the hilltop conjuring the mist-borne enchantment flowing out toward the Fir Domnann raiders.

But by the time the arrow reached its intended target, the target was gone.

The curse-caster yelped in shock as Ronan slammed into her and sent all the salvagers reeling. Sparrow fetched up against a moss-covered boulder with enough force to drive the breath from her lungs. Which was what Ronan had intended. No breath meant no speech. No speech meant no curses.

As she lay there gasping, he clambered to his feet and peered over the precipice of the hilltop to see the consequences of his rash act.

The cursed glimmering mist wavered . . . then shattered.

Sparrow's anguished cry tore through the air as her fragile enchantment blew away on the wind. Disrupted before it could fully form. The woad-painted Fir Domnann warriors below had already begun to slump forward, the patterns on their bodies dimming until they were just symbols again, painted in dark green pigment.

"I should kill you where you stand," Sparrow snarled.

Ronan turned a flat stare on her. "And you'd be dead where *you* stood if I hadn't intervened. But don't thank me or anything."

A frown ticked between Sparrow's big dark eyes and her gaze flicked to where Ronan's arm hung awkwardly. A smoldering raw gash of slow-welling blood dyed the sleeve of his tunic red. She plucked up the arrow that had wounded him, stuck deep in the turf beside her, and saw that the bronze arrowhead was still pulsing with a glimmering ember-glow that faded to nothing as she held it. She dropped the thing to the ground like it was a viper.

"Mórr's mercy," she gasped. "Who—what *did* this?"

Ronan shook his head. "I cannot tell you that. But it would seem you're not the only enchantress on this island."

"How did you know to find us here?" she asked.

"You didn't ask me for help at Samhain because of my charm and great beauty."

She raised an eyebrow at him. "Are you—"

"In a great amount of pain? Yes, thanks." In truth, the arrow had barely grazed him, but it had still done a deal of damage. Because of who'd shot it. Ronan sucked in a deep breath and turned to the other salvagers, daring any of them to give him grief for saving Sparrow's life.

Sparrow reached up and grabbed the front of his tunic, hauling him down behind the sod parapet of the hill, beside a leather satchel. It was overflowing with oddments of spells—bits of stone and slivers of driftwood and scraps of cloth—all of it dull and faded. Gathered over who knew how many months or years, now leached of the magic that the salvagers had distilled and poured into the conjuring he'd just disrupted. Wasted. Gone.

Mostly.

Sparrow used what little fading magic remained to salve Ronan's wound while he explained to her—without getting into details where Neve was concerned—that he'd had a premonition of Sparrow's death.

"Then that was my fate. You shouldn't have intervened."

"Neither should you. You're all meddling with things that are far better left un–meddled with. Trust me." The pain from his wound suddenly lessened beneath her fingers and he almost gasped with relief. There was still a dull ache to it, but Sparrow's ministrations had at least cooled the searing agony of Neve's uncanny flame.

"What do you think will happen when the Dagda finally goes under the Hill?" Sparrow asked quietly, gazing off into the distance at Brú na Bóinne.

"I have no idea," Ronan said, "And you don't either. Not really. I don't know who or what has convinced you otherwise, but the world is not going to go back to the way it was. The Wheel turns, Sparrow. It always has."

"Aye. And eventually it'll get back to where it was."

"With more mud in its spokes."

Some of that dirt was on him, he thought, as he struggled to raise himself up enough to look down at the battle. As he had predicted, without the aid of the curse, the Fir Domnann were in trouble and they knew it. If there was a leader among the raiders—and from that distance, Ronan couldn't honestly tell—they must have given the order to fall back. The retreat was chaos. But it was, at least, a retreat. Then a rout.

He turned back to see that he was alone on the hilltop. The others—Sparrow and her fellow salvagers—had vanished like the mist they'd tried to conjure. They'd be back, he knew. Bide their time and lick their wounds. Maybe try again. With, he feared, stronger magic gathered to their cause. Because whoever it was that had rallied them to this attempt would push them to another.

And what about your *magic?* he asked himself. *You could have helped them.*

He looked down at the small pale scar on his hand. He could have called on it, he thought. The darkling marks, the power he knew slept beneath his skin. Together with the salvagers, they might very well have wiped out the Dagda's warband and claimed Brú na Bóinne for the folk of the land . . .

And then what? Lead a Fir Bolg rebellion to victory against the Tuatha Dé?

The Tuatha Dé, on the whole, were very good at killing things, but with the queen-to-be, Úna, holding the reins of power, they might be even better at it. She was, by all accounts, the least mad member of the royal house. And that made her dangerous. Because ambition was always worse than passion when it came to such things. Ronan didn't like where his thoughts were taking him.

But if Ruad Rofhessa and his first daughter were gone, that would leave only Neve. It was ridiculous—dangerous, even—to imagine such an outrageous circumstance.

And yet . . . here he was, imagining just that.

⬤

WHEN SAKIR PULLED the horses into a tight turn and raced back toward Temair, Neve didn't object to leaving the battle. Still, the arrows in her quiver rattled, chattering restlessly, eager for flight. The sagaris at her belt knocked against her thigh, hungry for blood. Or so it seemed to her fevered imagination.

They crossed the river to safety and Sakir drove until they could no longer hear the muted cries and clashes of the conflict. Near a stand of birch, stark white against the darker forest, he eased the horses to a stop and turned toward the princess where she stood gripping the chariot rail.

"How did you do it?" Sakir's voice was quiet.

Neve avoided his gaze. "What?"

"The arrow. The fire."

"I'm not sure what you mean. An arrow is an arrow."

"Even when it's on fire, yes." When she didn't explain, he pressed her. "Your arrowhead burst into flame midflight."

She laughed a little and there was a wild edge to the sound that even she could hear. "Your eyes must have been playing games with you, Sakir," she said.

"A trick of the light."

She nodded and turned her face away. As much as he could grate on her nerves, she hated lying to Sakir. He was the closest thing she had to a confidant. Often, all she'd wanted to do was sit in the stable and talk to him. Listen to the tales of the Horse Lords. But this . . .

She was afraid of what he'd think of her if he knew what was happening—not that she even knew herself. She didn't think she could handle seeing disappointment in his eyes. Or worse, fear.

"It doesn't matter. I missed my shot," she said.

"Aye. You did." Sakir said. "Lucky for your father's warband that runner took down the raider's curse-caster. That was bravely done, whoever he was."

Neve nodded but said nothing. What Ronan had done had been brave. Noble even. And he'd done it without spilling any blood. While Neve had fully intended to. And her arrow had responded in kind. What if her father had been right? What if magic really was too dangerous to leave lying fallow in the fields and forests for anyone willing and able to gather it? Even—maybe especially—Neve herself.

Or what if it's there to be yours for the taking?

Neve shut her eyes to silence the whisper in her mind. *When Úna is queen,* Neve reminded herself, *she will finish what our father has started. She will make the land safe. Secure.*

Stagnant . . . And your kind will die out, never to return.

Her kind. And just what, exactly, was that?

As they drove back toward the palace in silence, Neve glanced down at her palm. There were lines—faint, but traceable—that hadn't been there before. Lines in a twisting triangle shape, like a knot made of three flames. Or—she peered at the sigil more closely—like the head of a wolf—ears and muzzle—staring up at her.

Beloved of the Wolf.

Neve Anann Eriu . . .

Little Scota. Maybe not so little, now.

———

SPARROW'S SALVE SPELL was wearing off, and Ronan found himself somewhat regretting his noble act. Neve's arrow had left a searing wound, black-edged and bleeding, branded upon Ronan's upper arm. Had it hit its intended mark, Sparrow would be very dead, and that wasn't something Ronan could reconcile with the Tuatha Dé princess he knew. She wasn't exactly a cold-hearted killer. And there was something else Ronan couldn't reconcile: *how* had Neve done it?

What kind of power—*really*—did she hold in the palm of her hand?

You might have found out if you hadn't driven her away when she sought your help, he chided himself. *Again.*

"You were right about the damned salvagers," Cavall muttered as he peeled the frayed edges of Ronan's tunic sleeve away from the seeping wound on his arm. "They're just not right in the head. The heart, maybe, but definitely not the head . . ."

As an apprentice smith, Cavall was something of an expert at treating burns and cuts, although he'd admonished Ronan that having suffered both in the same wound was a bit much, really. Ronan's head was swimming from the generous amount of mead Cavall had made him drink before mending his arm.

"I gave you the strong stuff," Cavall said. "This is going to sting."

Like a whole nest of hornets. Ronan managed not to scream outright, but there was a lot of wounded-animal groaning while Cavall cleaned and salved and stitched. When it was done and bandaged, Ronan stood and awkwardly hitched his cloak back on over his shoulders.

"Where are you going?" Cavall asked. "I'll come with you—"

Ronan shook his head and the firelit little room swung side to side. "Not tonight, Cavall. I need to go alone."

"Where? You can barely stand."

He shrugged a bit helplessly. "I'll know when I get there."

"*If* you get there. Whatever you're looking for, Ronan," Cavall said, a worried frown on his face, "make sure it wants to be found. But more than that, make sure you want to find it. Things that are hidden—not *lost*, hidden—well, it's been my experience they're hidden for a reason."

Cavall wasn't wrong. Ronan knew that. And he also knew that he *was* looking for something. He had been all his life. But it was only now, it seemed, that it was also looking for him. Hunting him. He pressed a hand to the bandage on his arm and hissed. He was a marked man. In more ways than one. Hunted by the very thing he'd been hunting for.

In the days following his first fateful meeting with young Neve, thirteen-year-old Ronan had spent all of his free time secretly practicing another bit of magic he'd stolen from a different grave. Unlike the fuath curse, *this* particular spell had been carefully, artfully stitched with silver thread onto a finely woven strip of indigo-dyed linen. A token of love, not hate. A speaking spell, used to communicate with the shade of a loved one passed on. Ronan had kept that one for himself.

So that he could ask the questions he needed answers to.

After that night with the fuath—and the ban sidhe and the girl—young Ronan had had a lot of questions. And so Ronan had gone at moonrise to a sacred spring deep in the forest. Staring down into a mirror of stars and darkness, he'd called upon the goddess of the waters to help him speak to the dead. And had been met with silence. His mother did not appear to console him or explain why she'd done what she had. His father did not return to tell him who he was.

The surface of the spring had remained black, blank, mute.

In all his young life, he'd never felt so alone.

"*There is no goddess here*," he'd said finally, bitterly. "*There are no gods in Eire. And no small wonder the Tuatha Dé conquered this land.*" Ronan had fed the strip of spell cloth to his torch, watching as the silver threads charred and the ashes floated down into the water. Tears fell from his eyes, igniting into bright flashes of indigo flame—just like the barrow girl's had—as they hit the water. Dark fire, so blue it was almost black, rippled outward.

The young orphan thief scrambled back from the water's edge as, rising from the spring like a wraith, a glittering mist twisted through the darkness toward him . . . enveloped him . . . and, as he'd screamed in pain and fear, the now-familiar patterns of writhing lines and sigils appeared on his skin, spiraling outward from the scar on his hand to wrap around his wrist like a bracelet. The marks crawled up his arm and encircled his neck, slithered like eels across his torso, down his other arm, and wrapped around his legs . . . and he'd felt himself begin to change into something inhuman.

Otherworldly.

Familiar . . .

That night, Ronan had decided there were no gods left in Eire, but there was definitely magic—far beyond curses and spells. He'd found it. And it had found him. Because of her. But Ronan knew, even then, that power and peril walked hand in hand.

So he would find the girl whose life he'd saved, who'd made him open that forbidden door and brought this affliction down upon him. And he would make her answer for what she'd done. He'd made himself that promise on that long-ago night.

It was high time he stopped letting Neve just walk away.

Ronan had an oath to keep.

XIII

SAKIR STABLED THE horses and stowed the chariot so that no one would know they'd been at Brú na Bóinne. He'd said very little to Neve, but it was clear he was troubled. She supposed she couldn't really blame him. After he'd retired to his quarters in the stable compound, Neve waited near the kennels, through dusk into darkness, for Fintan and the hounds to return.

It was clear to her now that the óglach had most likely been lured away to Blackwater as a distraction. A way to keep the spell-harrows away from Brú na Bóinne while the curse-casters did their work, helping the Fir Domnann in their fight against the Dagda. It had been a coordinated effort, but to what end? Was it an isolated incident, or a prelude to something bigger?

And what in the wide world had Ronan been doing there? If his aim all along had been to side with the Fir Domnann and the renegade magic salvagers, he'd done a wretched job of it.

It was dark when Fintan and his men returned after a fruitless day scouring Blackwater for anything so much as an ensorcelled sewing basket without any luck.

Yes, Fintan told Neve, they'd heard of the skirmish at the barrow. "The king didn't seem to think it signified anything of great import," Fintan said, spreading around fresh hay for the dogs to lie down on. "Just the usual Fir Domnann raiders, rabid and reckless, come ashore to burn and pillage as usual. He and his warriors handily put an end to the attempt, so I hear."

Neve recalled the conversation she'd had with Úna about rumors of ships. Invasion. And the Dagda's apparent disregard of those rumors.

"I see. Seems strange, if they were here to burn and pillage, why attack my father's barrow? It's just a great pile of stone," Neve said.

"Who knows?" Fintan grunted. "Maybe the fools think he's filled it to the beams with treasure."

"How likely do you think that is?" Neve pressed as he gave Thorn a going-over with an old horse brush. "That this attack meant nothing, I mean? No coming battle, no looming war?"

Fintan chewed on the corner of his thumbnail. "I—" He stopped and shook his head. "It's not my place to say anything. But . . ." He huffed a sharp sigh and seemed to come to a decision. "I trust you, lady. More'n I trust your da. These days, leastways. The dogs like you. And that, for me, speaks volumes."

Neve was startled by his admission. "Do you trust the chieftains?"

"Some, yes. Others . . . not with so much as an empty purse. But that's as may be with any chamber full of those with power and those who want it, isn't it? And there are those whose priorities run counter to the Dagda's, if you catch my meaning."

She did. Her father's obsession with his monument. The out-lawing of magic.

"What about Lorcan?" Neve asked, even though what she really wanted to ask was how Fintan felt about Úna, and her tacit support of their father's edicts.

Fintan opened his mouth to answer her, but all of a sudden, the quality of the light in the kennel yard shifted, growing brighter . . . and *darker* at the same time. Redder. The air filled with a skirling, hungry sound.

"The dog!" Neve exclaimed.

Fintan's eyes went wide and he drew his sword as his harrow hound leaped over her kennel fence and bounded past him, teeth bared and eyes burning with crimson fire—the source of the lurid illumination.

"Thorn!" Fintan shouted to no avail. He turned to Neve. "Stay here!"

He sprinted out of the courtyard, sword in hand, in pursuit of the dog. Echoes of the spell-harrow's eerie spectral wailing seemed to be coming from nowhere and everywhere at once, and Neve felt the same cold fear thrill through her veins as when she'd been on the run from the hounds in Blackwater.

She unsheathed her sagaris and grabbed a torch from the near-est wall sconce as Sakir came running from the stables, his eyes wide with alarm.

"I'm right behind you!" he shouted, loosening the axe at his belt.

They ran toward the howling, which took them toward the wing of the palace where Neve's own quarters were. Neve felt a growing dread in her heart, but there was no one there. Úna had already moved into her new, sprawling queen's apartment and now it was just Neve—and Emer—who occupied those rooms.

The carved doors were thrown wide and Neve skidded to a halt on the polished floor. The main chamber was dark and empty, except for Fintan and Thorn, standing brace-legged in the middle of the room, flared nostrils quivering and chest heaving. The way the creature had howled, Neve wouldn't have been surprised to find the whole room packed with slavering ban sidhe. But nothing, not a cushion or a curtain or a string of glass beads, seemed out of place.

"Fintan . . . what *is* it?" Neve gasped, out of breath, as Sakir strode into the room on her heels, axe in hand.

"I . . ." Fintan shook his head. "I do not know, lady."

"Mórr's blessed eyes! *What* is going on?" Emer squawked as she lurched out from behind a woven wicker screen in the adjoining room, hurriedly tugging her arms through the sleeves of her sleeping shift. "Have you and that bloody beast gone mad?" She stalked up to Fintan, her face flushed and big dark eyes blazing bright. "You're in the princess's private quarters. Show some respect—"

"Emer, wait." Neve stepped between the two of them before her bondswoman did something foolish that close to a cursefired harrow hound. "Fintan?"

Fintan had a firm grip on the harrow hound's silver collar, but the beast's eyes still burned with traces of a sullen, deep-red glow.

"There doesn't seem to be anything here," Fintan said, confounded. "See, Thorn's cursefire dies down to naught."

"Nothing but a poor handmaid terrified half out of her wits," Emer snapped.

Fintan knelt down, taking the hound's head in his hands and peering at her closely. "She's usually very dependable. But . . . I suppose chasing phantoms all day has her turned right around. Eh, girl?"

The dog huffed, and Sakir and Neve exchanged a glance.

"There's a full moon tomorrow night," Neve suggested, trying to make somewhat light of the scare. "Isn't everything just a bit touched with magic on such nights?"

Fintan shot her a look. "I'd be careful not to let your father's Druids hear such talk, Lady Neve," he said in a low voice. "Nor your lady sister."

"Of course," Neve said. "You may go, Fintan. Be assured, I'll call for you if anything else *untoward* should happen tonight."

"Well then"—he bent at the waist in a bow—"a pleasant night to you, Princess."

"And to you." Neve then turned to Sakir, who stood hovering, ready to fight but without anywhere to aim a blow. "Good night, Sakir."

Sakir hesitated. He cast another sweeping glance around the room and then nodded and stepped out over the threshold.

Neve sheathed her sagaris at her belt. "I am sorry you were frightened, Emer," she said. "I'll speak to Father about keeping the beasts out of the palace proper." She took a deep breath to steady her nerves. "Now, would you fetch a small tray from the kitchens?"

Emer stared pointedly at Neve's weapon, then at the leather archery guard on her wrist. She'd likely been fussing about the palace all day wondering where her mistress was, amidst word of the Fir Domnann attack. Neve wasn't about to tell her. "Please,

Emer. I've been practicing archery all day, and I fear my stomach will complain louder than that hound all night and keep us both from sleep."

Emer nodded with a huff and reached for the firebrand so she could navigate her way through the mostly darkened corridors. "I'll not be but a moment."

Once Emer had gone, Neve pulled the door shut and lit the brazier. Then she exhaled slowly and held out her hand to the flickering orange glow. Her palm was unmarked, but for the faint triangle of creases that remained quiescent. She'd been afraid that *she'd* somehow been the one to inadvertently ignite Thorn's cursefire. Just like she'd accidentally set her arrow alight at Brú na Bóinne.

It *had* been accidental, hadn't it? Because it would have been a terrible death for that salvager, had the thing actually hit its mark. Neve knew that. Something inside her felt bruised and she pressed her hand to her chest.

She stayed like that for a long moment before lifting the candle and walking into the deep alcove where her sleeping couch used to be. She slept now in the larger chamber, but she'd spent every night staring up at that ceiling and those walls, memorizing every line and shade of the mural that had been painted there by the Scathach's own artisans. As well as every crack and chip and faded, peeling patch that had appeared over recent years.

The coming of the Tuatha Dé to Eire.

She lifted the light to the procession of beautiful, godlike beings riding impossibly graceful steeds up through the sea surf and into a lush, fantastical forest landscape on a starry night. The troop of lords and ladies, decked in fine robes and rich jewels, were led by a woman—the Scathach—exiled ruler of the White-Walled City of Ankh-Tawy in the desert kingdom of Kemet, cloaked and hooded, her face hidden, and riding a silver-white horse. Her midnight mantle was stitched with celestial symbols and she had a long reed flute tucked into her belt beside a blue-jeweled dagger on her hip. She bore a lamp held high in her hand.

The mural used to shimmer with a subtle, barely discernible sparkling—the stars had winked, the seafoam glimmered like real, moonlit waves—the last traces of a harmless enchantment. As a child, Neve had delighted in the subtle, magical beauty of it. Úna had always wanted to paint the wall white.

Neve reached up and touched a fingertip to the Scathach's lantern. Beneath her touch, the painted flame flared to a tiny pinprick of light. Neve gasped and tensed, listening for howls, but the night remained silent. And the faint glimmer eased the strange ache inside her chest, even as it made her heart beat faster.

If only Ronan had been willing to teach me . . .

She lowered her hand and the gleam faded to nothing. The painted blue jewel in the hilt of the Scathach's dagger winked conspiratorially at her and Neve smiled.

Then she yawned and stretched, remembering that her sister was getting married on the morrow. Then there would be the Brú na Bóinne Stone Singing—the last one—at moonrise, and then feasting until dawn. Neve's gaze drifted over to the corner of the room where Emer had draped the gown Neve was to wear over a screen. She grimaced at the sight, as if she was already wearing it with the laces pulled too tight about her ribs . . .

Stop being ridiculous, she told herself. *There's nothing to be anxious about.*

She lay down on her old couch and her eyes drifted closed, the red glow of the brazier and the trooping Tuatha Dé procession fading to black. The silence all around her grew louder, like the pounding of distant waves on a shore, in time with her heartbeat. She heard the thready whine of a distant flute, and a whisper in her ear wound itself around the sound . . .

Daughter . . . Beloved . . . Queen . . .

War horns blared and a cry of joyous triumph from a sea of voices rang out.

And then a shout: *Dagda!*

Neve startled awake, gasping for breath, eyes wide in the darkness. She was alone. Emer still wasn't back with the food. Neve sat up and put her head in her hands for a moment, feeling beads of sweat on her brow. She opened the carved double doors and stepped onto the terrace, where the carefully pruned branches of the trees still bore the very last autumnal foliage, but the flowers were gone, leaving behind only a few withered blooms. Even still, Neve imagined she caught a whiff of heady floral perfume. Like lilies, only sweeter.

The water in the little pond reflected the shining stars like a dark mirror. Neve breathed deeply and tilted her head back, staring up into the night where clouds veiled the sky, hazing the moon's brightness. It took her a moment to realize the disconnect.

There are no stars shining . . .

Her gaze snapped back down to where the pond still sparkled. Neve stepped farther out onto the terrace, drawn by the tiny points of light strewn on the water like glittering beads.

No. Not like *glittering beads . . .*

Beads. One step closer and Neve could see them clearly now. All the shining, faceted, tiny jewels that had been painstakingly woven into the netting of Úna's wedding gown. It took a handful of heartbeats for the horrific realization to set in . . . and then Neve was running across the terrace, dropping to her knees on the stone.

"Úna . . ." Neve's voice cracked, an ugly crow call. "*Úna!*"

She reached for her sister, motionless at the bottom of the shallow little pool. The tiled bottom of the pond was covered in less than a handsbreadth of water—even as the stone terrace surrounding it was bone dry—and Úna lay at the center of it, her long, graceful limbs splayed out at odd angles, her wedding gown spread out all around her. Frantic, Neve scrambled into the pond and pulled her sister up, brushing away the long dark hair that curtained Úna's face. Her skin was pale and perfect in the moonlight, her lips tinged blue. And her dark eyes, open and staring.

Drowned . . .

A wide trickle of water ran from the corner of her mouth.

Neve heard a wolf howl somewhere in the distance—far beyond the palace walls—or maybe it was Thorn, and then she heard the sound of her own voice skirling up and out into the night, shredding the darkness, louder than a whole pack of harrow hounds belling, a wail of denial and grief.

She didn't know how long she knelt there in the cold, rocking Úna's lifeless body in her arms and keening her throat raw, but suddenly it seemed that the tiny garden was full of people. Surrounding her, reaching for her.

Emer was first, followed by Fintan and the other óglach on watch that night. Guards who'd heard the commotion. Servants pale with fear. There were others—a blur of faces—but Neve couldn't tell them apart. When several hands finally managed to pry her away from Úna, the world was spinning around her.

Through the haze, she saw Lorcan standing in the archway to the garden, his face a blank, carved mask. His eyes empty. His shoulder was heavily bandaged, the wound the Fir Domnann had given him seeping blood, though he didn't seem to notice.

As they carried Úna's body away, the last person Neve saw was Gofannon, framed in the doorway to the chamber, clutching a heavy night robe around his shoulders. He still wore his serpent torc, but his hair was unbraided, hanging loose about his face.

And his blue eyes were filled with tears.

XIV

I N THE GREAT Hall, where the fire had been stoked to roaring
life, Ruad Rofhessa, the mighty Dagda of the Tuatha Dé, vic-
torious that afternoon in battle, looked like a warrior who'd just
been beaten and laid low by a great enemy. His charcoal mane of
hair was unplaited and hung in wild tangles around his face. His
eyes were two burning coals, red-rimmed and sunken. His huge,
muscled frame looked shrunken, wasted, as he knelt on the stone
steps of the dais where Lorcan had lain Úna's body.

Neve felt as though she stood outside of herself, watching. Not
even breathing.

She looked from her father's ravaged, tear-streaked face to the
court ladies, a tangled knot of grieving beauty. They clung to each
other, hair unbound, garments loose, weeping in genuine sorrow.
Something, Neve thought, they never would have done for her. She
wouldn't have blamed them—Úna had been their companion, their
princess, and Neve had made as little effort to get to know any of

them as they had her. She felt a muted sense of regret for that. But then again, every feeling was muted in that moment. As if someone else was experiencing her emotions and inadequately relaying them to her, like an unskilled bard telling a half-remembered tale.

She looked over at Lorcan. Úna's betrothed stood beside the vacant throne chair, the hand of his uninjured arm balled into a fist at his side, looking like it wanted a weapon to clutch. Or something to hit.

Neve understood the feeling all too well. It occurred to her that Úna had been right about her. She'd never actually taken a moment to look—to really *look*—at Lorcan since they'd both grown up. Perhaps he would have made a fine Dagda after all. But now, Temair and the Tuatha Dé would never get the chance to know.

Because of her sister's death, on the very eve of her wedding. In one fell, incomprehensible stroke, the realm had lost their future queen and their future king. Neve felt the searing pain of Úna's loss turn to ice in her guts. She glanced over to where Fintan stood and recalled what he'd said to her earlier that evening about not trusting the chiefs. Or the Dagda . . .

How had such a thing happened?

And now that it *had*, who would carry on the Dagda's legacy? *His legacy* . . .

Her father's legacy wasn't peace or prosperity. It wasn't conquest beyond bloody brawling with an already conquered people. It wasn't anything. Yet. For now, it was a pile of stones in the curve of the river. Neve's thoughts spiraled away from her, flying like a sparrow at dusk, tumbling across the hills to Brú na Bóinne. She could see it in her mind's eye, the grassy dome of the mortuary temple, the ring of stones . . . all standing sentinel except for one final stone. The one Gofannon had said he would dedicate to Úna.

At Teg Duinn . . .

The words whispered in Neve's head, even as she closed her eyes against the dizzying sensation. Not Brú na Bóinne . . .

Teg Duinn . . .

House of Darkness. The portal to the underworld realms . . .

Her mouth gone dry and her palms slick with sweat, Neve silently backed out of the Great Hall, unnoticed. She ran through the deserted corridors of the palace, with a hand on the axe on her belt so it wouldn't rattle in its sheath.

Neve wasn't going to throw herself on her couch and mourn Úna's death. She was going to do something about it.

Neve wasn't at all surprised to find Sakir standing in the middle of the stable yard alone, waiting for her. He bowed his head as she slowed to a stop in front of him.

"Which horse should I saddle for you, lady?"

"It doesn't matter."

"Then I'll saddle two," Sakir said. He couldn't have known where she wanted to go, but he knew her well enough to know she couldn't stay in Temair that night.

"No, not this time, Sakir. I'm going alone."

"Where?"

"I can't tell you." She felt the tears threatening to flow and shook her head hard, willing them back because if she started to cry, she feared she might never stop. "No one must know."

Sakir nodded and looked up. "The moon will light your way," he said.

The thin veil of cloud had cleared off, and the moon—only a whisper away from full—was so big and bright that it seemed close enough to touch. Wolf song floated out into the night in homage and Neve felt the small hairs on the back of her neck lift.

Sakir reached out and put his hands on her shoulders.

"Beloved of the Wolf," he said. "Go and come back again." It was the only time she could remember someone calling her that without mockery or jest. Then he leaned forward and kissed her forehead—so swift and softly, she might have imagined it—and went to saddle her horse.

A part of Neve wanted—desperately—to call him back and tell him, yes, saddle two horses. Úna was gone and she felt so utterly alone and the only one who seemed to understand her—even if that was the very thing that drove her mad about him—was Sakir. The stable hand who was a prince.

You wouldn't be the first Tuatha Dé princess to lose her heart to a Horse Lord . . .

As Sakir led her mount out of the stable, Neve thought of the mural in her chamber, the lamp held high in the Scathach's hand as she rode beside *her* Scythian prince. And she remembered just how badly that had ended, for both of them.

FOR THE SECOND time that day, Neve found herself at Brú na Bóinne. She was faintly surprised to find the place unguarded, particularly after that day's attack. It gave her pause but didn't stop her from tethering her mount and walking the long straight path toward the barrow.

The massive curving wall of white stones that fronted the temple gleamed in the moonlight, and the smooth, sloping curve of the domed roof, covered in thick green mossy-soft sod, was dusted with tiny clusters of night-blooming wildflowers.

Alone, up close, Neve realized what a stunning achievement her father's final resting place was. The design of the structure itself seemed, at first glance, deceptively simple. A domed structure, a single entrance. But every stone was intricately carved with patterns that Neve could not even begin to comprehend. Years of construction and hundreds of masons and artisans and workers— each dedicated for half of each year to carving and hauling and raising stone—had built this marvel.

Her resolve wavered for a moment and she felt her throat tighten. *Don't cry*, she told herself. *You don't cry*. Not anymore. She remembered how her tears had conjured a ban sidhe from the Dead Ground. But there was no one buried in Brú na Bóinne.

Not yet . . .

Her boots made no sound as she walked the last few steps on the path and her fingers clenched around the sagaris hanging from her belt. For a brief moment, Neve wondered if she should leave the weapon behind. What was she going to do with it, after all? Fight a god to win her sister back? It seemed as if the glimmering mark on her palm would be more useful in such a case. Not that she even knew how to conjure it. Maybe Ronan hadn't wanted to teach her because he really was a salvager. Except he wasn't . . . was he? She didn't know.

All she knew was that, in the course of a single day she had *almost* lost her father, *had* lost her sister, and felt like she was losing her mind and somehow . . . somehow it all made her think of him. Nothing had been the same since that day in Blackwater. And now she stood at the very threshold of the Otherworld. Maybe.

She loosened the axe in its sheath but didn't remove it. Neve stepped over the elaborately carved kerbstone laid across the threshold. Entering the structure felt like walking through an icy waterfall and the skin on her arms and the back of her neck rippled into gooseflesh. The sudden, weighty silence—even after the hush of deep night outside—was deafening. Neve cursed herself for not bringing a pitch torch or a tallow candle and flint. But then her eyes began to adjust to the gloom inside the monument and the pale wash of moonlight spilling into the passageway from behind her.

No . . . With a shiver, she realized that the faint glow illuminating the long stone corridor was coming from somewhere in *front* of her. Neve froze and listened, straining to hear voices—the sound of breathing, the scuff of a boot or the butt of a spear on the earthen floor, something that would indicate the presence of another soul.

No. Something in her soul told Neve that she was the only living creature in the Great Barrow that night. But that didn't necessarily mean she was alone. She expected the air to be heavy, cold and damp, but instead, she felt a warm—almost hot—breeze sweep across her cheeks and forehead, laden with the sweet heavy scent of a flower she couldn't quite identify.

She pressed on.

The farther Neve stepped down the passage, the more she expected branching passages, chambers, statuary . . . *something*. But there was only a long narrow passageway leading deeper into the center of the barrow. There were no torches in sconces on the walls—no sconces at all even—and no way to tell where the light in front of her was coming from. But whatever it was, the glow grew brighter and brighter the closer Neve walked toward it, until finally, she stepped out into a single empty chamber.

It looked unfinished, barren of furnishings except for a lone, carved stone stele resting on a wooden sledge. In the center of the chamber, there was a small square pit dug into the earth, as if waiting for the stele to be stood up in that spot. The stone itself was plain and small, carved out of pale sand-colored stone, weathered and singularly unimpressive.

She turned in a slow circle and saw smaller niches on three sides, each housing a tall clay water jar. There was nothing else. Just cold stone walls and water jars, shadows and echoes.

Neve's desperate hope of a way, a path to find Úna, blew away like so much dust.

This is what her father believed would keep them safe?

"This?" she asked aloud, her voice shocking in the silence. "*This* is worth losing his sanity and his soul to?"

Her knees buckled. This was no Teg Duinn. No mystical portal. It was an empty tomb. And that was all.

Oh, my sister . . .

Dearest blood of mine . . .

The whispered anguish was Neve's, and not Neve's. Grief swept over her and she sank to the ground as if all her bones had turned to powder. She stayed like that, staring with unseeing eyes into the empty pit until she suddenly realized that there was something buried in the earth, gleaming faintly.

She dropped down into the dugout on hands and knees, clawing away the dirt. With a grim determination, she pried the object from the earth and lifted it up. The thing was crusted over with a thick layer of dirt, but there was the shine of what looked like gold along one edge. That's what had caught her eye. But the strange light in the chamber was growing dim, making it difficult to discern any details beyond the basic shape of the object—a mask, maybe, or perhaps the visor of a chieftain's helmet.

Neve raked at the dirt but could find nothing else, so she tucked the thing under her arm and climbed out of the hole. The chamber was near dark as she made her way back to the entrance, and her steps quickened until she was running by the time she burst back out into the night and the cool, soft air, where a ground mist had begun to rise. Her horse stood, dozing, where Neve had left him. But instead of mounting up and setting off back to Temair, she led the beast north toward the edge of the forest where she knew there was a hidden spring in a clearing.

At the edge of the clearing she stopped and dismounted, wrapping her mount's reins loosely around a branch of a lone hawthorn tree. There were strips of cloth embroidered with spell sigils tied to the tree—some still vibrant, some faded—that showed Neve wasn't the only one to have sought solace or supplication at the spring, sacred to some god or another. But it wasn't a place that anyone would venture in the deep darkness of middle night.

Except for a desperate, desolate princess.

Neve walked to the water's edge and sank to her knees, bending over the deep black mirror of the pool. The near-full moon peered like a wide eye over her shoulder, distantly curious, as she plunged the dirt-encrusted object into the ice-cold water. The earth fell away in clouds of silt as she worked at it with her fingers, slowly revealing the shape and details beneath. She'd been right. It was a half mask, like a helmet visor, made of metal and gilded, molded in the shape of a highly stylized animal with high pointed ears, a long snout, and sly eyeholes ringed with jet and blue lapis.

Khenti-Amentiu . . .

The wolf god of the Scathach stared up at Neve. Guardian of the Gates of Death.

Devourer of Souls, Lord of Vengeance, Keeper of my lost brother's light . . .

Neve frowned in confusion as she lifted the visor up so that it stared back at her, ears perked forward, muzzle pointed down . . . She raised her hand up beside it. The shape of the mask and the shape of the lines on her palm echoed each other.

As if in a dream, Neve turned the mask around and pressed it to her own face. The contours seemed as if they'd been sculpted to fit her features perfectly, settling on her cheeks and forehead, the metal warm and dry, as if she hadn't just plunged it into the spring pool. Neve held the mask in place with her hands and gazed out through the eyeholes at the dark forest around her. She closed her eyes for a moment.

And when she opened them . . .

The gasp that escaped her lungs was like a punch to the chest, winding her. Behind the golden wolf mask, Neve's eyes went wide.

The trees around her began to shift and change, blurred like smoke, and then vanished as the whole landscape transformed from a place of cool mist and moonlight and shadows to one of hot, dry darkness. She whirled in a circle. Gone were the trees and the green, folded hills. The near-full moon in the sky was now a sliver of a crescent, like the edge of a sickle blade, sharpened for reaping. In the far-off distance, Neve could see low dunes of shimmering, shifting sand.

She stiffened when she heard the music of a single, mournful reed flute and turned to look south. Where Brú na Bóinne would have stood, Neve saw a different structure, similar in size and height, only with squared, sloped walls and a flat roof instead of curved walls and a dome. Made of stone, umber colored in the starlight, not white. But it had the same single black doorway that her father's temple had. Like a gaping mouth without teeth.

Something that could swallow you whole.

Neve's nostrils flared, drawing in the sultry air, as her senses seemed to heighten. Smell, hearing, eyesight . . . And then a wave of something else. A foreign sensation like nothing Neve had ever felt before. Not like this. *Hunger.*

Not for sustenance, but for blood. For vengeance and conquest— *Neve Anann Eriu . . .*

—and most of all, for power.

Ravenous, overpowering, terrifying and terribly seductive all at once.

Neve . . .

The last note from the flute shivered in the air and was drowned out by the low, languid snarl of an animal, hunting in the darkness. Hunting her. Neve licked her lips, unafraid, almost eager for something to fight, something to kill—

"Neve!"

A lightning strike of pain lanced through her skull. The night turned crimson as she fell to her knees, clutching the sides of her head. She was desperate to tear the strange mask from her face, but it was as if it had melded with her flesh, gripping the bones of her face tighter and tighter . . .

With a terrible, anguished cry—like the sound of a soul torn from a body—Neve collapsed beside the sacred spring, motionless beneath the baleful eye of the moon.

XV

NEVE! DEATH AND Darkness! I thought you were dead!"

Ronan lifted the strange golden mask away from Neve's face and gasped in relief when he saw her eyelids flutter. He wrapped his arms around her and half lifted her from the ground, burying his face in her hair as she lurched up toward him. Her arms circled his ribs like iron bands, and she shuddered against his chest, gasping for breath. He knelt there for what seemed like a very long time, and she didn't let go, clinging to him as if a storm wind was coming to tear her away.

"Neve . . ." He said her name gently, stroking her hair. "Neve, it's me. It's Ronan."

He held her until her shaking subsided, enough so that she was able to lift her head and push the snarled hair back from her face. Ronan loosened his grip and she tilted her face up to look at him, the moonlight washing her features with a pale silver glow. She was startlingly lovely, Ronan thought. Her cheeks were dry, but her dark lashes were spangled with wetness that clung to them like stardust.

"I already promised," he said quietly.

She frowned at him in confusion. "Promised . . . ?"

"That I'd never tell anyone," he said. "About you crying."

"I don't cry," she whispered.

Her face was so close that he felt like he could fall into the depths of her gaze and drown. He noticed faint, fading red marks—almost like welts—on her forehead and cheeks where the mask had been. He touched one lightly with a fingertip and she reached up and caught his hand in her own. There was dirt beneath her fingernails.

"Neve—"

That was as far as he got before she leaned forward and stopped his breath with a kiss . . . and the world around him fell away, shattering into shards of moonlight. Her other hand reached around the back of his neck, tangling in his hair, as he pulled her close.

He forgot all about the darkling curse twisting in his veins that he'd decided long ago was all her fault. He forgot that she'd shot him with an otherworldly flaming arrow earlier that day. He forgot everything as her lips moved against his skin with a kind of ravenous hunger, sliding from his mouth across the prickling stubble on his cheek, hunting the pulse of his throat where it thrummed beneath his jaw, before moving up to pour whispered breath into his ear.

He heard Neve gasp when he kissed the hollow at the base of her throat and her head tipped backward. Ronan followed, his mouth searching for hers again, as she fell slowly back onto the cool, mossy bank. There was a mist rising all around them, gray and glittering, and her fingers dug into his flesh hard enough to leave bruises . . .

Then suddenly, sharply, he remembered the girl he was kissing so passionately had been weeping only moments earlier. *Almost weeping . . .*

"Princess," he whispered. *My queen . . .*

She looked up at him, her pupils so large that, for a moment, her eyes looked black, ringed only by a faint hint of dark gold. And in the darkness of her gaze, Ronan saw shadows moving. Her features twisted in an expression that seemed utterly foreign to her. A look that Ronan could only describe as *avarice*. The kind of hunger that went far beyond basic need.

"Neve . . ."

She blinked, suddenly herself again. "You keep saying my name."

"Just making sure it's really you in there." He did his best to smile at her. "I'm used to your knife at my throat, not your lips . . ."

Ronan brushed away the strands of dark hair that curtained her gaze. The roiling shadows—and the strange hunger—were gone. But he could sense a weight upon her that hadn't been there before. Neve's gaze drifted down to the linen bandage circling his arm and her brow darkened as she touched where blood had seeped through the cloth.

"What are you doing here, Ronan?" she asked, her voice hoarse.

Good question. He wished he had a good answer.

After Cavall had patched him up, Ronan had set off in the direction of Temair, stumbling along forest tracks, his head heavy, swimming with mead. What his plan was—if he'd actually managed to even get to the palace—would remain something of a mystery, even to himself. Perhaps especially to himself.

There were gaps in his memory. Images, sensations, thoughts and feelings, all of them jumbled and confused. Stars and the moon, then darkness and clouds, forest tracks and then a field. A wolf howling, somewhere close by . . . Blinding lights as the whole of the palace suddenly seemed to ignite like a massive pyre with blazing torch fire and the sounds of shouting. Then darkness again.

And then . . . here.

Ronan had awoken to find himself lying in the long grass on the far side of the sacred spring, cold and wet, his tunic and kilt sodden from the heavy dew. Or maybe rain. Had it rained? He wasn't sure . . . This grove was the place where, as a boy, he'd come seeking help from the gods and been denied. How—and *why*—he'd found his way back there that very night he had no idea. He only knew that he'd gone in search of Neve, only to have her find him there. Well, not find him, so much as startle him awake with her screams before she collapsed.

"I come here sometimes," he said. "To, uh, commune." He gestured to the spell ribbons and strings of beads hanging on the tree branches. It wasn't a lie. He had come here on occasion, for just such a thing. Just not lately . . . "I must have fallen asleep."

She tucked a damp strand of hair behind his ear. "Then why are you soaking wet?"

"I . . ." Ronan shook his head. "It's not important. Neve, what are *you* doing out here all alone in the middle of the night?" He held up the golden mask. "And why were you wearing this? Is it ceremonial? What's happened?"

Neve stared at the mask for a moment before stuffing it away in a pocket inside her cloak. Her face twisted with emotion and she said, "She's dead . . ."

"What?" he asked. "Who? *Who's* dead? Neve—"

"Úna. My sister is *dead.*"

For a moment, Ronan was too stunned to react. *Úna. The queen to be . . .*

Torches blazing in the palace compound. The sound of shouting. A wolf howling. The mask in his hand was carved in the shape of a wolf . . .

"An accident," he murmured, his voice a rasp. "Surely?"

The look on Neve's face chilled him to the marrow.

Sweet Macha, Lady of Peace. Ronan set down the mask and reached, very gently, for Neve's hands, stained with fresh, black earth and gripped with tension. The last time he'd held her hands, the lines crisscrossing her palms had shone like embers. Now they were etched with darkness, the dirt settling in the shape of a woven triangle. "Can you tell me what happened?"

"I was the one who found her." Neve's words were barely above a whisper. "She was lying in the pond. They'll say she drowned, but . . ."

The chill in Ronan's bones turned to deathly cold. "But what, Neve?"

"I don't think her death was an accident."

"Are you sure?"

"No." Neve shrugged, a helpless gesture that ill suited her. "And it doesn't matter anyway. Even if I had seen someone holding her down beneath the water, no one would believe *me.* The Dagda's *other* daughter, the one who everyone hopes will just scurry off into the hills one day and leave them all in peace. I should have done that long ago. Like my mother did . . ."

"They'll believe you," Ronan said firmly. "They'll have to. You're not the Dagda's *other* daughter anymore. You're the queen-in-waiting now, Neve. Surely you realize that."

"I most certainly am not!"

She snatched her hands away and the girl who'd kissed him only moments ago was nowhere to be found. She'd vanished like a dream, as if she'd never been.

"Don't act like you understand anything about the court. There's not a lord of the Tuatha Dé who'd take a step in that direction," Neve said. "My father himself would sooner break his own legs with his war club than risk his legacy with me. He'll shatter the sacred bloodline of descent before putting me anywhere near the throne. And his chieftains will all agree."

Ronan ached to take her in his arms again. He didn't. He wouldn't. Not unless she wanted him to. Like the kiss . . .

"I tried to bring her back," Neve said suddenly.

"What?"

"I went to Brú na Bóinne to find her and bring her back . . ."

Ronan felt his heart thud heavily in his chest. "What did you *do*, Neve?" He looked down to where her dirt-stained hands were knotted into fists in her lap. Neve and dead ground, barrow ground, was a perilous combination.

"I did nothing," she said quietly. "There was nothing *to* do. Nothing there."

"Nothing?" Ronan thought he could hear in her voice that there *had* been something there. But that, whatever it was, it wasn't what she had gone looking for.

"I know there have been whispers for years that my father has been building Teg Duinn." Neve laughed mirthlessly. "But it's not. My father's gone mad, and my sister isn't there for me to bring back."

Ronan didn't know how to console her. Silence filled the clearing until his ears rang with it. Then a mourning dove cooed beneath the trees and he felt as if a spell had been broken. Neve shivered and hugged herself.

"Daybreak's not far off," Ronan said. "They'll be looking for you . . ."

When she didn't answer, he looked to see her staring at his bandaged arm, plainly visible because Cavall had cut away the sleeve of his ruined tunic.

"You were at Dubhadh today," she said flatly. "I almost forgot. It seems like so long ago . . ."

"It's been an eventful day," he said. "For both of us, it would seem. I wasn't there to fight, if that's what you're thinking."

"I don't know what to think right now." She hooked a finger under the edge of the bandage and pulled the linen strip free. Ronan's throat grew tight as she slowly unwound the strip to reveal the wound she'd given him earlier.

"Admiring your handiwork?"

"How do you know it was me?" She studied him through narrowed eyes.

"It's obvious," Ronan said with a shrug that was more of a shiver as another strip of bandage uncoiled. "Another wrecked tunic. You've been trying to get me shirtless since Blackwater . . ."

He could feel the heat from her hands as she slid down the last layer of bandage.

"Careful," he breathed, catching her wrist. "I'm ticklish, remember?"

She gave him a small, fragile smile that swiftly faded as she looked closely at the wound, the flesh around the gash puckered and raw. Painful even to look at. "You're *burned*," she said.

"Flaming arrows will do that. Especially magic ones."

"I don't understand how I could do such a thing," Neve said. "Especially with magic so scarce now."

"It's not so much that magic is scarce." Ronan shrugged, not knowing quite how to explain. His own knowledge only went so deep and there were things—things about himself, even—that he didn't understand. "It's that, thanks mostly to your father's óglach, the spells to conjure the magic are. The wild magic of the land will always be there—to a greater or lesser degree—but the spells that give the folk of the land access to it, what we call small magics, are being stolen from them and hoarded."

Neve shook her head. "But I have no spells. I know no spells."

Ronan let go of her wrist. "Neve . . . I'm not sure how to say this. What you've done is . . . not *small* magic. There is a kind of power that flows from deep emotion. Intent. Passion. Tears. Sweat. Blood . . ." He could feel it, roiling through his own veins in that moment, ignited by her very closeness. The fire she kindled beneath his skin.

Neve leaned forward, her golden eyes glassy, almost feverish, and gently covered the sutured gash with her hand. For a moment, the dull aching heat vanished, as if Neve was pulling the fire of her arrow out of the wound. A sheen of sweat broke out on her brow and then, beneath her hand, a burst of pale gold fire suddenly bloomed.

Ronan screamed in pain and twisted away from her. His own darkling light shivered to the surface, lines of twisting sigils spiraling out from the old pale scar on his palm, writhing upward until his whole arm was covered shoulder to wrist with serpentine dark-light, swallowing Neve's golden flames and spilling indigo fire out into the forest clearing.

Half out of his mind with pain, Ronan bolted past Neve and plunged his arm into the cold spring up to his shoulder. The dark-light didn't so much extinguish as slough off his limb and writhe, glowing threads spiraling out beneath the surface of the water. Lying on his stomach at the edge of the spring, Ronan saw the reflection of his own face ripple and warp . . . and then the water itself seemed to come to life.

The water leaped like liquid flames up into the air, wrapping around him as he struggled and thrashed. Ronan thought he might drown—there, in the air, *above* the pool—until suddenly he was free. The liquid embrace exploded outward and the spring water fell back into the pool like rain. Ronan gasped and fell forward onto his hands and knees.

The surface of the sacred spring grew instantly, eerily calm, flat and mirror-like, and—in the instant before a cloud blotted out the moon—he glimpsed his face again.

Only it wasn't *his* face. Not exactly. The cheekbones and jawline stood out in sharp relief and his eyes were wide and completely black. His skin had taken on a silvery, rippling sheen. He scrambled back to find that his fingers had grown longer—like talons, almost—with pale, translucent webbing between them . . .

"Fomori!"

He whirled around to see Neve staring at him, open-mouthed.

"You're a shapeshifter!" she gasped.

The look of stark horror on her face cut him far deeper than any blade or claw. He wasn't Fomori. It was impossible . . .

He reached for her. "Neve—"

She scrambled back and, in the blink of an eye, she'd drawn the axe from her belt, slashing it at him in a wide, whistling swing.

Ronan felt the kiss of the blade edge across his torso as it sliced through his tunic, a breath away from eviscerating him. He staggered back and lost his footing at the edge of the spring.

With a startled cry, he fell backward and sank into the dark, frigid water.

XVI

RONAN SANK DEEPER and deeper into the sacred spring's watery embrace until he floated there, suspended in the blackness and the silence and the stillness. The thundering of his heart in his ears slowed to a deep, sonorous drumbeat and he felt warm. Peaceful. Powerful. Something inside him told him that he could stay there. Forever, if he wanted to. That he could breathe in the water, wrap it around him like a king's cloak, see through the darkness as if he stood in bright sunlight . . .

And that terrified him. Because of what it would mean.

Before the air in his lungs ran dry—before the moment he would be forced to discover if he really *could* breathe underwater— he kicked and swam upward, breaking the surface. Ronan pulled himself onto the mossy bank, ducking with almost casual ease as Neve's axe whipped past his head, missing him by a hair as it cartwheeled through the air and disappeared into the spring pool with barely a splash.

XVIII

*T*HERE WAS TO be no ceremony for Úna. No body. No funeral. No one had expected the princess to die and so there had been no barrow built for her, and Ruad Rofhessa refused to have her body raised on a pyre. Instead, the Dagda's Druids would perform rites for the princess, Neve was told. And that would be that. Úna had failed their father by dying, she thought bitterly, and so their father would hold no celebration of her life, her spirit.

Instead, a smaller gathering than usual of Tuatha Dé lords and ladies trooped out into the drab fog of evening, hoods up, heads down, for the final Singing of the Stone. Neve had saddled one of her horses and ridden out on her own, leaving Sakir to gather with his own folk before they returned to the Golden Vale. At Brú na Bóinne, Neve dismounted and joined the rest of the gathering waiting for the ritual to begin, casting furtive glances at the

Ronan stood up, chest heaving, spring water running from his torso and limbs, dripping from his fingertips. He held out a hand, fingers splayed wide as a cloud passed and the moon shone down once more on his normal, *human* fingertips . . .

"What *are* you?" Neve asked in a low, harsh whisper.

"A thief," he snapped, his hand clenching into a fist at her reaction. "An ex-Druid. Apprentice, really. I thought we'd been over this."

"Try Fomori."

"I'm *not.*"

"In Blackwater. I saw you in the river. I thought it was the water-wight. But it was *you.*" She shook her head. "Úna never believed me. I told her your kind would be back one day. I just didn't think they would look like you."

He walked toward her. "Neve, listen to me—"

"No!" she snarled. "I know what I saw."

Ronan backed off a step, but her accusation had lit a fire in him. "And naturally," he said, "you just happen to know what a Fomori looks like, do you? Is that it? Something that hasn't been seen in this land since your people—*your* folk, Princess Neve of the Mighty and Glorious Tuatha Dé—drove them bloodily from this land?" He was shouting now, gripping a handful of his ruined tunic, pink with blood from the shallow cut from her axe. "Is that what you're telling me?"

"While *you* didn't tell *me* anything!" Neve shouted back. "You lied to me! 'I steal magic,' you said. You *are* magic."

Ronan's indignation faded in the face of her stricken, wounded expression. The heat seeped out of him, leaving him feeling numb. Neve wasn't angry. She was hurt. Betrayed. By him.

"I trusted you," she said.

"Well, that was your mistake, wasn't it?" he said. "You don't know me, Neve. You don't know anything about me. And the one thing you've assumed disgusts you. I can see it in your face."

"That's not true!"

He laughed humorlessly. "Do you know I've been looking for you? Every day after that night seven years ago. I looked for you."

She frowned at him in confusion. "Why?"

"Because I thought I was cursed. After that night at the barrows. And I did learn one or two things from my failed Druid apprenticeship." His jaw clenched as he struggled to find the words for what he was trying to say. "Sometimes an enchantment done can be *un*done. But you see, there's a trick to it. You need to have all the same basic elements of the original magic gathered together again. I thought I needed *you*."

Her eyes shone gold in the moonlight. Like they had almost every night in his dreams when he was younger. Dreams that had faded over time . . . until suddenly they'd manifested in this nightmarish reality. Now her eyes were filled with fear and age-old hatred.

Ronan drew himself up. "Now I can see that there's nothing you can do for me. I once thought that you were probably just a Fir Bolg river rat, like me. Maybe if you had been, we could have fixed me together. But you're not. You're Tuatha Dé and a princess, and you're not even from the same realm as my kind. Whatever *my* kind truly is. You can't fix me, Neve. You can't fix my broken folk. You can only trample us into the ground from the backs of your infernal horses. Just like the Scathach did."

"I'm not—"

"My enemy? If that were true, then *you* wouldn't think of me as *yours*." He sighed, suddenly infinitely weary. "I grieve with you this night on the death of your sister, Princess. My heart wishes her safe journey—"

"Don't." She stood. Slowly, as if she thought he might attack her. "Don't speak of her. Or me. I think you were right the first time. We should stay far away from each other from now on, thief. For both our sakes."

"I have a name," Ronan said quietly, staring down at his hands, blue-white in the moonlight.

"So do I." Neve backed away from him until she reached her horse and then swung herself up onto its back. "It is Neve Anann Eriu of the Tuatha Dé, Beloved of the Wolf. Don't speak it. And I won't speak yours. And maybe whatever gods or demons have thrust us together for their amusement will grow bored and turn their attentions elsewhere, and leave us to our separate fates. I do not wish to see your face—if that even *is* your real face—ever again, Fomori. And I should think you'd feel the same. If there's one thing I've learned from stories told around a hearth fire, it's that our kinds don't mix well."

After she was gone, Ronan went back to kneel at the edge of the spring. The golden mask was gone. He hadn't seen her pick it up, but she must have taken it with her. She'd left something else behind, though. The light of the moon reflected on the bronze blade edge of her sleek war axe, lying in the depths of the pool, too far out of reach. He ran his fingertips across the still water, ruffling the surface and distorting the moon's visage.

Neve *had* found something in Brú na Bóinne that night. He knew it, because the water knew it. And now, because of who—

what—Ronan was, he knew the water would never lie to him. While he'd been submerged in the spring's embrace, it had whispered the name for what he was, and that name had not been Fomori. He hadn't lied about that.

He wished he could say the same about Neve.

He wished he knew where he'd been that night, too.

He wished the water could tell him *that* . . . but he was afraid to know the answer.

Almost as afraid as when the water had named him: Fé Fíada. *Lord of the Mist.*

Ronan the ex-Druid apprentice knew what that was.

And it terrified him to his very soul.

NEVE REENTERED TEMAIR the same way she'd left it that night— by way of the hidden gate—and Sakir was waiting for her. He gestured her forward, easing the door shut behind her. There was no one else there to see her return.

"The court has retired to their chambers," he said quietly. "But no one is sleeping. The whole palace is restless. Be careful if you don't wish to be seen."

He reached for her horse's bridle and waited while she threw a leg over his neck and slid to the ground. Sakir's gaze flicked to the empty sagaris sheath at her hip. She considered telling him about Ronan, but dismissed that thought. What could she possibly say that would make any kind of sense?

"I've misplaced my axe," she said. "Can you find me another one?"

"Of course—"

"One with a blade made of iron. *Pure* iron."

Sakir hesitated, but only for an instant. Iron, at least high-quality iron befitting a Tuatha Dé princess—the *only* Tuatha Dé princess—would be costly, far more expensive than bronze. And yet she knew he would make it happen. He nodded once and said, "You shall have it."

"Where is my father?"

"Gone." His hands paused for a moment unsaddling the horse. "Along with the architect, the Druids, and some of the chieftains. They took your sister away."

"Where?"

He shook his head. "I don't know, lady."

Neve swallowed hard, jaw clenched, then turned to go.

"Neve."

She turned to look back at him.

"I'm sorry."

Sakir's sympathy dragged across her skin like an unsharpened blade. If there was one thing that just might break her that night, it was softness from him. She needed him to be hard. And sharp. A weapon she could use. She didn't even know, yet, what for. But her mind was churning with everything that had happened that night and her gut was telling her to be ready for what was next.

"This isn't an ending, Sakir," she said. "This is but the beginning of something terrible. Find me another axe, Sakir. And rest well tonight. I'll need your strength for what is to come."

Emer dozed fitfully on her pallet in the small room beyond Neve's sleeping chamber. When she eased the door to her apartments shut, Neve could hear her murmuring in dreams. The brazier beside Neve's own bed glowed sullenly, casting just enough light for Neve to make her way toward the doors that led out to the garden. She paused, her hand on the ring handle. For a fleeting moment, she imagined she could push the door open and Úna would be standing there, ready to chastise her for still not having changed out of the tunic and breeches that stank of horse and sweat.

Neve eased the door open and stepped out onto the terrace.

She padded carefully, soundlessly, over to the edge of the empty pond.

Empty . . .

Neve remembered the water running out of the corners of Una's mouth when she lifted her head. Her mind conjured up a horrid image of Úna standing at the edge of the pool, her screams muffled by living water that forced itself down her throat into her lungs, her body wrapped in an unbreakable, liquid embrace—

Ronan . . .

She'd never seen magic like the kind Ronan had called up in the sacred grove that night—whether he'd meant to or not—because it was the kind of magic that didn't exist in Eire anymore. Neither did Ronan's kind. Fomori. Shapeshifter. An extinct impossibility. One she'd seen with her own eyes. Shot with her own arrow.

Kissed with your own lips.

Why she'd kissed him she didn't know. She'd never kissed anyone like that. Ever.

Grief—and shock and anger—had twisted her emotions up inside of her that night, she told herself. But that *wasn't* it. No, kissing Ronan had been a thing outside of everything else. Something that, if she was honest with herself, she'd wanted—had wanted ever since their mad dash through Blackwater Town with spell-harrows howling at their heels—but that was before she knew what he was.

Now that Neve knew the truth of what was hidden behind that iron-gray gaze and that slow, sly, crooked smile . . . Now that she'd seen his eyes turn black, watched his skin ripple with a silver sheen, his features sharpen to become lean and feral . . . Fomori. Shapeshifter . . . A monster from fables to frighten children.

In spite of what Neve desperately wanted to believe, the truth of the matter was simply that Ronan was, at his very essence, her ancient enemy. And she was his. Úna had been, too.

Úna's wedding gown had been dry. Ronan had been soaking wet. Fomori.

Shapeshifter.

Thief . . .

Neve would make Ronan pay for what he'd stolen from her.

And she would do it alone. If she went to her father, he would throw her from his chambers for spouting childish nonsense about monsters. Lorcan and the rest of the chieftains would simply think she was mad—unhinged by grief—and they wouldn't be entirely wrong about that. She was. Enough to enter what she'd thought might well be Teg Duinn that night.

Neve reached into the inner pocket of her cloak and pulled out the golden wolf mask. She lifted it up and stared into its dark eyes. It almost seemed to be grinning at her. A wily hunter. She thought of her father's harrow hounds on the hunt and what Thorn and her pack would do to Ronan if they were to hunt *him* down.

Did she really wish *that* fate on him? Did she hate him that much?

Did he murder your beloved sibling? whispered a voice in the darkness.

Neve shuddered as she remembered how the water from the sacred spring had risen up out of the pool to engulf Ronan in a sinuous, viscous embrace. Like a lover. Or a serpent coiling around its prey. Which was it? Did it matter? Whether Ronan controlled the element or it controlled him, what difference did it make? The result had been the same. Úna was dead. And Ronan had been right about one thing, even if she'd been unwilling in the moment to admit it, even if her father would tear the stars from the sky to deny her . . . Neve was now the queen-in-waiting.

Little Scota, said a smiling voice in her head. *Beloved of the Wolf. No . . . You are a* king *in waiting.*

XVII

WHEN NEVE AWOKE, the sunlight lancing through a crack in the heavy curtains told her it was late mid-morning. Head full of fleeting, forgotten dreams, she shoved aside the bedclothes and swung her feet down onto the cold stone floor. For a brief, blissful moment, all was well in the world. The gown she would wear to Úna's wedding that afternoon was hanging on the dressing screen, waiting for her and . . .

No. Oh, no . . . Úna . . .

Úna was dead.

The realization hit her like a fist. There would be no wedding. No celebrations—

"I left out your gown," came Emer's voice from archway to the main chamber. "But I can air out one of your other dresses if you don't want to wear that one. The gods know you have enough of them languishing in trunks from lack of use."

She flitted about the rooms in her usual fashion, but there was an edge to her. Like she'd laced her own dress too tight just to keep herself from falling apart. Her small, angular face was pale and drawn except for two spots of anxious color on her cheeks, beneath her big dark eyes, which were still puffy from sleep. Or maybe weeping.

Neve scrubbed her palms over her face. "Emer, why would I need a gown?"

"For the Singing of the Stone, of course," she answered, not looking at Neve, as if she were already bracing for the coming outburst.

"The Singing—you must be joking!" Neve lurched toward her, mouth open in disbelief. "The Dagda isn't seriously going to go through with that ridiculous ritual after what's happened!"

She reached for her cloak, her hand brushing the golden wolf mask, still tucked in its pocket, as if she would go hunting the palace halls for her father in her nightshift. "I won't let this madness trample my sister's honor into the dust. Just so he can pretend he's some kind of hero from a bruidean bard's tale—"

"Stop!" Emer barred Neve's way, her gaze bright with uncharacteristic anger. "Just *stop* right there, now, Neve. You're not going to march into the chambers of a man who's grieving the loss of his daughter just as much as you're grieving the loss of your sister. I won't allow it. I know what it's like to lose someone. I know what it's like to lose *everyone*. My father died when I was barely old enough to know he was my father. My mother did everything short of selling the heart out of her body to keep the fire in the hearth burning and even when her wee small magic wasn't enough for that, it was still too much and I lost her because of it. Because of . . . well." Her head twitched to one side, and she blinked rapidly. "You get over it, and you get on. Eventually. But first you grieve and there's no one to tell you which way is the right or wrong way."

"You really think that's what my father is doing?" Neve asked.

"I think he's trying to carry on," Emer said. "To show the kingdom that the Tuatha Dé are not defeated by death."

"But *aren't* we?" Neve sat on the edge of a trunk, staring at her hands, still faintly dirt-stained. "Úna is dead, Emer. I might as well be for all I matter. The line of the Dagda will end with my father."

Emer gazed at Neve for a long moment, head tilted to the side. Then she turned and pulled out a dress that was dyed a shade of green so dark it was almost black. Neve was silent while Emer helped her dress, pulling her thick dark hair back and securing it with a jeweled pin in a fashion that, in the silver mirror's reflection, made her look older. Made her look just a little more like Úna.

Her sister's pale cold visage flashed through Neve's mind. But her eyes were black. Like Ronan's had been—

Stop, she told herself. *Stop thinking of him.*

It was cold enough to wrap Neve's head in a cloud of her own breath when she stepped outside. She heard a commotion beyond the walls and discovered that, while she'd been asleep that morning, Temair had received visitors.

A contingent of Scythians from the Golden Vale—the herd-lands to the south.

Growing up, Úna had never developed the same love for horses that Neve had, but she'd actively courted the loyalty of the Horse Lords in recent years. Ruad Rofhessa considered his Scythian troops largely ceremonial, preferring to rely on the óglach. But Úna, Neve had come to realize, had understood the power of commanding a cavalry in times of war. It seemed she'd invited the fiercely independent Horse Lords of the Golden Vale to her wedding. Now, her funeral.

Sakir met Neve on the path and walked with her out to the largest tent—an opulent orange-and-red-striped affair, swagged with long fringe and tassels that echoed the manes and tails of the Scythian horses. A tall, lean man with dark-brown hair and a beard stepped out to meet them.

"This is Cormac, my uncle." Sakir nodded to him. "He is a chief of the tribe, leader of my clan. First Horse Lord of Eire, holder of the Golden Vale. Uncle, this is Neve Anann Eriu, second daughter of the Dagda, Ruad Rofhessa, Lord of the Tuatha Dé, High King of Temair."

Cormac inclined his head, a warm smile creasing the corners of his beard. "Lady Neve," he said. "May your days run free and long, and your horizon be as far off as forever."

"Farther off than my sister's, I can but hope," Neve replied, swallowing a knot in her throat. "I apologize, I am a poor substitute to welcome you to Temair on her behalf, but I thank you with all my heart for coming."

"My people grieve with you on this deep loss, Princess. Your sister rides with the wind now, but we who are still earthbound shall miss her," Cormac said. He paused before continuing, "My nephew tells me your love of horses nearly rivals a Scythian's. May I show you something?"

Sakir excused himself while Cormac led Neve over to one of Temair's paddocks, where the Scythian cavalry horses had been left to graze. Cormac pointed to a pair of magnificent silvery-white horses.

"Descendants of the Scathach's own favorite stallion," he said. "A matched pair, trained to the chariot. They were to be a wedding gift for the queen-to-be."

Neve felt her throat constrict. "I've never seen any creature so beautiful."

"It would please me greatly if you would accept them," he said. "Now that your sister cannot."

Neve stood there, digging her fingernails into her palms to keep from weeping. Cormac seemed undisturbed by her silence, the two of them watching the horses graze, their long silvery manes lifting in the breeze.

"You look just like her," Cormac said after a moment. "Like Anann, I mean."

"You knew my mother?" she asked.

"Knew her?" He laughed quietly. "I damned near married her."

Neve stared at the Horse Lord, not quite sure if she'd heard him right. His profile was similar to Sakir's; he had the same strong nose and high, angular forehead, but his complexion was weathered. The skin around his green eyes fanned out in fine lines, carved there by sun and wind as he watched over his herds.

Cormac glanced sideways at Neve. "It was a *very* long time ago." He shrugged. "I was her father's—your grandfather's—charioteer. *Your* father, Ruad Rofhessa, was the son of his First Spear chief. And my closest friend."

"I've never heard him speak of you in that way," Neve said.

"I'm not entirely surprised," Cormac said ruefully. "Like I said, it was a long time ago. And, well, the way things worked out between the two of them . . ."

"You mean the way they *didn't*?" Neve scoffed.

"Anann was always a woman of strong opinions, which she made little effort to keep from others." He rested his arms on the paddock fence. "In truth, it was one of the things I found most attractive about her. It made her seem less like all the others at court and, well—"

"More like a Scythian?"

Cormac chuckled. "Yes."

"Then why didn't she go to the Golden Vale when she left Temair?" Neve asked.

"Because she is still the queen," Cormac said.

"She loved you, then."

He hesitated. "So she told me, lady. At the time. And so I believed her."

"Why didn't she marry you then?" Neve wondered. "If you were in love—"

"The Lia Fail did not speak for me." The words dropped from his mouth like stones themselves, hard and cold.

The Lia Fail again, Neve thought. So-called Stone of Destiny. According to her bedtime tale of the Scathach, it was the Stone that had always decreed who would be worthy to rule the Tuatha Dé. Úna had dismissed the ritual with the Stone as some sort of Druid fakery to install whoever their most favored candidate was upon the king's throne. But considering her recent otherworldly experiences, Neve wasn't so sure.

Perhaps it did not speak for him because he was not worthy. . .

"That hardly seems like something my mother would care about," Neve said, trying to sound offhand.

"*She* didn't." Cormac laughed bitterly. "But the Tuatha Dé chieftains most certainly did. Your mother—strong opinions notwithstanding—was still beholden to the will of the clan lords to a great degree."

"So . . . the Stone spoke for my father?"

Cormac looked down at the palms of his hands as if he might find the answer to her question there. "It did," he said finally. "And I vouched for him. If *I* could not marry Anann, then, at the very least, I wanted her to marry a good man. A strong warrior able to protect the realm. A fine friend . . ."

"*You* heard the Stone speak for him?"

"Ruad said it did."

"He *said*?" Neve peered at Cormac. She felt a shiver along her spine. "You didn't hear the Stone and yet you vouched for him. You lied to the chieftains."

Lies. . .

"Did I?" He shot a sharp glance at her. "Was the Stone wrong? He *is* the Dagda."

It was Neve's turn to laugh—a sound like a startled bird in her own ears. "There are Dagdas," she said, recalling the words of the Faoladh seer, "and there are Dagdas, Horse Lord."

"Ruad Rofhessa is a great warrior and a mighty king," he said stiffly. "Eire is at peace, thanks to your father, and the kingdom prospers."

"And the Stone itself has vanished," Neve said, half to herself. "Almost as if it will never again be needed."

"I don't think I take your meaning, Princess."

Neve wasn't entirely certain herself where her thoughts were leading her, but she felt compelled to chase them. Like the hound after the hare . . .

"I only meant that, as much as I honor my father, I do not think he is immortal," she said. "If there is to be another Dagda, should we not search for the Stone of Destiny?"

"It's just a hidebound old ritual," Cormac said.

"The same hidebound old ritual that kept *you* from the throne?"

Cormac could hardly argue with that. "I don't know what to tell you, Princess," he said. "But I do know this—when Anann was mistress of Temair, very little happened within its walls that escaped her keen eye. If you're that curious, perhaps she might know of the Stone's whereabouts."

"Perhaps," Neve murmured. She shook herself loose from her racing thoughts. "But you must forgive me, lord," she said, mustering a little laugh. "You've been a guest at Temair for the length of a lark's song and I've already drawn you into weighty matters of hearts and stones."

He inclined his head graciously. "No apologies, Lady Neve. I welcome your honesty and I'm very glad to know you." Then his gaze flicked up over her shoulder. "I suspect I'm not alone in that."

Neve turned to see Sakir approaching from the Scythian tents. He'd changed into attire more befitting his station among his own people. Which was, Neve kept forgetting, that of a prince—Sakir, son of Farsa, Chief Horse Lord of Eire, Keeper of the Dagda's Herds in Temair. Suddenly her charioteer was nowhere to be found beneath several embellished layers of princely finery. The long, fitted tunic in a rich midnight-blue cloth over soft-sueded breeches still managed to emphasize his lean, athletic build—just in a much more refined way than his usual gear.

"Not bad," she said as he approached. "For a stable boy."

"I'm glad you approve, lady." Sakir bent his head in a gesture that was not quite a bow. Then he leaned in and whispered in her ear, "I didn't think it was fair to remain comfortable while you have to suffer through all that proper attire."

"How kind of you to inconvenience yourself so lushly," she whispered back, striving to maintain their usual banter. Although she would never say so out loud, Neve deeply appreciated his attempts at making her feel normal.

But then Sakir paused and said, "You look like a queen."

Neve made the mistake then of looking into his clear hazel eyes and she saw there, writ plain, everything Sakir was thinking and feeling in that unguarded moment. And he knew that she saw it. Neve's breath caught in her throat.

This time, he didn't even bother to try and hide behind his usual cool half smile. He simply bowed and headed off in the direction of the paddocks.

Neve wondered if he would look at her the same way if he could see inside her heart in that moment. If he knew the fire that had ignited her arrow the day before begged to set the world on fire. Like the Scathach had.

Little Scota . . .

"Away with you!"

The sound of her father's angry voice shook Neve from her dark reverie. She turned to see him approaching, fist gripping his war club, face a deep shade of crimson.

"Away," he barked again. "Here's no place for the likes of you."

Unworthy. A thief upon the throne . . .

"Father, I—" Neve steadied herself and clenched her hand around the faint stirrings of heat she could feel blooming there. She wasn't sure what had sparked her father's fury this time, but she needed to find a way to tell him about Ronan . . . and the potential threat of a Fomori presence in Eire once again—

The Dagda's thundercloud gaze swung from Neve to Cormac, the friend who—if he was to be believed—had lied for Ruad Rofhessa so that he could sit upon the throne.

"Nor you, Horse Lord. I did not summon you here."

"And a welcome sight you are to my heart's eyes, too," Cormac answered back, his tone mildly amused. He gestured toward his tent. "Shall we speak more privately, old friend?"

The Dagda glared at him but stalked inside, as if Neve had already disappeared into nothingness. Cormac followed, dropping the tent flaps closed behind him. Neve pressed herself to the side of the tent, out of sight of anyone walking casually by, and listened, heart pounding.

"You did not have to summon me," the Horse Lord was saying. "I came at the invitation of the Princess Úna to celebrate her wedding."

"With a full contingent of cavalry?" the Dagda scoffed.

"You would have had me bring anything less than a full honor guard?" Cormac asked. "You would have stomached that insult at the marriage of your firstborn, queen-to-be of the whole of the realm, of which—I'm sure I have no need to remind you, my lord—the Golden Vale is a bountiful part?"

"There isn't going to be a wedding now, so you're free to return there as soon as you can pack your gear," Neve's father snapped. "I'm sure your herd misses you greatly. I know how very beloved you are. Old friend."

Beneath the rasping sarcasm, Neve detected something in her father's voice that she'd never heard before. Hurt. If Cormac hadn't told her of the history between the two men—and her mother—she wouldn't have believed her ears. But it seemed that the past truly had left an unhealed wound on the Dagda's soul.

A long moment of silence stretched out between the two men inside the tent.

Cormac was the first to break it. "Ruad, I grieve deeply with you for your daughter's death. As much as for our broken ties of brotherhood, which once were like bands of forged iron. If you need my men, my horses—"

"For what?"

Another pause. Then, "I have ears, my lord."

"You mean spies."

Cormac laughed. "Why would I need spies? Are we not allies?"

"And why would I need your warband?" Ruad Rofhessa's voice was like a lash. "Temair has her own warband. I know what you've heard. Lies and distortions. Fir Domnann? There have always been raids on our coasts and there always will be. You want my óglach to ride out and defend every empty beach? Against what actual threat? Are you like my chieftains? A pack of superstitious old women who fear monsters beneath their beds at night? Do you not have faith in your king, Cormac?"

"Ruad—"

"The Lia Fail chose *me*!" Neve jumped back at the sound of a fist slamming on a table or trunk. "The gods have spoken. I alone will keep this island safe and prosperous!"

Cormac's answer was grim. "For all our sakes, I truly hope so."

"I'm done with this foolishness," Ruad Rofhessa said. "Stay or go. I care not. Just don't give me an excuse to send my óglach *your* way. I know the folk of the Vale are too soft to have given up all their small magics. It would be a shame if the harrow hounds caught the scent of anything that might set them off."

Neve ducked out of sight as the tent flaps burst outward like the wings of a startled falcon, and the Dagda shouldered his way outside, stalking back toward the palace without so much as a backward glance.

So the chieftains were beginning to question her father's judgement, Neve thought. She'd been right about that. Her fingers traced the contours of the golden wolf visor still carefully tucked in the pocket of her cloak. As her anger faded, the stirrings of a plan began to form in her mind.

"*You look like a queen,*" Sakir had told her.

"*You're the queen-in-waiting now, Neve,*" Ronan had said. "*Surely you realize that . . .*"

And finally, another voice spoke in her mind, newly familiar.

Why wait?

Dagda's chief advisers. She caught more than a few of them, heads together, muttering darkly to one another, and where normally they would have stood together behind their king, that night there were gaps and distance between the chieftains and the Lord of Temair.

The Dagda was an island. Until he caught sight of Neve.

With a jerk of his head, Ruad Rofhessa beckoned her to his side. Staring straight ahead, Neve walked slowly over to stand with him. It was entirely for show, she knew. Or maybe it was because, without Úna, her father truly was alone. Even if he didn't really know it.

As she took her place at his side, the ritual commenced. The Druids began their incantation—an ominous dirge to Neve's ears—and wisps of mist rose and gathered into a heavy, pearlescent gray fog. Thicker, it seemed to her, than what the Druids usually conjured up to disguise their fakery. As the last sentinel stone—Úna's stone—started to lift, Neve added her voice to the singing, if only to honor her sister, in a way that a meaningless slab of rock never could.

The stone slid forward and dropped into the hole in the ground with a resounding boom that shook the very earth beneath their feet. An invisible force flowed outward from the circle of stones, slamming into the Tuatha Dé like a sudden gale-force wind and nearly knocking some of them from their feet. Cloaks and robes lifted and snapped like war banners streaming. The fog that cloaked the plain bloomed outward and vanished, revealing the Great Barrow of Brú na Bóinne, surrounded by the full, complete circle of sentinel stones.

And crowned with a cluster of shadowy figures.

Neve heard surprised gasps and confused murmurings from the gathered crowd. And then silence descended as, one by one, they noticed the band of women, dressed for war and still as statues, dark silhouettes against the leaden sky.

"Faoladh," Neve whispered, her heart leaping in her chest.

The pale-haired Faoladh leader—Cliona was her name, Neve remembered—along with their seeress, Aevinn; the brawling redhead; and five or six others rose to standing from where they had crouched, hidden in the shadows and mist in front of the Great Barrow's entrance. Before that moment, she'd taken them for stones, so still they were.

The effect was impressive—more than one fearless tuath warlord took an involuntary step back as the Faoladh walked toward them. Neve noticed they'd donned armor that was entirely Tuatha Dé. Archaic in style, more ornate than what the óglach wore, but with similar decorative motifs and flourishes. Spoils of war. Trophies taken by their Faoladh forebearers and worn, Neve suspected, purely for the occasion.

Why? Neve wondered. What were they playing at?

"Dagda of the Tuatha Dé!" Cliona's cry rang out into the darkness. "The Faoladh of Eire bring you greetings and our continued oath of fealty to your throne, Chosen of the Lia Fail. Úna Ruad Macha is blessed in death. She walks before to prepare the way for the Dagda, and we are bound to serve to preserve the Light in the Darkness in the coming days. And there is a great darkness coming." Cliona narrowed her eyes at the crowd then. "When the Dagda of Eire calls upon us, the Faoladh will be ready. The Daughters of the Wolf, teeth and claws, bone and blood and spirit, are yours to command. Let all men know this."

There was a subtle emphasis on the word "all." And that told Neve everything she needed to know. Cliona of the Faoladh had just issued a challenge and a warning, not to the Dagda's enemies, but to the Dagda's allies.

That's why they're here, Neve thought, suddenly understanding. With Úna dead, the knives were already being sharpened, aimed at the target painted on Ruad Rofhessa's back. And the Faoladh knew, whether it was through Aevinn's visions or a result of the blood oath they'd sworn, that the Dagda was in peril. And the one thing the Faoladh needed, above all else, was a Dagda who could grant the return of their riastrad. No Dagda meant no Faoladh. Ever again.

Her father had yet to roar at them to begone. Could it be that he understood their mutual risk might, instead, be their mutual reward? Neve glanced over to where Gofannon stood and saw in his shrewd expression that *he* understood the situation perfectly.

He began to murmur words beneath his breath, and the sentinel stones began to glow. The light flickered around the Faoladh, dancing about their heads in fiery shapes like pointed ears and muzzles, ephemeral echoes of Neve's golden mask. Or the three-pointed sigil on her palm . . . She tightened her fist, silently willing her own uncanny flame to remain hidden. Gofannon conjured a momentary illusion of monstrous, magnificent transformation over the warriors, that then flared to a brilliant, blinding burst of light for a moment, before snuffing out like a tallow candle in the wind.

A lone wolf howl echoed across the plain, and the clouds overhead began to clear, like a veil being drawn aside between the realms. The guttering pitch torches steadied and began to burn brightly again, and Neve saw the Faoladh were gone. Vanished.

Before the gathered lords and ladies had a chance to question what they'd seen, Ruad Rofhessa strode forward to stand between the last two sentinel stones, feet braced wide, crimson cloak spread behind him like a river of blood.

"Tuatha Dé," he said in a surprisingly quiet voice that still carried with its deep, sonorous rumble. "My most beloved and blessed folk. This night, in the shadow of my deep grief, I rejoice in the light of this, my greatest achievement. For the good of our people and our place, this is my gift and my legacy to you, as commanded by our gods. You see how this monument is already fortified and protected by the powers of Eire. By its Faoladh warriors in waiting, blood-bound to the throne of Temair. By the gathered magic of this land."

More like stolen and jealously hoarded, Neve thought. She also noticed that her father hadn't explicitly said that *he* had accepted the pledge of the Faoladh.

She stole another glance at Gofannon and saw a light flicker and fade in his eyes that only Neve was, in that moment, close enough to perceive. She also saw that there was a sheen of sweat on his forehead and his jaw was tightly clenched, as if with great effort or concentration. So, even the great sorcerer was taxed when it came to using magic, it seemed. He clearly hadn't been expecting the Faoladh to appear, either, but he was certainly clever enough to use it to his lord's advantage.

"You heard the words of these guardians," Ruad Rofhessa continued, gesturing to the now-empty slope of the Great Barrow. "Úna, my beloved daughter, has gone before me, as a harbinger. As a queen among the dead. Her spirit will prepare this barrow for its purpose." A muscle in his neck twitched convulsively at what must have been a great effort to sound sincere. "A purpose I was born and chosen for—the continuation and protection of the Tuatha Dé, lords of this green land. Return now to Temair and rejoice. We Tuatha Dé will endure. Eire will endure. The Dagda, and all Dagdas to come, will endure."

By the time he was done speaking, Neve almost believed him. So too, by their expressions, did most of the folk gathered there. Whatever else the Faoladh had intended that night, they'd done that much. The Faoladh, and Gofannon. And the Dagda's quick, clever tongue.

There are Dagdas and there are Dagdas, Neve thought.

Aevinn had said that to her, and she'd said it to Cormac. Cormac, who had then planted a seed of doubt in her mind about her father and his claim to the throne. And the power that went with it.

My father is a liar. Neve shook her head. *A good one. He'll never break the Scathach's enchantment and restore their riastrad. If he wasn't the Lia Fail's true choice, I don't even know if he can . . . In another lifetime, he probably would have gotten on well with Ronan.*

But then, at the thought of Ronan, Neve remembered something he'd said to her.

"Sometimes an enchantment done can be undone."

Maybe her conversation with Cormac had planted a seed of hope, too.

She lingered behind as the assembly headed back toward the palace, a somberly triumphant Dagda riding at their head. What if Neve could give the Faoladh back their power—their *real* power, not a Druid's showy tricks—and then . . . what? Command them herself? There had to be a way . . .

Of course, there is a way.

The desire had been simmering deep inside her since . . . when? Since she was a child, truthfully. But she'd never had a path to that destiny. Not like she did now. Now, especially if there was any truth to what Cormac had said, Neve could—just like she'd always dreamed—become the Dagda herself. Then *she* could call upon the Faoladh to become her warband. The only problem was that she needed a warband to *become* the Dagda . . . She stopped and smiled to herself.

The solution to her problem was the problem itself—a serpent devouring its own tail. She'd always thought the Scathach foolish for turning her rage against the Faoladh instead of turning them, truly, to her cause. Perhaps she wouldn't have come to such an end if she had.

The voice in her head whispered, *Perhaps . . .*

But now she was grateful she had. Because it gave Neve the chance *she* needed.

An enchantment once done could be undone.

If you have all the right elements.

Neve hesitated, glancing back over her shoulder, but Brú na Bóinne was silent, slumbering. She gathered her horse's reins and reached into her cloak pocket for the wolf mask. She winced against the remembered pain of the first time she'd donned the golden visor, and steeled herself as she lifted it to her face once again, closing her eyes.

The hot wind of Khenti-Amentiu's desert, the Scathach's desert, washed over her, and she opened her eyes again. The landscape spread out before her, shimmering. Not quite like sand dunes this time, but more as if the hills and vales that were already there had been dusted with embers in the darkness.

She focused her will on finding the Faoladh, bound as they were by the Scathach's dark curse. Neve heard the song of a wolf, soft and mournful, beckoning, coming from somewhere to the west, where the glimmering seemed brighter. She froze, listening, and then urged her horse into a trot, following the cry. It led her to one of the abandoned clusters of ancient barrows that dotted the floodplain of An Bhóinn. A brooding, forlorn place, given a wide berth by most reasonable folk, called Cnóbha, the Cave of the Moon.

She could see a group of figures, black shapes against the darkness, hunched around a fire at the center of a half circle of tumbled stones sticking out of the earth like rotted teeth. Neve dismounted and slipped the mask off, dropping it back into the folds of her cloak as she walked toward them.

Cliona beckoned her over with a wave of her hand.

"Been waiting for you, Princess," she said, lifting a drinking horn to her lips. Aevinn gave Neve a faint smile.

Neve sank down onto her haunches in front of the fire. "This night you offered your services to my father, to stand with him against a coming darkness."

Cliona and Aevinn exchanged a glance. Cliona nodded. "Aye. Your ears work, at least."

"And we all know just how much that offer—as it currently stands—is worth," Neve continued. "Tell me this: what good are you and your women without your riastrad?"

"The Dagda's last little princess mocks us," Grian said from the shadows.

"My name is Neve. I don't like the title 'princess,' and I'm not mocking you." She glanced around at the circle of women who crouched upon the stones around the fire, like statues waiting to be brought to life with a spell. "I'm serious. And you know that—otherwise, why are you here, waiting for me?"

Aevinn looked away.

"All Fomori carry at least a trace of transformative magic in their veins, is that not true?" Neve asked.

"There are no more—"

"They *did*," Neve pressed. "When there *were* Fomori, yes?"

Cliona's eyes narrowed, trying to see the trap in the question.

"Yes," Grian answered for her. "It's true, but to varying degrees—"

"Grian—"

"Well, that's what you've always told us, isn't it, Cliona?" She turned to the other Faoladh, unwilling to hold her tongue. "And you, Aevinn? That we Faoladh carried in our souls the strongest of those magics—our riastrad, our sacred battle madness that brings on the change—but that there were others, highborn Fomori, the Fé Fíada—Lords of the Mist—who could use the power to command the very elements to their bidding."

There was that name again. Fé Fíada. Fomori royalty, Glynnis had called them at Úna's celebration. Neve thought of Ronan, and of how the spring water had wrapped him in an embrace, called to him by the magic flowing beneath his skin—his marked *silver* skin. Now she had a name for what he truly was. Not Fir Bolg. Not even just Fomori. Fomori royalty. Powerful beyond measure.

A Lord of the Mist.

Fé Fíada.

"Grian speaks out of turn," Cliona said flatly, "but she speaks truth. Still—what of it? We are all that are left."

"Do you really think the Scathach managed to eradicate every single Fomori that ever lived?" Neve asked.

"There weren't that many of us Fomori to begin with," a black-haired woman with a streak of silver at her temple said. "All the Fomori that weren't Faoladh were either killed or driven away."

"Or went deep into hiding, maybe," Neve argued. "So deep their descendants forgot who—or *what*—they even were."

Cliona's glance sharpened.

"What could you do with the blood of your kind?" Neve asked quietly. "Blood that still carried the magic of the Fomori?" *Or, better still, Fomori royalty . . .*

"We could restore our own." Aevinn spoke cautiously. "We could use it to call upon the riastrad. We would become the warriors we were always meant to be."

"And what would you do with that gift?" Neve asked, fingers gripping the cold, golden weight of the mask beneath her cloak.

Cliona leaned forward, as if straining at invisible bonds. "Pledge it in service to the one who'd given it to us."

"But you are already pledged in service to the Dagda," Neve challenged, leaning forward herself. "To the Chosen of the Lia Fail. That vow is unbreakable."

Aevinn put a hand on Cliona's shoulder and said, "There are Dagdas . . ."

"And there are Dagdas." Neve nodded.

Even Elchmar, the first to claim the title of Dagda, had succumbed under its weight and disappeared into the wild mists of Eire. The untamed magic of the land was as hungry as it was pitiless, and even the Chosen of the Lia Fail might not stand against it. Not without drawing upon the likes of the Faoladh and their riastrad.

There were blood oaths, and blood oaths . . .

The thief Ronan killed your sister. Spill his *blood and make it count.*

The blood of the boy from the barrows. The young man she'd kissed . . .

He's a Fé Fíada beast. A threat and an assassin and more powerful than you could know. He cannot live.

Neve held out her hand for Cliona's drinking horn. The Faoladh leader handed it over to her and Neve drank deeply of the sweet mead, then passed the horn back, smiling coldly.

"Well, then . . . ," she said, "I have an idea that might make things a *great* deal easier. For you and for me."

XIX

Ronan needed spells. For himself and . . . well. For himself. That was all. So long as none of the salvagers spotted him there, he wasn't too proud to go begging. In fact, he was getting desperate enough not to care even if they did. There were days when his skin felt like it was drenched in molten honey and crawling with bees, humming with the darkling magic that coursed through him, stronger each time it manifested. Which it had—in mercifully brief bouts—twice now since the last time he'd seen Neve, sparked by nightmares. It was a damned lucky thing Cavall had been spending most nights sleeping at the forge lately. But if the change happened in daylight . . .

"Ill-omened," muttered an ancient crone, peering at the angry purple sky as Ronan passed her market stall. A bitter wind shook the bare tree branches like a Druid rattling bones for a soothcasting. "Dark days ahead, young lad. Look to your loved ones . . ."

"Had I loved ones to look to, old mother, I would." He tossed her a small copper coin for a wrinkled apple from her basket.

"Desperate times . . ."

Ronan took a bite of the sour fruit and ducked beneath a stone archway carved with a particular rune, the entrance to a narrow alley that led to a ramshackle collection of windowless huts. The last vestige of Blackwater's dark market.

Most folk in town had never been down that alley, kept away by a remarkably effective spell that was so subtle as to be almost imperceptible. It did little more than make it uncomfortable for the unwitting to even look in that direction—let alone go that way—but it was still faint enough so as not to spark cursefire in a harrow hound. It left those folk that still possessed any kind of spells or spellcraft free to deal in them, so long as they didn't actually cast them there.

Ronan knocked on the lintel of a tiny, tucked-away hut and entered the shadowed doorway. Right into the point of a knife, held by a tall man dressed in long gray robes.

"Clearly you were expecting me," Ronan said dryly.

"Macha's bloody teeth. Not *you*." The man sheathed the blade. "I thought I sensed something actually *worth* killing at my door."

"Sorry, no. Can't sell my parts for anything above three-day-old prices."

"You're still a disappointment, I see."

"I stole a new shirt," Ronan said, shrugging. "You should've seen me yesterday."

"There's blood stains on it."

Ronan glanced down at where stubborn seepage from Neve's arrow wound had marked his sleeve with a streak of rust.

"Like I said," Ronan said with a shrug.

The man's eyes narrowed. His mouth twitched, then bent into a grin as he laughed and held out his hand.

"Eolas," Ronan said, clasping his wrist. "It's good to see you, my old friend."

"I would say the same of you, my young friend," Eolas said. "Except I know that if you're here, it's likely not for good."

"I don't even know myself, to be fair," Ronan admitted. "But for good or ill, I could use your help."

He gestured Ronan over to a low table beneath a hanging lantern, littered with wax tablets and scrolls held flat by earthen mugs set on their corners. Ronan actually recognized one or two of them from his time as an apprentice.

Eolas had been a Druid master and one of the archive keepers of the Order—the one who'd turned a blind eye every time young Ronan got his nose into something he shouldn't. Until he couldn't anymore, and then he'd reluctantly banished the lad. And told him that it was, in all likelihood, for his own good.

He was also the first of a handful of Druids to leave the Order once Gofannon and the Dagda began to build Brú na Bóinne, refusing to help them hoard the magic to do it. In the years after his disavowal, Eolas had been one of Ronan's best customers, back when he'd been selling stolen incantations. How ironic, Ronan thought, that he was the one who now needed to beg illicit spells from his old master.

"Sit," Eolas said, running a hand through his silvering hair. "Just try not to set anything alight with all those stray magic sparks you're shedding . . ."

Ronan frowned and glanced down reflexively but, of course, saw nothing out of the ordinary. "That obvious?" he asked.

"Not yet. But it will be soon." Eolas poured a cup of mead for them both. When he looked up, Ronan could see traces of Druid Sight twisting and flitting like ghosts in his gaze. "I assume that's why you're here," he continued. "What have you gotten yourself into now, lad?"

Ronan took a deep breath and told him. Everything.

He told him about Neve—from their first meeting to their last, in the sacred grove—about the ban sidhe she'd conjured then and her uncanny fire now. He told him about his own darkling sigils, and the transformations . . . Everything. Everything except the small suspicion in the back of his mind that he'd done something he couldn't remember. Something terrible. Deadly . . .

"Fé Fíada," Eolas murmured, a look in his eyes that wasn't quite awe, but something a stone's throw from it. "Not a guest I'd ever imagined entertaining at my humble table. Always knew there was something interesting about you, lad." He emptied his mug in a long swallow and refilled it. "They'll kill you very dead if they get their hands on you. That demon-clever fiend Gofannon and the Order—they're little more than his thralls now, with the óglach and their dogs squirming under their black thumbs . . ."

Ronan knew that well enough. What he didn't know was why. "What hold does Gofannon have over them? Over the Dagda himself?" he wondered aloud. "I rarely saw the man when I was in the Order."

"Few of us did. He arrived one day in our midst—sailed over from Cymru, he said—with a sacred vision of the Dagda's destiny and enough sweet oil on his tongue to convince the Druid council to help him make it come to pass."

Not the first time such a thing had happened among the Druid order, to be sure. A prophecy, well-prophesied, was a powerful thing. But it was no concern of Ronan's. Especially now that he and Neve were no concern of each other's.

"What about the girl? Neve?" He gestured with his hand as if he held fire in the cage of his fingers. "What does your Druid learning tell you about that?"

"The Princess?" Eolas shrugged. "She is Tuatha Dé. The magic of Eire does not speak to them the way it does to the true folk of the land. Which is not to say that her own forebearer did not bear a powerful magic of *her* own . . ." He gestured to the old scar on Ronan's palm. "My guess is that the girl's interaction with you has marked her somehow. Perhaps your Fé called to the power of her ancestress sleeping in her blood."

The Scathach. Ronan groaned. "Well, that's not worrying at all . . ."

But also not at all beyond the realm of possibility, he thought. If he closed his eyes, even for a moment, Ronan's Druid senses— the training he'd received from Eolas himself—would take over and he could almost *see* the connection between him and Neve stretching out like ethereal filaments, pulled taut but unbreakable. He could feel the searing shimmer of the darkling marks on his skin at the very thought, the liquid fire of her mouth on his. He felt her in his soul like a thorn beneath the skin.

"It should be worrying," Eolas said. "For her, I mean. If that power manifests in the presence of her father's hounds, the Dagda might soon find himself without any daughters at all."

Which was the same reason Ronan had sought out Eolas for himself. "I need a veil," he said. "A glamour, something to hide this . . ."

"Gift?"

"Curse."

"It's not a curse," Eolas snapped, reminding Ronan of the sometimes harsh teacher he had been in his youth. "It's an inheritance, boy. A birthright. Cherish it."

Ronan's mind drifted back to the moment the spring waters had engulfed him, transforming him into something at once terrible and magnificent. Finding himself—his altered self—reflected in Neve's golden eyes . . . and seeing the fear and hatred in her gaze at what he really, truly was.

Ronan held up his hand and watched Eolas's eyes widen as he stopped fighting and allowed the Fé to take over for a moment. His fingers grew long, taloned, webbed with iridescent skin. The darklight sigils spread out to wrap around his forearm.

"I can't cherish it if it gets me killed," he said, then shook his arm sharply, willing it back to normal.

Eolas whistled low and leaned back in his chair.

"I remember you used to keep a store of small-magic spells—handy in certain situations for a thief—that you, uh, liberated from the Druid Order," Ronan said, wiping the sudden sheen of sweat on his brow.

"Aye . . ." Eolas pulled a small chest off a high shelf and fished out a small handful of what looked like silver coins. He dropped them, one by one, into the palm of Ronan's hand. "I remember how useful you used to find them."

"They were beneficial for us both, I seem to recall."

Like smaller, portable versions of the spell that kept the dark market veiled, the magic the "coins" contained was so slight and so benign as to be undetectable by the óglach spell-harrows, and a few of them, with engravings on both sides, served a kind of dual purpose—a hide and seek spell—that could be used to either keep a thing hidden or find a thing lost. Ronan had used them on occasion to procure other, more lucrative enchantments for Eolas. And remain elusive while he did so.

Ronan slipped them into a pocket in his satchel and stood.

Eolas stayed seated, staring into the dark liquid in his cup. "Ronan," he said quietly, lifting his head, his gaze flickering again with Druid Sight, "when you leave here today, don't come back looking for me again. I won't be here to find if you do."

Ronan hesitated. He would miss Eolas and their very occasional friendship. But he nodded and said, "I understand."

"The gods watch over you, Ronan of the Sea."

"Thank you—"

"That wasn't a blessing," Eolas said. "Just an observation."

Ronan ducked out of the house, making his way back into the market square, and the first thing he noticed was that it was deserted. In the near distance, he heard the bone-chilling wail of a harrow hound on the hunt.

His heart leaped into his throat as he saw the salvager Nym, pelting down a side street, followed hard at his heels by a pair of spell-harrows, eyes blazing crimson. Ronan squeezed his eyes shut at the sound of the salvager's truncated scream.

He dug into his satchel and pulled out a coin, whispering the word inscribed on it, and felt the air shiver around him. As he went to tuck the charm away, a vision of Neve flashed through his mind—the memory of her pleading for his help when she'd sought him out in Blackwater.

"*You did this—you have to help me!*" she'd said. "*My chamber garden is close enough to the harrow kennels that I can hear them howl when it's time to be fed. I'd rather not be their next meal.*"

"It's none of your business, Ronan," he admonished himself. "*She's* none of your business. She made that damnably clear, remember?" And what could he do, with Neve behind the high stone walls of Temair, a place Ronan would never be allowed to set foot?

The howls of the spell-harrows faded, but Ronan could still hear the panicked cries of the folk in the market. When those, too, drifted to silence, he turned down a street and ran home, the long way around. By the time he got back to the little house he shared with Cavall, his heart was pounding in his ears.

He pushed aside the leather door curtain and ducked inside to see that the apprentice blacksmith had been busy. An axe lay gleaming in the middle of the single rough wooden table they shared infrequent meals at. It was sleek and elegant in design, with a long handle and wickedly curved blade.

Ronan had seen one very like it recently. "Who is that for?" he asked warily.

"Someone who appreciates my talent," Cavall murmured. "Finally. This lovely thing"—he picked it up and spun it slowly in his hand, catching the lamplight with the blade—"is destined for the palace, if you can believe it."

Ronan's chill deepened down to his marrow.

He could more than believe it. In fact, he knew who it was for, and why it had been commissioned. Because his last encounter with a weapon like that was when Neve had thrown one at his head. It was an uncommon weapon, so of course she would have wanted a replacement for the one she'd left behind, sunken in the depths of the sacred spring. Ronan felt a sharp tightening in his chest when he realized the new blade was crafted of iron, not bronze. Hadn't he been the one to tell her—all those years ago— that iron could disrupt magic?

And destroy monsters . . .

"Who—*exactly*—at the palace is that for?" he asked, needing to be wrong, and knowing he wasn't. "Cavall?"

"Hm?" Cavall glanced over at him. "Oh, ah . . . not really sure?" He shrugged. "Might be for the Dagda himself, for all I know! Had a visit to the forge from one of the horse folk—you know, the king's mercenaries—arrogant sort, but he had a purse full of coin and a promise of more to come, and a satchel full of high-grade iron ore. And I have a mighty tolerance for arrogant sorts under the right circumstances. Gave me very specific instructions and said I could deliver it direct to the palace when it was done." He wiped a scrap of sheepskin over the blade to buff away a nonexistent smudge. "You don't get that silvery luster from just any old iron, even rare enough as that is. No, *this* came from far away—someplace with a name I can't even wrap my lips around." Cavall lowered his voice and looked around, even though he and Ronan were, of course, the only people in their hut. "And the heat needed to forge such a metal takes a very *special* fire if you take my meaning . . ."

"I take it." Ronan shook his head. "I take it to mean you risked getting yourself killed using magic to fan your flames. Cavall, it's just an axe. Not exactly worth getting yourself torn to pieces by spell-harrows."

"Don't worry, I'm careful as a new mum with a pretty babe."

"Well enough, fool," Ronan snapped. "But that thing still *reeks* of magic. I can smell it from here. How do you propose to deliver it without bringing the hounds down on your neck?"

Cavall blinked a couple of times. "What?"

"Are you just going to walk up to the main gates of the palace—the palace guarded by óglach and their magic-devouring hounds—and introduce yourself?"

"Huh." A frown ticked between the smith's brows. "I didn't think of that . . ."

"You didn't *think*." Ronan reached for the axe and picked it up. The skin on the palm of his hand tingled with needle pricks and he could feel the flickering ghost flames of the fire magic Cavall had used. It might have even called Ronan's Fé to manifest if he hadn't just cast one of the coin enchantments Eolas had given him. He didn't ask Cavall who'd conjured the forge fire for him. Sparrow, probably, or one of her wayward ilk. He thought of Nym in the marketplace and shuddered.

"You'd be torn to pieces within a hundred paces of the walls of Temair," he said. "And then Ne—and then who*ever* commissioned the damn thing can walk right out into the field where you fell and take it from your dead fingers."

And then what if the fire magic still left lingering in that blade calls forth her *flames?* he thought.

The inside of Ronan's skull echoed with Eolas's ominous words: "*If that power manifests in the presence of her father's hounds, the Dagda might soon find himself without any daughters at all . . .*"

"How do you propose I collect on my services then?" Cavall complained.

Ronan hesitated, chewing on his lip, and then said, "I'll do it."

Ronan could use one of the precious coins to wrap a veil around the axe. And then—more importantly—he could give one to Neve, too. Keep her safe. Hidden. Of course, there was every chance she might just have him arrested by the óglach on sight. But as much as he tried not to care, Ronan knew he wouldn't be able to live with himself if Neve came to harm because of his inaction.

Cavall agreed, in equal measure relieved that Ronan was rescuing him from his predicament and reluctant to part with his masterpiece. He went to go find a scrap of leather fine enough to wrap the thing in, and Ronan waited with both dread and desire at the thought of seeing Neve again.

When he held the sagaris up, the iron blade seemed to grin at him in the firelight. A monster killer . . . delivered into the hands of its mistress by the monster himself.

XX

$\mathcal{T}$HE WIND GUSTED down out of the western hills, sending icy gray rain hammering on the shutters of Neve's chamber windows. It seemed to her as if the weather for the past several days had been a mirror of her moods, swinging wildly between bleak gray gloom and furious cloudbursts. She'd done her best to stay far away from anyone who might provoke her in one direction or another, but it wasn't as if she could avoid herself. Or her own grim thoughts.

Her oath to the Faoladh and what the restoration of their riastrad would mean, both to her and to the whole kingdom, was the ragged shipwreck spar Neve clung to in the middle of her storms. And yet every so often her mind would catch on a stray thought, and her feelings for Ronan would start to rise up, complicated by the knowledge of what he had done—and by the guilt that she had let him get close enough to do it.

Neve's throat constricted around a knot of unshed tears as she remembered how Ronan had looked beneath the moonlight as the spring water had spun up to entangle him. How his skin had rippled with a silvery sheen, the angles of his face sharpening, his eyes widening into obsidian pools. Beautiful.

Monstrous . . .

And, Neve thought with growing, bitter certainty, probably the last thing her sister had seen before she drowned, standing in the middle of Neve's garden.

Ronan of Blackwater.

Men are not to be trusted, whispered the silken-smoke voice in her head that was becoming her near constant companion. *Men you show your heart to, even less so.*

She reached beneath her pillow for the golden mask she kept hidden there and gazed into its shadow-cast wolf's eyes.

Love is only an impediment to power.

Neve looked up from the mask to the mural on the wall above her, at the painted figure of Elchmar riding beside the Scathach, proud and handsome. His mount leading the way just ahead of hers, hand on the hilt of his sword like a conquering hero, even though it was *she* who had led the Tuatha Dé on their perilous journey. In the days before he and his brother had both betrayed her and stolen the throne of Temair. The lantern in the Scathach's hand was cunningly painted to seem as if its flame illuminated his features, while she remained in shadow, cloaked in midnight, hooded and mysterious.

Neve reached out to the mural, but stopped short of laying her hand upon it this time, for fear the fiery sigil would appear on her palm again. If only Ronan had shown her *how* to call the fire from her veins—willingly—and how *not* to. For weeks now, every time she heard the óglach guards calling to each other in the courtyards, or the harrow hounds belling in the distance, she froze in fear.

What am I? she wondered, over and over again. *What have I become?*

Does it matter? the voice answered with a beguiling smile Neve could hear. *You are powerful.*

"Powerful . . ." Neve almost laughed at the thought.

So powerful she couldn't even walk beyond the walls of the palace on her own.

Not that there was anywhere to go. Not with the Horse Lords still encamped in the fields to the southwest—Sakir's uncle, Cormac, finding endless reasons to delay the Scythians' return to the Golden Vale. And to the north and east, several other encampments of tuath warbands had sprung up, clusters of tents sprouting almost overnight like mushrooms.

Neve couldn't get a straight answer from anyone on who was summoning the tuaths, or why, but she suspected the appearance of the Faoladh at the Stone Singing—with their cryptic warning of a darkness to come—likely had something to do with it. The chieftains might have conferred with Úna, she thought. But not with her.

They fear you.

Ridiculous . . .

They will.

"They used to fear the Dagda," she said out loud.

The chosen ruler with his mighty war club. But those days seemed a faded memory now. The Faoladh show of swearing renewed allegiance might have staved off the inevitable, but it was clear there were long knives out for the king of the Tuatha Dé. And it was his own damned fault for being so wrapped up in his delusions of destiny and grandeur, carving his legacy upon the land . . .

But what made her think that she was any more worthy than her father to sit upon the throne?

Ask your mother, the whisper-voice answered. *The blood of the first Dagda runs through* her *veins, not Ruad Rofhessa's. Your veins. Daughter of daughters of queens . . .*

Neve reached up to find that the wolf mask—in her hands only moments earlier—rested lightly on her face. Neve gently lifted it free. There was no pain this time and that, in itself, made her mouth go dry with apprehension. She wasn't so sure if this was something she should be getting used to. Restless, she stood to fetch her cloak and tucked the golden relic in her pocket so that Emer would not happen upon it.

That same blood had run through Úna's veins, too, she thought as she slipped out of her room into the empty corridor. And see how much the fates cared for that?

The storm had blown over and the sun was setting behind iron-gray clouds, bleeding crimson into black, as Neve headed toward the stables. Sakir was probably with his uncle, but at least she could spend time with her horses. They cared about apples. Not destiny.

In the wake of Úna's death, most of the court seemed to have assumed it had been an accident or even by her own hand, impossible as that was. But the Dagda's mistrust of his own lords had grown such that he only relied on the counsel of Gofannon and the Druid Order, their phantom-pale robes haunting halls and courtyards. Neve ducked down a branching corridor to avoid a prowling clot of Druids and instead passed through the main chambers of the palace. Her father was back at his monument, preparing for the consecration of the Great Barrow at Midwinter, so she had no fear of crossing his path. But as she neared the Great Hall, Neve heard a cacophony of muffled voices coming from her father's throne chamber.

Angry voices.

Neve paused outside the massive carved-oak doors. It wasn't open revolt among the lords, not yet—even with rumors the óglach had already come close to direct conflict with more than one chieftain—but perhaps that was about to change.

She peered through a gap between the doors and listened.

"He squats like a mushroom out on that damned hill, doing nothing while no trade ships from Cymru or Alba have made the crossing," one hardened chieftain with long black braids and battle scars complained loudly. "Not since just before Samhain."

"That's just shite weather and time of year, Balar," answered another voice, rough and salt-scored, as if the speaker had spent his life on the waves or never out of sight of them.

"Well then how do you explain rumors of empty lands north of the Neck?" Balar pressed. "Or talk of ships massing in the Northern Sea?"

The Neck was a narrowing of the land in the realm of Alba, across the Eirish Sea. The folk north of the Neck were said to be a strange, warlike people. It stood to reason that if they'd abandoned their settlements, it could mean they were gathering elsewhere in preparation for a campaign.

"It amazes me how rumors seem to be able to make the crossing, but not trade ships," Soren said dryly.

Multiple voices bubbled up again like a cauldron overboiling. Then a quieter voice suggested, "Maybe the prophecies are coming true."

A silence descended. Neve leaned in. The lords of the Tuatha Dé all kept Druids in their courts for counsel, and the wiser ones paid attention to their auguries. If only because their own fortunes often depended on them. The Druids made sure of that.

"What prophecies?" Balar brayed, stoking the flame of his own bravado. "You mean the ravings of those mad wolf women at Brú na Bóinne? The Dagda should ha' given the order to cut them down right then."

"And who would have followed it?" asked another. "The Faoladh near wiped the mad queen Scathach off the face of the world. They might be the Dagda's strongest weapon if the legends *are* true—"

"You'd trust that pack of bitches? I'd rather call up the bloody Horse Lords first—"

"Watch that wagging-dog tongue of yours." Farsa's voice lashed through the room. "Or I'll tie it to my saddle and slap my horse's arse!"

As the room burst into another cacophony of arguments and insults, Neve wondered where Cormac was. And, more importantly, where his loyalties truly lay. The tuath chieftains looked upon their Scythian counterparts as little more than mercenaries, but the fact that there was a sizable number of them camped outside the walls of the palace clearly made them nervous. The lords bellowed at each other until, finally, the air in the room must have run out and there was a momentary lull.

"This talk of 'darkness on the horizon,'" one of the northern chieftains said in a deep, quiet voice. "Even if it *is* just spit in a rainstorm, Soren, shouldn't the warriors of the Tuatha Dé at least be ready?"

Soren rubbed a gnarled hand over his face. As the Dagda's First Spear chief, his loyalty to Neve's father was unfailing. But she also knew that Soren was an infinitely pragmatic man. "Aye," he said with a laden sigh. "And very like that's why you're all standing here in this hall right now, isn't it?"

"*We* came for a wedding," said a chieftain with a western lilt.

"Aye," said another. "And stayed for a funeral."

"The Dagda's mind grows weak," Balar said.

And *that* was something Neve had never heard uttered out loud before. Beneath her cloak, the edges of the wolf mask bit into her fingers as she gripped it.

Be strong. You will need strength. Beyond what any expect of you. And soon.

She held her breath, almost leaning on the doors.

Banach, a chieftain Neve recognized who hailed from Laigin in the south, cleared his throat and took a step forward. "Perhaps . . . we need a new Dagda," he suggested.

"Ruad Rofhessa's daughter died before she could produce an heir," one of the lesser lords of Temair remarked dryly. "Or weren't you party to that information in your remote little corner of the realm?"

"There *is* no other Dagda," Farsa snapped. "Not one of *my* folk will serve at any rate. The Lia Fail spoke for Ruad Rofhessa. My own brother Cormac stood witness."

There is your answer, Little Scota! That is your key . . .

"The horse folk have pledged their loyalty and service to the true kings of Temair down through generations," he continued. "We are the Sons of Elchmar and we will not break faith now."

Seize this chance. Lay the banquet table and invite them all to feast . . .

"You're quite correct, Horse Lord," Lorcan said, stepping forward to join his father beside the throne. "The Dagda is the Dagda through blood and Destiny. There is no other path. And I will—"

Lorcan swallowed whatever he was about to say next, as Neve Anann Eriu, sole daughter of the Dagda, shoved open the Great Hall's double doors.

She stalked into the middle of the chamber to stand in the firelight cast by the Dagda's hearth. Shocked silence descended on the room. Most of the lords assembled there towered over her. And most of them took a step back, widening the ring where she stood, turning in a slow circle to look at them all, one by one.

"My lords," Neve said by way of greeting, a preternatural calm settling over her. "You are all, I think, forgetting something. The Dagda has *two* daughters."

After the moment of stunned silence, the reaction of those assembled was, to Neve's mind, laughably predictable. Equal portions incredulity and derision. She ignored the jeers and stood, hands clasped tightly beneath her cloak, a faint smile on her lips.

"And you are forgetting something else," she said. "You—each and every one of you gathered here beneath this roof—know full well that the *only* voice that matters when it comes to proclaiming the rightful ruler of the Tuatha Dé is the voice of the Lia Fail. Not my father's, and not any one of yours."

Neve noticed sharpened gazes from the chieftains canny enough to realize what Neve had just insinuated. They may not have thought much of her before that moment, but now they thought of her as marriageable. A path, perhaps, to getting within arm's reach of kingship for one lucky lordling.

Neve meant for them to keep thinking that. Until such time as she'd gathered the means to prove them wrong. In every way.

"Do you think Eire is invulnerable, lords?" she asked. "Impervious to assault? I don't think that. I can't *know* that. I only know this: in the face of a darkness rising—and darkness follows dusk follows bright daylight, always—an unjust kingdom will never stand. A false king will ever come to ruin. And faithless tuaths will, in the end, burn to ash and scatter on the winds."

Neve wasn't sure where the words she spoke came from, but they flowed from her mouth like a prophecy, silencing all dissenters.

"Carrion crows squabble over another's kill until it's cold, my lords. Wolves band together in the hunt to share the spoils. I am the daughter of the Dagda, but I am also the Beloved of the Wolf. I will defend this kingdom to my death. Which among you can say the same?"

She didn't give them time to respond, knowing how they likely would. She just turned and swept back out through the doors, leaving a hall of chieftains murmuring in her wake.

XXI

*T*HE NIGHT WAS cold, but Neve took the long path to the little garden off her mother's old apartments, just so she could stop her hands from shaking beneath her cloak. She'd never done anything quite like that performance before the tuaths and wasn't sure if she should be proud or wary of herself for doing it. The withered tree still stood there, but when Neve sank to her knees and leaned her head against the rough bark, she thought she caught the faintest scent of apples. And where she'd pressed her palm against the trunk, there was a faint gold mark glimmering there. Like a three-pointed sigil.

Neve stood slowly. Even though Midwinter was fast approaching, there was a fresh new branch, thin and fragile, angling skyward. And a single leaf unfurled beneath the moonlight.

Only one of the torches in her chambers was lit when Neve eased the door open and slipped back inside, and the brasier coals burned low and red.

"Emer?" she called softly. "Are you awake?"

"Your handmaiden has stepped away," said a voice from the shadows of her sleeping alcove.

Neve saw a familiar figure standing near her couch, looking up at the mural on her wall. "Lord Gofannon . . ." She swallowed the sudden sour taste of fear, but she could feel her heart racing in her chest. What was he doing there? Were the lords still arguing in the hall? And where was her father?

"She's gone to attend the Dagda at my behest," Gofannon continued.

"I thought he was at the Great Barrow."

"He was. We returned not long ago, and he has retired to his chambers," Gofannon said. "He is unsettled in his mind tonight and I thought one of Emer's remedies might ease him into a restful sleep."

That didn't explain why Gofannon was there in *her* chambers.

"Also, I wished to speak with you, and had hoped to find you here . . . ?"

"My apologies," she said, forcing an unperturbed smile back onto her lips, ignoring the unasked question of where, exactly, she *had* been at that time of night. "I wasn't expecting company at this late hour."

"Of course not," Gofannon said and offered her a courtly apologetic bow. "Nor would I have intruded if I hadn't thought it a matter of utmost urgency."

"Enough to conveniently dispatch my handmaiden and wait here in the darkness for me to return?" Neve kept her smile where it was and moved to take up the torch, lighting another with its flame and returning it to its sconce.

"Lady . . ." Gofannon stepped toward her, his brow furrowed with concern. "I say this gently, for I know how much you love him. Your father is in ill health."

"If you knew how much *he* loved *me*, you wouldn't take the care to be gentle," Neve said. "What exactly do you mean by 'ill health,' Master Gofannon?"

"He's dying."

Her smile fled and Neve felt a hollow pit open up inside her, just below her heart.

"Just as well he has somewhere to go when he's dead, then, isn't it?" she said, the words spilling from her lips before she realized it.

Gofannon took a deep breath. "You are angry."

"You're very perceptive."

"Lady . . . will you come take just a bit more of this night's air and sit with me?" He crossed to the tall carved-oak doors that led out into Neve's private garden and opened them, gesturing for her to lead the way. "Please."

Neve shivered as a rush of cold swept through her chambers, stirring the air that was close and stale, tainted with the acrid smell of pitch smoke because Neve had adamantly refused to open the garden doors since the night Úna died, and hadn't let Emer do so, either. She drew her cloak close and brushed past the architect, preceding him along the pebbled walkway, toward where a stone bench stood under the barren branches of a weeping willow.

The garden was unkempt. The shrubs bore clumps of dead and withered flowers, and the water in the pond was black and stagnant and stank. Even Emer's meticulously tended herb and medicines garden was nothing but a patch of wilted leaves. Not that it mattered. Nothing mattered in that moment.

The Dagda was dying.

Father . . .

"The chief of the Tuatha Dé is mighty beyond measure, but his great strength wanes. And with it, his mind weakens," Gofannon said, echoing the lords in the Great Hall that night. "I do not mean to say his demise is *imminent*, lady—forgive me—but . . . the realm and the king are as one. As falters the Dagda, so falters the land. Temair must be prepared for new blood upon her throne. *Your* blood."

Neve froze as if the touch of moonlight had turned her to stone. Her pulse thundered in her ears.

"*You* are what this realm needs, Neve Anann Eriu," Gofannon pressed on. "Bright fire. The spirit of your ancestress lives in you, I can see it clearly."

Little Scota . . .

A surge of excitement—followed hard by one of cold dread—washed over her at the thought of how the Druid sorcerer's proposal seemed to align so very closely with her own embryonic scheme. It meant that there was more at work than she could have possibly accounted for in her own machinations.

Use it. Use him . . .

"I know I can convince your father to proclaim me his choice as marriage-son and heir," Gofannon pressed on. "You would be Queen Consort and rule at my side. I know you must think me old, but I'm not so very decrepit." A faint, almost rueful smile bent the corners of his mouth. "I was a very young man when I first came to this island, you know. Barely older than you are now."

Neve remembered Sakir's suspicions that Gofannon was Scythian. She studied the Druid's profile and wondered if her charioteer was right. What other secrets could he be keeping? How long had he been planning on claiming the throne? She suddenly remembered the tears in his eyes on the night of Úna's death and wondered if he hadn't had a very similar conversation with her.

Does it matter? He is a tool. A weapon. Use him as one . . .

"Master Gofannon—"

"You needn't love me," he assured her. "Of course. And I have the highest regard for you—for your spirit, your strength. Together, lady, we could restore a brilliant sheen to Temair's faded glory. I believe it is your destiny."

"I find your proposal intriguing, Lord Gofannon," Neve said, digging the nails of her left hand so hard into her palm she felt the skin break. She chose her next words carefully. *Very* carefully. Almost as if she could hear the whisper of them in her mind before she gave them voice. Like she had in the Great Hall. "And I am honored," she continued. "I know the general opinions of the court where I am concerned. No"—she held up her other hand, smiling graciously—"do not deny them. But my sister left me footsteps in which to tread. Eire is what is most important, and I can think of no one who has done more for the glory of the realm than you."

Gofannon's smile widened and Neve leaned into it. Just a touch.

"But . . . ," she continued, as if the thought were just that moment occurring to her, "there will need to be assurances."

"Lady?"

"For the people. Legitimacy, Gofannon." She tilted her head and looked at him. "A rightful transfer of power from Dagda to Dagda. If, say, in front of a gathering of the Tuatha Dé, the Lia Fail were to speak for *you* . . ."

Gofannon's gaze narrowed. "The Lia Fail."

"The Stone of Destiny. The Herald of Kings—"

"Yes," he interrupted her, his tone sharp at the edges. "I know what it is."

"But do you know *where* it is?" Neve sat back.

What Neve had said earlier to the chieftains about the Lia Fail—about bringing it before the tuaths for a kingmaking—might just as well have been a bard's tale. The truth of it, of course, was that she had no idea where—or even if—the Stone still existed. For all she knew, Ruad Rofhessa had smashed it into rubble before she was even born. But if Neve could entice the Druid sorcerer into revealing its current state . . .

She could challenge her father's legitimacy to the throne. Bring the Lia Fail to court and make him place his hand upon it in front of the gathered lords of the tuaths. Watch the truth dawn in their eyes as the Stone remained mute beneath Ruad Rofhessa's touch . . .

Then stop him before his madness went any further. Before Brú na Bóinne was consecrated at Midwinter and the darkness the Faoladh seeress had told her of descended upon them. Because in Neve's mind, those two things were inextricably linked.

"Lady Neve." Gofannon smiled. "I was right about you. You are not to be underestimated," he said and reached for her hand—the one she hadn't scored bloody with her nails, thankfully—and placed a kiss on her knuckles.

"I'm glad you think—"

"Of course, the Stone of Destiny has been sadly lost over the years since your father's making," he continued. "But I'm certain the Druid Order can . . . fashion a suitable replacement. For—as you say—the benefit of the people."

Neve's heart dropped into her stomach. That wasn't what she wanted at all. Her growing confidence in her plan vanished like mist on an ill wind.

"It shall be done," Gofannon said. "On the morning of the Winter Solstice, you and I will announce our betrothal at the ritual of the rising sun."

With that understanding, and the sound of Emer returning, Gofannon bent his head over her hand. "I shall take my leave of you now, my lady."

Neve nodded faintly, and decided she would take hers, too. From Temair.

She had thought herself so clever, earlier. Clever enough to match wits with a Druid master. A sorcerer. Now there was no avenue left for her but to escape. And only one place she could think of to go.

"Neve!" Emer poked her head into the garden. Her gaze flicked back and forth from Neve to Gofannon, taking in their clasped hands. "Lady," she said in a voice thick with disapproval. "It's biting cold. Come inside."

Gofannon's long fingers squeezed hers once and then let go. "My queen," he murmured, quietly enough that Emer wouldn't hear. "I will fulfill my promise to you. This I vow."

He stood and bowed himself out.

Neve held her breath until she knew she was finally, completely alone. Then she began to tremble like the lone leaf on her mother's apple tree. She sat there at the edge of the fetid pond and pressed her hands together to keep herself from shattering to pieces. The blood from her nails made her palm slick. And warm. And glimmering . . . The sigil on her right hand suddenly flared to life.

Neve swore and dropped to her knees, rubbing her hands on the dead, damp moss, willing the flame to snuff out before the harrow hounds caught wind. It did, reluctantly, but before its light died, Neve's eye was caught by a gleam in the darkness.

What in the name of Light . . .

The brief flare of otherworldly illumination had reflected off something.

Something hidden beneath a low-spreading juniper bush. Neve knelt down and carefully ran her hand over the rocks and soil of the garden bed. The pungent tang of Emer's abandoned herbs filled her nostrils as she reached beneath the shrub, fingertips skimming the ground . . .

There.

And *there.*

Two objects hidden beneath the juniper. She drew forth one and then the other. The first was a thin, brittle strip of stone, crudely scratched with a line of symbols. The second was a small knife, the plain, dull-gray blade forged of cheap iron. Neither was hers. Nor had they been Úna's. Neve was certain of that much— her sister never would have had use for such things.

Behind her, the doors opened and Emer stepped back out onto the terrace. "Is his fancy lordship gone?" she asked, startling Neve. "What did he want?"

"Nothing . . ." Neve stood, slipping the knife and stone into an inside pocket of her cloak, beside the wolf mask that was still nestled there. She stepped past Emer, who closed the doors behind them after a long look out at the bleak little garden. "He wanted to convey his sympathies for Úna's passing."

She hated lying to Emer, who'd been a true friend and done her best to look after Neve over the last several months. But she also couldn't tell her why he'd really been there. Or that she planned to escape in the morning, both to avoid the fate he'd just offered her and because she really wasn't sure how much longer she could control her cursed flame.

"How magnanimous of him." Emer snorted. "Could he not have picked a civilized hour?" She plucked Neve's cloak off her shoulders and hung it on a peg, then stabbed at the sullen coals in the brazier with a poker, coaxing warmth into the room. "Now," she said. "To bed, lady. Before you catch your death."

Emer retired to her sleeping pallet and Neve dutifully crawled into bed, burrowing under the heap of blankets and furs and staring at the ceiling.

Aye, she thought, listening for her handmaiden's breath to settle into a deep, somnolent rhythm. *Or my death catches me.*

XXII

Ronan stood at the gates of Temair, wreathed in a fog of his own breath, as he waited impatiently for the guard to return. The sun climbed reluctantly over the horizon as he did, spilling moody orange light out over the gray landscape, and he rolled an eye at the sky. He couldn't smell snow—not yet, but soon. It was less than one full moon until the shortest day—which, of course, meant the longest night—of the year.

The damp chill had worked its way between the layers of his tunic and cloak; his feet were stiff and cold inside his worn boots. He found himself wondering, not for the first time that morning, why he hadn't just stayed in bed. And then a shiver that had nothing to do with the weather crawled down his spine as he saw one of the Dagda's óglach striding down the path with a harrow hound loping along at his side.

It took a supreme effort of will not to just drop the sheepskin-wrapped bundle he carried and bolt for the nearest stand of trees as the massive beast dragged its handler in his direction. But it seemed that Eolas's veiling spell had effectively worked its small magic on Cavall's axe and—hopefully—on Ronan's own particular gifts, should his Fé decide to act up inopportunely. For the moment, it seemed the darklight remained content to stay quiescent beneath his skin.

"He's a handsome beast," Ronan said, standing rooted to the ground as the hound nosed at him, huffing great noisy breaths out of its huge wet nose.

"Yes," the óglach said. "She is."

"Ah." Ronan lifted a tentative hand to scratch behind the dog's ear. "Sorry, my lady. No offense meant . . ."

The óglach snorted in mild amusement. "Come on, Thorn, girl. Nothing for you to eat here."

As if to confirm that, the beast licked Ronan's knuckles, then stood and shook itself, massive head swinging up so that Ronan looked down into two liquid black pools staring up at him. He held his breath, waiting for the cursefire to suddenly kindle in the depths of the beast's gaze. But then they were gone, heading off toward the clusters of tents pitched in the field.

Ronan felt as though his knees had turned to a pair of boiled puddings. The veil he'd cast had held—clearly—but he really hadn't been expecting to test its efficacy in such close quarters. He wiped the sticky hound drool from the back of his hand and took a deep breath to steady his heartbeat.

"You," called a voice. "You're waiting for me?"

Ronan saw a young man walking toward him, cloak thrown back over his shoulders.

"You're Sakir?" Ronan asked. "The Scythian?"

"I don't know you," he said by way of answer.

"I'll take that as a yes," Ronan said. "You don't have to know me. I'm just a messenger."

"Then tell me your message and be gone."

"No." He shook his head. "It's not for you."

"But *that* is." Sakir the Scythian pointed to the roughly axe-shaped bundle in the crook of Ronan's arm.

"No . . ." Ronan held up the bundle and looked at it, one eyebrow raised. "I don't think this is, either. But I'll happily give both to their intended recipient: Princess Neve."

Ronan knew Sakir the Scythian hadn't told Cavall who he was making the axe for, but his guess was obviously the right one. The Horse Lord gazed at the upstart "messenger" through narrowed eyes.

"How—"

"I just know."

"And you have some kind of strange delusion that I'm actually going to let you anywhere near her." Sakir took a step toward him, casually shifting his cloak enough to reveal the axe at his own belt. "Interesting. Here's what I think—"

"She's in danger," Ronan said.

"Is that a threat?"

"That's what danger usually means, yes."

"You're either very foolish or—"

"You can stop right there." Ronan put up a hand, his tone gone flinty. "I thoroughly acknowledge my foolishness in being here. Happy to do so. Just get me to the princess." He took a calculated risk. "Before the spark becomes a fire that grows too big to snuff out."

From his expression, Ronan could tell Sakir knew exactly what he was talking about. Which meant he knew about Neve's sigil flame. The fact that he had clearly said nothing to the óglach about it meant that maybe he could be trusted. To what degree, Ronan didn't know. But it was better than nothing.

"Who are you?" Sakir asked.

"Like I said. I'm just the messenger."

"Do you have a name, messenger?"

"Ronan," he said, as a measure of good faith. "Of Blackwater Town."

"Follow me." He turned on his heel, headed toward the stables at a swift walk.

Ronan caught up with him in short order and they strode side by side through relatively deserted yards and walkways. He noticed that Sakir chose a route that would likely avoid any gatherings where he might to be called upon to explain the presence of a Fir Bolg outsider. Which Ronan clearly was, judging from the ragged hem of his cloak and his worn leather leggings. He was well aware that, to Tuatha Dé nobles, he probably looked like a bandit or an assassin for hire. The Scythian was probably regretting leading him into the heart of the palace compound, but Ronan hadn't really given him much choice.

Suddenly, Sakir fetched up short and stuttered to a stop. "Oh no . . ."

"What?" Ronan asked. "What's wrong?"

"Damn!"

Sakir ran to a fence enclosing what looked to be a small paddock behind stables and jumped up on the middle rung, scanning wildly before running into the stable and then back again.

"What are you doing?" Ronan called with increasing alarm as Sakir ran past him and shoved aside a curtain of ivy that had perfectly concealed what looked like an ancient door in the stone wall and thrust his way through. When he didn't reappear after a long moment, Ronan ducked his head through the archway to see the Scythian crouched and staring at the cold-hardened ground.

He swore and stood and turned in a circle, searching the horizon. Ronan knew it could only mean one thing.

"She's gone. Isn't she?"

"Her chariot, her horses—the ones my uncle gave her," Sakir spat, clearly upset. "She's the only one who uses them and she doesn't ride out without me. And in the time I've wasted with you, the sun has climbed just high enough over the hills to have melted any hoofprints or wheel tracks in the frost . . ."

In three strides, Sakir had pinned Ronan with a forearm to his throat before Ronan could lift a hand to defend himself. Not that he even tried.

"Where is she gone to?" Sakir snarled.

"Why in hell would you think I'd know?"

Sakir slammed Ronan's shoulders against the wall. "*You're* here and *she's* gone," he said. "After not having left the palace since her sister's death, this morning she decides to ride out alone and in defiance of her father. I find the timing suspect. Now I ask myself—why would Neve decide to leave Temair the very moment *you* arrive? What reason would she have to fear you?"

"I assure you," Ronan answered through clenched teeth against the increasing pressure on his windpipe, "I couldn't make that girl do something against her will if I tried. I'm not sure anyone can. And I can see that you are concerned about her well-being, so I'm going to pretend I didn't notice that your hands are still on me. Much, I imagine, in the same way that *you're* going to pretend there isn't a knife at your guts right now."

The blade pressing against Sakir's abdomen, just below his ribcage, with enough pressure to have likely pierced his tunic—although not his flesh, not yet—was anything but pretend.

"If you let go of me and step back a pace, we can both ignore these little indiscretions," Ronan continued. "Then you can tell me what the hell is going on and maybe we can try to find Neve together, before she gets herself in trouble. Which she likely already has."

Even with his blade, Ronan had no way of knowing how the Scythian would react. He waited patiently for him to decide.

After a long moment of stillness, Sakir took a step back and released Ronan. Ronan's mouth quirked, and he handed over the sheepskin-wrapped sagaris. Sakir let out a long breath and nodded at Ronan, who slid his dagger back into the sheath at his belt. Sakir glanced at the dagger and then frowned in recognition.

Ronan lifted a shoulder in a shrug. "She loaned it to me."

"None of my business," Sakir said, although it was fairly clear that he considered anything to do with Neve most definitely his business.

He shouldered Ronan aside and stalked back to the stable building to retrieve a bridle and saddle blanket. He stowed the axe bundle in a leather satchel and slung the strap over his torso.

"If you don't know where she's gone, how do you propose to find her?" Ronan asked.

Sakir paused, clearly unwilling to admit that he didn't readily have an answer to that question. There were, Ronan knew, a multitude of directions in which Neve could have gone. Almost every road in the vicinity that could accommodate a chariot passed near or through Temair. When Sakir didn't—*couldn't*—answer, Ronan drew a breath, already regretting what he was about to say, but saying it anyway.

"That axe." He nodded at the travel satchel. "It's for her, isn't it? Forged to replace the one she, uh . . . lost. I couldn't help but notice it has an iron blade. Does the original?"

"What?"

"The axe. The one Neve—Princess Neve—lost. Is it made of iron, too?"

Sakir shook his head. "No. Bronze. I gave it to her. No iron at all."

A bit of luck. "Then I might be able to help," Ronan said. "But I can't do it here." If any part of that first axe had been forged of iron, it would disrupt any enchantment he could conjure. Bronze he could work with.

The Scythian's eyes narrowed and he ran a dour, appraising glance over Ronan head to toe and shook his head doubtfully. But he plucked a second bridle from a peg on the stable wall and held it out to him. "Can you ride a horse?"

"Usually only if I've stolen it first," Ronan muttered, eyeing the proffered tack. He reached out to take the bridle from Sakir, who gestured to a stall occupied by a cloudy-gray gelding and slid the latch back on another that held a leggy black mare.

"Let's go, then."

Ronan slipped the bridle over the gray's head. "You said you didn't know where she's gone," he grunted.

Sakir was already mounted and ready. "You said you did. Let's go."

Ronan took the lead and they rode out at a gallop, heading north. It wasn't long before they'd crossed An Bhóinn and circled west of the Dagda's mortuary temple. Ronan kept his gaze fixed firmly between his horse's ears, avoiding looking too long at the dome of stone and sod that was still, even that close to Midwinter, a shocking hue of vibrant green. It was unnatural, Ronan thought. As if the place gave off its own warmth that kept the grass growing meadow-bright. Soon enough, they'd reached the trees and the hidden path that led to the sacred spring that cascaded down rocks into a dark blue pool. Ronan slid from the back of his mount at the edge of the clearing and tethered him.

"Why are we here?" Sakir asked. "Where's Neve? You—"

"I don't know. Yet."

The Scythian was off his horse with his axe in his hand in the blink of an eye. "Don't try my patience, Blackwater—"

"And *don't* put your hand on me again." Ronan's own hand shot out and twisted Sakir's free hand behind his back, yanking it upward. Hard. "I'm not some Fir Bolg peasant you can threaten with your fine, fancy blade, Scythian."

"What are you then?" Sakir asked through clenched teeth.

"When I figure that out, maybe I'll let you know. In the meantime, let's not try each *other's* patience." He let go of Sakir and shoved him away to arm's length.

"What are we doing here?" Sakir asked again.

"I think I can find her." Ronan walked toward the gently murmuring spring. "I just need a little help. A spell."

"Magic is outlawed in Eire, Fir Bolg. Especially this close to Temair," Sakir said, following. "You should know that—"

"Yes, *of course* I know that, Scythian," Ronan snapped in irritation. "Whose magic do you think it was in the first place? And the Dagda outlawed it for most, yes. Not for me. Not exactly . . ."

Sakir narrowed his eyes as he looked at him, nostrils flaring as if he could sniff out the lies Ronan was about to tell. "What are you . . . a Druid?"

"Ex." Ronan shrugged. "Apprentice. That's *all* I am. And before you ask—no, they didn't kick me out of the Order."

"Why don't I believe you?" Sakir asked. "About either thing?"

"Because there's a chance you might not be a complete idiot," Ronan murmured, retrieving the silver spell coin he'd used to veil Cavall's axe from his belt pouch. "Do you want to find our princess or not?"

Sakir nodded warily.

"Then hold this." He handed Sakir the coin. "Stand back. And . . . I don't know." Ronan waved him away. "Just stand back." He unclasped his cloak and tossed it aside, along with the dagger he wore on his belt. And then he stripped off the shirt he wore, laying it on top of the pile.

"I tend to ruin tunics," he explained. "This could get a bit wet, and I've only got the one after . . . never mind."

Sakir took a few careful steps backward with an expression of extreme skepticism. Ronan ignored him and closed his eyes, letting his awareness sink into himself, and into the clearing and into the traces of magic that still clung to the place like frost or cobwebs or starlight. In the coursing of the blood through his veins, and in the beating of his heart. Especially that. It wasn't just the water in the wellspring that spoke to him. It was the weapon. Because it was *hers*. He needed to find Neve. To tell her . . .

Stop.

Time enough for that once he'd retrieved it, he thought. First things first.

One thing at a time, Ronan . . .

He glanced back over his shoulder at Sakir. "When I told you I was an ex-Druid?"

"You said apprentice."

"Yes. Well . . . just assume that this is something I learned in the Order."

Ronan dropped to one knee and plunged his hand into the spring. In the blink of an eye, the darkling marks appeared, blooming up from beneath his skin and clawing their way up Ronan's arm, snaking in spirals past his still-healing shoulder wound and spreading across his chest and down his torso. The indigo darkness billowed in clouds from his fingertips out into the crystalline water of the pool, and the glassy surface began to heave and writhe. A thick, shimmering mist rose up and piled in drifts all around Ronan where he knelt, shushing and whispering softly, seductively . . .

Each time Ronan tapped into the power inside himself, it was easier. And so much harder to come back from. And each time, the water whispered more secrets to him. This time, when he looked deeply, he saw her face reflected. Neve. Only . . . no. Her eyes were different. Brown, not gold. And her face was thinner, brows arched higher . . . and she was drowning. Screaming soundlessly as water poured down her throat—

"What in the name of Light—"

That was as far as Sakir got before a geyser exploded from the pond, a column of silvery un-light bursting skyward, twisting like a living entity to wrap itself around Ronan. Instead of fighting it—like he'd done the last time, with Neve—Ronan shoved aside the fear and leaned into the water's embrace, reaching his arms out wide and letting the transformative power flow through him. It was as if he and the sacred spring were one.

Ronan stretched out his hands and saw that his skin rippled with a silver sheen, and his fingers grew longer, taloned and webbed. He could *feel* his eyes turn black, his pupils widening impossibly to take in the smallest detail of the world around him. He knew that if he inhaled in that moment, he could breathe in the water that cocooned him without drowning . . .

She couldn't. Úna . . .

The image of Neve's sister, water wrapping around her face like a scarf, pouring down her throat, swam up before his eyes again. Was *that* what had happened to her? Was that what Neve thought he'd done? He imagined what he'd looked like to her the night she'd found Úna . . . when he'd first fully manifested as Fé Fíada . . .

No. I didn't . . .

He could breathe water if he wanted to, right then. He held his breath instead. To do otherwise would mean wholly becoming something he wasn't sure he was ready for. Something he'd only ever read about in forbidden Druid lore. He concentrated, instead, on reaching down into the pool and wrapping a fist of water around the weapon, working it free from a rock fissure and lifting it up . . .

Gently . . .

Inside Ronan's head, the whispering of the water, enveloping Neve's sagaris, grew to a roaring.

There!

The axe shot out of the pool, arcing high above the water. Liquid tendrils grasped at it like fingers, flailed, and then flew apart, raining back down into the spring in a shower of droplets. The sagaris plummeted back toward the pool, but Ronan hadn't the strength left to catch it.

"*No—*"

Sakir lunged past him and stretched out his hand, snatching the spinning bronze axe out of the air, saving it from being lost in the depths of the spring once more.

Ronan collapsed to his knees, his dark hair curtaining his face, as the spring water sloughed off his body. He stayed there for a long moment, reckoning with the reflection that stared up at him. The last time he'd looked into those eyes it had been under cover of night and moonlight, but now, beneath the light of the sun, he could see—truly *see*—what he'd become. What he *was*. Silver-skinned and black-eyed, feral and angular, sleek . . . the darklight sigils still moving, liquid beneath his skin.

After a long moment, the transformation began to fade.

He sat back on his haunches and reached for his shirt, rubbing it over his face and arms like a towel, and then glanced over at his Scythian companion.

Sakir stood there, holding Neve's axe in one hand. "What was *that*?" he demanded.

"That was nothing." Ronan bent over the pool and, cupping his hands, drank from the spring. The water was ice cold—but it was just water—and it helped to douse the fire burning in his chest. The blood in his veins felt still like venom, coursing just beneath his skin, but that, too, was fading. "Just a bit of Druid conjuring . . . that's all. Gods," he muttered, still a bit astonished at how he'd been able to *will* the spring water to do his bidding. "That would have made thieving so much easier, had I known."

The sigils had fully faded by the time he climbed back to his feet, wobbling a bit.

Sakir put out his free hand to steady him, but his gaze was hard. "How did you know this was down there?" he asked, hefting the axe.

Ronan shrugged out of his grip and shook the wet hair out of his face. "I knew because the last time I saw Neve, I was standing right here, and she threw it at my head. She missed. Barely."

"And why did she do that?"

Ronan stared down into the dark, cold mirror of the sacred spring. His reflection stared back at him, rippling and distorted and strange. "Well, for one thing, I'm fairly certain she thinks I killed her sister."

"Did you?" Sakir asked, his voice low, dangerous.

"I... don't know," Ronan said. "I'm not exactly myself when... I change, and it makes it hard to remember. I might have. If I did, I would dearly wish to know why."

To Sakir's credit, he didn't just outright bury the axe in Ronan's chest.

"May I see that?" Ronan asked, gesturing to it.

Sakir handed over the weapon with the kind of unconscious flourish that spoke of his intimate familiarity with such a weapon. Ronan reminded himself silently to stay on the Scythian's good side—as much as that was even possible.

"And the coin?" he asked.

The pale winter sun held little warmth that day, but it was still able to spark fire from the inscribed surface of the little silver disk as Sakir dropped it into Ronan's palm. He flipped it over to see that the other side—the one with the veiling spell he'd used earlier—was duller, almost tarnished-looking, its power depleted. He flipped it back over to the shiny side and held it in a cage of his fingers, Neve's sagaris gripped in his other fist.

Before he'd reencountered the Tuatha Dé princess, Ronan wouldn't have even considered what he was about to attempt possible. But ever since she had reentered his life, all of the knowledge he'd stored up in his young, thirsty mind from those early Druid apprentice days had begun to bubble up. The existence he'd assumed would always be stagnant—a thief, a peasant, a nobody—had fallen away. He felt like the young boy in the barrow again. Fearless, dauntless, willing to dare for things that mattered.

She mattered.

Even if she hated him. Even if she had cause to.

He could—he *would*—find her.

Employed in a straightforward manner, the spell on the coin could find, say, a lost axe. Like the one he held in his hand. But Ronan thought he could manipulate the spell, delve deeper into the workings so that it would find not the object, but its owner. This spellwork could only—*maybe*—work with a person who had a soul-deep connection to said object. It was a gamble, but the connection between Neve and a sharp thing she'd tried to kill him with . . . good enough.

He felt the axe handle grow warm in his hand.

He closed his eyes and clearly pictured the young woman holding it.

A figure, cloaked, hooded, turning toward him and pushing the cowl back away from her face to reveal . . . a mask. Golden, in the shape of a wolf. The lupine visage stared at him with equally golden eyes. The face behind the mask he knew all too well, framed with waves of dark hair blowing in a stiff salt breeze. He looked past her—over Neve's shoulder—and saw the sea at her back. But the perspective confused him for a moment. The lines of waves, breakers rolling endlessly landward, were very far away . . . and below. Far below. But there was also water nearby, fresh, not salt . . . Not sea, not even a lake, really. More like a glorified pond. He could see it. A circle of water, split by a causeway leading to a *crannog*—a small, round stone fort—in the middle. All of it situated on the plateau of a commanding promontory, soaring precipices dropping straight down into the crashing surf of a grim gray sea—

"I know where that is!" Sakir exclaimed. "An Bhinn Mhór— the Great Cliff. I went there once with my uncle when I was a boy. Less than two days' fast ride due north from here. We might even catch her on the way if we hurry."

Ronan hadn't been aware he'd been describing the place out loud. The coin in his hand was blackened, both sides now. He flipped it with his thumb into the sacred pool with a whisper of thanks for the added strength the waters had granted him. As the Scythian charioteer went to fetch their horses, Ronan glanced back into the pool, and faint stirrings of his own augury showed him an image of Neve again, only standing on the deck of her chariot, driving hard.

Chased by pale, ghostly apparitions.

XXIII

NEVE HAD HIDDEN around a corner of the stable wall, cloaked in deep-blue early-morning shadows, as one of the gate guards hailed Sakir and told him of a messenger from Blackwater waiting at the main gate. Her heart lurched a bit, wondering if it was the delivery of her new sagaris—and wondering if she could wait one more day to find out.

She couldn't. Not after last night with the council meeting. With Gofannon.

So she'd risen, dressed, and was out in the stable yard with her bow and a traveling pack before the sun was up or Emer was even close to shaking herself loose from the deep dreams that had kept her tossing and muttering throughout the night.

The last thing Neve had done before leaving was to find the silver cuff she'd had made for Emer—the one with the symbol of a freedwoman of Temair inscribed on it—and placed it on the low table beside Emer's cot. Neve had planned to give it to her, along with the freedom it conveyed, on Úna's wedding day, but the aftermath of her death had overtaken them. Emer, she knew, would understand what it meant upon waking.

Unfortunately, Neve wasn't the only early riser in the palace that day.

"Neve?"

She turned to see Lorcan striding across the small empty stable yard and her heart sank. "Just going for a walk," she said.

"I see. With a traveling pack . . ." His eyes flicked to the leather satchel over her shoulder, then to her other shoulder. "And a bow . . ." Then to her hip. "And a sword."

Neve smiled sweetly at him. "I misplaced my axe."

He crossed his arms over his chest, muscles bulging. Years of soldiering had definitely changed him. She tightened her grip on the hilt of her sword. His gaze never wavered from her face, but she could tell he'd registered the movement.

"Please don't try to stop me, Lorcan."

"I wasn't going to stop you. I *was* going to open the main gate for you." He nodded at the secret portal behind her, where she'd already pushed the ivy screen to the side. "I guess I should have known that you of all people wouldn't need help escaping this place. You always won our games of hide-and-find."

"You're helping me?"

He shrugged a shoulder and his armor creaked. "You made quite an impression among the noble lords in the Great Hall last night."

"Nothing they wanted to hear, I'm sure."

"Everything they needed to hear, if you ask me." He glanced back toward where the palace slumbered in the predawn light.

"We both know there's a storm brewing on the horizon, Neve. Úna's death, the Faoladh returning, the increased raids and threats of war—it's all connected." He shook his head. "The Dagda is . . . distracted. He cannot—or will not—see what is happening right in front of him and I think *you* might be our best hope to deal with that storm, whatever it becomes, when it hits."

She looked at him sideways. "You really think that?"

"I think it would be a mistake to underestimate you." He grinned ruefully. "To be fair, I've thought that since you knocked my tooth out."

"I guess I owe you an apology for that."

"Saving my life in that skirmish at Brú na Bóinne makes up for it, I think."

"I don't know what you're—"

"Don't bother denying it, Neve. I know it was you." He shook his head. "Even with that silly helmet on. Sakir doesn't ride out with anyone else in his chariot. Ever."

Neve felt her face go red, as if they were children still and Lorcan had caught her stealing cakes from the kitchen.

"I also saw what happened *after*," Lorcan continued. "The whole warband owes you that victory for taking out that spell caster. Even if they don't know it. And I'm truly sorry for all those times I told you girls can't fight. *You* can fight. You can *win*. And I'll be there to help you when you do."

Neve felt her throat tighten. "You would have been the Dagda if my sister had lived," she said. "You would have been worthy."

"The 'Good God,'" he mused. "I was never comfortable with that title. But I also know it would have been Úna, not me, who would have worn the cloak of its power. I was fine with that. I don't want the throne. I never did. I only ever wanted her. And she wanted what was best for Temair, I think. Truly." He cocked his head to the side, looking at her. "What do *you* want?"

"I want what's best for Eire," Neve said. "*All* of it. Tuatha Dé and Fir Bolg alike."

He nodded, satisfied with that answer. "Where are you going?"

"North," she said, with a groan of reluctance. "To An Bhinn Mhór."

"Ah." Lorcan nodded again. "I understand."

Having known her all her life, he would.

"Ha." Neve shook her head. "I hope *she* does."

"I'm sure, at least, it will be a great comfort to Queen Anann to see you again," Lorcan said in a stilted tone.

"No, it won't be. But it's all right." Neve smiled wanly. "I don't need my mother. I need answers. And Eire needs her queen."

He looked at her, unblinking. "She does at that."

Neve turned and went inside the barn, where she'd already yoked the matched pair of silver-white horses Cormac had gifted her to her chariot. She led them through the gate and out into the overgrown field beyond, slung her traveling pack onto the chariot floor, and secured her bow to the side rail, where there was a hol-ster with a leather tie-down.

Then she turned back to Lorcan. "Thank you."

"What will you do when you get there?" Lorcan asked.

"I don't exactly know. Yet. But I will . . ."

What Neve *did* know was that there was a driving instinct deep inside her, guiding her actions, helping her, and she was starting to rely on its counsel. The only problem was, she was starting to wonder just who, exactly, that instinct belonged to. Her father's words came back to her from the night after the Stone Singing, when she and Úna had stood in his chamber.

"*You want to be like the Scathach? Is* that *what you want? You want to crack the Lia Fail to dust with your reckless will?*"

As the Dagda's fury echoed in her mind, two things occurred to her. Ruad Rofhessa was afraid of the Lia Fail. Therefore the Lia Fail must still exist. Somewhere, somehow, contrary to what Gofannon had just told her the night before.

A spark of hope rekindled in Neve's heart.

"Pick up the track that leads due north," Lorcan said. "Then take the trader road curving east before crossing An Bhóinn."

Neve frowned. "That route will add almost a half day of travel."

"Aye. But that way you'll avoid traversing the boglands. They're nothing but marsh-wights to lead you astray with pretty lights and treacherous pathways through sloughs that can swallow whole caravans without a trace."

"Duly noted." She grinned. "The trader road it is. I'm not *that* desperate to see my mother."

She pulled her hood close around her face and slapped the reins. The landscape rolled away in front of her, cresting in waves of gray and green into the purple-hilled distance. Neve crouched down lower over the front rail of the chariot, calling to the horses, and they surged down the road at a gallop, leaving a cloud of glittering frost in her chariot wake.

NEVE DROVE NEARLY without stopping as a bleached-white sun transited overhead. The days were so short at that time of year, but she still would have had a good few hours of daylight left were it not for the overcast that had grown thicker and bleaker as she'd traveled north. With the sky a dusky purple and her horses wreathed in steam and smoky breath, she looked for a place to hunker down until the morrow.

A thin tendril of smoke rising in a lazy spiral drifted above the trees ahead as she passed a stone marker on the roadside crudely carved with the symbol of a bruidean. Neve turned off the trader track and followed a short winding path that led to a clearing with a sod-roofed hovel, barely more than a cattle byre. A pale skinny lad loped out to take her horses by the bridle and lead her chariot around back to a lean-to structure that served as stalls for travelers with horses. It was clear that they didn't get many of those—the thing could barely accommodate two beasts and the boy was flummoxed by the chariot harnesses—so Neve dropped a coin in his palm and told him to go stoke the fire inside instead and tell his master to open the good beer. She could handle the horses herself. When the boy didn't move right away, she turned back to find him staring down at the silver in his hand, jaw hanging. She grinned at him and folded his fingers closed over it. He ducked his head wordlessly in thanks and scuttled off.

Neve went to work on the traces, her muscles protesting after so long standing on the deck of the chariot, but froze when one of her horses whickered low—a warning sound—and the other stamped a hoof and flicked his ears forward. Neve listened and heard it, too. Hoofbeats. Voices.

Men. Not traders—not gruff enough—and not óglach. Not enough ring and creak of armor. She shushed her horses and made her way to the side of the bruidean, peering around cautiously. There were men there on horseback. Druids. Three of them, in their pale hooded robes. She almost would have preferred óglach.

They bore no weapons beyond the bronze daggers at their belts, but Neve suspected they didn't need them. She'd begun to feel something as she rode throughout the day, farther and farther from Temair and Brú na Bóinne. In places, here and there, a certain shivering in the air . . . the glimmering off pools and waterfalls that was more than just sun-sparkle . . . the whispers beneath trees that were more than just wind . . . Maybe wild magic still thrived in the remoter places in the land. The thought both thrilled and terrified her. She much preferred the Druids to have limited access to that kind of power. Especially if they were looking to use it on her.

"A woman," one of them was saying. "Driving a chariot with a pair of matched horses. Pale, like silver."

It occurred to Neve belatedly that, if she'd been thinking, she could have ridden out on any one of the other horses in the Dagda's stables. The dun mare or the chestnut gelding. Something a little less conspicuous than the matched silver pair of chariot ponies and the fast, light war chariot they pulled.

"He doesn't know what silver is," said his companion. "Look at the poor fool."

From where she hid, Neve reached into her belt pouch and fished out another silver coin, holding it up so the lad could see it, and put a finger to her lips. The boy's expression never wavered. He didn't look directly at her. He just nodded at the Druids and stood holding out his hand, which they ignored.

"I'll wager he still knows what a woman is," the first Druid said.

"In a place like this?" scoffed the second.

The third made a crude joke about she-goats that made his fellows laugh as they dismounted and carelessly tossed their horses' reins at the lad.

"If you see her, you will keep her here and tell us immediately. Understand?"

Neve held her breath.

The lad nodded again, meekly. The trio of Druids shouldered past him, throwing up clots of mud from their boots as they stomped toward the little bruidean. The boy waited for a few long moments after the wooden door had banged shut, then led their horses back around to where Neve waited with her own.

"Why are they hunting you?" he asked, head tilting to one side as he regarded her.

Neve hesitated. From her chariot alone, it was obvious she was highborn, likely from Temair, probably Tuatha Dé. She had money. Did she dare gamble that was enough to buy his silence? Or would he betray her presence if he thought the Druids would offer him a greater reward than she could?

A dark whisper reminded her she also had a quiver full of arrows that she could set aflame with a thought. The image of the stable boy lying on the ground with a still-smoldering shaft protruding from the center of his bony chest flashed through her mind and she squeezed her eyes shut. She took the gamble instead.

"They are hunting me because they fear me," Neve whispered. "Because I am going to try to become the new Dagda."

"One day soon?"

She nodded. "Maybe."

He seemed to consider this. "Will you have to fight?"

She nodded again.

"Will you win?"

Oh, yes . . .

"I will."

That seemed to satisfy him. "I'd like to say I've done a service for the Dagda."

She grinned and held the coin out. "For your loyalty."

"I don't need no more silver, lady. Got nothing to spend it on here." He grinned at her and shrugged. "Sending those bastards goose hunting is payment enough. I can wait awhile and then go tell 'em you arrived, all right, and headed direct back to the trade road when you saw their horses."

"I would be in your debt." She put a hand on his shoulder. "Please, if you won't take silver, take these."

Neve emptied her purse of coppers into his palm. He nodded in thanks and pointed to a barely discernible path beneath a tunnel formed by curved fir boughs woven together so thick overhead the path disappeared into a midnight of shadows.

"There's a track the woodsmen use. It's narrow, and twisty, but it's fair flat and hard-packed. Your cartwheels should ne' have trouble on it. Comes out in the marshes on the other side. There's those there that can help you further. Maybe. It's not the safest . . ."

"Nothing is these days," she said, stepping up onto the chariot deck.

Neve drove the woodman track at breakneck speed—one misstep by the horses or a fallen branch and she would turn her chariot into kindling. But with the sun sinking into the west, bleeding red fire through the trees, Neve didn't have much choice.

There is no other choice, she thought. This is the only way.

The fact that Gofannon had loosed his Druids on her trail told her, without doubt, she was doing the right thing. He was afraid of what she might do, or what she might discover. He was afraid of her.

He should be.

She raced on, heading north and west until the sun had set and the swift cloak of night overtook her. She could only hope the bruidean lad had been convincing. And that, even if the Druids had discovered his duplicity, it was too dark now for them to do anything about it. When not even her horses could see to go on, she pulled the chariot as far off the track as she could, into a tiny clearing offering a scant bit of shelter from the bitter wind. She picketed the horses on a line she strung between two trees, working their harness fastenings free with numb cold fingers, and wrapped herself in her cloak, sinking down into a deep drift of fallen leaves beneath a rock shelf.

"Finally," Neve said wryly, as she struggled to keep her teeth from chattering. "Glorious freedom from the confines of the palace."

The absurdity of the situation was damned near comical, she thought. The most autonomy she'd ever experienced, and here she was, a fugitive in almost every sense. Running from her father, his Druids, her fate, her *heart* . . . It might have been that last one that cut the deepest. She thought about how it had felt to kiss Ronan. Like finding a missing piece of herself. What was it going to feel like, she wondered, when the moment came when she had to deliver Ronan and that piece of herself over to the Faoladh? And then watch as they destroyed her thief, spilling his lifeblood so that they could become warriors and she could become a king. She would have to carry that with her for the rest of *her* life.

A king bears the weight of every subject's death upon his back. That is what it means to be king.

Neve couldn't argue with that. She just wasn't sure she was supposed to be the *cause* of those deaths. The lines on the palm of her hand tingled and she reached into her cloak. In the blackness of the night-bound forest, the only light was the faint golden gleam of the three-pointed sigil on her hand. A wolf-shaped flame, shining through the eyes of the wolf mask she now held up in front of her face.

She could still feel the moment when Ronan had reached for her, with a touch that had somehow ignited fire beneath her skin . . . Her throat ached—as if remembering the tears she'd told him, as a girl, she would not ever shed—and a rogue wave of loneliness crashed over her.

Loneliness is weakness, whispered the voice in her head that had become her near-constant companion. *Do not give in to it. How will you conquer with no stomach for hardship? For sacrifice?*

"I'm not looking to conquer anyone," she said, gazing into the wolf's golden eyes. "Only to protect my own."

That's what all good conquerors say. In the beginning . . .

The mask seemed to grin as the light from her sigil began to fade. Neve tucked it back into her pocket, pausing for a moment when her fingers brushed the iron knife and stone shard she'd found in her garden. She'd forgotten she'd stuffed them into her pocket after her conversation with Gofannon. She curled into a ball on the hard ground.

⁕

AFTER A FITFUL night of dozing only to wake with every snapping twig, Neve wolfed down a few strips of dried meat and half a lavender cake—provisions that she'd pilfered from the kitchen stores— and hitched the horses back up. Every muscle and joint ached and she longed to sink into her copper tub back at the palace.

The sun was barely above the horizon when Neve reached the edge of the thick woods where the trees gave way to scrub and then the marshes Lorcan and the boy at the bruidean had told her of, cut through by a broad river flowing sluggishly through the boggy fens. Neve could see a river crossing where a perilously rickety barge was tethered and tended to by a bent-backed old man in a seal-skin cowl. He lifted his head as she approached, and Neve could see by his milky-white eyes that he was entirely blind. But his ear twitched in her direction and his nose wrinkled and he said, before she'd even opened her mouth, "Two horse, a cart—wicker and narrow—and one . . . boy. No—girl. Alone, eh? You know where you're headed?"

Neve blinked at him, bemused. "I know well enough."

He snorted, spat, and held out his hand. "Crossing'll cost you three coins in gold—one for each beating heart—and a silver for the cart."

She paid the man and stepped down to let him lead her horses onto the barge.

"You'll want to head due north," the ferryman said, even though she hadn't told him her planned destination. "If you find yourself lost, follow the hooded crow if one appears. Don't look for lights in the trees, don't listen for music from the streams."

"Thank you," Neve said, pressing an extra coin into the old man's calloused palm.

But he gave it back, telling her, "Give thanks to the goddess Macha when you see her. For it was she who told me to tell you."

Macha? He must think I'm Fir Bolg, Neve thought.

As the old man cast off, he suddenly cocked his head. "Who follows?"

Neve's stomach knotted in fear.

"Horses . . . men . . . three of each . . . Huh." The old man sniffed at the air. "They smell of barrows and carrion. Magic eaters, are they?"

"Child!" one of the Druids called out from the riverbank. "You would do well to cross back over. We are no threat to you."

Neve's hand went to the place where her axe should have been on her hip. "Old father, I—"

"Don't you worry, lass," the ferryman said, white-eyed gaze roaming an unseen landscape ahead. "I've no burning inclination to turn back. I smell no silver on them. Hear no gold. And they can't cross if my barge is on the other side."

Neve clutched the splintery rail, leaning toward the far bank as if she could urge the barge faster by sheer will. "Where's the nearest ford?"

"Halfway between here and the coast."

She exhaled. A full morning's ride. They would never catch her.

The barge thumped against the landing on the far bank and Neve almost cheered as she mounted the chariot and urged the horses down the driftwood causeway. But when she glanced back over her shoulder, she saw the three Druids had dismounted and were walking to the river's edge.

Together, they crouched down in the reeds and, even from where she was, Neve could hear a thrum ripple through the air as they began to chant. The surface of the river began to churn with wild magic, called by Druid voices.

Water-wights.

The ancient ferryman suddenly swung his barge pole up and across, cracking the spiny back of the first creature to heave itself up onto the barge deck. A second followed hard behind, a mouth full of ragged eel teeth bared in a hideous grimace. It lunged for the ferryman.

"Old father!" Neve screamed as the creature snapped its teeth shut on the old man's throat and took him over the rail into the water.

More creatures scrabbled and clawed at the barge itself, dragging it away from shore, back toward the other side. Shaking from the swiftness of the old man's demise, Neve reached for her bow.

She drew an arrow from her quiver, hands sweat-slick upon bow and string as she drew back toward her ear, sighted down the arrow shaft, and loosed. But unlike at Brú na Bóinne during the raid, this time there was no spark from her sigil that ignited her arrow. The missile struck one of the wights and it screeched and thrashed and sank beneath the surface. But the other monsters kept on, dragging the barge farther into the center of the river. Neve shot another arrow and another with the same results. Fire would have helped immensely, but her sigil flame refused to flare to life.

"Fair enough," she murmured through clenched teeth. "I'll do it myself . . ."

There was a leather oilskin hanging from the barge's center post that the old man would have used to fill the little lanterns hanging from the bow and stern. She aimed at the oilskin and loosed, her shot tearing a gash in it and sending oil spilling out onto the deck of the barge. Then she drew another arrow and aimed at the stern lantern. It fell to the deck, shattering and sending sparks flying. The barge burst into roiling flame, like a funeral pyre afloat in the middle of the river, shrouded in crimson fire and black smoke.

The water-wights screamed in fear and pain and disappeared, abandoning the burning craft to its fate. Neve holstered her bow and slapped the reins, urging her horses to a gallop. Behind her, angry shouts from the thwarted Druids and the hideous shrieks of water-wights faded into the mist like a nightmare before the light of dawn.

XXIV

RONAN FELT AS if they'd crossed over the borders of the Otherworld. The landscape of Eire's northern reaches was a blur of mists and moors, green and purple heather that looked as though it had yet to feel the touch of winter's chill, even that late in the season. Stardust points of light glimmered, beckoning and mischievous, in the hollows of the hills.

Magic . . .

Ronan and Sakir had forded a river in the barely shimmering light of dawn—Sakir having to swim the horses across in lieu of a ferry crossing—after a night of terrible sleep in an abandoned hunting shelter, and now they were here. The land was brimming with wild magic, Ronan realized. He kept his eyes fixed on the back of Sakir's head to avoid straying off the path, led by whispers of faint, seductive song, into the bogs, where he and his horse would be lost as if they'd never been—

"There!" Sakir suddenly shouted, a gust of wind snatching the word from his mouth. He thrust out an arm, pointing directly ahead, as they crested a low, rocky rise.

An Bhinn Mhór. The Great Cliff.

The plateau before them formed the curve of a promontory—like the prow of a giant's ship—that jutted out into the Northern Sea and then abruptly fell away into deep and fathomless blue.

Ronan could hear the crashing of the waves beyond, a sonorous rhythmic booming he could feel marrow deep in his bones. He could only imagine what the soaring cliffs looked like to someone in a ship on the sea—a majestic, foreboding headland that was the highest northern point of the whole island. The rolling terrain was dotted with gorse and stands of trees twisted by the salt wind, and in the middle of the plateau a small, slate-blue lake lay, like a mirror with a broken edge set down upon a ragged cushion. In the center of the lake, there was an island. Built there long ago by the hands of men, stones piled upon stones to form a crannog—a tiny fortress, accessed by a single causeway—with a neat sod-roofed *broch*: a roundhouse complete with a paddock occupied by a pair of goats and a single horse grazing on scrub grass. A wind-raveled skein of smoke rose from the hole at the center of the broch's roof. Someone was home.

"There she is!" Sakir pointed below and to the right of them, toward a shallow crevasse half hidden by a stand of scrubby trees, where a pair of silvery horses were running flat out, pulling a chariot behind them. "She's in trouble . . ."

"Of course she is," Ronan said.

Cloak and dark hair streaming behind her, Neve was bent low over the front rail of her chariot, slapping the reins, urging on the horses, which were already galloping madly. Ronan put a hand up to shade his eyes from the sun and scanned the terrain. Three riders, pale robes flapping like the wings of hunting owls, were closing fast on Neve from both sides and behind.

Ronan went cold. "Druids." He spat the word like a curse.

He and Sakir put their heels to their horses.

Ronan angled his toward the nearest Druid closing on Neve's left flank, drawing the iron dagger from its sheath that Neve had given him. He wasn't above appreciating the irony of that: his only weapon was a blade the Druid Order would have never let him carry, which had once belonged to the princess they now hunted like prey.

Ronan's own quarry was so focused on catching up with Neve that he didn't notice the thief pulling neck and neck with his own mount, but Neve's eyes went wide at the sight of him charging up. She ducked as the Druid pulled a long bronze dagger from his belt and slashed at her. There was no way for her to defend herself or fight back. She couldn't let go of the reins. As the Druid raised his dagger high, Ronan hauled on the reins of his horse, crashing his mount into the Druid's, and thrust his own blade between the priest's exposed ribs. The man screamed, clawing at the blade as he fell from his horse and tumbled beneath the wheels of Neve's chariot.

"What are you *doing* here?" Neve shouted at him. The daggers that flew from her eyes were near as lethal as the bloodied blade in his fist.

"You're welcome!" he shouted back. "Head for the causeway! We've got these bastards . . ."

Neve didn't argue. She slapped the reins again and her chariot surged ahead of him. Ronan glanced over to see Sakir dispatch his own target with an acrobatic leap onto the man's horse. He broke the Druid's neck with a wrenching heave before throwing him to the ground and taking up the reins of his mount. It gave Ronan an instant appreciation for Scythian horsemanship. But any sense of triumph was short-lived. The last Druid—clearly the canniest—had dropped back from the chase when Sakir and Ronan appeared, and now switched tactics.

As Neve peeled right, thundering toward the narrow stone bridge on the eastern edge of the lake, the Druid galloped—not toward the bridge but to the southern shore of the water. His horse nearly threw him over its head when it came to a sudden, bucking stop at the edge of the reeds, and Ronan knew there was something in that water that the animal was afraid of. Not just afraid of, deathly terrified by—and it was something only a Druid could wake. And only in a place where the magic still flowed through the land as blood through veins. Like the magic coursing beneath Ronan's own skin. He could feel it but he still didn't know how to use it—not without doing more harm than good—and he nearly screamed at the cruel frustration.

He didn't have time.

Whatever spells the priests of the Order had equipped themselves with on their mission to find the Dagda's daughter, they'd been either very lucky . . . or very knowledgeable. Ronan suspected the latter. There was lore in the archives that would have told them of this place. Its secrets. Its magic.

Its monsters . . .

The Druid's chanting, even from that distance, was like thunder in Ronan's ears. His own horse reared, lashing out with his hooves as the surface of the lake suddenly erupted like a geyser.

A serpentine creature, the length of a trade ship, rose thrashing from the brackish depths, its lidless amber eyes burning with ancient anger. Lightning crackled along the surface of skin the color of decay, coated in thick green-black lichen, draped in slimy weeds torn from the lakebed and hanging from its sinewy neck like a mane. Its mouth was wide enough to swallow a man whole, and it clawed at the air with talons like cauldron hooks.

"Beithir-Nimh!" Ronan shouted in warning. "Storm serpent!"

He'd heard of this creature. Read of it. Thought that—like the gods he refused to believe in—it was nothing more than a myth. When time and tide permitted, Ronan thought, he was clearly going to have to reexamine a few of his long-held beliefs.

The serpent's tail whipped in a great arc, slamming down onto the causeway, throwing stones into the air. Neve yelped in alarm and crouched down low in her chariot, covering her head as rocks fell like rain all around her.

THE PORTAL GATE at the other end of the causeway stood open, but Neve couldn't see anyone in the enclosure of the crannog beyond. Her chariot had just reached the foot of the causeway when the waters of the lake began to ripple, and her horses stuttered to a stop, snorting and stamping, eyes rolling white.

More water-wights? she thought, reaching over her shoulder to pull an arrow from her quiver. She nocked and sighted, pulling the bowstring back beside her ear with the fluid, continuous motion Sakir had drilled into her, sweeping for her target . . .

And then a monster rose up before her.

Startled, she loosed her shot. The arrow split the air with a whine and hit its mark, sinking deep into the thing's eye socket. It writhed and whipped its head around, slamming it against the rocky shore to dislodge the missile. Neve's horses—Scythian-bred without fear—flattened their ears against their skulls, lips drawn back from their teeth. The serpent screamed a raucous challenge in return, thick black blood dripping unheeded down its face, and hammered its tail down on the causeway.

Neve ducked for cover and when she lifted her head again, it was to the sight of lightning bolts striking the ground all around the perimeter of the lake. Over the sounds of the creature roaring, she heard Ronan scream a warning and saw the last Druid had mounted his horse again and was riding hard toward her, cutting off her chance to turn back. Neve spat an oath, drew the bronze-bladed sword she carried in lieu of her sagaris, and snapped the reins, crying, "*Hyah!*"

The chariot surged forward, and so did the monster. One taloned foot grappled at the side of the cart. Neve slashed down with her blade and the creature's severed limb spun away out over the water. Suddenly, the way ahead was clear.

Neve shouted in triumph. Sakir shouted in warning. And Ronan shouted for them to get the hell out of harm's way. Together the three of them—Ronan and Sakir on horseback, Neve in her chariot—thundered across the causeway and through the stone arch to safety. At least, Neve's chariot did.

Neve herself flew backward off the cart deck as if she'd slammed into a solid, invisible wall, every muscle and nerve jolted with a shock of pain like she'd been hit by one of the lightning strikes. Her arrows spilled out from her quiver all around her, clattering on the stones of the causeway, but her bow lay on the deck of her chariot. On the *other* side of whatever unseen barrier she'd just hit. She didn't know where her sword was. Probably at the bottom of the lake.

The space between Neve and her chariot—and Ronan and Sakir, now safe in the little courtyard beyond—crackled and flared with uncanny fire. The magical barrier had let the two men through easily but seemed to think Neve was a threat—which, fair enough, the Druid and the dragon were targeting *her*, after all, not them— leaving Neve with absolutely nowhere to run. From the other end of the causeway, Beithir-Nimh surged toward her, howling and slathering, teeth and talons and oily black skin reflecting the blood-red rays of the sun setting behind the crannog.

But when Neve looked past the monstrous apparition, she saw the moon rising, shining like silver as it lifted above the horizon. And she smiled.

For she was still, in spite of everything else, Neve Anann Eriu, Beloved of the Wolf. She for whom the sun set and the moon rose . . .

Calmly, as if she had all the time in the world, Neve drew forth the golden wolf mask from her cloak and slipped it on over her face. The twilight sky shifted from red to gold and the fog of fear and rage cleared from her gaze. She lifted her hand to see the sigil on her palm was incandescent, gilded by the power that flowed through her.

At her feet, the scattered arrows began to rattle upon the stones of the causeway, before lifting up into the air and hovering around her, as if nocked and aimed by a whole battalion of ghost archers.

In the far distance, she could hear wolf song.

Neve's lips curled back in a feral snarl. With a thought, the arrowheads ignited, roaring to blazing life. Her dark hair lifted back from her face, and she shouted a war command in a language she didn't know.

And the flaming arrows flew.

⚬

RONAN WATCHED, HIS jaw hanging open as dozens of fiery missiles tore through the air and through Beithir-Nimh, drawing streamers of sooty black smoke from the storm serpent, who shrieked and climbed into the sky in a grotesque dance, twisting and writhing through the air only to fall back into the lake, which churned and spat bolts of lightning into the dusky air.

As Beithir-Nimh sank out of sight, clawing the air with ragged talons, the spell barrier that protected Queen Anann's island home shivered and dissipated. At the other end of the causeway, the Druid on his horse, realizing defeat, wheeled and galloped off into the deepening shadows. It was over in moments. The causeway empty, the lake still and serene . . .

"You told me you were the one who taught her how to fight," Ronan murmured to Sakir, standing at his side. "You teach her how to do *that?*"

Sakir shook his head, astonished, as Neve in her wolf mask staggered through the archway toward Ronan.

"He didn't teach me how to do this, either." She slammed her fist into the side of Ronan's head, knocking him unconscious.

XXV

NEVE STEPPED OVER Ronan's prone form and lurched a few steps before nearly collapsing herself. Sakir reached for her, half carrying her over to a wooden bench in the crannog's neat little courtyard. Wordlessly, Sakir settled Neve on the bench.

"You can tie the horses to the rail over there," Neve said by way of greeting, waving at a hitching rail between a goat pen and vegetable garden. "And him." Neve nodded at where Ronan lay on the ground. "Tie him to the rail, too."

Sakir paused. "He's the reason we came after you. He came to me with a warning. For you."

"And you believed him?"

"I'm here."

"That's not the same thing," she said, finally lifting the golden wolf visor off her face. "He's here, too, and I don't trust him. Tie him up, Sakir."

"Truthfully?" Sakir shrugged. "With pleasure."

He dragged the Fir Bolg thief by the cowl of his cloak across the yard and secured him by the wrists, arms stretched out wide, to the hitching rail. He was tying the last knot as Ronan started to come to and groaned in protest.

Even though the sun had set, there was still enough ambient light in the yard to see clearly, although Neve couldn't say for certain where it was coming from. It seemed warmer in the courtyard, too, the sea winds less biting, the air perfumed as if with unseen apple blossoms.

Sakir noticed it too. He raised an eyebrow at her and said, "Magic."

"Of course, there's magic here." A cloaked figure stepped out from around the side of the crannog and lifted a hand to push back a deep hood.

Neve saw a woman's face that was nearly as familiar as her own, her dark tresses wound into a plait.

"The Dagda's spell-harrow hounds only hunt so far," Queen Anann explained. "Although I see you had three other hunters at your heels, daughter. You must have rattled quite a few cages back in Temair."

Neve took a moment to look at the woman she hadn't seen since she was a young child. Exile, self-imposed or otherwise, seemed to have agreed with Anann. Her features had only lightly and lovingly been touched by the passage of time. Strands of silver lent her long braid a frosted sheen, and there was a fine network of lines fanning out from the corners of her deep, dark brown eyes beneath high, arched brows. She wore a long, belted tunic, dyed the color of the sea, over suede leggings and boots that laced up past her knees. The only jewelry she wore was a slender silver torc that rested on her collarbones. But even lacking queenly finery, she was still—quite obviously—a Queen of Eire.

"Did you know there was a dragon living in your lake?" Neve asked.

Anann smiled wryly. "Beithir-Nimh was one of the reasons I chose this place. I do hope he's not too angry with me after all that ruckus . . ." She paused and nodded at Ronan, who hung limply from the rail. "I thought *he* was with you."

Neve frowned, gazing down at the mask in her hands. He was everything that *wasn't* with her. No matter how much she might have once wanted him to be.

"He's with himself," she said, slipping the mask into her cloak pocket, ignoring her mother's sharp glance at the relic as she did.

Ronan's head half lifted and then dropped forward again. Neve's knuckles throbbed at her side. She'd hit him hard, she knew. She was glad of it.

Murdering Fomori.

Anann didn't question her daughter further, just beckoned Neve and Sakir into the broch. Although modest, the single-room dwelling was spotless and the furnishings opulent. The rugs underfoot and hanging on the walls were thick and woven in jewel-toned threads, scenes of myth and legend, and there were couches for sitting and sleeping covered in thick furs and piled with tasselled throws and pillows. Lanterns hung from the rafters casting warm light throughout.

"There's stew," the queen said, gesturing at a cauldron swinging over a fire. "You're probably hungry. Not one of you looks as if you packed enough provisions for an afternoon in a meadow."

"Indeed." Sakir nodded. "We followed your daughter in some haste, lady."

Anann ran a glance over Sakir head to toe. "You're Scythian," she said, not a question. "And near in blood to Lord Cormac, I suspect."

"He is my uncle, lady," Sakir said.

"You're Farsa's boy." She stepped forward and looked at him more closely, then sighed. "I *have* been away for a long time. I remember the day you were born, Sakir. Úna was just a babe in arms and Neve wasn't yet a spark . . ."

Úna . . . Neve's throat closed around her sister's name and would not allow her to speak it. To tell her of her firstborn daughter's fate. She swallowed hard and pushed past the pain of it. Anann deserved to know, and to hear it from Neve. "Mother . . . Úna is—"

"Stop." The word rang out like the crack of a whip. Anann's eyes squeezed shut. "I already know," she said.

"You knew? Then why didn't you come back for the funeral?"

"Because I *couldn't.*" Anann opened her eyes and looked her daughter directly in the face. Neve saw a soul-deep sorrow. "And there wouldn't have been any point. Was there a ritual? A pyre or singing or solemn speeches? Did the funeral ease your pain?"

Neve glared silently at her mother. No. There hadn't been anything like that. And no, it wouldn't have eased her pain if there had. But having her mother there might have.

"Exactly." Anann shook her head and, for a moment, the years weighed heavier on her face. "I can—and *do*—mourn well enough here on my own. For many things. Alone." Anann ran a hand over her brow. "So. Daughter. Well met and welcome. Why have you come here?"

Neve remained staunchly undaunted by her mother's cool demeanor. "You don't know?" she said, crossing her arms. She'd had her whole life to accept the fact that her mother had chosen not to be her mother and, to be fair, she *had* mostly accepted it. Mostly. "You knew about Úna. You seem to know about everything."

"I'm not a Druid, my dear," Anann said, waving a hand at the brazier and murmuring a word that made it burn brighter, as if to directly contradict herself. "I can't read entrails or divine the future from the flights of birds. Although, to be fair, I don't think most Druids can either. No, the knowledge I have comes to me through tangible, earthly sources—mostly. Human ones. Messengers. Informants."

"Spies."

"Even so." Her mouth twitched upward at one corner. "And since no one warned me of *your* arrival, I expect that means no one at the court of Temair knows you're here."

"Lorcan knows." Neve shrugged. "Father's new First—"

"First Spear. I know." Anann nodded. "And he didn't send word ahead of your arrival. Interesting. I suppose that means he likes you. Good."

"You know Lorcan?"

"Soren's boy, yes, of course. I get most of my court missives from him—"

"*What?*"

"And he receives my reports in return, which I mostly glean from fisherfolk and traders hereabouts. And the odd, minor bit of spellcraft when I can manage it . . ."

Neve gaped at her mother. So *that* was it. The increased presence of the tuath warriors, the rumors of ships and warriors gathering across the sea . . . It all came from *her*, funneled through Lorcan. *They* were the ones preparing Temair for war—in spite of the Dagda's indecision.

Úna had been right to choose Lorcan for her king-to-be. And Anann had been wrong—so very wrong—to leave Ruad Rofhessa to rule alone in the Great Hall . . .

"Did you know that Lorcan was to be Úna's husband?" she asked.

"I knew that they were betrothed." Anann's jaw tightened, the muscles on the sides of her throat jumping. "I also knew Lorcan's kingship would never come to pass. I didn't know *how*, though. And I chose to spare Lorcan that particular foreknowledge. That might have been a mistake. I've made one or two of those in my time . . ."

"How—"

"Now." Anann put up a hand. "*You* were about to tell me of your business here. Surely you didn't just come all the way up here for the view."

All right then, Neve thought. *Straight to the heart of the matter.* "I need to know if the Lia Fail ever spoke for Father," she said. "Did it call him to the Throne of Destiny?"

"Ah." Anann nodded once, slowly, regarding her youngest through keen eyes. "That's a very strange and dangerous thing for you to ask, now, isn't it?"

Neve steadfastly ignored Sakir, who had gone very still. "Ruad never heard the Lia Fail speak," she asked again, "did he?"

"No."

"How do you know?" Neve pressed.

"Because *I* heard it speak." Anann's dark eyes glittered as she laughed grimly.

"You did? But how?"

"When I was the Dagda's Queen Consort, I did something absolutely forbidden to any girl or woman of the Tuatha Dé. I laid hands upon the Lia Fail. The Stone of Destiny. It was such a beautiful thing, carved with all those intricate symbols, gilded in electrum. It shone as if there was a fire lit within it. Few dared go near it, for its touch is agony, sometimes even death, to the unworthy, and not many dare to hazard that chance. But for weeks I'd dreamed about it whispering to me, and then, one night, I couldn't sleep and I found myself standing before it in the darkness beneath the stars. Alone. I reached out . . ." She shrugged.

"What did you hear?" Neve asked, leaning forward. "What did it sound like?"

"Like . . . music. And battle. Wind and waves, the turning of the world . . ." Anann's dark eyes grew unfocused. "A whisper and a shout. A cry of ineffable joy for the finding of a true king. But . . . it didn't cry for *me*. I knew that."

The queen's dark eyes snapped back into focus again, gleaming in the firelight, and locked onto Neve's face. Neve felt her heart creeping up into her throat in fear.

"Not for me," Anann continued. "But I bore within me a child that night."

Neve shook her head. "Wait—"

"*That's* who the Lia Fail cried out for." Anann's gaze brimmed with unnamed emotion as she looked at her daughter. "One who could become a true Dagda."

Neve took a deep breath, the full force of understanding what her mother had just said thundering down upon her. "I came here to find out if what Cormac said was true. To learn if I could lawfully *challenge* the Dagda's legitimacy to rule," Neve said. "And now you're saying I *am* the Dagda—"

"No. You came here to ask me what you *could* be. I'm telling you what you *are*. If you want it. And maybe a great deal more." Anann reached out a slender hand and touched Neve's cheek. "But it is up to *you*, Neve. When you were born a girl, I knew that the chiefs would never allow it. Women cannot rule the Tuatha Dé. The memory of the Scathach's transgressions is too ingrained in them."

"So instead of supporting any claim *I* might have had to the throne," Neve said quietly, her words hard as stones, "you threw me in a river the night I was born. As an offering to a wolf god, like some tender piece of meat, because I was a girl."

Anann shook her head, her hand dropping back to her side. "That's not how it happened at all," she said, before frowning at Neve in annoyance. "And that's wolf *goddess*. Don't be disrespectful."

"Goddess? Khenti-Amentiu is—"

"Is the Tuatha Dé god of death. The Opener of the Ways—he who takes the form of the golden desert wolf—and was the patron of Queen Neith, the Scathach, yes. In Kemet. But *you*, daughter, are beloved of the she-wolf *goddess*, Macha. Here, in Eire."

"A goddess . . . ," Neve murmured, drifting over to sink down on one of the couches before her knees gave out on her. "A *Fir Bolg* goddess . . ."

"A Fomori goddess, if you want to be precise. And *yes*, I did *present* you to her," Anann said. "Because she is one of the greatest powers in *this* realm. I did it so she could claim you for her own and bestow her protection upon you. I knew that you would need that and it was the only way I could give that to you. Now do you understand?"

There are wolves and there are wolves . . .

Neve shook her head and whispered, "No."

"You are the child of two tribes, Neve. You are a *bridge*."

"That's not possible," Neve said flatly.

"And yet here you are, daughter."

When Neve didn't respond, Anann sighed and nodded at Sakir, who had remained like a statue throughout the entire exchange.

"He's a handsome one," she said lightly. "Very like his uncle."

The shift in her mother's tone snapped Neve out of her stupor. "Spare me your reminiscences," she said. "I know about you and Cormac. And you and Father. And . . . and all of it. The Stone. The lies. That much I understand."

"I don't," Sakir said, suddenly coming back to life. "I don't understand at *all*."

"My mother and your uncle were in love," Neve explained as briskly as possible, so as not to have to dwell on her mother's romantic entanglements. "And then she married my father instead, when the Lia Fail decided Cormac wasn't worthy."

"But . . . that doesn't make sense," Sakir said. "Why didn't Cormac fight for you if he loved you? *Make* himself worthy? He is a Scythian. With a Scythian's honor." He glanced at Neve. And then quickly glanced away.

"He would say his honor got the best of him when he stepped aside." Anann shrugged. "*I* say it was his pride. When the Lia Fail did not speak for him, that was the end of us. I was heartbroken that the wailing of some ancient relic meant more to him than our love. Of course, that was before I heard it for myself. Then there was Ruad . . . and, truthfully, he deserved better than to have my affections already spoken for, but that was just the way of it. Years later, after Úna was born, Cormac came to me again in secret." The lantern flames in the crannog flickered restlessly, as if reflecting Anann's inner turmoil. "At least I *thought* it was Cormac."

Neve closed her eyes. "I'm not certain I want to hear this . . ."

"It was a Fomori man. One of the Fé Fíada," Anann said softly.

A monster . . .

"A Mist Lord," Neve murmured.

Anann nodded, focused on some inner distant vision. "One of the last. Alone in my chambers, he revealed his true self to me. Told me he had gazed on me in the woods. Watched me ride in the meadows . . . And I had never seen anything—anyone—so wondrous in all my life."

Neve didn't tell her mother that *she* had. Instead, she pushed away the image of Ronan transformed and said, "Ruad Rofhessa is not my father."

Anann shook her head.

Sakir stood there speechless at the revelation, like a man spell-struck.

Something dark and dangerous moved through Neve's mind at the realization of what she truly was. She could feel it, even if she could not yet make her mouth form the words. And, in spite of everything, every belief she'd held until that very moment, it felt . . . right. *Good.* A strange smile spread slowly across her face. She knew, without seeing her reflection, that it was a cold, terrible expression. She turned her face away from Sakir and her mother so they could not see and said, "Tell me again why a woman cannot be king of Eire."

Little Scota . . .

"The first *queen* almost was," Anann said. "You've heard of most of her atrocities, I'm sure, but her worst one took place right outside this door."

"Worse than drowning her enemies in an underground chamber?" Sakir asked. "Or cutting off her Scythian lover's hand so he couldn't challenge her for the throne?"

The queen shrugged. "Maybe a little worse."

Neve and Sakir exchanged a glance.

"The Scathach wanted there to be no means for her own people to ever return to their far-distant home," Anann continued. "And she wanted to make an example of those who'd opposed her conquest. So she filled the hundred magnificent ships the Tuatha Dé had sailed to Eire full of Fomori captives and set them adrift off the north coast." Anann pointed out the door of the broch. "Just out there."

"At least she let them live," Sakir said.

"Oh no." Anann shook her head. "As the winds caught their sails, she ordered her archers, stationed on the headland, to set them all alight with flaming arrows."

Neve's hand clenched convulsively into a fist.

"Afterward," the queen continued, "displeased at what she perceived as hesitation from some of the bowmen, she ordered Elchmar's Scythian charioteers to drive the archers over the cliff's edge to their deaths. All of them."

Neve closed her eyes, trying not to picture it in her mind, to no avail.

"It was too much even for Elchmar's soul to bear," Anann said. "He could not bring himself to kill her, but he and his sorcerer brother devised a spell that would forever bind the Scathach, trapping her soul with the power of the Lia Fail and consigning her to the Beyond Realms. She remains there to this day, a queen among the dead. Elchmar became the very first Dagda instead, and the Scathach's bloodline continued on through her daughter, Fea—a babe at the time of her mother's transgressions—passing down to me, and now you. But . . ." Anann's lip twisted in an expression of delicate umbrage. "As women were no longer allowed within a spear's throw of the throne, there needed to be a test of worth among the men who would claim the title. The power of the Lia Fail cries out only for the true *worthy* kings of the Tuatha Dé, and that is why it was used. So that the unworthy might never sit upon the Throne of Destiny."

"But what then became of the Lia Fail itself?" Neve asked, leaning forward like a leashed hound on the hunt catching a scent.

Anann's brow creased. "I don't know. When Ruad claimed the throne with a lie, the Stone began to corrupt. It lost its luster. Slowly at first, but eventually, as the years wore on, the markings began to fade. The electrum flaked away and the Stone itself began to crumble. And then, after you were born, it disappeared. I don't know where it is now."

The blood thundered in Neve's ears. She hadn't seen it—hadn't been *looking* for it—but the Lia Fail had been right in front of her eyes, and she hadn't recognized it. She reached for her mother's hand and said, "I do. I know where it is."

Anann covered Neve's hand with hers. "Then you also know what you must do."

She did. And it both thrilled and terrified her.

XXVI

RONAN DRIFTED IN and out of wakefulness, hanging from the hitching rail in the crannog yard. He probably should have just waited by the gate back at Temair, he mused in a lucid moment. Given Sakir Neve's axe and one or two of Eolas's spell coins, wished him and his chaos-curse of a princess good luck, brushed the whole matter from his hands like so much dust, and walked away.

In the wicker pen, one of Queen Anann's goats bleated as if in agreement, and Ronan lifted his head again, blinking to clear his sight. For a moment, it felt as if the earth and sky and stars all spiraled around the place, before his head became too heavy and fell back onto his chest.

Then a shadow crouched in front of him, and a fist grabbed a handful of his hair.

"Wake up, thief," Neve said, lifting his head up and staring directly into his eyes. "And listen."

The planes and contours of her face, curves and lines limned in moonglow, left Ronan a bit breathless, even under the circumstances. She was, he had to admit, heartbreakingly beautiful.

"My mother has just told me that I am, in all likelihood, the one true Dagda of this land," she said. "And that in no way gives me the right to deal justice to you. Not yet. But you will tell me the truth, or I will go back inside and inform her that you murdered my sister."

"And then the queen will feed me to her lake serpent," Ronan murmured, grinning crookedly. "Understood. What would you like to know, Princess?"

"Did you kill Úna?"

He looked into her eyes for a very long moment.

"I might have," he said quietly. "I don't—and I tell you this *truthfully*—I do not know for sure. But I fear there's a good chance I might have . . ."

"Why would you do such a thing?"

"Perhaps . . . I was angry after the battle at Brú na Bóinne? You almost killed a friend of mine—you almost killed *me*. Perhaps I just thought you would make a better queen than your sister." He shook his head as much as Neve's grip on his hair allowed. "Perhaps—and I have long suspected this, ever since that day in the marketplace with you—it's because I am no longer in control of my own destiny, and there is something driving me that is not born of my own free will." His gaze lowered to the bare patch of ground between them. "Or perhaps you were right. And it's simply in my nature because I'm Fomori—more than that, I'm Fé Fíada, a monster."

He couldn't even muster the necessary sarcasm he normally would have for such a revelation. Not now, not with her. Not when he'd essentially resigned himself to his fate resting in the fiery, unforgiving palm of Neve's hand. He could still feel the wound on his shoulder and wondered how much more a flaming arrow to his *heart* would hurt.

"You were right, Neve. And I can't continue to lie to myself. Or you. Especially you, Neve. You were right when you said it never ends well between our kind—"

"Well," she said. "It turns out I *am* your kind."

He blinked, knocked out of his bleak reverie by her words. "Fir Bolg?"

"Fomori." She lifted a shoulder. "Fé Fíada, actually. The same as you."

"That . . . was not what I was expecting you to say."

"It wasn't what I was expecting to hear," she said, and there was a strange little hitch in her voice. "From my mother, no less. And if you're a monster, then so am I."

"I . . . all right, look." He took a moment to collect his thoughts. "I've been hit in the head, and I'm tied up, and I'm probably not thinking clearly. Please explain to me—in *simple* terms, look you—what you mean by that? Also, does this explain the flaming arrow trick? Because I've really been wondering—"

She let go of his hair and Ronan's head fell forward again. Neve reached for the iron-bladed dagger on his hip and used it to cut through the ropes that held him to the horse rail. Freed from the restraints, Ronan fell face-first into the dirt, his arms bloodless and numb.

As feeling began to rush back to his fingertips, he hissed in pain and struggled to rise to his knees. Neve still held his knife in one hand, pointing at his heart—he couldn't entirely blame her—but in her other hand she held another, small and crudely fashioned, but also made of iron.

Ronan frowned at her, not understanding.

"Two days ago," Neve said, "I went back out into my private garden, where I'd found Úna. No one had been out there since that night. I found this hidden under a bush." She laid the blade on the ground in front of him and her hand disappeared beneath her cloak.

"I see . . ."

"I also found this, lying next to it."

She produced a stone shard, crudely carved with a line of symbols running along one side. At the sight of it, Ronan scrambled back, his shoulder jamming painfully up against the hitching rail post. "For the love of Mórr, be *careful!*" he exclaimed.

Neve's eyes narrowed as she stared at him, judging his reaction. "What *is* it?"

Ronan was silent for a long moment, his emotions swinging wildly between relief and horror.

"Ronan?" Neve pressed. "What—"

"Exoneration," he whispered, feeling the truth of that word course through him in a wave so strong he almost collapsed again. "Neve . . . I didn't kill Úna. This *proves* it."

Crouched before him in the moonlight, a curse in one hand and an iron dagger in the other, Neve took a slow deep breath and—without lowering the dagger—said, "Tell me."

"Your sister drowned. You—and I—thought my . . ." He searched for the word.

"Your Fé," Neve said quietly.

"My . . . Fé. Yes. I thought it—thought *I*—was responsible," he said. "I can speak to water. Mold it, shape it, command it, even . . ." He reached very carefully for the stone shard, holding it up between them. "So can this."

"What is it?"

"This . . . is the fuath curse I cast the night when we first met."

Neve's hand tightened on the dagger hilt. "This is not the convincing argument for your innocence you think it is," she said.

"But it *is*. For more than one reason. The fuath is an elemental water demon, a conjuration of pure hate, and it is unfathomably dangerous. You know both of those things better than most. If I was going to kill someone—drown them like Úna was drowned—why would I call on such a dangerous curse, when I possessed the power *myself* to do it?"

"What if you didn't know you had that power yet?" Neve argued. "You seemed just as surprised as I was at the sacred spring. As if it was the first time that had ever happened."

"Not the first time, no." He shook his head. "Just the first time in a very *long* time. But even so. Even if I had decided, instead, to summon the fuath, I would need to be prepared to destroy it after it had carried out its horrific task. I would need to carry iron. But why would I use *this*"—he picked up the pitted, ragged-edged little knife—"a blade so barely serviceable that I might risk my own life, when I already carried *your* blade on my hip?"

A light dawned in Neve's eyes as she realized the simple truth of what he was saying. The dagger would have been a far more effective means of dispatching a fuath.

"Iron and demons . . . ," she said quietly.

For a moment, Ronan could once more see the scared, brave, defiant little girl who'd killed a demon with a pickaxe. And he knew, then, he'd fallen in love with her that very moment, all those years ago. Childish, unrealized, and everlasting.

Her gaze shifted to the stone. "You said this is yours?"

"Not mine." He shook his head. "I threw the stone away that night and haven't seen it since. Not until this very moment."

"Is it active?" Neve raised an eyebrow at him. "Dangerous still?"

"Always. Unless you chisel off the incantation or shatter the stone to pieces, and then I still wouldn't turn my back on the shards. And I would never willingly call upon that kind of malice ever again."

Neve tucked the stone back into her cloak pocket. "Someone did."

Ronan nodded. "Someone did, indeed. Someone very angry."

She spun the dagger in her palm and handed it back to him. The blue stone set in the pommel winked at him as Ronan took it and slid it back into the sheath at his belt.

"I'm curious," he said. "How did you come by this blade? You said it had been handed down."

"My mother left it for me, so I assumed it had been hers." She glanced over her shoulder at the broch and then turned back to him and shrugged. "I never thought to ask. Why?"

"It's just that one doesn't come across so fine a weapon as this very often. And it looks older. Much older."

"Ah. You think it was *hers*?" she asked, and reached beneath her cloak for the gilded wolf mask. "Like I think this was?"

Mine. Yours. Ours . . .

"I don't know. I'm just happy to carry it in service to my queen." He canted his head in the closest he'd ever come to a bow. "And I don't mean the Scathach."

"Don't call me that."

"What? Scathach?"

"Queen." Neve leaned toward him and her eyes were pale gold in the moonlight, glittering dangerously. "When I take the throne—and I *will* take the throne—I'll do it as the Dagda. I'll do it as a king."

Ronan felt a swell of fierce pride in his chest. He realized in that moment that he'd do anything in his power to help her kingship come to pass. Not just because of how he felt about her—although he could not even begin to deny that—but because she might just be the best, brightest hope for the future of Eire. All of Eire.

"I'd be lying if I didn't say I feared for you, Neve," he said, closing a hand over top of hers where she held the mask with cold fingers. "I honestly don't know if you're being hunted or lured— or if you're just following your destiny of your own accord—but you're riding headlong into peril, either way."

"And I'd be lying if I said I didn't agree." She offered a shrug that was almost a shiver. "Perhaps when I am Dagda, I will appoint you as my adviser."

He laughed. "You'll have plenty of Druids scrabbling for that honor. I'd rather oversee the royal treasury."

"You never told me how you came to be an apprentice Druid," she said quietly.

"There is a Fir Bolg ballad," he said. "You might know the tune—it's a late-night favorite in the bruideans, usually when everyone is drunk and weepy—about a lovely young fisherwife whose husband died valiantly in battle, and how she was so stricken with grief she walked with her newborn into the sea . . ."

Neve nodded. "When I was a girl, that was always one of my favorite tales when the bards played in the Great Hall," she said.

"The babe was too lovely and so the sea gave him . . . back." She stared at him, her mouth drifting open.

Ronan dipped his head and affected a humble shrug. "I don't know about the *lovely* part. I suppose that might have been a bit of artistic embellishment . . ."

Neve's astonishment gave way to a small smile shaded with sadness for his inauspicious beginning in life. "I've seen a few newborns," she said, "and they're not beautiful . . . You were probably still red and wrinkly and—"

"*Don't* make me summon the óglach, Princess."

"Right." Her eyes glinted in the darkness. "I'm sure you were quite striking . . ."

A strained silence stretched out, broken only by the cry of sea birds. There was too much between Ronan and Neve that was made of hurt. But there was even more that seemed drawn from the same heart, beating in two different bodies. A shared destiny they could not deny.

"I wonder if all the Fé Fíada wound up near drowned by their mothers as babes," Neve asked, that familiar starry wetness spangling her lashes. Her eyes full again of the tears she refused to shed in front of him.

She was so close, all Ronan had to do was reach out and take her hand. "Neve . . ."

She lifted her fingers to his lips, pressing them gently to silence. "I'm *sorry*," she said, a whisper. "I never should have doubted you, and I never should have said the hateful things I did. You have saved me and you have stood for me. And you had no earthly reason to. The very least I can do is ask your forgiveness."

"You have it," he murmured against her fingertips. "You don't need it but—"

She pressed him to silence again. "Be sure of that," she said. "Of your forgiveness. Because I *will* ask you to stand by my side in the coming days. Against our own kind, should it come to that."

"I don't have a kind, Princess. Any more than you do."

"You have me." Her expression shifted a bit then, became troubled. "Ronan, I have to tell you something. I made an oath I'm going to break . . ."

"Was it to me?"

"No—"

"Then I don't care." Ronan reached up a hand beneath the wave of Neve's dark hair, his fingers gripping the back of her neck as he pulled her closer to him. Her lips curved into a smile beneath his and he inhaled the scent of her hair—lavender and vervain—as she pressed closer to him until he could feel her heart beating. The wolf mask slipped from her grasp and her hands moved up his back, fingers kneading his muscles. As her lips moved across his, the tip of her tongue tasting the corner of his mouth, a sliver of Ronan's awareness searched for the lie—for the part of Neve that wasn't her. For the hidden hunger that had urged her to kiss him on the bank of the sacred spring. The twisted skein of *other* coiled somewhere deep inside her soul that even she was barely aware of . . .

This time, he sensed none of that.

The kiss was all Neve's. Ronan's own soul felt like a song with wings as they melted together, shared breath and hearts beating in time beneath the moon. After a long enough while that his lips were tingling, Ronan pulled back, just far enough so that he could look into Neve's face. She reached up and lightly ran a finger from the top of his forehead, down the center of his nose, over his lips, his chin, the column of his throat—as if trying to memorize his profile in that moment—to rest in the hollow between his collarbones.

He could feel his pulse beating against the sharp curve of her fingernail. And, like hoofbeats approaching in the distance, he could feel the darkling magic in his blood pulsing deep inside his chest. He noticed there was already a hint of ground mist rising in the yard beyond the circle of firelight, and he took a deep breath to steady himself.

"Was that really you?" Neve asked in a thready whisper. "The babe from the ballad?"

"Famed in song and story." He grinned ruefully.

"When this is over," she said, "they'll have to write more verses to tell our tale."

"Let's hope it has a happy ending," he said, a bit more dire than he intended. "I'd hate to have to make a bard shed tears."

"I see you've untied the lad." Anann's voice carried over to them. She appeared in the doorway to the broch, her darkened silhouette lined with the glow of the hearth fire inside. "Does that mean you've worked through your little disagreement?"

Neve rolled an eye at Ronan as she picked up the mask and stood.

"At least come inside and eat," Anann said. "Before I send the three of you riding off back into the maelstrom."

XXVII

"Does Father—does Ruad—know the truth about me?" Neve asked, setting down the bowl of stew she'd barely touched. "That I'm not his?"

"I'm faithless, Neve," Anann said. "Not cruel. Of course not."

"Then why did you leave Temair?"

"Because that damned Druid architect Gofannon knew." She sighed ruefully. "I don't know exactly how, but he knew. He threatened to tell Ruad, and I already suspected that he'd had something to do with Ruad's lies about the Lia Fail, so I took him seriously. I did the only thing, under the circumstances, that I could. I made a bargain with Gofannon that I would leave and he would stay silent. I made him swear it on an oath stone carved with a curse should he break his promise."

Neve felt her throat tighten. Her mother hadn't left because she'd been a disappointment. She hadn't thrown Neve into the river to die. Everything Anann had done, she'd done to try and protect Neve. Offered up her newborn to a terrifying wolf goddess, not knowing if she'd be watched over or devoured or just left to sink beneath the waves on the river. She'd left her home and family and palace behind. Renounced her very queenship, all to protect the daughter who would grow up resenting her for that sacrifice.

"Gofannon offered me a bargain, too," Neve said quietly. "Become Queen Consort. *His* Queen Consort."

Ronan made an outraged choking noise. Sakir's expression turned murderous.

"He said he would take the throne himself," Neve continued, "to save the realm from the coming storm of chaos. He said Father is . . . He said Ruad is dying."

Anann went a bit pale at that.

"But isn't that what they've been preparing for all this time?" Sakir asked. "Isn't that what the Great Barrow is for? To channel the Dagda's spirit once he passes on and make of it a protective force for the realm?"

"Unless that's not what it's for at all," Neve said, her head full of whispers.

Beneath the folds of her cloak, her thumb traced the edges of the wolf mask, rubbing a raw groove in her flesh as her mind churned, fitting together pieces like an artist crafting a mosaic from shards of broken glass. She felt her thumb begin to bleed. The whispers grew louder. "Didn't the Scathach have an architect back in Kemet? Wasn't Elchmar's brother the sorcerer who built her banquet hall for her—the one that flooded and became a tomb for her enemies?"

She stood and paced over to the fire in the hearth, staring into the flames and casting her mind back to the conversation she'd had with Gofannon. About her axe, about the stone maze in the far-off country he'd told her of—the labyrinth, he'd called it—and how both those things—the maze that was really a prison and the banquet hall that was really a death trap—were built to seem as one thing but were actually another.

What if Brú na Bóinne was like that? What if it truly *was* Teg Duinn? Not a tomb, not a temple, but the doorway to the Beyond Realms, and Neve just hadn't known enough to know how to open the door when she'd ventured inside to find Úna?

Doors work both ways. They let things in . . . and out.

As she stared into the flames of her mother's fire, Neve saw images moving before her mind's eye, like the procession of Tuatha Dé pictured in the mural on her chamber wall. Only this time, she saw a figure she'd never noticed before, riding behind Elchmar and the Scathach. A bearded man with auburn hair and mild blue eyes . . . and a torc around his neck in the shape of a serpent.

"Sakir, in the Horse Lords' legends, what happened to the Scythians?" Neve asked, her voice rasping in her throat. The fire seemed to be whispering secrets to her in its language of crackle and hiss. "To Elchmar and his sorcerer brother?"

"Elchmar diminished and disappeared into the wilderness," Sakir answered. "His brother's fate, as far as I know, is lost to the fog of time. Not even his name remains."

"You told me Gofannon had the look of a Scythian," Neve said, the image of the mural in her mind growing brighter in the flames before her, shimmering. The horses galloping, the bearded man's eyes fixed on the woman who rode before him . . .

"Yes, a *living* Scythian," Sakir said, realizing what Neve was turning over in her mind. "Neve, you can't possibly believe . . . "

A gout of flame billowed from the fallen log, and Neve saw the flashing image of the structure she'd glimpsed that night by the sacred spring—umber stone, sloped windowless walls, and a single entrance—and a man in flowing robes, waiting. A woman in a midnight cloak, walking out of the shadowed archway as a heavy stone door shut behind her with a sonorous boom. The sound of distant rushing water . . .

"It's *him*," Neve murmured. "It has to be. Gofannon is the Scathach's sorcerer. They're bound to each other because of the Lia Fail spell. She cannot escape the realm of the dead, he cannot escape the realm of the living . . ."

"They must come together to undo what has been done," Ronan finished her thought, echoing what he had told her before about magic and how a spell once cast could not be sundered unless all its original elements were gathered again.

Neve felt a surge of heat race up her arm, and the fiery visions cleared from her sight. She drew her hand out from beneath her cloak and saw that the lines of the sigil on her palm weren't glowing, but they were stained with blood from the gash on her thumb.

She turned to face her mother and Ronan and Sakir.

"*Neve* . . ." Her mother's eyes grew wide. "Where did you get *that*?"

Neve lifted up a hand to her face, to find the wolf mask resting on her cheekbones. With a gasp, Neve lifted the mask from her face, and the images faded from her mind. There was a bright line of crimson, beading along the gilded edge of the mask.

She wiped it away on her cloak.

"The mask *is* hers," Ronan said, rising to his feet and taking a step toward Neve. "It must be the Scathach's."

"Then you must be extremely careful with it," Anann said.

"I have a better idea." Sakir was on his feet, too. "Throw it into the fire—"

"No!" Neve stuffed the mask back into her cloak. "I found it for a reason."

"What if it was her reason, not yours?" Anann asked. "The Scathach is not to be underestimated, my daughter—"

"Neither am I," Neve said. "I am *your* daughter. Not hers. And I can handle this. It was buried in the Great Barrow chamber, which means Gofannon didn't want it to be found. Maybe that means it can be used against him."

"If he is who you say he is," Sakir argued, "then no mask will stand in his way. Gofannon is powerful almost beyond measure."

"*Was*," Ronan said quietly.

They all turned to look at him.

"The amount of magic it would have taken to bind the Scathach with the Lia Fail would have been enormous," Ronan explained. "Gofannon would have been rendered a mere shell of himself. It's likely taken him all this time to regain any substantial amount of the power he must have once had."

"And now, what?" Sakir challenged him. "He's had a change of heart? He wants to release his mad mistress back into the world?"

"Or she *wants* to be released." Ronan shrugged. "And has simply convinced him, through their bond, to make it happen. But the *power* it would take to call a soul back into this world from the Beyond Realms would be—"

"They have the power," Neve cut in. "The Druids have been gathering up the magic of the land, siphoning it off, funneling it into Brú na Bóinne. Gofannon and Father didn't ban wild magic because it was dangerous, but because they—*he*—needed it. As much as they could glean—every scrap they could land their hands on. It will become Teg Duinn, in a way."

"The barrow is to be consecrated at Midwinter," Sakir said in horror.

"Which, I predict, should be right about when the looming invasion reaches the mouth of An Bhóinn," Anann said with a heavy sigh. "I dearly hope Lorcan has managed to gather enough warriors."

"This cannot be a coincidence," Sakir said. "An invasion armada possibly headed this way, within days of the completion of the Great Barrow—"

"No." Neve shook her head. "That is *her* doing, too. The Scathach works her will through Gofannon. It's how he knew I wasn't Ruad's daughter. When you touched the Stone, Mother, *she* told him."

Little Scota . . .

"And whether he is complicit or coerced—it hardly matters at this point—I think Gofannon fully intends to release the Scathach back into the world of the living, in the very same moment that a warband arrives on Temair's doorstep."

"I think you're right," Anann said. "Unless Temair's true king can stop them."

"The ships," Sakir said suddenly, his brow creased in a frown as if this was a thing that he'd been turning over in his mind. "The ones the Scathach ordered fired on, with the Fomori captives. Did they *all* burn and sink?"

Anann shook her head. "There's no way to know for certain, but I think survivors could very well have made it to the shores of Alba. Lived, maybe even thrived, there. Replenished their numbers down through the long years—"

"That's what you fear, isn't it?" Ronan interrupted. "Not a clutch of Fir Domnann raiders, but an armada of Fomori, bent on reclaiming what was once taken from them."

Anann's expression was exceedingly grim.

"They are coming," Neve said.

"But the Fomori were *her* enemy," Sakir said. "Why would they—"

"The Fomori weren't the ones who imprisoned her with the Lia Fail," Neve countered. "The Tuatha Dé did that. Her Scythian Horse Lords did that. Gofannon came here from across the Eirish Sea. If he spent time there, forged ties, kept in contact with them through the years until the time was ripe and then prompted them to this invasion, then they likely don't even know who they'll truly be fighting *for*. They just know it's to bring down the Tuatha Dé."

"So . . . what?" he pressed. "You think she means to set these Alban Fomori and the Tuatha Dé at each other's throats, let them destroy one another, and then swoop in like a raven onto a spent battlefield to pick over the spoils left behind?"

Ronan laughed mirthlessly. "From everything we've learned of Neve's revered ancestress so far, I don't imagine she's above exacting a little vengeance alongside a victory, do you?"

Neve picked up a birch log and tossed it on the fire, making the flames leap and claw back the shadows. "Then I suppose it's up to us," she said, "to see to it she gets neither."

"I think I might have something that could help you," Anann said. "Something else that once belonged to her. It's yours now, if you want it." She glanced at Ronan and Sakir. "Why don't you two go see to the horses?"

—◦◦◦◦—

RONAN STEPPED OUTSIDE into the crannog yard, followed by Neve's charioteer, who brushed past him—not *quite* shoving him out of the way—and went to go check on the horses, tethered to the same hitching rail that Ronan had so recently been freed from. Ronan followed, harboring a fairly good idea of who it was that had tied the knots.

"What will you do, Fir Bolg?" Sakir asked, feeding sheaves of sweet hay to the horses.

"I'm not sure what you mean, Scythian," Ronan said, rubbing at the rawness of his wrists. "What will I do about what?"

Sakir nodded in the direction Neve had gone. "What are you willing to do to put her on the Dagda's throne?"

"Anything," Ronan answered without thinking. "Everything. Whatever it takes." Then he did pause to think about it for a moment and added, "If I have to, I'll die for her."

"Well, then." The Horse Lord nodded. "You do that. Me . . . I'll kill for her."

"I'll remember that."

Sakir dropped a hand to the axe at his belt. Bronze bladed. Ronan wagered it wouldn't kill a demon, perhaps, but the way Sakir handled it, it could certainly kill him. The charioteer handed Ronan a leather water pail to fill for the horses and headed for the lake causeway.

"Where are you going?" Ronan called after him.

"I've never seen the sun rise over the ocean," Sakir said over his shoulder. "I'd like to do that just once, I think, before we go to war."

———

THE GOLDEN VISOR glared up at Neve with reproachful, empty eyes. She'd laid it down on the couch next to her, waiting as her mother rummaged through an oak trunk. Neve reached down and picked up the wolfen visage, her fingertips prickling on the gilded surface.

You are far from home, Khenti-Amentiu, she whispered in her mind to the Scathach's golden wolf god. *Stay in your realm of the dead. Keep her there as your queen. Do not send me borrowed trouble. I will find my own place and my own power. And I will defend both with my life. And my death.*

"Ah," her mother said. "Here it is . . ."

Neve looked up and her eyes went wide with astonishment.

"I thought you might find this useful when it came time." Anann held out an armload of exquisitely wrought armor, partially comprised of a tunic made of hundreds of individual overlapping scales—like dragon skin—forged of black Korinthian bronze with a patina so dark, they shone almost purple in the firelight.

Neve took the armor from Anann. It was surprisingly light and would allow for a great degree of mobility, she could tell just by the way it felt. Her mother's eyes were bright with pride as she placed a helm on top of the pile. Neve could see the notches in the front and sides that weren't just decorative, but designed to accommodate the Scathach's golden wolf visor.

Anann smiled. "I think *you'll* wear it better."

"I . . . I'm not sure what to say. Thank you for this," Neve said. "For believing I might one day be worthy to wear it. You're probably the only one who ever thought so."

Anann put a hand on Neve's cheek, and shook her head. "Ach," she murmured. "What a mess I made all those years ago . . . You, my mad, weird girl, are the only thing pure and perfect to come out of it all. I did right by leaving you to grow up under your sister's wing."

"I will find out who took her from us, Mother. I swear it." Neve ran a fingertip over the brim of the helmet, blinking away a sudden blurriness. "I miss her so much."

Anann smiled sadly. "Then you must find her again. In the deepest places in your heart and your mind, there she is. And when you need her, she will be there."

Neve uttered a little laugh. "Maybe," she said, trying to smile, "I'll just think of her as living on a strange little island in the middle of a lake on a windswept cliff somewhere. Like someone else I used to miss and found again."

"I think that's a lovely thought," Anann said, her eyes shining brightly. Then the exiled queen hugged her youngest, her only daughter, and said, "Give them hell, my king."

At that moment, Sakir ran through the door to the broch. "You might not have to give it to them," he said, panting. "It looks like they're bringing it to us . . ."

"What is it?"

"I saw the Alban ships on the horizon, sailing down from the north."

Neve felt every muscle in her body tense. "How many?"

"Too many."

"Is my chariot ready?" Neve asked, knowing it would be.

Sakir nodded.

"Will you come with me, Mother?" she asked Anann.

The queen shook her head. "I'm not a warrior. In Temair, I'll only be a distraction and a point of contention. You'll be better off without me."

Neve gave her a brief, only slightly brittle hug. Then she picked up the golden mask and added it to the pile of armor she carried.

"Let's hurry. Where's Ronan?" she asked.

"He's out on the headland," Sakir answered over his shoulder.

Neve frowned. "What's he doing out there?"

"That . . . you'll have to see for yourself."

She stalked outside and, once across the causeway, broke into a run, Sakir at her heels. The pull of magic coming from the north felt almost like it was tugging at Neve's skin.

As she ran, Neve could see a lone figure standing at the edge of the cliff drop, bathed in the light of the moon. Ronan was so near the edge of the precipice Neve was afraid he might fall into the sea. But as she got close, she saw that, in fact, the sea was rising to meet *him*.

He stood with his legs braced, arms stretched wide and head back. His cloak and tunic rested in a heap behind him and his dark hair was loose and blown back from his face. The darkling sigils, the marks of his Mist Lord power, moved beneath his silvered skin, beneath the seawater that flowed up over the edge of the cliff to clothe his outstretched limbs like finest-spun threads of silver, winding Ronan in a shimmering cocoon.

Neve watched as the seawater gathered, then began to billow out from Ronan's shrouded form, turning into thick plumes of mist. With a sweeping gesture, Ronan brought his arms together and pushed the fogbank in the direction of the ships, still barely more than specks on the horizon—too many specks. Slowly, like a pack of hounds on the hunt, the roiling fog billows crept over the edge of the cliff and began to crawl across the obsidian sea waves toward the armada. Beneath them the water grew still as a stagnant pond, the white foam lines of waves diminishing. The moon, riding low, turned from pale yellow to a sullen, dull orange and then disappeared altogether behind the thick obscuring haze.

As the fog drifted out to meet the ships, Ronan shuddered and dropped to his knees at the edge of the cliff. Neve ran toward him, pulling him back before he toppled over the sheer drop. He collapsed on his back on the damp grass, the silvered sheen on his skin fading and his face slowly shifting back from the sharp, angular contours of his Fé Fíada form. His eyes opened, still completely black, fathomless, and for a moment, Neve could see herself reflected in them as if she were trapped behind the mirror of his gaze.

Then Ronan squeezed his eyes shut, and when he opened them again, they were the silver-flecked dark gray she'd always known.

"That might slow them down," he gasped, chest heaving. "I hope . . ."

Ronan's efforts had drained him, and he looked hollowed—like some of the life had actually been sucked out of him—but what he'd done was certainly impressive. Directly over the crannog, the sky was still clear, star-spattered. But when Neve looked back out seaward, she saw that the fog he'd conjured was like an impenetrable wall. Without a hint of wind to stir their sails, no moon or stars or sight of land to guide them, and no way to tell where the rocks and shoals might lie, the armada would be rendered helpless. Motionless. For now.

She smiled down at Ronan, astonished and grateful for the gift of time he'd granted them. And just a little frightened.

If he was the last true Fé Fíada left in Eire—the last one except for *her*—then he was clearly intending to make the most of it. She stood and helped him to his feet.

"How long do we have?" she asked.

"Maybe a day. Two if the weather lends a hand and a good Midwinter gloom rolls in."

"They'll most likely head for the mouth of An Bhóinn as soon as they can," Neve said, chewing on her lip and dredging the memories of war in her head that weren't hers. "As soon as your mist lets them."

"Then I suppose we'll just have to get there first," Ronan said.

XXVIII

THEY RODE AS far into the night as they could, stopping to rest for only brief naps taken in shifts. The weather conditions the next day seemed happy to cooperate with Ronan's sea fog conjuration, and the sun never appeared in the sky as anything more than the far-off-seeming eye of a petulant sky god, dull orange and mostly hidden in heavy cloud. By the time the sun had dropped down behind the western hills again, Neve and Ronan and Sakir were crossing An Bhóinn.

With no hint of the invading Fomori enemy in sight, Neve breathed a profound sigh of relief. It was a feeling that wouldn't last.

They could see the fires of Temair blazing from a far distance. And not just the watch fires and the bonfires in the field camps beyond the walls; it seemed to Neve as if every pitch torch and lantern in the land had been gathered and set alight. The darkness above the palace glowed a shade of pulsing, angry orange that bled out into the night sky.

Her chariot raced toward the curved stone walls, threading through the jumble of encampments. The multitude of tents that had cropped up along the walls over the last few weeks had bloomed outward, spilling into the adjacent fields like invasive weeds.

Lorcan has *been busy*, Neve thought as they drove past tuath gatherings, some of whom leaped to their feet to catch glimpses of her as she rode past. *There must be thousands of warriors here.* And it would be up to her to lead them in battle. They just didn't know that yet.

In the far fields, Neve could see—just from the rows of picketed horses—that Cormac's contingent of Scythians from the Golden Vale had also increased. They'd set up camp where Sakir often took Neve to practice her spear throwing and archery. Not only had the Horse Lord not gone home, as the Dagda had commanded him to do, it seemed he had increased Temair's cavalry contingent substantially. At Lorcan's prompting, Neve dearly hoped.

The last thing she needed was Cormac thinking he could take the opportunity to challenge the Dagda. She would have enough trouble trying to convince the tuath chieftains to follow her into battle. If it even came to that. There were so many things that could take her down before she even got there, but at least she didn't have to worry about the presence of the Druids at court for now. She couldn't help but notice the lack of pale-robed figures—word must have gotten back to them from the Druid who'd escaped at An Bhinn Mhór.

She saw Cormac stalking between rows of horses in battle dress. Beneath the brim of his helmet, the Scythian's gaze was flinty— hard and sharp, and eager—and his face bore the look of a man who had not been in a fight in a long time . . . and who'd just remembered how much he missed it. There was a look of craving about him and, for a moment, Neve could see why her mother had been enamored of the Horse Lord. His every move was purposeful and precise and energetic. He carried himself like a leader, charismatic and persuasive. Neve tried to picture *him* wielding the Dagda's war club instead of Ruad Rofhessa and sitting on the Throne of Destiny.

But, for some reason, the image would not form in her mind.

She watched as Banach and Balar, two of the more powerful tuath chieftains, confronted Cormac.

"And what will you contribute to the defense of Temair, spawn of Elchmar?" Balar sneered. "Your years of experience in battle? When have your precious horsemen ever ridden out on their prancing ponies in support of this Dagda?"

"Just because you were too much of a wee babe to remember when it happened, Lord Balar, does not mean that it didn't," Cormac answered. "But I'm sure *your* tender years spent cattle raiding have served you well—if not your fellow chieftains."

Neve pulled her chariot to a stop and stepped down from the deck intending to quell the dissent. Before she could intervene, a voice hailed her.

"Princess!" The shout rang out over the clamor of the encampment. "Lady Neve!"

She saw the Dagda's commander of the óglach heading toward her at a run.

"Fintan!" Neve called, stripping off her gloves. "Please, I need you to gather the chieftains in the Great Hall for council—"

"Lady, you must go to your father—"

"I must speak to the chieftains first, Fintan. Father'll be angry, I know, but that can't be helped." She waved for Ronan to accompany her. "I have urgent news and—"

"Neve!"

She pulled up short. Fintan had never addressed her that way before.

"Your father, Princess . . ." The óglach chief's face contorted and his mouth worked as though trying to bite back the words it said. "He's not . . . *angry*. But you must go to him. *Now*."

Neve shared a look with Ronan as he dismounted.

"I'll come with you," he said.

"Sakir!" she called. "Find out from your uncle what's going on out here."

"Aye." He shook his head in disgust. "As soon as I can elbow through that crowd of haggling fishwives . . ." He moved off toward the crowd.

"Fintan," Neve said, "send one of your men to call the council to assemble, and take me to my father."

Neve hitched her traveling satchel and arrow quiver up on her shoulders and handed Ronan her bow. They followed the óglach chief through the halls and corridors of the palace, ablaze with torchlight.

Outside the door of the Dagda's chambers, Neve shrugged off her quiver and left it and her bow leaning against the wall. Before she pushed open the massive door, carved in relief with heroic scenes from the lives of Dagdas past and present, Fintan put a hand on her shoulder.

"You should know before you see him. The Dagda is not . . ."

"Well?" Neve asked. "Sober? In his right mind?"

"Long for this realm."

That shocked her to stillness. She had not expected it to be so soon. "Where is Gofannon?" she asked quietly.

"I've not seen the man in days," Fintan said, his expression one of distaste. "Mind, I've not looked for him."

Neve nodded and he stepped aside and pushed the door open for her. The air in the room was close and stale. Sour-smelling. The torches in the wall sconces burned low—some guttering, a few already extinguished—and an acrid haze of smoke drifted through the outer chambers.

Neve turned to Fintan angrily. "Who attends the king?"

"He'll let none near." The óglach chief shrugged helplessly. "Not for a day and a half now. Roars like a wounded bear and threatens anyone who approaches the bed. He's still himself, lady. In many ways."

That much was evident when a cup suddenly soared through the air to shatter against the wall beside Neve's head. She flinched, ducking pottery shards as she heard Ruad Rofhessa raggedly bellowing profanities from the chamber beyond. Cautiously, she peeked her head around the doorframe.

The Dagda lay on the massive sleeping couch in his chambers, twisted in the bedclothes like a corpse already wrapped in a funeral shroud. His face was mottled red and gray, and his eyes were sunk deep in his head. The tattoos on his cheeks were black in the gloom and his mouth hung slack. His war club rested on a bronze stand beside the bed. When Neve took a torch from the stand and moved it closer, the sputtering flames seemed to burn brighter in her presence, and the Dagda flinched, weakly lifting a hand as if to fend off an attacker.

"It's too bright in here . . . ," he muttered peevishly, his head rolling on a sweat-stained pillow, hair and beard tangled like a thorn hedge. Eyes like smoldering coals narrowed as he tried to focus on Neve's face. "Anann . . . ?" He squinted at her. "Is it you?"

"It's Neve, Father." The last word stuck a little in her throat.

But the sight of him like this had driven almost all of the bleak, black feelings over what he'd become out of Neve's heart. Ruad Rofhessa had done great and terrible things in his lifetime. He'd been a liar and he'd been lied to. He'd striven for the mantle of the gods, in brash defiance of his charted destiny. But here, now, at what seemed close to the end, he was just a man. One that Neve had both loved and hated. The hate somehow didn't seem as important.

"Neve . . . ," Ruad managed before he stiffened in agony, gasping for breath.

"Rest easy, now," she said and rested a hand on his shoulder. "The Druids—"

"They say there is nothing they can do," he rasped. "I'm dying, not deaf . . ."

Neve's senses, seemingly heightened since her Fé had manifested, set off a warning tingle in the back of her skull. Her nostrils flared as she recognized the smell of dark earth, a faint mushroomy mustiness . . . and sweetness. The suspicion that had been growing in her mind, since the moment she learned Ronan hadn't murdered Úna, walked a step closer to truth. It made her want to weep for what was to come.

"Is Emer still at court?" she asked Fintan.

He nodded.

"Find her. Tell her to bring what medicines she has." As Fintan hurried out, Neve turned to Ronan, who stood in a corner of the room. "I need a moment alone."

"I'll be right outside," he said and let himself out into the Dagda's private garden.

Neve went back to the Dagda's bedside and looked down at the man who'd always seemed a mountain to her. His chest was sunken and his hands, those fingers that had always seemed able to crush a man's skull, were limp on the bedcover, the nails tinged purple. It seemed to her as if he was already halfway over the threshold to the Otherworld.

But then he spoke, and it seemed that whatever it was that was destroying his body had clarified his mind. His voice was low but clear and cogent.

"Forgive me," he said, then winced. When the wave of pain had passed, she could see in his gaze a serenity she had never seen in him. "I have treated you badly. I have betrayed the Tuatha Dé. I am a victim of my own blinding pride, and I fear I have unleashed a darkness on this land."

"No," Neve said urgently. "You haven't. Not yet. There's still a chance—"

"Not for me. You. *You* can stop it. I should have trusted you, daughter."

"I . . . I'm not your—"

"I know. I've always known. The Stone knows." He chuckled, a low grinding rasp in the back of his throat. "Sometimes, I would sit with the Lia Fail . . . just sit and listen to it as it mocked me. As it whispered your name. The envy in my heart was a forge fire burning, Neve. None of this is your fault and I have acted cruelly."

"The Lia Fail is the stone in the barrow chamber, isn't it?" she asked. "That's what that crumbling old relic is."

He nodded.

"And the barrow itself—"

His hand reached for hers convulsively. "I was deceived by Gofannon. Neve, daughter—"

"I know," she said. "He's gone from court, but I will find him."

Neve wrapped her fingers around his, her hands so small next to his massive ones. Like she was still the little girl standing in front of his great throne, dirty and defiant, proclaiming she would defend the honor of the Dagda while he glowered down at her with thinning patience.

"Devious bastard," Ruad murmured. "Played upon my pride like a harp. All these years. I was to be a hero. A guardian for Tuatha Dé and Fir Bolg alike . . . for all of Eire. When he knew I was at the end . . . he told me . . . told . . ." His face contorted in pain. "Do not lay me to rest in that house of lies, Neve."

"It's the Scathach's way back into the world, isn't it?"

His gaze shifted to her, clear and sharp. "Only if *you* let her through."

"I swear on the blade of my axe, she will not set one foot back into this world." She squeezed his hand. "Rest easy now, Father . . ."

His head lolled on the pillow and he lapsed back into unconsciousness, his breath rasping shallowly. Neve bent low over him and there was that musty tang in her nostrils again. She heard footsteps and turned to see Emer hovering at the threshold, a leather bag clutched tight in her hands. Her large eyes were fixed on the Dagda until she noticed Neve. Then she shook herself and came over to the bed with a bare semblance of her usual bustle.

Neve stood quietly, watching as Emer bent over the Dagda, peering in his eyes and rummaging in her medicine bag . . .

"It's not a curse, is it?" Neve asked.

Without looking at Neve, Emer shook her head, fingers probing the Dagda's temples, his jaw.

"Makes sense," Neve continued. "I suppose you had to resort to plain old poison when you couldn't find these."

Emer froze as Neve tossed the curse stone and blade she'd found hidden in her garden onto the bed. When Emer finally straightened to look Neve in the eyes, Neve barely recognized her. Gone were the warmth and humor she'd always known in her handmaiden. Emer's gaze flicked down to the fuath curse and back up to Neve's face.

In that moment, the door to the garden swung open, and Ronan stepped inside. Confusion swept over his face as he looked from Emer to Neve.

"Sparrow," he said. "What are *you* doing here?"

His eyes narrowed as he saw the stone and the dagger lying on the bed, and confusion turned to disgust and he cursed under his breath. "You did this?" he asked. "I should have let Neve's arrow take you at Brú na Bóinne."

So Emer was a salvager, Neve thought. The pain she felt at her betrayal was muted by Emer's reasons for betraying, leaving only ugly sorrow in its place.

"The Dagda is beyond saving, isn't he?" Neve asked quietly.

"Yes." Emer nodded. "Well, there is someone who *could* save him . . ."

"Who?"

"My mother could have," she said, the words so brittle they sounded like they might shatter. "With her magic. Before the

Dagda and his wretched Druids stole it from her. Before his óglach and their bloody dogs drove her from her home. She might have taught me how to cure such an affliction, but she abandoned me before I was old enough to learn. I only taught myself how to cause it. Now his fate lies in the hands of the gods. And they don't answer many prayers these days."

"After all these years," Neve said. "How could you, Emer?"

Emer looked at her as if she were mad. "How can you ask me that when you know what real magic—wild magic—feels like? You do, don't you? I can *smell* it on you." Emer turned to Ronan. "And you. Traitor to your own kind."

Ronan didn't bother to deny it.

"When the Tuatha Dé drove the Fomori out, we thought it would be better," Emer said, her voice harsh as crow call. "And it was, for a while. The magic of this land was left to bloom and blossom in its *own* way, strange and wild, and the folk of the land—*my* folk—were able to use it to our benefit. To *our* good for once. Never taking too much, always giving thanks, letting the wells refill and replenish. For generations. Right until *your* father stole it all away."

Emer looked down at the Dagda and Neve half expected her to reach for the iron knife and plunge it into his chest. But she didn't have to—Ruad Rofhessa would be dead soon enough.

"But why Úna?" Neve asked. "You had no cause to harm her. She would have been a good and prosperous queen to this land."

"You can tell yourself that," Emer said. "*She* did. But I knew better. So mild and gentle she was, they all say. Well, Eire isn't meant to be a mild and gentle land. There is *mystery* here greater than any tribe, and that mystery—strange, wondrous, dark, and dangerous—is the lifeblood of Eire. *She* didn't believe in magic at all. She was glad, in her heart, that it had been outlawed, and she would have kept it that way, continuing the Dagda's legacy."

Neve couldn't deny the bare truth of Emer's words. Still . . .

"Úna loved you," Neve said, the sound of her voice flayed raw.

"She *owned* me. She could have given me my freedom, but instead she handed me over to her little sister—like an outgrown toy—and told herself the lie that it was a kindness." Emer held up her arm to show the silver freedwoman cuff Neve had left her. "You, lady, were always more honest than your kin, even though it wasn't always to your benefit. I'll give you that much, I suppose. That I'll die at your hand means I won't be killed by a liar, at least."

"You're not going to die by my hand, Emer." Neve shook her head.

"His then?" She twitched her head in Ronan's direction. "Traitor to his own?"

"Not by the hand of anyone under my command," Neve said. "And, thanks to you, everyone in Temair will soon be under my command. I suppose I should thank you—"

Emer lunged across the bed and snatched up the fuath curse.

Neve swore as Emer bolted for the door, her lips already forming the hideous words that would call the demon forth. Ronan made a desperate grab for her but she was as swift and nimble as her namesake in flight.

Neve didn't know if Emer meant to unleash the fuath on her or her father or all of them, but when the poison-green light spun into demonic being, Emer was closest.

And so the demon turned its malevolence on her.

Emer's screams tore the air, echoing off the stone walls of the corridor, as the demon drove vaporous claws into her chest, digging for her beating heart. Neve's arrow got there first. Emer stiffened, hands clutching at the air for a moment before she dropped to the ground in a heap. In the distance, too far away to make a difference, the harrow hounds sent up a frenzied cry.

The fuath turned glowing, hate-filled eyes on Neve . . . and smiled.

It bounded down the hall toward her, shrieking hate . . .

And the crude iron dagger punched through its throat.

Ronan, arm still extended, stood panting beside Neve, his eyes not quite completely black, in the same way that she could feel hers weren't quite completely gold. As she watched, the few darkling marks that had appeared on his wrists began to fade. She looked down at her own hands and saw the gleam of her own dark-gold markings shimmer away to nothing.

At the other end of the corridor, Fintan stared in astonishment, with Thorn straining against her leash.

Neve froze. "Fintan—"

Red-eyed with cursefire, the harrow hound tore free and bounded down the corridor toward her, jaws snapping. Neve threw her arm up in front of her face, bracing for the moment when teeth and claws tore her flesh. It never came.

Thorn's howls turned to querulous whines as she reached Neve.

Neve cracked open one eye and peered down to see the harrow hound crouching on her belly at Neve's feet, the crimson fire fading from her eyes. Neve slowly crouched down and held her hand out to Thorn, who nuzzled her still faintly glowing palm. It was an unexpected vindication for Neve. A sign that maybe—

just *maybe*—she was on the right path. She lifted her head to see Fintan standing there, sword in hand, and a look on his face she couldn't quite interpret.

"Is Ruad Rofhessa gone over the Great Dark River?" he asked, his voice ragged.

Neve shook her head, but Ronan said quietly, "If he hasn't yet, it's only that he stands on the bank, awaiting the boat that will ferry him across."

Fintan dropped to one knee, head bowed. "Then my life and sword are yours, my king," he said to Neve. "The heart and soul in my body. I pledge my destiny in service to the true Dagda, for that is what you surely are."

Neve opened her mouth to protest, but Thorn rolled over on her side and presented her belly.

"I've seen magic in my time and I've seen *magic*, lady. Thorn, with all her cursefire ablaze in her eyes a bare moment ago, lays her head at your feet."

"If only to have me scratch her ears," Neve said, embarrassed by Fintan's devotion. There was more—much more—to be done before she could truly lay claim to the óglach chief's offered oath. "I'm still just Neve, Fintan. Not the Dagda yet. But I need to convince the lords of the Tuatha Dé of the exact opposite, and I need your help. We stand at the threshold of two battles this night, my friend. One for the soul of Eire . . . and one for her body. I will tell you everything on the way."

Fintan collected himself and sheathed his blade.

Suddenly, there was a loud crash from the Dagda's chamber and Neve spun on her heel and ran back inside.

Ruad Rofhessa was half risen from his bed, gasping for breath, his war club knocked from its stand onto the stone floor and a table with a mead jug tipped over, the dark reddish drink pooling like spilled blood. Neve rushed to his side and put an arm across his chest, easing him back onto the pillow. His gaze, feverish and roaming, settled on her face and he smiled. A silly, awkward grin, like a little boy's.

He lifted a hand to her cheek and it was cool and dry.

"Beloved of the Wolf," he said. It was the first time he'd ever called her that.

Neve felt tears prickling at the corners of her eyes. *"Father . . ."*

"Be brave," he said, the grin fading to a smile that was serene and full of a new, strange, and secret wisdom. "The stones . . . the stones will show you the way . . ."

"I don't—"

"Tell Úna I loved her . . ."

And then the mighty Dagda, high chieftain and king of the Tuatha Dé, Lord of Temair and of all the realm of Eire, was gone. Neve felt his last breath shudder through his massive frame. She thought she could almost see his wraith rise and vanish into the darkness. Then there was stillness. Emptiness. A space where there had been a spirit. His eyes were closed; she didn't need to do that for him. She just lifted his hands and laid them on his chest and, bending over, kissed him on the forehead.

Back out in the hallway, the curse stone lay on the floor beside Emer's hand, her fingers curled loosely around emptiness. The strip of chiseled flint had shattered into a dozen or more pieces. Ronan pulled a cloth from his satchel and began to gather them up, careful not to leave even the tiniest shard behind. Neve bent and gently drew Emer's—Sparrow's—shawl over her face.

Neve stood, feeling numb but knowing that wouldn't last long. She whispered a plea for forgiveness—for them both—hoping Emer's wraith might still be near enough to hear.

Then she turned to Ronan and said, "I need you."

"You have me."

She turned to Fintan. "Call all the tuath chieftains to meet at my father's Great Barrow." It was her first real command as Dagda in all but name. "Assemble the óglach. Ready them for battle. And find the Druid Gofannon, wherever he has gone."

XXIX

SAKIR FASTENED THE last buckle on the breastplate over top of the Korinthian scale armor Queen Anann had given Neve. There was power sleeping in the Scathach's battle dress, Neve could tell. She could feel it. And that, she knew, made it a risk. But like the Faoladh when they'd appeared in armor before the Dagda and his lords, Neve knew that tonight, she needed to make the right kind of impression. Still, risk was one thing and recklessness another, and so, before donning the ancient armor, Neve had locked her wolf mask away in a trunk. She wasn't about to hand over the reins to the Scathach entirely, no matter how much she was beginning to relish the ride.

Sakir tucked away the buckle strap and his fingers, Neve saw, were shaking. Something she'd never seen before. She reached out and took his hands in hers.

"Sakir . . ."

He stared down at their hands, not speaking. Not moving.

"What is it?"

"I was never supposed to teach you how to fight," he said quietly. "But I did. Even knowing—somehow I always knew—that one day you'd take what you learned from me and ride into battle."

Her fingers tightened on his. "Then it's good you taught me well."

"I shouldn't have taught you at all." He looked away from her. "Because then I wouldn't be standing here on the very edge of losing you."

"You're going to have to work a great deal harder to lose me, Horse Lord," Neve said. "You're the one driving my chariot."

Sakir swallowed thickly. "Just don't do anything stupid, like fall off," he said, his voice gruff as he added a belated "my king."

He lifted the Scathach's helmet from Neve's dressing table and settled it on her head, over the long dark hair she'd braided tightly down her back. As the heavy bronze pressed down on her brow, the whispers in Neve's head grew to a roar, like a deluge from a thunderstorm crashing down a mountain crevasse. Neve lifted her hands to the sides of her head, almost tearing the helmet off for fear she would drown. But she fought the impulse. Neve lowered her hands and looked at where the mark on her palm glimmered just enough to remind her of its power.

Half the blood in her veins might have been Tuatha Dé, but the other half was Fé Fíada. Her armor was the Scathach's, but her greatest weapon was her sigil flame. Two sides of the same coin and she needed both. Working together, not fighting each other. The Scathach seemed to realize that. Neve took a deep breath and the noise in her mind receded like a wave, back into a whisper as the enormity of what she was about to do settled on her like a

cloak. She would need to convince the warlords not just to prepare for the coming battle, but to follow *her* into the thick of it.

She looked at Sakir and nodded.

He stalked over to her chamber door and flung it wide. Neve
stepped out into the corridor to see Ronan waiting there, outfit-
ted in a suit of óglach armor that Fintan must have scrounged for
him. He wore the Scathach's iron dagger on his hip. Neve carried
her new iron-bladed sagaris on hers.

She held her arms out by her sides. "Well? How do I look?"

"It's a bit much for everyday mischief," Ronan said, tilting his
head as he took in her majesty from head to toe. "But for a kingmaking, I think it nicely hits the mark."

She arched a brow at him. "Your king requires you to bear arms.
Fortunately, I happen to have a spare." She nodded at Sakir, who
handed Ronan her original sagaris—the one with the bronze blade.

"Hit your enemy with the sharp side," Sakir said dryly, loosening his own axe in its sheath. "You'll get the hang of it. Probably."

"Or I won't." Ronan shrugged. "And then *you'll* have to swing
an axe with each hand. Hope you can drive a chariot with your
teeth."

Sakir grinned in response.

"The bastard probably could, too," Ronan muttered as Neve
swept past the two of them, black cloak billowing in her wake.

Ronan and Sakir fell into step behind her, and, flanked by the
two of them, Neve stalked through the palace corridors and out
into the courtyard, where her chariot and two horses stood ready.

As they crossed the river, Neve could see the gathering of tuath
chieftains and high-ranking lords of Temair clustered outside the
stone circle of her father's temple. She could hear the swell of

confusion and anger when the lords saw who it was who'd called them there, and her hands grew slick with sweat on the reins.

She saw Lorcan standing beside Úna's stone with his father, Soren, who gave her a slight nod of his head as she approached. As did Farsa, her father's Horse Lord, who then locked eyes with Sakir, a fierce pride shining in his gaze. Neve knew the support of those three alone would carry some weight. But the others . . . A knot tightened in her stomach. As she drove her chariot through the crowd, she could feel the wariness, the animosity, the outright hostility, but she'd be damned if she'd allow it any room to breathe. The scales of her armor whispered dragon strength to her limbs as she drew her chariot to a stop at the head of the gathering. The brim of her helmet gripped her brow like a royal diadem. The cuirass that wrapped around her torso held her straight and tall as any conquering hero.

Now. Seize Destiny by the throat and make it bow to you.

"The Dagda is dead," Neve declared to the gathered lords. "His spirit has traveled to the Beyond Realms." The silence that descended on the plain was louder than thunder. "The Throne of Destiny is not an empty chair," she continued before anyone could react. "It cannot be. The Lia Fail's voice will sound for the new Tuatha Dé king. The Stone stands in the chamber at the center of Brú na Bóinne and this night you will hear its mighty shout."

"Shout for *who*, Princess?" asked Balar.

Neve slowly swept the gathering with her gaze—as if she might be searching for the chieftain that the Lia Fail could claim worthy—and then said, simply: "For me."

At Neve's words, a surge of vitriol poured forth. It was silenced in the next moment by the deafening clamor of war horns as

Lorcan and his father, Soren, sounded the carnyx—the tall bronze wolf-headed war horns that, up until that night, had stood on either side of the Throne of Destiny in the throne room of Temair. Lorcan hadn't lied, Neve thought, when he'd told her he believed in her.

Neve weathered the outburst of the warlords, one hand resting on her sagaris, until the ringing of the horns faded over the distant hills.

"This is a jest," Balar sneered. "A Dagda is a chieftain, with a tuath warband of his own to command. You have a stable hand and"—he flicked a hand first at Sakir and then at Ronan in his borrowed armor—"from the looks of it, a Fir Bolg peasant dressed up in some óglach's castoffs." Laughter rang out from the gathered crowd.

"I understand the doubt some—most—of you harbor," Neve said, ignoring the jibe. "That's why I will prove this night that my place is upon the Throne of Destiny."

And what will you do if the Lia Fail betrays you in that moment? It betrayed me . . .

Neve closed her eyes. *I'm not you.*

Are you so very sure of that, Little Scota?

Neve opened her eyes and felt herself break out in a cold sweat beneath the Scathach's helmet. What if this was all a ruse? What if Gofannon had planned it this way all along? She might yet lay her hand upon the Stone and find out her destiny was—what had her mother said?—agony. Or death. What if that was the price of the Scathach's resurrection? A sacrifice? What if the Scathach, herself long trapped in the Lia Fail, had lied to Neve's mother all those years ago?

In the cave of her skull, Neve's fears ran rampant, chased by an echo of wild laughter. But outwardly, she kept her expression utterly composed.

"Of course," she continued, "you are welcome to return to Temair, if you so wish. My óglach and their harrow hounds will be more than happy to escort you and ensure your safety and comfort within the palace walls until my return. At which time," Neve added, "I would be delighted to discuss the matter of tuath fealty at more leisure."

Clever girl . . .

Neve turned away so they couldn't see the flush on her cheeks or notice how her pulse fluttered like the heart of a hunted hare, and, for a moment, Neve thought she saw a shadowy figure standing in the doorway of the temple, as if waiting to welcome her. Or warn her away . . . Then, in the blink of an eye, the figure blurred and shifted, and now she saw the dark shape of a wolf, clearly outlined against the white wall of the temple. It turned and walked into the temple's dark entrance.

Neve was Beloved of the Wolf. But was it the right wolf, under the circumstances? The Lia Fail had come from Kemet. It belonged to the Tuatha Dé. But the source of Neve's own power was a gift of the gods of Eire. Her mother had told her she was a bridge. What if she was wrong? How could Neve possibly think she could unite the folk of Eire under her banner, when there was a battle still raging within herself?

And what if, when she touched the Stone, the wrong side won that battle?

Only one way to find out.

Neve stepped down off the deck of her chariot. Ronan and Sakir dismounted and flanked her as she walked forward, through the now completed circle of stones, and stopped in front of the yawning portal.

"If the Lia Fail remains silent," she said quietly to them, "I won't be coming back out."

Sakir's eyes went wide and he opened his mouth as if to protest.

"And you will tear down the stones in this circle," Neve continued quickly. "So the magic of the land that my father and Gofannon trapped in this barrow can be free in Eire once more. But you must then close up the portal before the Scathach can escape. Do I make myself clear?"

Ronan nodded and after a long hesitation, Sakir did, too.

Lorcan and Soren joined them a few moments later with torches and spears, and together, they turned to face the gathered warriors spread out over most of the floodplain. The air was thick with fraught anticipation.

"We are not alone!" Soren suddenly called out in warning as a gang of shadows crested the curving slope of the Great Barrow and ran toward them, moving like wraiths.

Neve reached for her sagaris and shouted, "No! I have not summoned you—"

One of the shadows charged Ronan, knocking him off his feet. He hit the ground hard enough to knock the wind from his lungs and was pinned to the ground with a knee on his chest and a pair of crossed swords at his throat.

"*Stop*—"

"He bears the Scathach's blue-jeweled blade!" his assailant shouted over Neve's protest. "The vision is true!" Then she pushed back the hood of her dark cloak, and he found himself staring up at the leader of the Faoladh.

"Cliona—"

"My lovely thief," she said, a moment of regret flickering in her forest-green gaze. "I should have known it would be you . . ."

She divested Ronan of both his new sagaris and the iron dagger—handing the latter to Aevinn—and stood back while two of her Faoladh sisters took Ronan by the arms and dragged him up to a kneeling position. The circle of Tuatha Dé lords stood by, watching in astonishment, clearly not understanding what exactly was happening. For his part, neither did Ronan. Not until Aevinn stepped toward where Neve stood, axe held at the ready.

"Mighty Faoladh," Neve said, eyes darting from Cliona to Aevinn, her breathing quick and shallow, "your presence is most welcome at these proceedings, only I must speak with you first. The oath I swore—"

"I have seen the death of Ruad Rofhessa in the eye of my mind," Aevinn cried out. "The ravens have heralded his passing. The Dagda of the Tuatha Dé is gone. There is no Dagda now to free us from our curse. Therefore, we demand the blood sacrifice that *you*, Neve Anann Eriu, have hitherto promised us!"

She pointed with the iron dagger at Ronan.

"*What?*" Ronan turned to Neve. "What blood sacrifice? Does she mean—"

"No!" Neve shook her head. "This is *not* what I meant to happen, Faoladh."

You made a blood promise, Little Scota. You'll find those aren't easily broken.

"No. Ronan—"

"My Sight leads us to this man," Aevinn said, her eyes white-rimmed, teeth bared in a terrifying grimace. "The one who bears the Scathach's blade upon his hip. His is the blood we will spill this night! The last Fomori blood in all of Eire . . ."

He shook his head in vigorous protest. "I'm *not* the last! What are you—"

Aevinn slashed through the air with the Scathach's iron dagger and Ronan yelped in pain as a line of dark blood welled up on his cheek, flaring with a spark of indigo light as it dripped onto the ground.

"No!" Neve shouted. "Stop. *Stop!*"

The iron dagger hovered in the air above Ronan's head. All around Neve the circle of tuath chieftains watched, waiting. There would be no help from them. Not until Neve had proved herself.

"I go now—right *now*—to seek the cry of the Lia Fail," Neve said. "Once the Stone of Destiny grants me my kingship, I'll grant you your freedom. I swear it. I'll give you back your rias-trad *without* the need for Fomori blood. Without the need for *any* blood."

Aevinn's fingers twitched convulsively on the iron dagger's hilt, but Cliona licked her lips and put a hand on the seeress's shoulder.

"We won't wait much longer," Cliona said. Then she turned back to Ronan, wild longing flooding her gaze. "We *can't.*"

Neve nodded. She knew the hunger she saw in the eyes of the Faoladh wasn't something she could stave off for long. She looked at Ronan where he lay upon the ground and bit her lip to keep from pleading for his life. He stared back at her, his gray eyes fearless in that moment. Whether that was because he believed in her, or simply because he had accepted whatever fate awaited him, she couldn't tell. And she wished she felt that same bravery.

Instead, she felt as if she was wagering her kingdom and her life—and Ronan's—on a deadly game of Hare and Hunter. And she knew as well as any Fir Bolg peasant, the winner always cheated.

Without another word, Neve turned and walked forward alone, between the two stones that flanked the avenue leading to the great barrow of Brú na Bóinne.

—◦◦◦—

Neve stepped over the threshold and the portal swallowed her whole, her dark cloak and black bronze helmet blending into the shadows. Ronan fervently hoped that if there was anything about the barrow that meant her ill, it would choke. Not least because he knew that, if she didn't return, he was a dead man on his knees. The sound of the word "Fomori" had sent an instinctive, time-honored revulsion shuddering through the gathered Tuatha Dé lords. Any hope Ronan might have held out for their aid had vanished with the revelation of his true nature.

But he couldn't possibly have cared less in that moment.

His only concern was Neve, and whether she would survive the touch of the Lia Fail. But if she did, her people would have to accept her as Dagda. Regardless, even, of the unsavory company she kept. Ronan could feel the stars wheeling overhead as they all waited for . . . something. He couldn't even fathom what that something would be. What, exactly, happened during a kingmaking? He didn't know. He'd never been to one.

The night seemed to stretch on into infinity and still Neve didn't reappear. There was no sound, no movement from within the barrow. Ronan could hear his heartbeat thrumming in his ears, louder and louder the longer the silence spooled out. He closed his eyes, listening and *listening* . . . An age passed. And then another. Ronan felt a blooming terror begin to creep around his heart at the thought that Neve might be hurt. Or worse.

"We will wait no longer," Cliona said finally, as she took the blade from Aevinn's hand.

"No!" Sakir cried. "She *will* return—"

He lunged forward but Grian took his legs out from under him and pinned him to the ground, a blade pressed against his spine.

Ronan swallowed the thick knot of apprehension in his throat. "Cliona, please—"

"The Faoladh will spill the blood of this Fomori man tonight," Cliona proclaimed, her voice raised so that the gathered warriors would hear her every word. "We will claim his power for our own, in the breach of the Dagda's passing without an heir."

She moved like lightning and Ronan shouted in pain as another slash of the blade—just above the borrowed armor he wore—opened a gash along the side of his neck. Ronan watched, numb with shock, as blood poured down his neck and began to pool on the ground before him.

Aevinn began a low, sonorous chant. A thin mist began to rise in a circle around Ronan, shifting in hue from pearly silver to a deep, dark crimson.

The circle of Tuatha Dé warlords backed away in dread as the mist began to spread across the ground, creeping toward the Faoladh. With each warrior sister the red fog touched, Ronan let out a tortured gasp.

"With thanks and honor for his sacrifice," Cliona continued, her face tipped up toward the moon. "Macha shall receive our offering and once more bestow the power of our riastrad upon us."

Ronan lifted his head weakly, struggling to focus on the barrow. On the shadows he saw moving there. He didn't believe in gods, but he struggled to form his own plea to the wolf goddess in that moment. But before he could reach for the words, the bone-chilling howl of a wolf sounded from the barrow.

Everyone turned to see a tall figure, a woman cloaked in profound darkness, standing on top of Brú na Bóinne. Faceless, golden-eyed, she vanished as his vision began to grow dim, and a wolf—a huge, coal-black wolf—stood in her place, long white teeth bared in a frightful grimace.

A wolf on a wide green hill . . .

A wave of sound crashed over the gathering, hammering all but the strongest warrior to their hands and knees. Indescribably glorious and terrifying all at once, it was the voice of the Lia Fail unleashed.

The Lia Fail was not of Eire, but Eire recognized its power.

The roar and music swelled, bursting like the blasts from a hundred carnyx, just as Queen Anann had described—but also so much more. There was a crack of lightning and a rolling crash of thunder, the clashing of a thousand swords against a thousand shields, the shouts of a joyous celebration in a feast hall after a bountiful harvest, and the voices of women raised in sweet songs that wove between the cries of triumph in battle.

And it was all for her. For Neve Anann Eriu . . .

The Lia Fail, having been denied its true king for too many years, made certain to let the gathered lords and warriors know it had made its choice. In no uncertain terms. The cry of the Stone of Destiny faded into a filled silence.

And Ronan of Blackwater collapsed in a widening pool of blood.

XXX

NEVE STAGGERED BACK out through the barrow's portal and almost fell to her knees.

As she thrust her arms out in front of her, she saw the serpentine sigils that flowed beneath the surface of her skin in glimmering gold.

"Ronan!" Neve cried, rushing toward where he was splayed out on the ground, a wound on his neck spilling a river of blood. He struggled to lift his head and as their gazes met, Neve saw there was no anger or hate or even reproach for what she'd promised the Faoladh.

It was awe . . . and pride. He was proud of her. More than that.

And Neve wasn't about to lose him.

The firewolf sigil on her palm ignited. With savagely focused intent, Neve thrust her hand into the air—a beacon shining in the night—and reached out with her own Fé, gathering the red mist of Ronan's dread sacrifice and drawing it back toward him, wrapping the two of them in a tenebrous whirlwind that could not dim her light. She dropped to her knees on the blood-wet ground and lifted his hand, pressing the glow of her palm on the scar he'd earned the first night they'd met as children, all those years ago.

His lips moved, barely breathing a word, and she leaned closer to him to hear.

"Tickles," Ronan said in a ragged whisper.

Neve felt a sob stick in her throat, and her shoulders shook as she saw the lines of his darklight sigils beginning to appear, ever so faintly. They grew darker, stronger. The edges of the wound on Ronan's neck closed before her eyes and color flooded back into his alabaster-white face.

Neve heard him cry out from the midst of the maelstrom that surrounded them, even as she heard the Faoladh howling as Aevinn's riastrad spell began to unravel.

But Neve wasn't finished.

She needed Ronan—more than she'd ever thought possible—and she needed him alive. But she also needed her Faoladh warband if she was to become a functioning Dagda and fight the coming battle. She would be damned if she couldn't have both.

With Macha's blessing.

And mine. The Faoladh have always been mine.

Now they will be again . . .

The Scathach's words seethed with an ugly note of triumph and Neve felt her resolve weaken. But in that moment, the goddess Macha silenced the whispers of the Scathach with her own wolf-song voice.

In the echoing hush that followed, Neve was free to grasp that fearsome, feral power with all her soul. She could barely contain it. And why should she? She was Beloved of the Wolf. She was the Dagda. And her first act as Eire's new-chosen king would be to undo the terrible curse that never should have been cast upon the sisterhood of warriors who stood before her.

The light that seemed to burn beneath Neve's skin shot from her fingertips like forked lightning, branching and splitting through the air to strike right at the heart of every single one of the Faoladh. The sight and sound of the Fomori magic flowing back into that band of warriors, maybe a hundred of them altogether, gathered in the darkness—daughters of daughters of daughters who'd lived so long without the thing that defined their very souls—was beyond overwhelming. It was savage and glorious and beautiful. The whole floodplain surrounding the Great Barrow was bathed in a burst of golden light.

Neve stepped up on the deck of her chariot and raised her arms as the moon lifted up over the hills. Cliona threw back her head and howled. The sound that poured from her throat was chilling. The others joined in, the howls turned to snarls, and the Faoladh—right before the astonished eyes of the gathered Tuatha Dé—transformed.

The faces of the women altered, their eyes becoming larger and darker, the hair on their heads growing wilder, fuller. Sinews stretched torturously and joints elongated, angling up and back. The transformed Faoladh were a perfect blending, a balance between human and beast: standing upright on limbs longer and more heavily muscled, fingers longer and stronger, ending in heavy black claws that looked capable of rending shield and flesh. Cliona stepped out in front of her band, her skin a pale silvery color like her wild locks and her blue eyes wide and canted upward at the outer corners. Her face had taken on a wolfen aspect, drawn forward over a wider mouth full of very long, very sharp teeth.

The shapeshifting happened in the blink of an eye, followed closely by the shouts of alarm and surprise from the Tuatha Dé warriors and the rasp and hiss of their swords, drawn reflexively.

"How like you my warband, Lord Balar?" Neve called out.

The massive brute of a warrior cast his glance over the Faoladh assembled at Neve's back. Living weapons, capable of speed and strength and brutally efficient violence in service of their new leader.

And then a huge, fierce grin split his face.

"I like them very much, my king!" Balar shouted, breaking into a half-mad laugh as if the coming battle was there to be charged headlong into that very moment. "*These* are king's warriors to fight side by side with. The bards will have to sing their throats raw and harp their fingers bloody to record the deeds of a warband with such monstrous valor!"

With Balar and the chieftains satisfied, she needed one last gesture, Neve thought. For the Horse Lords gathered there. And to show the Tuatha Dé that she could use her magic—control it—with purpose. That it was not something to be feared or suppressed, the way her father had. She took up the reins of her chariot and flickering flames began to dance along the traces, flowing down the sides of the chariot, and the horses—the magnificent pair of matched silver chariot horses—began to gleam, shining like two pale white-gold comets, lighting up the night, burning without heat, without destruction.

Without fear.

Lorcan was the first lord to draw his sword and drop to one knee, jamming the point of the blade into the soil.

"My sword and my life in service," he said in a clear and ringing voice, "to this soil, to this realm, to my king, the Dagda Neve Anann Eriu. Chosen of the Stone of Destiny, long and just may you rule over the mighty Tuatha Dé."

"That, my lords," Neve said, "will be up to all of you gathered here tonight. I, for one, do not think that we will fail."

XXXI

Neve's unexpected kingmaking that night was a heady victory, tinged with the sorrow of the Dagda's passing. It would take some doing, Neve suspected, before she could begin to untangle the knots of feeling she had packed away in her heart about Ruad Rofhessa. He hadn't, in the end and after all, been her father. And they'd both—in some way—known it. But there were times growing up when he *had* been.

Back in the stable yard, alone except for Sakir and Ronan, she stepped down from her chariot and stumbled over her own feet. Sakir reached to steady her, but Ronan got there first.

He wrapped an arm around her shoulder and said, "I think your majesty has likely had enough excitement for one day."

Neve pushed herself upright with a hand against his chest and tugged the helmet from her head. She nodded to Sakir, who tipped one of his ironic half bows in her direction. *That much, at least, hasn't changed,* she thought. *The moment these two start treating me with proper respect, all is lost.*

"I want Lorcan to speak to Cliona about sending out parties of Faoladh to search for Gofannon and any of his wretched Druids who haven't already fled for the farthest hills. If any are still around, the Dagda's Wolves should be able to track them down. I'll also need current rosters of men and equipment from each of the tuaths drawn up. And a full tally of my Scythian contingent—men and mounts. You will be my official emissary to the Horse Lords, Sakir," she said. "I know the Dagda didn't see the need for additional cavalry to protect Temair, but I most certainly do."

"That's because you are wise well beyond your years, my king," Sakir said, the dryness of his tone effectively blunting such courtly flattery. But she could tell he truly meant it when he said, "I am honored to act in such capacity."

"Good. See to it, my friend." She gripped his arm and together they shared a long glance. The stable rats were in charge of the whole palace, now, it seemed. They'd best not muck it up.

As she made her way back to her apartments, Neve could feel a subtle change in the air. The corridors had extra guards posted at every entrance, and half the torches lining the walls had burned out, and yet the darkness somehow felt less heavy, the halls less constricted. As if, with the Dagda's passing, his madness had begun to lift. Like a curse unraveling . . . But there was yet more work to be done. Much more.

Neve and Ronan reached the door to her chambers and she bid him good night. "Fintan will find you sleeping quarters," she said, reaching for the helmet in his hands.

Ronan didn't move.

Neve lifted an eyebrow at him. "What? You're staring."

"You look . . ." He dipped his head for a moment. Then he lifted his gaze again and said, "You'll need help. With . . . your armor. The fastenings."

"I'll get Emer to—" No. No, she wouldn't. "I'm sure I can manage it myself."

"You'll wind up sleeping standing up." Ronan said. He lifted a hand to the bronze fitting holding her cloak attached to the top of her cuirass. "I managed to figure out mine. It was only a little less complicated than you. Than *yours*, I mean." His iron-gray gaze turned smoky in the dim light of the corridor. "Let me help you."

Neve shook her head, smiling, and slowly backed away so her shoulder blades pushed the door to her chamber open. She invited Ronan in with a nod of her head.

The rooms were quiet. Dark. Cold. No bustling, no brazier already lit and glowing, no nightclothes laid out or mug of mulled cider waiting. And none of the humor and homely wisdom. Nor the companionship that Neve had always—she now saw, too late—taken for granted. She lit the brazier herself with a spark of her Fé, and the effort almost caused her to pass out. She had stretched herself to the breaking point—well past, to be truthful—without even fully realizing it. And clearly, she still had a lot to learn about her gifts.

"Hang on, now," Ronan was there to catch her again as she teetered. "Didn't we decide you'd had enough for the day?"

He steadied her and undid the fasteners of her cloak so he could lift the weight of it off her shoulders. Neve stood there, mesmerized by the movement of his long, nimble thief's fingers as he worked the ties and fastenings, divesting her of her armor, one piece at a time. The corner of his mouth lifted in a hint of his usual sardonic smile as he raised her arms up to rest on his shoulders and reached for the buckles on the sides of her cuirass.

"Ah, sweet freedom," Ronan murmured, as the rigid carapace fell away.

Neve felt her ribcage expand with breath, unimpeded, and almost wept with relief.

Ronan set aside the armor and led her over to the couch, the scale mail tunic she still wore hissing as she moved. Ronan undid the leather ties that fastened it at the shoulders and the whole thing slid to the floor like the shed skin of a serpent. Holding his hands, Neve stepped out of the circle of dragon scales. She wore only a sleeveless tunic and leggings and her whole body felt light as air—as if she might float away if he let go of her.

She didn't want him to let go.

He didn't seem inclined to.

Neve tilted her head up so she could look into Ronan's gray eyes. He was good at hiding his true feelings—like any decent thief—but there in the darkness, she could sense one emotion too strong for him to truly hide.

"What are you afraid of, king's thief?" she asked.

"You," Ronan answered. "For you . . . *of* you . . ."

"I felt the same when I saw what you could do at the sacred spring. Who you really are."

She lifted a hand to his face. Remembering how different—and how very much the same—he seemed when he called upon his Fomori magic. It was as if the Fé clarified him, burning away all the defenses, all of the disguises, stripping him to the core, down to the very essence of what made him Ronan.

"I'm not about to lob an axe at you, if that's what you mean," Ronan said.

"You're angry about the Faoladh." She lifted her other hand, framing his face.

He raised an eyebrow at her. "You made a deal to sacrifice me to a pack of berserker warrior women—who I *thought* were my friends."

"Forgive me, Ronan. I made that bargain when I thought you were a murderer," she said. "And they are your friends, still."

"They cut my throat," he murmured, his voice going a bit thready as Neve leaned forward and pressed her mouth to the place on his neck where the knife wound had been.

"Are you sure?" she whispered, feeling his pulse beat against her lips. "I can't seem to find the scar . . ."

"It was right below the one *you* left when you tried to rob me in the marketplace," Ronan gasped. "Look harder."

He wound her in an embrace that was almost tighter than her armor, but Neve didn't complain. He dipped his head forward so that his mouth could find hers, and the kiss took her breath away. So very far away that she felt her legs give out on her at last. Before she could fall, Ronan swept her up in his arms and carried her across the room to the alcove with her sleeping couch. They were still kissing as he laid her gently down, but as he sat beside her, he pulled away just far enough so he could look into her eyes.

"Most kings," he murmured, "would have a poor thief executed for such brazen behavior."

"I'm keeping that option in reserve." Neve pulled him close for another kiss.

He started laughing against the corner of her mouth when she couldn't stifle the yawn that overtook her. "I said brazen, not boring . . ."

The lamplight gleamed in Ronan's eyes as he smiled and began working his fingers through her hair, slowly loosening her braid and drawing the long dark waves forward to curtain her shoulders.

"There is nothing boring about you, Ronan of Blackwater. It might have been a more peaceful life for you if there had been. Maybe longer, too." She shook her head slowly and her hair sifted through his hands like silk. "But you were given to me by the wolf goddess and I would not dishonor myself or insult her by returning that gift. Even though I might wish to, before our tale is fully told."

A frown line ticked between his brows. "Why would you wish such a thing?"

"Because, fool"—she reached up to gently smooth the crease with a fingertip—"it would be a grievous wound on my heart if anything should happen to you."

His frown faded and he smiled his slow, sly smile down at her.

"You should rest," he said and started to stand.

Neve wrapped her hand around his wrist. "You should stay," she said.

"Neve—"

"Gofannon has not been found," she argued. "I need . . . sleep. And protection. You will take the watch." She tilted her chin up, daring him to defy her royal decree.

His smile never faltered, just softened into something deeper as he looked at her. By the dim orange glow of the brazier, he stripped off what remained of his own armor, and sat down beside her on the bed. The palace was silent all around them as the newly made Dagda of the Tuatha Dé, Lord of Eire, Ruler of the Realm, King Among the Living, Beloved of the Wolf lay her head in his lap and was sound asleep before the king's royal thief could draw another breath.

⸺◆⸻

NEVE WOKE TO the sound of a distant flute in her ears and the perfume of lilies in her nostrils. The feeling of a desert wind kissing her cheeks . . .

Dreams, she thought, still muddled with sleep. *Whose dreams are these? They are not mine . . .*

In the pale golden light of morning seeping in through the high windows of her chamber, Neve rolled her head to see Ronan lying beside her, deep in slumber. Now *that* dream had been all hers, she thought as she lay there, her gaze tracing the lines of his face in repose, the lines of his neck and shoulder—the scar from her arrow healing in a shallow sickle curve—and his chest, rising and falling like waves on the sea. She would have stayed like that, just watching him, forever. But she could already hear voices outside.

The palace was astir, and the Dagda must be, too.

Her gaze drifted up, over Ronan's head, to the mural painted on the wall. The same image she'd woken to every morning of her life. Almost. The figure she'd seen in her mother's hearth fire was painted there now: the sorcerer Gofannon, revealed for who he truly was. But there were other changes, too. Elchmar's hand, resting on the hilt of his sword, now gleamed silver. As for the Scathach, the sight of her made Neve's breath catch in her throat.

Her hood was pushed back and, for the first time in her life, Neve could see her face. Or, at least, she would have . . . except the Scathach was wearing the golden wolf mask, framed by the mane of her dark, shining hair.

Like a story passed down from bard to bard through the years, details shifting, some details fading while others sharpened. Or altered. *Ships*, Neve thought, pushing herself up to sitting. *More of them. And shadows rising up from the river . . .*

"What is it?" Ronan's voice drifted up to her. "What's wrong?" She looked down to see his face still soft with sleep. "Nothing."

But when he looked over his shoulder to see what she'd been staring at, Neve watched his eyes grow dark. She could tell he could sense it too—the magic of the painting. The shifting course of fate it represented. The coming storm. Neve didn't know if the most dangerous threat was the invading Fomori ships in the east or the one building inside her. But she did know that having Ronan there pushed the whispering in her mind just a bit further away.

If Sakir was Neve's weapon in the coming battle, Ronan was Neve's shield.

She bent down to kiss his lips, and, in spite of the overwhelming urge to spend the morning engaged in that pursuit, she slipped from Ronan's embrace and padded across the room to find something befitting a Dagda. The closest she could come was a fitted forest-green tunic and leggings, to which she added a twisted golden torc around her neck and gold bracelets around her wrists.

IN THE HALL that had been Ruad Rofhessa's, the fire in the great hearth was stoked high, and lords of twelve tuaths awaited their

Dagda. Neve held her first war council. She listened to reports and asked questions about armor and weapons and supplies and fortifications. About tents and blacksmiths and horses. And how they would treat the wounded on the field.

They didn't yet know whether the invaders in the ships Ronan had temporarily becalmed in the North Sea with his Fé would come overland from a coastal anchorage or sail upriver. But even the most fractious of the warlords agreed: Brú na Bóinne would be their ultimate destination. Everyone in that hall had now witnessed the power Ruad Rofhessa and Gofannon had gathered there and knew it would be the prize the Fomori sought. Power that neither Neve nor any of her lords had any idea how to safely render harmless, should they lose. And so loss was not an option.

"Would help some if every Druid in the land hadn't suddenly vanished like a herd of deer at the snap of a twig," muttered Soren. "Treacherous bastards . . ."

"But it still doesn't mean we can just move the warband there and leave Temair unprotected," Lorcan said.

"Aye," Cliona agreed from where she leaned against an ornately carved pillar, looking only slightly out of place in her worn leathers and wild hair. "The invaders could just as easily shift their target and raze this fine and lovely palace to the ground to draw us back here or split our numbers."

True enough. After much discussion, Neve decided to leave the bulk of the warband camped in the fields outside the palace walls, with a smaller contingent at the barrow and her Scythian cavalry ready to mobilize at the blast of a carnyx horn.

"I want staggered scouting parties on either side of An Bhóinn," Neve said, gesturing at the serpentine line inscribed in the wax surface of the map table in front of her. "Here and here. And there." She pointed to the places along the river course. "And I want them reporting to you every hour," she told Lorcan and Soren, "not every few hours." She turned to Cliona. "I want to know if the birds seem restless or the river turns muddy where it's normally clear. If there is so much as a mild breeze blowing the wrong direction or a patch of stray mist that doesn't belong on a hill, I want to know about it."

Cliona gave her a nod of acknowledgement. Her Faoladh knew the terrain better than anyone.

"This isn't just a Fir Domnann raid," Neve continued. "These aren't cattle poachers or northern marauders wandering up and down the coast looking for easy pickings. The greatest weapon they have is unseen and unknown. They could be bringing magic back to a land that has been stripped of that very same thing. We are depleted, thanks to Gofannon and my father. We do not know *what* they are. Eyes and ears, my good lords. Eyes and ears . . ."

She dismissed the council, leaving Balar and Banach to wrangle the warlords. Cormac had been absent from the council and so Neve went to find her Scythian emissary outside the palace walls in the Horse Lords' camp. She headed in that direction, graciously ignoring the two unobtrusive shadows she'd grown ever since waking up that morning. The king's personal guard, drawn from the ranks of the óglach at Fintan's behest. She hadn't wanted to offend him, so she tolerated their presence and would continue to do so for at least another day or two. Maybe.

As she headed toward the main gate, Neve couldn't help but shake her head ruefully, wondering what Úna would have thought of it all. She probably would have laughed and said, "*You got what you wanted, little cub. Didn't I tell you to be mindful what you wish for?*"

"What I wish for most is to have you back," she sighed as she walked among the rows of tents and leather horse troughs. This would be so much easier with Úna there, the two of them ruling side by side . . .

Would it? She never wanted the same things for this realm as you do.

As we *do . . .*

Sakir hailed her from the clearing in front of Cormac's tent.

"Where's Cormac?" she asked. "I need to talk to him about cavalry deployment."

"He rode out hunting before sunrise," Sakir said. "The stew pots over the campfires were lacking meat, I'm told."

Neve frowned. "I need him here."

Sakir lifted the tent flap and gestured her inside. "I have the tallies you wanted. And I can send a scout into the forest to find my uncle."

Neve ducked inside and Sakir went to retrieve a stack of wax writing tablets. Neve sat on a cushioned bench and Sakir poured her a small cup of sweetened fermented mare's milk. She sipped the drink, lost in thought. Sakir waited patiently, knowing her. Knowing there was more she'd come to talk about than troop manifests.

Knowing she'd tell him eventually.

He's a Scythian. You cannot trust him. In the end, he will betray you, just as—

"Stop!" Neve slammed her cup down on the table, spilling her drink onto the lacquered surface. She closed her eyes and took a deep breath in the silence that followed.

When she opened her eyes again, her Horse Lord was staring at her.

"Sakir . . I fear my mind is not my own."

"Tell me."

She told. About the whispers. About the shifting visions in the mural the Scathach had painted in her own room all the long years ago. About how she feared that in preparing for the coming battle she had already lost. Because that was what the Scathach wanted her to do.

"You think the Scathach is using you," Sakir said, "to make her whole scheme come to pass."

"If I sit by and do nothing and, through my inaction, Gofannon opens the portal to the Otherworld . . ."

"Or," he said, "if, through your actions, Gofannon opens the portal . . ."

"I cannot know one way or the other. I'm second-guessing myself at every turn and she *knows* that." She cast a rueful grin his way. "I sound mad, I know."

"You sound like Neve," he said, returning the grin. "And that is enormously reassuring. Have you told Ronan about all of this?"

She shook her head. "He would do everything he could to keep me from riding out in battle, if I did."

"I knew there had to be something I liked about him," Sakir said dryly.

"Sakir . . ." Neve put her cup down and looked him in the eyes. "You are my most loyal friend." She pretended not to notice his expression at her use of that last word. "Swear to me, on your life and the lives of the Horse Lords and the continuance of the herd . . . that if it comes down to it—if I lose control of myself to the Scathach—that you will . . . end me."

The blood drained from his face. "I cannot—"

"You *must*," she said. "I've only just begun to realize how much power I *truly* hold in my hands. I'm nowhere near to controlling it yet. And it cannot fall to someone like her. Can you imagine the Scathach commanding the magic of the Fé Fíada? Sakir . . . her whispers, in my head, they are . . ." A shudder wracked Neve's spine. She inhaled deeply and finished her drink. "You're the only one I trust to do such a thing."

Sakir's mouth hardened and his eyes grew dark. "It is no great honor, my king, this thing you ask of me."

"And yet, my lord, you better than anyone know why I ask it."

The muscles of his jaw worked and for a moment, Neve actually thought he would tell her to leave the tent.

"What do you think *she* would do to the Horse Lords?" Neve asked. "What vengeance would she wreak? Think about what the Scathach did to the archers who hesitated to fire on the ships bearing the defeated Fomori." She reached for his hand, knowing it would make it easier and so much harder for him at the same time. "I don't know if I have control of the reins on this, Sakir. And I can't risk taking the Tuatha Dé to war unless I know *someone* does."

His fingers squeezed hers once. Then he let go. "You have my promise."

"That's all I need." She stood. "Now, if we're lucky, you won't have to keep it."

XXXII

THE SCOUT REPORTS found her wherever she was in the palace that morning—which seemed like everywhere—and all of them came back with nothing out of the ordinary. Each time she breathed a sigh of relief, followed by one of growing apprehension. By the time the sun had reached the zenith of its brief transit across the sky that day, she was anxious to address one duty that couldn't wait, but that she didn't know how to accomplish.

Fintan had posted an honor guard at the doors of the Dagda's chambers, where his body still lay, shrouded in his crimson war cloak. But since every single Druid had fled, there was no one at court to prepare Ruad Rofhessa for his final journey. Neve found herself strangely paralyzed by the dilemma until Ronan finally took her by the shoulders.

"I think I know someone who can help," he said a bit hesitantly. "That is, if you'll allow it."

"Who?" Neve asked, wary of his tone.

"His name is Swift." Ronan frowned. "He's . . . Well, to be honest, I'm not quite sure what exactly he is. Many things, I think. A fisherman, of sorts."

Neve frowned. "A fisherman?"

Ronan nodded. "He lives in Baile Sláine. The first time I encountered Swift was enough to make me ask around about him. I was told he lives in a good stout roundhouse with stone walls and a thatched roof—a reward from the king for a duty rendered, some years ago—and I think he'll know what to do."

As Neve heard Ronan echo back her own words—spoken over mugs of brown beer in a musty little Blackwater bruidean—she understood the rightness of it.

They rode out together, north to the village of Baile Sláine, where, with a few discreet inquiries, it didn't take long to find where the old man sat beside his fire in a tidy little riverside house. When they ducked inside the leather-curtained doorway, they found three cups of honey mead poured and set out on a little table.

"I've long awaited—*hoped* for—this day," Swift said, when they'd settled themselves on stools at his behest. "Oh, not the death of that old ruffian, to be sure. Didn't want that . . ."

"The last thing he told me," Neve said, "was not to lay him to rest in the Great Barrow. He realized too late that it was not what he thought it would be."

"Late wisdom is still wisdom." Swift sighed. "And his intentions, it must be said, were pure. At least in the beginning. Pure things are so often easily corruptible, my dear. Of course I will help you. Deliver the king of Temair to me, and we who deal with such things among the Fir Bolg will prepare him properly, so that you may send him skyward. That is, if you prevail, and if the Tuatha Dé ride out the coming storm."

"You mean the battle brewing over Brú na Bóinne, don't you?" Ronan asked. "Do you know what will happen?"

Swift's eyes glittered darkly. "That I cannot say." He shrugged and refilled their cups—and his own. "This is not the working of the gods of this isle, and so what lies beyond that portal is barred from my sight. What I do know is this: you are the thread that binds the two halves of this tapestry, Neve Anann Eriu. The bridge that spans the chasm between two peoples."

"My mother said something like that to me," Neve said quietly.

"Your mother is wise beyond reckoning. Stole many a young man's heart, I remember." He frowned. "Give her my respects when next you see her. And . . . take the south road back to Temair, through the forest. Not the river path." Swift was staring intently at the flames of his fire, his eyes tracking things only he could see.

Neve and Ronan exchanged a glance. The river track was the easier ride, but they both knew enough not to ignore the old fisherman's suggestion.

———

THE SUN WAS already near to setting by the time they left Baile Sláine. It would be full dark by the time they reached Temair. A sense of foreboding settled on Neve's shoulders as they rode, their shadows lengthening across the frost-crisp meadows. The sun would rise again on the shortest day of the year. Followed by the longest night . . . and then, the moment of sunrise when the Dagda would have consecrated his monument, had he still lived. That moment, Neve knew, was the hinge point—what Gofannon had been working toward—and what she had to keep from happening.

Beneath the black lace canopy of the tree branches, the crimson sky turned mauve then violet then indigo. Neve's eyes seemed to adjust to the darkness better than she was used to, but she turned to Ronan, about to ask if she should try to conjure a Fé flame to help light their way. She bit down on her words when he suddenly reached for her horse's bridle with one hand and put a finger to his lips with the other. He cocked his head and listened and, after a moment, Neve heard it, too.

Voices. Low, murmuring, nearby . . .

There was a rocky outcropping off to the side of the path near a small waterfall and a rushing stream. As quietly as possible, they dismounted and left their horses tethered to a tree on the path, moving soundlessly on foot near an abandoned mud hut— probably an old fishing camp—on the banks of the stream. The roof of the little hovel was half caved in, clearly deserted. Ronan beckoned her forward, into the shell, and out the other side to where there was an escarpment. He crouched low and crawled to the edge of a precipice. Neve followed close behind. Peering over the edge, she could just make out the mouth of a cave on the far side of the stream, fronted by a clearing marked with a standing stone.

A meeting place. Shadows moving beneath the trees.

This, somehow, was what Swift had wanted them to stumble upon.

"The Lia Fail spoke for *her*," said a male voice, deep and strong, carrying over the chatter of the icy stream running down the hillside. "Again. Not for me. Not for him. For *her*. It is the will of the gods—"

"And so it is part of our design," a second male voice answered, the tone mocking. "What don't you understand about that? Do you want your queen or don't you?"

The response was a murmur, too low to hear.

"The Stone of Destiny will burn before it drowns, my old friend," the first voice said. "As it once did, so very long ago. Then we can both have our queens back again. And fulfill *our* destinies. You have yearned for yours for a long time, I know, denied your heart's desires by the Lia Fail itself. But I assure you, I have yearned a great deal longer."

A muted jingle of horse tack and the voices moved off into the distance.

Ronan turned to Neve and could tell by her expression—and the fact that she was reaching for her axe—she'd recognized at least one of the speakers, if not both. He opened his mouth to ask, just as a shadow rose up behind her.

And then another.

The two men, scouts or guards on watch for the meeting that had just taken place, were as surprised to find Neve and Ronan as they were to be found. Ronan didn't bother shouting a warning—Neve was already ducking out of the way—and instead dove for the nearest man, punching wildly until he could manage to focus enough to draw on the darklight of his Fé magic. When he did, the power behind a single blow drove the man's head into the soft mud of the stream bank and he slumped over, unconscious. Or maybe dead. Ronan didn't care which.

"Neve!" He scrambled to climb back up the stream bank where the Dagda of Eire grappled frantically with a warrior determined to make her reign a very short one.

NEVE STRUGGLED AND kicked, pinned beneath her attacker and barely able to grab for the man's wrist as his blade descended. Her assailant grinned and bore down with his short sword, the point less than a handsbreadth from her throat. With a cry, Neve twisted to the side and sank her teeth into his forearm. He dropped his blade with a scream, but Neve just bit harder. Blood welled up in her mouth and she spat it in the warrior's eyes, blinding him.

The bitter iron taste stirred fire in Neve.

She felt a sudden, fierce flood of strength course through her limbs. A flame kindled behind her eyes, flared to a blaze, and a voice, deep and sonorous, that was *not* the Scathach's spoke hungrily to her heart.

"*Daughter,*" it said. "*Beloved . . .*"

Over the sound of her own ragged breathing, Neve heard a splash and a low, muted growl from the ferns at the edge of the stream. The enemy scout's hands splayed out like talons, grasping for her throat. The ferocity of the attack gave her no time to concentrate, to summon the newfound power of her Fé, and she was no match for his brute strength, but the growling sounded again—louder, closer this time—and Neve brought her knee up into the man's midsection and was rewarded with the crack of a rib and a sharp grunt of agony. He staggered back and she kicked him hard in the stomach. His steps faltered, feet sinking in the soft mud at the edge of the stream.

A dark, ragged-edged shadow rose up behind him . . .

And then he was gone.

His truncated scream barely split the air, drowned out by the gnashing of teeth. Blood, hot and acrid, splashed across Neve's cheek as a huge black wolf thrashed in the shallows, its mighty jaws clenched in a death grip on the limp, lifeless scout's corpse.

Neve watched in horrid fascination as the great beast's eyes glowed with golden fire in the darkness, before the monstrous creature dragged the body out into the churning water and disappeared from sight. On the far bank, Neve thought for an instant that she saw a tall, cloaked figure staring back at her, with the same golden eyes as the wolf.

Then all was emptiness and shadows beneath the trees.

She looked back at Ronan, who stood staring at her in stunned silence.

"Kings do not die in mud huts," she said and stalked back toward the road where they had left their mounts. "And they do not abide treachery. Come. There is a lord back in Temair I require answers from."

―――

"DAMN HIS EYES!"

Ronan flinched as Neve slammed her fist down on the edge of the wax map table in the Great Hall hard enough to crack the wood. There was still dried blood at the corner of her mouth and on her cheek. She hadn't wasted any time going to her quarters once they had returned to the palace.

Instead, she'd ridden immediately to the Scythian encampment. And discovered it half empty.

Furious, Neve had summoned Sakir to the Great Hall, where she paced, mud-spattered and bloodied, waiting for him to arrive with some sort of explanation. He had none.

"Elchmar was a traitor to *his* queen," she snarled, pacing like a caged animal. "And Cormac clearly sees fit to follow in that same time-honored tradition. I would drive him and his seditious cavalry over a cliff, too, given the chance—"

"Neve." Sakir's voice was quiet and low, holding a warning. Ronan didn't think the charioteer had ever seen that particular side of his princess. He didn't think anyone had.

"Is there not a Horse Lord living who will not betray the Tuatha Dé?" Neve raged.

"Neve, *listen* to yourself," Sakir said, leaning toward her. Ronan remembered in that moment that Sakir, too, was of royal blood. An actual descendant—many generations removed—of Elchmar, in the same way Neve was. Barring the voice of the Lia Fail, Sakir had nearly the same claim to the throne as she did.

"*Look* at yourself," Sakir continued. "This isn't you."

That brought her up short. Neve's eyes flared. After a moment of effort, Neve heaved a sigh and her fists clenched and unclenched before she spoke again.

"Is that what you think, too?" she asked Ronan sharply. "That I'm not acting like myself?"

Ronan hesitated. But he knew flattery and falsehoods had been the death of Ruad Rofhessa, and Ronan would be damned if he'd be party to the same thing happening to her.

"In my—albeit brief—acquaintance with your Lord of Horse, I've learned that he is unflinchingly honest. Blunt, if you will. Irritating. And usually right," he said. "He's not wrong now, Neve."

She threw her hands in the air and stalked across the room to the throne dais. She had yet to sit upon the Dagda's great chair, where her father's war club rested. After a moment, she turned back around to face them, visibly calmer.

"Your uncle took my cavalry," Neve said. "After meeting secretly in the forest with the Scathach's sorcerer. Our *enemy*."

"Cormac didn't *take* them," Sakir countered. "They went *with* him. There is a difference. And I would remind my king that at no time in our history has any Dagda offered Scythians true equal status on the same footing as any one of the tuaths. My folk are still seen as mercenaries, kept hidden away from civilized Tuatha Dé folk in our Vale. Hired swords and horseflesh at the beck and call of whoever rules over the Tuatha Dé. Ruad Rofhessa was no different. Can you blame them?"

"Yet your uncle was the one who could have stopped my father from taking the Throne of Destiny in the first place," Neve snapped, the embers in her gaze flaring again. "Ronan and I have told you what we heard in the forest. Now that the Dagda is gone, Cormac seems to think if he helps Gofannon release the Scathach back into the world, he'll somehow have a chance at winning Anann back to his side when this is all over and done! Explain *that* particular madness to me, if you can."

The fight went out of Sakir. He just looked at Neve and said, "He loves her."

Ronan looked away from the raw emotion in the young Horse Lord's eyes, which he knew had nothing to do with Cormac and Anann. A weighty silence settled on the hall.

"That's not love, my dear friend," Neve said softly. "That's selfishness."

"The curse of the Scythians, it seems, where Tuatha Dé women are involved."

All the fight went out of Neve then, too. She folded down onto the steps below the throne and ran a hand through her tangled hair.

"I need you, Sakir," she said. "And that, too, is a kind of selfishness. But I will lose this coming battle without you." She looked over at Ronan. "Both of you. And I cannot lose."

"No," Sakir said. "You cannot. The Scathach, at least, could flee from her first kingdom in the east. There's nothing west of Eire but the edge of the world. You will have to do better."

"Half the horse folk left with Cormac," Neve said, chastened by her Horse Lord's rebuke. "Will the ones who remain follow me?"

He was silent for a long moment, contemplating her words, which had come in the form of a question, not a command. Then he shrugged and said, "You set your chariot and horses aflame at your kingmaking."

Neve's mouth twitched in the shadow of a grin. "Too much?"

"If you hadn't done that, you might have lost more of us," Sakir said wryly. "But all the young warriors saw a promise of glory in those flames. Most of them have yet to even see a cattle raid, but they all want the chance to ride their own comets into the songs."

"Tell them the Dagda will commission a contest of epic poems celebrating their deeds once we win," Ronan said.

"I already did." Sakir shrugged. "I also promised them tuath status and land to settle here in the north."

Neve looked at them both, then nodded. "When all of this is over and done," Neve said, "bring me a map and a pot of ink and they shall have it. All of it."

Sakir gave his usual enigmatic bow.

Neve stood to leave.

"I'm going to go now and wash my face," she said. "Then I'm going to review your troops and pledge my loyalty to them and ask the same in return. And if the fates decide I should meet Cormac on the field of battle, and I show him any less mercy than my father would have? It will still be more than my mother might grant him, should she ever learn of his treachery."

XXXIII

THE SNOW THAT fell softly from pale gray skies that dawn didn't stay upon the ground, just sparkled and spun in the chill breezes racing down from the hills to the west. A blizzard would have been a blessing. A good, raging blizzard would keep Gofannon from the field, Neve thought as she watched the rising sun doing its best to poke holes in the overcast. Too much to hope for. Far too much. This day was destined.

She dropped the tent flap and finished braiding her hair just before Ronan lifted the flap again and poked his head in through opening.

"Lorcan has sent a rider," he said as he entered the tent. "We were right. The Alban ships have landed and the Fomori are marching on Temair. They'll find naught but empty fields and farms along the way. As you ordered, we sent out word for any Fir Bolg to take shelter in the hills to the west until this is over. The Blackwater bruideans, of course, are still open for business."

Ronan was trying to distract her from worrying, she knew. But Neve still felt like she could feel every footstep of the approaching warriors in her bones. She could only pray to Macha that her plan had worked.

After she'd addressed Sakir's Scythian troops the day before, she'd ordered the bulk of them to quietly pull back, away from the fields outside Temair, and to make camp in the thick forests to the northwest, within swift striking distance of Brú na Bóinne. Then she'd gathered the tuath chieftains and told them of her plan. Neve had spent the sleepless night in a tent beneath the oaks, listening to the whickering of horses and terrified that, come the dawn, she'd be wrong. Catastrophically wrong.

She had been right.

Whether it was some hint of the Scathach's battle genius filtering through to her or just Neve's own instincts and the counsel of her lords, she'd instructed the gathered tuaths' warbands to remain stationed and battle ready outside the walls of Temair, under the command of Lorcan and his father, Soren. She'd left enough horses, captained by Farsa, along with their still-pitched tents and camp trappings, to give the impression of the full Scythian contingent—all that Cormac had left her, at least. Then she'd gathered a cavalry force, handpicked her own royal warband, led by Balar and Banach, and had Cliona summon the rest of the Faoladh.

And run.

Neve was gambling that, if Gofannon's scouts saw that the might of the Dagda's warriors were still camped outside the walls of Temair, Gofannon would send most of his invading force there, to keep the Tuatha Dé occupied, while he led a smaller force against a seemingly undefended Brú na Bóinne. Which meant that, consequently, Neve could take a smaller—but still formidable—force there to engage them while her tuaths could retreat behind the palace walls if necessary.

In essence, using Gofannon's distraction strategy against him.

Clever girl . . .

"What's the character of the attacking forces?" Neve asked.

"Do you mean are they monsters like me?" Ronan countered wryly.

"Or me, I suppose," she said as he lifted her cuirass up around her torso.

"Some look to be lesser Fomori, according to Lorcan," he said. "Berserkers, fierce, but they're none of them Fé Fíada, as far as the scouts have reported. I think the gathered Tuatha Dé can very likely handle them. They're more than spoiling for this fight."

"I should be with them," Neve said.

"*Let* them fight," Ronan said gently. "Let them fight for *you*. Stick to the battle plan we've drawn up."

She sighed and, after Ronan settled her helmet over her braided hair, reached for the golden wolf visor to fit it into place. Ronan wrapped his fingers around hers before she could do so and said, "Maybe where we're going, you should leave Khenti-Amentiu behind . . ."

Neve hesitated, feeling the seductive pull of the golden relic. The way it seemed to enhance and channel her own Fé . . . But he was right. They were going to war with the Scathach's forces. Neve didn't need to carry the semblance of the Scathach's god of death onto the battlefield, no matter how powerful it made her feel. She nodded again and let go of the visor. Ronan placed it carefully on a camp stool and handed Neve her sagaris instead. Then he fastened her war cloak on her shoulders and stepped back.

"Neve . . . when this is over—"

"Stop. Whatever you have to say to me now," Neve whispered, "you'll just have to stay alive long enough to say it later."

Ronan nodded, his gray eyes full of all the things he hadn't yet told her. He turned to go wrangle the Faoladh, who would be acting as Neve's vanguard on the field, once it came time for them to join in the fray. At the door to the tent, he stopped and strode back to Neve, wrapping her in a fierce embrace, his mouth locking on hers in a searing kiss.

"What I'm going to live long enough for . . . ," Ronan said as he pulled away, "is to do that again."

Then he went to go find the Dagda's Wolves.

———

"PLEASE. FOR MY sake—for the *Dagda's* sake"—Ronan gripped Cliona hard by the shoulders—"don't do anything extravagantly stupid out there. That goes for Grian and the rest, too."

Cliona grinned at him in a way that made him pity the poor souls she would encounter on the field that day. He yelped as she bit his hand—not entirely playfully—to make him let go, before loping off to join her pack.

Alone for a moment in the swirling chaos of preparation, Ronan went to retrieve a long bundle, wrapped in leather, that was strapped to his saddle. He returned and held it out to Neve, a tight grin on his face. "Do you think you can you manage that

little flaming arrow trick of yours again today, with a little something added?"

Neve nodded warily.

"Then these might come in handy." He unwrapped the bundle.
Carefully.

Ronan had been awake all night, using pitch from the torches
to adhere each shard of Emer's broken curse stone to an arrow.
There were thirteen arrows in total.

Neve's eyes went a bit wide, but she took the arrows from him
and, willing her fingers not to tremble, slid them into her quiver,
alongside the shafts already there. Then she stepped up onto the
deck of her chariot, behind Sakir, and Ronan mounted his horse.

At Neve's signal, the carnyx brayed.

The fearsome challenge rang out through the frosted air and the
Dagda's warband broke into a charge. As the warriors reached the
edge of the floodplain of An Bhóinn, they broke from the trees,
and the Faoladh out in front of the horses and chariots blurred
like smoke, shifting from women to weapons, running with inhuman speed and a palpable joy at finally—*finally*—realizing their
true natures.

Ronan could almost see the shades of their ancestress Faoladh
running with them, joining in the battle howl as they burst from
the trees.

<hr>

IN THE DISTANCE, Neve could see the enemy warband massing
on the other side of the Great Barrow of Ruad Rofhessa. At
a glance, she estimated more than a thousand warriors who'd

sailed there on the ships from Alba. Many more. Supported by Cormac's cavalry. Neve's chariot was near the leading edge of the wedge-shaped attack formation as the first wave of her warband met the invaders with an ear-shattering clamor of war cries and weapons.

She could see, from the deck of her chariot, the Faoladh tearing into their targets with howling ferocity that was met and very nearly matched. But Neve was stunned to discover that the Scathach's fearsome Fomori enemies—the warrior race her ancestors had deemed worthy of extinction—were hardly the monsters she had been expecting. Warriors, certainly. But human, mostly. It was true there was a strangeness to them. Their bodies seemed almost fluid, moving and reacting with the characteristics of bird and beast—similar to the Faoladh if nowhere near the same extent—and they fought ferociously, but they did not deserve the reputation the first Tuatha Dé had burdened them with. Worthy foes, not monstrous ones.

None of which meant Neve was inclined to let them win.

All around her, inspired by the sight of the Faoladh, Neve's own tuath warriors surged forward, joining the wolf women in hewing through the enemy ranks. Neve saw Balar towering above a clot of Fomori, carving flesh with two broad-bladed swords. Banach's long spear cleared circles all about him, while his kin warriors darted in and out of the line of attackers with shorter staves, quick as serpents' tongues, leaving bodies behind, keeping the invaders from completely encircling Brú na Bóinne.

But as the tide of battle ebbed for a moment, leaving a field strewn with bodies, Neve signaled to Ronan and her battle captains, who circled back to her.

"Something's wrong," she said. "They're planning something. Cormac has pulled back his horsemen when they need cavalry support the most."

"Is it possible he's now betraying Gofannon too?" Ronan suggested.

"Aye." Balar nodded. "Maybe. We cut through their ranks like a scythe through barley—"

"*There*." Sakir pointed. "Something's happening . . ."

A dark, glittering fog was rising from the surface of the river, creeping across the plain. And there were shadows in the fog.

Eyes . . . teeth . . . wraiths . . . Every dead invader on the field suddenly lurched back to life, ashen-skinned and black-eyed.

Did you think it would be so easy? the voice in Neve's head screeched with insatiable bloodlust. *It's war, Little Scota . . . war—*

Shut up!

"Go!" Neve shouted. "*Go!*"

The wraiths flowed up, spilling over the banks of An Bhóinn, tattered scraps of long-dead spirits slithering across the plain. They were not nearly so easily killed a second time. Or a third.

Neve struck the head off one of them as Sakir whipped the chariot horses to a gallop, and still the headless thing's body flailed its sword at her, slicing across her upper arm and drawing a thin line of blood. She hissed in pain and slapped Sakir's shoulder, urging him to head back to where their lines were re-forming.

Neve saw Cliona in the midst of a knot of enemy fighters— alive and dead, both—her pale mane of hair matted with blood, but a maniacal grin splitting her lupine features. Aevinn was more fully transformed than Cliona—her limbs bristled with dark gray fur and she bore a fearsome, sharp-toothed muzzle—as she fought back to back with her warrior sister. The two of them went about rending their enemies into pieces too small to keep fighting, but even the Faoladh were losing ground.

Fintan and his óglach fought fiercely with their hounds, suffused with a crimson glow of cursefire, but sheer numbers threatened to overwhelm them, too. And the tuath warbands struggled to maintain footholds as corpse warriors filled spaces that had been empty save for scattered bodies.

"There are too many," Neve shouted to Banach. "Call them back. *Call them all back!*"

The carnyx brayed and the Tuatha Dé warband fell away from the engagement like a wave rolling back out to sea. They gathered on the western edge of the plain and the Fomori invaders did not follow, contenting themselves instead to close in a defensive circle around the standing stone ring.

"How are they doing this?" Fintan asked, gasping for breath and grappling with a bloody-mouthed, crimson-eyed Thorn, fighting to keep her from charging back into the fray. "That"—he pointed at the vile fog seeping up from the river—"that is a black Druid spell. Like a fuath spell, only multiplied. I can tell that much even without Thorn's cursefire. But it would take a whole Order of those twisted bastards to cast something like that. Where are they?"

Neve glanced at where Ronan rode beside her and could tell by the look on his face that he knew. Suddenly, with dread certainty—through Druid prescience or just plain instinct—Ronan knew.

"They aren't here," he said and thrust out an arm, pointing at Brú na Bóinne. "*He* is. Gofannon is *already* inside. He's in there, opening the door to the dead, using all of the wild magic his Druids gathered, and channeling those spirits into the warriors he's brought over from Alba. The longer it goes on, the wider the door swings and the more wraiths he'll be able to conjure. They'll just keep coming. All the way back to the souls of the first Fomori the Scathach murdered."

"An army of mindless thralls, all for her," Neve murmured, the horror of what Ronan was saying sinking in.

"And then," Ronan continued grimly, "once the door is open wide, there'll be nothing to stop her from stepping through. And that"—he pointed at the growing number of wraiths—"will be hers to command. The Scathach will be unstoppable. She'll conquer this realm all over again and nothing will stand in her way this time."

Fintan swore. "If he stays in there, he's won . . ."

"Get me there," Neve said quietly.

Sakir shook his head. "The barrow is surrounded. There's no way—"

"Just *get* me there!" Neve urged. "Look—the Fomori aren't entering the stone circle."

"It must act like the barrier to their magic," Ronan said.

"But not mine," Neve said slowly, understanding. "I'm Tuatha Dé as much as I'm Fomori. A bridge, remember? And if I can get inside, maybe I can stop him. Stop *her* from coming back."

"Once the Scathach crosses back over," Ronan said quietly, "it'll be too late."

"Then I'll have to take the fight to her." She locked eyes with him. "On *her* side."

For a moment, Ronan looked as if he would throw Neve over his saddle and ride off with her in the other direction before he would let that happen. But then he swallowed hard and smiled his sly smile. "I'll wager three silver pieces on *that* contest."

Sakir shook his head again but said, "All right. I'll get you to the barrow."

Fintan nodded. "*We'll* get you to the barrow."

Cliona limped up to them, favoring a wounded leg. "Aye," she said. "All of us."

CLIONA AND HER Faoladh were a collective mess of blood and dirt. The left side of Grian's face was a mask of blood from a gash on her forehead. She'd never looked happier. Almost as happy as Balar—whom she stepped up beside—and he seemed to be missing an eye.

"Warriors of the Tuatha Dé!" he bellowed. "Horse Lords and Ladies of the Wolf! For the glory of our Dagda, Neve Anann Eriu, and the kingdom of Eire!"

Her army surged forward, crying fury.

The Scythians fanned out in front with Sakir driving just behind the middle point and the Faoladh on either side of Neve's chariot, providing ferocious defensive cover. The fuath arrows Neve shot from the deck of her chariot carved a path through the enemy ranks, blooming into fuath-shaped flames, devouring whatever wraith they hit before bursting into screeching columns of smoke and desiccated ash. Ronan—silver-skinned and black-eyed in his Fé Fíada form—used his magic to draw off any traces of An Bhóinn water sustaining them and channel it outward in waves to sweep Cormac's cavalry away from the stones.

It was enough—*just* enough—to force an opening.

Enough for them to reach the ring of stones, where Neve's warband turned and formed a wall between her and Gofannon's forces. Over the din of the fighting behind them, Neve shouted for Sakir to halt her chariot just outside of the ring, between the last two stones raised. She jumped down beside the one that Gofannon himself had dedicated to Úna, carving her tuath mark on its surface.

"*The stones will show you the way,*" Ruad Rofhessa had said to her. Almost the last thing he'd said before he himself had crossed over into the Beyond Realms. The very last thing had been "*Tell Úna I loved her . . .*"

Seeing Úna's tuath mark hit Neve like a lightning strike. She pressed a hand over the familiar marking and felt its power seep beneath her skin. But she could also sense it wasn't the key to opening the door to Teg Duinn. No . . .

That Gofannon had carved for Neve, on *her* stone.

Which meant he was expecting her to use it.

"Neve!" Ronan shouted at her over his shoulder. "They're coming!"

She spun around and saw that the line of Faoladh was failing. Ronan's Fé was breaching in places. She didn't have much time. Neve ran over to her stone and lifted her right hand to the sigil there. She was unsurprised to see a triangle pattern that matched the firewolf on the palm of her hand. It pulsed with a faint, silver-white light. As she pressed her hand down, Neve felt a strange, shimmering warmth . . . and then the marking appeared on the *back* of her hand as if it had floated up through her flesh like water.

"*Neve!*"

She paused.

You must. This is your destiny. As much as it is his. As much as it is mine . . .

Neve stepped forward between the stones and felt as though she had walked into a cave of darkness. The sky grew instantly dark and stars appeared above her head, spinning so fast they made her dizzy.

Then a ruddy torchlight spilled out of the black maw of the barrow portal.

And Cormac stepped out to meet her.

"Don't do this, Horse Lord," Neve said.

"I would beg the same of you, lady."

"I am no lady to you. I am your king. Stand aside."

"I have no king. I never have. I thought you knew that."

It might have been a trick of the torchlight, but she thought she might have seen a silvery gleam reflecting off the back of his hand. But then Cormac threw the torch on the ground between them, casting a ring of flickering yellow light, and unsheathed his sagaris.

"If I believed in the power of kings," Cormac said, "then I would have claimed the throne, and then I would have had the only thing in life I ever wanted."

Neve drew her own sagaris and braced herself in a wide fighting stance—like Cormac's nephew had taught her to—and waited for his first blow. It came, as she suspected, as an underhand swing. Cormac was used to fighting from horseback and his instincts were all to aim low and to the side. Neve ducked and ran past him, aiming a blow high at his shoulder that just grazed his cheek, drawing a thin thread of blood.

"Cormac—"

He cut short her words with a snarl and another lunge, swinging wide with his axe and catching Neve's shoulder with the heel of the blade, drawing a red ribbon from her, too. She hissed in pain and the pain of the wound sparked a flame inside her.

Neve spun around and blocked another side swing of the Horse Lord's axe with her own, twisting as she did and wrenching his arm upward. Then she reached out with her other hand—where the firewolf sigil burned on her palm—and beckoned the flames of Cormac's torch to obey her. The firebrand flared, sending a column of sparks into his face.

Cormac threw one hand up, momentarily blinded, and Neve brought her axe down in a savage arc, severing Cormac's axe hand at the wrist.

The silent shriek of triumph that echoed in her head almost drove Neve to her knees—seemingly louder than Cormac's cry of pain as he bent forward, clutching the bleeding stump of his arm. He screamed again before collapsing in a writhing heap on the ground.

"There will be no Scythian sorcerer this time to mend you with living silver and make you whole, Horse Lord," Neve said in a voice that sounded alien in her own ears. As she stepped over him, she saw that while they'd fought, the sky had grown lighter by the moment. The longest night of the year was coming to a galloping swift end within the circle of stones . . .

Whatever Neve was about to do, she had to do it soon.

I don't know what that is, she thought.

No. You know *what to do*, said the voice in her head. *You've always known.*

Neve looked down and was unsurprised to find that she some-how held the Scathach's golden wolf visor in her hands. Slowly, she lifted it to her face, slotting it into place on her helmet.

Yes. Since the first days. I have always known . . .

⸻※⸻

RONAN WATCHED FROM beyond the stone circle as Cormac fell to his knees. His heart soared in joy at Neve's triumph over him . . . and then dropped into the pit of his stomach as he caught a glimpse of bright gold flashing beneath the brim of her black bronze helmet.

"Death and Darkness!" Ronan swore, leaping down off his horse and running for the circle. "No—*stop*! Neve!"

"What are you doing?" Sakir demanded, grabbing him by the shoulder.

"The mask—didn't you see?" He angrily shrugged off Sakir's hand. "She's wearing the damned wolf mask! That's *not* Neve. It's the Scathach—"

Sakir glanced at the iron dagger in Ronan's fist. "You're mad!"

"No—*she* is!" Ronan shoved Sakir out of his way. "If *she* enters the chamber now, we'll lose everything!"

He thrust his arms out wide, shoving aside his exhaustion, and called the river to his bidding. The darklight sigils appeared again on his skin, and a rolling bloom of indigo mist flowed across the ground, catching at Neve's ankles as she ran.

With a shouted curse, she stumbled forward onto her hands and knees. Just long enough for Ronan to catch up with her at the entrance to the barrow. She scrabbled at the turf, lunging for the darkness, as he reached for her shoulders and dragged her back away from the entrance, spinning her around to face him.

Her eyes, gazing out at him from under the golden visor, were black. Ronan thrust the blade of his iron knife up under Neve's chin, drawing a thin line of blood as he sliced through the leather strap holding on her helmet. He tore the helmet from Neve's head and flung it—and the cursed mask—away, down the long stone corridor into the barrow, watching as it disappeared into the darkness.

Her eyes flashed golden in the same instant Ronan heard the slap of Sakir's bow.

And the wasp-whine of an arrow in flight.

XXXIV

O H, NO . . ." NEVE whispered, loud as a scream in her head. "Ronan . . . *no* . . ."

Sakir was Neve's weapon. Ronan was her shield . . .

One had killed for her. The other had died.

"No . . ."

Neve wrapped her arms around her thief as he sank slowly to the ground. His gray eyes went dark as she watched, helpless to save him this time. The arrow that had struck Ronan, slipping through the gap of his borrowed óglach armor and sinking deep between his ribs, had been meant for her. Because she'd commanded Sakir to end her if the need arose. And it *had*. Or it would have, if not for Ronan.

She glanced back to where she could see Sakir with his bow, silhouetted between the stones, and felt her heart crack in her chest, as surely as if Sakir had hit his intended mark. Neve couldn't even take the time to weep—in a moment when time for her was untethered from the world—but she also would not let Ronan die in vain. She laid his body down just inside the barrow entrance. She loosened his fingers from the iron dagger she'd given him what seemed like an age ago, and shoved the blade into her own belt.

In that very moment, in the sky above the circle of stones, the wheeling stars began to fade as the sun rose with an impossible swiftness. The first rays of light raced across the frost-white grass to kiss the face of Brú na Bóinne. It was the dawning of the day after the longest night of the year. And just as Gofannon the architect had so cleverly designed it, the first fair beams of the rising sun on that one singular morning of the year poured into a small, hidden opening above the entrance to the barrow and down the long stone corridor that led to the barrow's chamber.

Neve heard herself gasp in astonishment. She followed the light, as if walking down a pathway of molten gold. Her third time entering the barrow.

The last time . . .

As she entered the chamber, she saw Gofannon standing in the center, his hands pressed to the seemingly unremarkable stone that Neve now recognized was the Lia Fail, the Stone of Destiny. His face was rigid with agony as the power of the stone flowed through him. When the sun's rays spilled into the chamber, they burst into flame on the floor. Neve watched as the fires bent and curved around the room, tracing a spiral pattern on the stone floor, a blazing trail snaking its way toward the Lia Fail.

Neve wasn't about to wait and find out what would happen if the flames reached the stone. She drew her sagaris and ran to the first of the three water urns, smashing it open.

"Stop!" Gofannon screamed, wrenching his hands free from the Lia Fail.

As the water gushed from the broken clay jar, she ran to the second and then the third. The green water rushed onto the floor of the chamber and cascaded over the flames, extinguishing them before the fires reached Gofannon—and the Stone of Destiny.

"No!" he shouted. "The Stone must *burn* first before it *drowns*!"

She turned to face him, the breath heaving in her lungs.

"For all these long years," he said, "I've been trying to stop the Scathach from clawing her way back into this realm . . ."

"*Stop* her?"

A wave of incandescent triumph surged up inside of Neve and, for a moment, Neve thought the Scathach's gloating might overwhelm her.

"Yes." He glared furiously at her. "Stop her. For centuries, I've been waiting for this moment to destroy this cursed Stone and shut the portal forever. Now *you've* wrenched the door off and invited her in! The Scathach will take your soul and make it her own and there is nothing either of us can do to stop her." He sank to his knees in the pooling water, the palms of his hands blistered and bloody. "You were my best hope, Neve Anann Eriu. I will *never* be free of her now . . ." His voice cracked on a note of heartbreaking despair, but there was a gleam of twisted elation in his blue gaze, too. "And neither will you."

Neve tightened her grip on her axe.

"I won't be defeated by a dead queen," she snarled and shoved aside the Scathach's mocking laughter in her mind.

"You don't understand." Gofannon shook his head. "*We* will die, and *she* will live. She will rule Eire, wrapped in a veil of darkness, and we will watch from beyond that veil while everything good and pure about this realm is destroyed. And Khenti-Amentiu, her dread god of death, will feast on the banquet of souls she serves him up for all eternity."

"Why would I let *her* wolf god feed on my realm," Neve said, her teeth bared in a snarl, "when I have my own wolf goddess to protect it?"

Wild laughter spilled from Gofannon's lips. "Can your wolf breathe underwater?"

Neve looked to see that water from the broken urns still cascaded from the shattered ceramic husks, spilling forth in foaming white cataracts, as if An Bhóinn were being channeled directly through the barrow. The water climbed up her ankles, rising faster than she would have imagined possible.

"The underground hall in Kemet," Neve said. "You did that. Flooded it with water and drowned the Scathach's enemies."

"That, and more." Gofannon nodded, profoundly weary. "I would have done anything to assuage her madness. I loved her. Beyond measure, beyond reason. Deeper even than Elchmar, my brother, who loved her with all his soul and hated her with all his heart." He closed his eyes. He seemed content to kneel there and accept his fate as the water rose almost up to the serpent torc that ringed his neck.

Neve searched frantically for the way out, which seemed to have disappeared beneath the rising water. Neve began to tread water to keep above the deluge but soon enough her head was butting the stone roof, and soon after, water filled her nostrils, pouring down her throat and into her lungs.

Neve's sagaris slipped from her fingers and she caught a gleam from the firewolf sigil on the back of her hand before everything began fading through the murk.

Darkness wrapped soft arms around Neve as she fell back into an endless embrace. Down through the doorway of Teg Duinn into the realm of the dead.

XXXV

"Wake up, Little Scota . . ."

The notes of a flute, high and sweet, sounded in her ears.

Neve opened her eyes, gasping for air, but found she could breathe easily.

She was standing in the courtyard of her mother's crannog—or so it seemed. The sky above was a mellow blue and the lake was crystal clear. The whole place was bursting with wildflowers in bloom.

And Neve could sense, just beyond the shores of the lake, a multitude of lost souls dwelling there. Restless and wandering, like the fluttering of moth wings outside the circle of firelight on a summer night.

I'm in the Beyond Realms . . .

"So we are."

Neve's heart lurched in her chest as a woman walked out of the broch. She wore the armor Neve's mother had given her, the upper half of her face obscured by the gilded wolf visor.

"I know who you are," Neve said. "I know *what* you are."

She reached for a weapon and found that she was dressed in a plain tunic and leggings. The leather belt she'd given to Ronan in Blackwater circled her waist, her iron dagger hanging from it, and on her feet were boots worn soft from her days of careless adventuring.

"Then you should know this," the Scathach said. "I can give you all that freedom again." She smiled, tucking a flute into her belt. Her eyes, behind the visor, were dark brown, ringed with kohl, and glittering with sharp intelligence. Ambition. Madness. "It's what you want, yes?" she asked, with a hint of the accent from her home far away. Far in the past. "Freedom . . . escape from the walls of the palace . . ."

"Not anymore," Neve said. "It's my palace now."

"Is it?" The smile turned cold. Frightful. "You're only one little girl."

"I am a king—"

"And I am *queen*," the Scathach snarled. "And which one of us rules *this* realm?"

"Stay here then," Neve said. "You shall not have Eire. Neither of us will. It belongs to its folk and deserves a protector. Not a tyrant."

Three long strides and the Scathach was in front of her. "Don't be such a fool. You couldn't wait to call yourself king and yet you only exist because of me. Because I was strong enough—stronger than any of them—and I led my people, my army to the shores of Eire. I *conquered*!"

"You destroyed," Neve said.

The Scathach backhanded Neve across the face with her armored hand. As Neve staggered back, the Scathach grabbed the iron dagger at Neve's hip.

"This," she hissed, "doesn't belong to you . . ."

The Scathach placed the gray blade against Neve's throat.

"We both know what iron does to the magic of this land, don't we?" She was so close that the golden muzzle of her wolf visor brushed Neve's cheek. "I ended many a Fomori life with this blade. Even some Fé Fíada. I'm glad to have it back to add one more filthy Fomori to that tally . . ."

She lifted the blade high to plunge it into Neve's heart, but Neve grabbed her wrist with one hand as she slapped her other palm flat against the center of the Scathach's armored chest. The symbol Neve had lifted from Úna's sentinel stone—her sister's tuath mark—blazed like a firebrand on the queen's armor before sinking into it, into the Scathach herself.

The Scathach gasped as she felt its burn blooming around her heart.

Macha hear my heart, Neve prayed fervently. *Grant my wish . . . Give me back my sister, a true and worthy queen among these dead souls . . .*

On Neve's other hand, her firewolf sigil flared to life.

A figure, shining with what seemed like moonlight, appeared at the end of the crannog's causeway.

"No . . ." The Scathach's eyes went black with fury.

The figure walked up to Neve and the light dimmed enough for Neve to look upon the face of her beloved sister.

"Didn't I tell you to be mindful what you wish for, little cub?" Úna asked with a gentle smile.

"No!" the Scathach shouted, twisting out of Neve's grip and throwing her to the ground. "I didn't get my brother back—you don't get *her*!"

Neve landed hard on her hands and knees—to find that her sagaris had found its way into the Beyond Realms with her. It lay on the ground at the roots of an apple tree in bloom. Neve reached for it and, looking up, saw the leather chin strap of the Scathach's helmet hanging free from when Ronan had cut it.

Neve lunged to her feet, long-handled axe held in both hands, and threw all of her weight behind a blow that knocked the dead queen to her knees and sent her visored helmet flying across the little courtyard.

The wolf mask bounced across the ground and lay still for a moment behind a veil of shimmering dust. Its visage seemed to grin, and its dark empty eyes filled with sullen orange light. Then the air surrounding it blurred and a massive golden wolf, lean and long-limbed, stood there, snarling.

"Khenti-Amentiu!" Neve shouted at the god-monster. "You have no dominion over this realm. Not anymore."

The wolf bared its teeth, legs bunching as it prepared to leap.

"Go back to your own and find another warrior queen to feed you souls," Neve cried. "The souls of Eire belong to Macha and the gods of Eriu."

She hurled her iron-bladed sagaris at the golden wolf in the moment it lunged forward. As the Scathach screamed, the war axe tumbled through the air, striking the wolf in the chest and throwing it back through the dusky air to land in an unmoving heap in the courtyard. The Scathach stood, shocked to stillness, and Neve held her breath. The wolf god's body blurred before her eyes as moth-winged clouds of lost souls poured over the walls of the crannog and swarmed around the fallen god, coalescing into a monstrous, writhing wolf-shape made of wailing wraiths. With red eyes. And teeth . . . The wolf-shaped soul cloud grew massive, roiling like a thunderstorm, incorporeal and terrifying. It leaped at Neve—

And Úna stepped in front of her, arms raised.

The phantom wolf god of Kemet hit Úna like a wave dashing on a rock, exploding into a crimson shower of blood and embers with a final echoing shriek.

Úna turned and walked back to Neve through that shimmering veil, scattering it into nothing.

"Emer was right, you know," she said quietly. "I didn't believe in the magic of the land. And I was afraid of *her* . . ." She turned her gaze on the Scathach, who staggered to her feet, blazing hatred twisting her face. "Of our shared blood. And look where my fear has led us. I'm so sorry, little cub . . . I couldn't make things right in Temair, but maybe I can here."

The Scathach lurched toward them but Úna thrust out her hand, fingers spread wide, toward the mad queen.

"*That*," she said, "belongs to me."

Her tuath mark, branded on the Scathach's cuirass, flared to brilliance then faded to nothing. Only to reappear in its rightful place on Úna's outstretched arm. The figure at the center of the spiral design—the one Úna would never explain to Neve, but kept as her own secret—began to glow, pulsing like a heartbeat. The Scathach cried out—in fear or awe, Neve couldn't tell—before she, too, faded from sight.

Neve watched in astonishment as her sister's features flowed like water, shifting between her face and the Scathach's . . . finally resolving into a combination of the two.

"I will rule here," Úna said, her voice deeper, smokier, than it had been in life, but still hers, twined with the Scathach's. "*We* will rule. With benevolence and care for the dead ones who deserved a better fate . . . Go back and do the same, for those living, little cub. Do what I failed to do. Welcome the Fomori back to their ancestral homes. Extend your hand across the water to the Fir Domnann. I am proud of you . . ."

Then she vanished into the rising morning mist.

Two tears, one for each queen, fell from Neve's golden eyes.

The waters of the lake surrounding the little crannog suddenly rose up around Neve and curled inward, crashing over her like a wave. She thrashed wildly, sinking beneath the deluge, the water rushing into her lungs, drowning her.

The light of her firewolf sigil flared like a tiny sun . . .

And then there were fingers clamped around her wrist.

Ronan's fingers, webbed and taloned.

He pulled her limp body against his as the water in the chamber of the Great Barrow emptied in a whirlpool rush. But not fast enough. Neve was dying and she *knew* she was dying. Through a haze, she saw Ronan, his gray eyes black and flickering with lightning, lift his arms above her, fingers stretched wide. The darkling marks glowed indigo, rippling across his silvered features as his Fé gift called to the water in Neve's lungs, drawing swirling tendrils out of her mouth and nose.

She gasped—an excruciating draw of breath—and he bent over her, fastening his mouth upon hers, and drew the last of the drowning water from her with his kiss. The pain was searing, burning in her chest and throat, but suddenly Neve could breathe again. She curled in on herself on the chamber floor, chest heaving. Ronan knelt beside her.

The light of his magic was just bright enough for her to see his face as the contours of his cheeks softened and his eyes shifted back to the silver-flecked gray she so loved.

"How . . . ?" She struggled to sit up, reaching for his chest, where she'd seen Sakir's arrow sink deep. "I was sure he'd pierced your heart . . ."

Ronan grinned down at her. "Shapeshifter," he said. "I'm not even sure where my heart is. At least . . . I wasn't. Until now."

"Just like a thief," she said, her voice raw and rasping. "Stealing life back for me out of the jaws of the gods of death . . ."

"I just wanted my dagger back," Ronan said, his eyes gleaming with wetness that might have been tears. "I've grown so very fond of her."

XXXVI

WHEN NEVE AND Ronan emerged from Brú na Bóinne, the sun was just lifting over the horizon. It seemed that they'd been in the Beyond Realms for far longer than either of them realized. Throughout the whole of the shortest day and the longest night of the year, in fact.

But Sakir and her Faoladh and her warband were there, waiting for her.

"We kept vigil after the battle and throughout the night," Cliona said. "The stone circle wouldn't let any of the rest of us through to fetch you back."

"The battle—what happened?" Neve asked, gazing around at them, most of them bloodied and bandaged.

Balar's lone eye glittered at her. "Do you think we would have delivered anything less than victory to you, my king? And against a valiant adversary, if you want the truth of it. The ones who weren't possessed of those bloody wraiths, at least. And once those faded, too, we knew you'd most like bested Gofannon." He nodded to a cluster of tents pitched near the barrows of Dubhadh. "They're over there now, those that surrendered. Along with those that Lorcan and the lords took captive at Temair. We brought the captives here to await your command."

"I want to speak with them," Neve said. "First give them meat and mead. Tend to any wounds. It is beyond time we begin to right the Scathach's transgressions."

"Well, you've made a fair start with us," Cliona said.

Neve reached out to put a hand on her shoulder, then thought better of it and threw her arms around the Faoladh in a fierce embrace. "You were loyal to me far beyond your oath," she said. "I will not forget that."

The gleam in Cliona's eyes when she released her told Neve Cliona wasn't about to let her.

When Sakir drove Neve's chariot up, she ran to him and leaped onto the deck to throw her arms around her Scythian charioteer. "Thank you."

"Thank me? I damn near killed you," Sakir said, nodding at Ronan, who sauntered up in Neve's wake. "I *did* kill him."

"You did as I asked," she said. "You both did. Where is Cormac?"

"Gone," Sakir said. "I stanched his wound and told him he was exiled from the Golden Vale, on pain of death, should he return. I gave him provisions and a horse and told him to go."

"That was generous of you," Ronan said.

"Not really." Sakir shrugged. "I gave him *your* horse."

Neve bit back a smile. "A moment?" she asked Ronan.

He looked at the two of them and nodded, then walked away, muttering about finding Cliona, as she'd most likely have procured a supply of mead.

Sakir turned back to Neve. "I couldn't . . . I had to let him go. I'm sorry—"

"Don't be." She reached for his hand. "There's been enough blood shed over something so simple as love, Sakir."

"Is it simple?" he asked, his hazel eyes bright with both the happiness and the hurt of having her back again in the world.

"The simplest," she said. "Cormac will find his way. Or he won't. As simple as that. For all of us. But that is for another day."

———⟨⟩———

THEY MADE CAMP in the fields outside the Great Barrow. Swift the Fisherman, true to his word, led a procession there, with a wain bearing the body of Ruad Rofhessa, washed and dressed in rich robes, his coal-black hair combed and braided with gold rings. A shield lay on his chest and his war club rested at his feet. They built a massive pyre on top of Brú na Bóinne so Neve could keep her promise to the Dagda not to bury him within. Ruad Rofhessa was laid to rest on the platform built on the scaffolding of long logs, set ablaze with her own magic.

The whole court of the Tuatha Dé, and those of the Fomori who'd accepted her invitation of peace, sang as the sparks from his pyre rose high into the night to join with the stars. The Faoladh howled and drank and fought anything that came within reach, in honor of his passing, and the Scythians raced their chariots up and down the plain of An Bhóinn with torches blazing.

Neve ordered Lorcan to seal up the mouth of the Great Barrow and ordained that, once the fire had burned out, it be left to the sheep to graze there and the wildflowers to bloom. They would, eventually, in brilliant abundance, as the magic crept back into the land, seeping into the earth and the air. And the water.

Neve wished that Emer was still there to see it.

As she stood there, the heat of her father's fire on her face, and Sakir and Ronan standing at her sides, she could feel the subtle warmth of the firewolf sigil on her right hand. The end of the first day after the longest night of the year.

From that point on, the Light would continue to gain ground over the Darkness. Triumphing a little more each dawn. And then, each dusk the sun would set and the moon would rise, and Neve Anann Eriu, Beloved of the Wolf, would sleep the sleep of a rightful king beneath the stars in the sky over a realm united against any who would seek to conquer her.

In the distance, Neve heard the Faoladh sisters shouting and carousing with the warriors of the tuaths.

"You're going to have to find a way to keep them all busy now, you know," Ronan said, wrapping an arm around her. "All these warriors of yours are going to be looking for trouble now that you've gone and given them such a sweet taste of it."

Neve leaned her head on his shoulder. She searched inside herself for the whisper-voice that used to be there and found only blissful silence. But some other sense made her turn and look outward, to the east. Toward Alba.

There was something there, still. Something that knew of Neve's victory and would not abide it. And in her heart, Neve knew that one day—maybe soon—they would all have more than enough trouble to keep them busy. And when that day came, Neve would climb aboard her chariot once more, and set her horses aflame.

And the gods themselves would see her fire.

ACKNOWLEDGMENTS

It's been a long, strange, stormy journey that has brought Neve and her family and friends—and foes, let's not forget foes—to life. The past couple of years have been challenging, to say the least, in ways both micro and macro, and I'm profoundly grateful to everyone who helped me see this story through to its release out into the wild.

As always, my boundless thanks go to Jessica Regel, captain of the ship at Helm Literary, and the lodestar to my own wandering vessel. Always pointing the way and lighting a path, the second you stop believing my weird ramblings will amount to something is the day I hang up the oars. So, you know. Don't do that.

Then there's my gratitude and sheer giddy delight at being given the opportunity to work with the spectacular Zando. Molly Stern is a force of nature and has assembled an impossibly talented crew.

First and foremost, my editrix extraordinaire, the magnificent and utterly unstoppable Tiffany Liao. This trip has been as much yours as mine and there's no one else I'd have rather had on this journey. I meant what I said: I'd go with you to the ends of the Earth, Tiff. And maybe a little beyond.

Massive thanks to director of publicity Chloe Texier-Rose, marketing manager Allegra Green, director of marketing Nathalie Ramirez, and head of sales Andrew Rein. Your collective dedication, expertise, and commitment to getting this book out there into the hands and minds of readers are beyond gratifying. You guys rock.

As for the book itself, for the glorious package wrapped around my words—and the great care and attention taken to make sure they were always the *right* words in the *right* order—my eternal thanks to the design and editorial teams. To cover designer Evan Gaffney and illustrator Tal Goretsky, I haven't been able to stop staring and smiling at the gorgeous cover of this book since the day it landed in my inbox. I know. That's a lot of days. It's a *lot* of gorgeous.

As for keeping the insides worthy of that outside, my undying gratitude to managing editor Sarah Schneider, copy editor Rachel Kowal, proofreader Hilary Roberts, and editorial assistant TJ Ohler. You guys have my back. Thank you.

Love and gratitude, always and forever, to my family. Especially, this time around, to Karen and Dean—for helping us find a place where I could write in peace and making sure we got there relatively intact. I owe you guys.

Thank you, Butters. You've been with me for every single book. The best office assistant I could have ever hoped for and an even better pal. And Daisy? Office manager par excellence and toothless green-eyed beauty. Don't worry, you two, Hawkeye the IT guy is taking good care of the place. Lots of fish in the break room. And the hallway. And the bathroom.

My final thanks, as always, is reserved for John. Every time. But especially this time. Because without you, this story would still be a collection of desperate characters set adrift on the seas of my brain, searching the horizon for somewhere to call home. Thank you for giving them a place to drop anchor. And for always being mine.

ABOUT THE AUTHOR

LESLEY LIVINGSTON is the award-winning author of the *Wondrous Strange* trilogy and the *Valiant* trilogy. She holds a master's degree in English from the University of Toronto and was a principal performer in a Shakespearean theater company, specializing in performances for teen audiences, for more than a decade. She resides in Ontario, Canada.

lesleylivingston.com

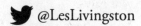 @LesLivingston

@LesleyLivingston